Lifelong romance addict J[...] break from her career as a [...] a family and found her call[...] author instead. She now lives in New Zealand, and finds that writing feeds her very real obsession with happy endings and the endorphin rush they create. You can follow her at jcharroway.com, and on Facebook, X and Instagram.

Three-times Golden Heart® finalist **Tina Beckett** learned to pack her suitcases almost before she learned to read. Born to a military family, she has lived in the United States, Puerto Rico, Portugal and Brazil. In addition to travelling, Tina loves to cuddle with her pug, Alex, spend time with her family, and hit the trails on her horse. Learn more about Tina from her website, or 'friend' her on Facebook.

Also by JC Harroway

Nurse's Secret Royal Fling
Forbidden Fiji Nights with Her Rival
The Midwife's Secret Fling

Buenos Aires Docs miniseries

Secretly Dating the Baby Doc

Also by Tina Beckett

Tempting the Off-Limits Nurse
Las Vegas Night with Her Best Friend

Buenos Aires Docs miniseries

ER Doc's Miracle Triplets

Alaska Emergency Docs miniseries

Reunion with the ER Doctor

Discover more at millsandboon.co.uk.

MANHATTAN MARRIAGE REUNION

JC HARROWAY

NEW YORK NIGHTS WITH MR RIGHT

TINA BECKETT

All rights reserved including the right of reproduction in whole or
in part in any form. This edition is published by arrangement with
Harlequin Enterprises ULC.

This is a work of fiction. Names, characters, places, locations
and incidents are purely fictional and bear no relationship
to any real life individuals, living or dead, or to any actual places,
business establishments, locations, events or incidents.
Any resemblance is entirely coincidental.

This book is sold subject to the condition that it shall not, by way of
trade or otherwise, be lent, resold, hired out or otherwise circulated
without the prior consent of the publisher in any form of binding
or cover other than that in which it is published and without a
similar condition including this condition being imposed on
the subsequent purchaser.

® and TM are trademarks owned and used by the trademark owner
and/or its licensee. Trademarks marked with ® are registered with the
United Kingdom Patent Office and/or the Office for Harmonisation in
the Internal Market and in other countries.

First published in Great Britain 2025
by Mills & Boon, an imprint of HarperCollins*Publishers* Ltd,
1 London Bridge Street, London, SE1 9GF

www.harpercollins.co.uk

HarperCollins*Publishers* Macken House, 39/40 Mayor Street Upper,
Dublin 1, D01 C9W8, Ireland

Manhattan Marriage Reunion © 2025 JC Harroway

New York Nights with Mr Right © 2025 Tina Beckett

ISBN: 978-0-263-32499-0

03/25

MIX
Paper | Supporting
responsible forestry
FSC™ C007454

This book contains FSC™ certified paper
and other controlled sources to ensure responsible forest management.

For more information visit www.harpercollins.co.uk/green.

Printed and Bound in the UK using 100% Renewable Electricity
at CPI Group (UK) Ltd, Croydon, CR0 4YY

MANHATTAN MARRIAGE REUNION

JC HARROWAY

MILLS & BOON

To G. Thanks for our twenty-eight-year marriage,
inspiration for the HEA my characters
are always chasing. x

CHAPTER ONE

UNDERNEATH HER SURGICAL mask Harper Dunn wore the serene expression she'd practised in the mirror and entered Theatre Six from the scrub room, her nerves stretched taut. Her locum position at Manhattan Memorial Hospital, or MMH, meant that seeing *him* was inevitable. Not that she had any intention of allowing one inconvenient ex-husband to stand between her and a coveted position as lead congenital heart surgeon at Manhattan's biggest hospital.

She glanced around the operating room, immediately spying the tall athletic build of Logan Grant. Even with his back to her and dressed in generic green surgical gowns, his stature and the way he carried himself were instantly recognisable. Of course, she'd once traced every inch of his body with her fingertips, her lips, her adoring kisses. But now that the time had come to actually face the man she'd once loved, a man she hadn't seen for ten years, she felt sick to her stomach.

A scrub nurse appeared before her, holding out a sterile gown.

'Thank you,' Harper said, trying to control her body's fight, flight or freeze response as she slipped her arms through the sleeves and pulled on sterile gloves. While the nurse tied her into the gown, Harper looked up, her eyes locking with Logan's.

'Dr Grant,' she said in a clear and unruffled voice, relieved to have got in the first word, even if she was struggling to breathe and speak at the same time. She might be over him, but he was still the last person to whom she wanted to show any hint of weakness. After mutually deciding to divorce and after Harper had fled to London to reinvent herself, they hadn't stayed friends.

'Harper,' he replied, the deep rumble of his voice reigniting long-forgotten memories: her name said a hundred different ways—with laughter, in frustration, on a passionate groan as he'd held her so tightly, she'd been certain they would last for ever, more fool her. She should have known better than to rely on love.

But Logan's voice also lacked surprise.

'I see you were expecting me,' she said. As a senior neonatal congenital heart surgeon at Manhattan Memorial and acting clinical lead, Logan would, of course, know everything that happened in his department.

'I was,' he said with a tilt of his head. 'Welcome.'

No doubt he was also aware that she'd applied for a permanent job he probably already considered his. Too bad she was there to challenge his assumptions...

'Should we get the awkward personal conversation over with?' she asked, clasping her sterile hands together in front of her as she joined him near the monitors used to display the patient's scans and X-rays. 'Or shall we skip straight to discussing the patient before he arrives?'

The corners of Logan's brown eyes crinkled as if he was smiling beneath his mask. The expression was so familiar, it triggered an automatic download of memories from the four years they'd been a couple. Their electric first meeting at a medical school party, the triumphant smile on his face when she'd agreed to marry him a mere two years later, his look of defeat when he'd finally accepted their two-year marriage was over and reluctantly signed the divorce papers. But she hadn't taken it personally; Logan simply hated to fail.

'It's good to see you, Harper,' he said, catching her immediately off guard in his typically competitive way.

'Is it? Really?' she asked dryly, trying not to notice the new scattering of grey hair at his temples that only made him seem mature and distinguished, not older. No doubt he was regarded as something of a silver fox around MMH. He'd always been a classically tall, dark and handsome man.

'I find that hard to believe,' she added, forcing herself to stand close to him, as if he were just another colleague. 'Having your ex-wife apply for the permanent clinical lead position you want must surely be unsettling. I'll essentially be your senior. What a tricky professional dynamic that will be.' She looked up. She'd once loved that he was so much taller than her, six foot three to her five foot six. Now she resented his height advantage.

'If it comes to that...' he said evenly with a dubious raised brow. 'The job isn't yours yet. And just because we're in competition professionally, there's no need to come out fighting.' His eyes narrowed a fraction with the challenge she'd been expecting.

'How else can I make you understand that I'm no longer the old Harper,' she countered with a flick of a glance. 'The one who avoided confrontation at any cost, the one so madly in love with you I'd all but bent myself into the shape of a pretzel trying to fit into your world?' With his pretentious and wealthy family in particular.

'I never asked you to do that,' he said quietly, his stare intense.

'Don't worry,' she bluffed. 'Our divorce was good for me. Not to mention my time at the London Children's Hospital working with Bill McIntyre has considerably bulked out my CV. So I'd say the race for the clinical lead will be a fair fight.' Now that she was back, her ex needed to understand she was there to stay. Her father, Charlie, needed her.

'Well, in that case, may the best surgeon win,' he said, with his trademark confidence, something she'd once found wildly attractive when they'd first met, but now considered irrelevant.

Smirking, she congratulated herself. 'I see *you* haven't changed.'

'And you truly have?' he asked, fire glinting in the depths of his irises.

Because to look into his eyes was to remember the thousand times she'd made love to him, held him through his darkest times, laughed with him over life's little things and soaked up his beautiful smile like a wilting sunflower absorbs rain, Harper pretended to study the baby's radiological images. In truth, knowing that she'd be operating alongside Logan this morning, she'd already scoured the test results and patient files meticulously in preparation for this surgery *and* come in early to examine the baby and meet his concerned parents.

'Definitely,' she said. 'Unlike when we were married, I'm no longer a pushover, willing to tolerate things for an easy life. I've learned a lot about myself these past ten years.'

'Really? Did you learn that you're done with serious relationships?' he asked. 'Because *I'd* heard you were still single.'

Her mouth gaped open under her mask, her scowl blurring her vision. Trust Logan to get straight under her skin. 'Who from?' she asked, outraged, and then thought better of the question. 'You know what, don't bother answering that. My personal life is none of your business. And you know what they say—once bitten, twice shy. One ex-husband is enough for me.'

She met his stare, her chin raised defiantly as she fought her own rampant curiosity. Shamefully, she had occasionally cyber-stalked him over the years, keeping tabs on where he worked, telling herself that, one day, if she ever wanted to return to New York, he might become professional competition. Although she couldn't explain why she'd checked the marriage announcements, from time to time.

'How's Charlie?' he asked, changing the subject, as if he was doing a much better job of being unaffected by her than she was of him, as if they were two old acquaintances catching up, as if this hostile force field separating them was a figment of her imagination.

'My father is fine, thank you.' She glanced away. He didn't need to know that the main reason she'd returned to Manhattan was because her beloved dad, who'd never remarried after Harper's mother had left them both when Harper was ten years old, had developed brittle type 2 diabetes.

'And your family? Biddie and Carter?' she asked about

his parents, more out of an attempt at nonchalance than genuine interest. She didn't wish the Grants ill. It had been Logan who'd far too often abandoned her to their stifling interference and expectations, which had played a big part in the demise of her and Logan's marriage. Growing up in Staten Island from a single parent family, Harper had never quite made the grade with the Grants, who came from old money, ran the most lavish charity galas the city had ever seen and owned large chunks of prime Manhattan real estate.

'They were well the last time I saw them, thanks,' he said, glancing at the anaesthetic room as if in search of their tiny patient. 'I'll let them know you asked after them.'

'Last time? Does that mean your parents have actually backed off from trying to run every aspect of your life?' She sniggered. 'Surely it can't be true...'

When they'd been together, his pushy, social-climbing parents had enjoyed throwing their money around, frequently suggesting influential allies they should meet, expecting the newly married couple at every high-profile social function the city had to offer. With such high expectations resting on his shoulders, Logan had grown up feeling as if he had something to prove. A career in medicine had been *his* choice, not theirs. The Grants had urged their eldest son to join the family business, a historic, billion-dollar real estate empire founded by Logan's great-grandfather that made the family a permanent fixture on the world's rich list.

'I run my own life,' he said looking mildly uncomfortable. 'But maybe we should discuss the case before our patient arrives.'

'Fine.' Harper wasn't there to become once more embroiled in Logan's elite brand of family drama. She had her dad to worry about, and Charlie Dunn only had Harper. 'But you don't need to worry; I'm well prepared. I've obviously reviewed baby Connor's case,' she said, eager to steer her thoughts away from her sudden flare of curiosity about her ex-husband. 'So I'm up to speed.'

She kept her eyes glued to the screen and on Connor's ECHO images, aware that Logan was close, too close for comfort. But it was time to forget that she'd once known everything about this man, to forget the painful past she'd left behind ten years ago and focus on the complex surgery ahead. 'Are there any particular complications you anticipate that we should discuss?'

In the induction room, the anaesthetist was prepping their tiny patient—a two-week-old boy with tetralogy of Fallot, a rare, life-threatening congenital heart malformation featuring a ventricular septal defect, pulmonary valve stenosis, a displaced aorta and an enlarged right ventricle.

'The ventricular septal defect is large,' Logan said, tilting his chin towards the images on the screen. 'But it should patch well.'

Harper nodded, sceptical that they could set aside their personal history and work together; something they'd never done before. 'Are you replacing the pulmonary valve or performing a valvuloplasty?'

'I prefer to decide once I've seen the anatomy,' he said, glancing sideways so she felt his eyes on her. 'What's your preferred method?'

Harper looked up sharply. The Logan she'd known had

been so self-assured, it had rarely occurred to him that opinions differing from his existed.

'I agree,' she said hesitantly, the words sticking in her throat. 'I like to decide once I'm in there. Although I can't quite believe you're asking for my opinion.'

Over the course of their tumultuous two-year marriage, there'd been little upon which they'd agreed. Where they lived—his apartment was bigger and better, thanks to his trust fund, with views of Central Park. Work compromises—at three years her senior, he'd qualified first and therefore had already begun to establish himself in a career before Harper. Family expectations— her father, Charlie, was an ordinary down-to-earth guy, a now-retired high school science teacher. By comparison, the Grants relished the glitz and glamour of Manhattan, always seen at the right parties with the right people, and had expected the same of their son and by extension, Harper, too. A young woman with eye-watering student debt and abandonment issues had stuck out like a sore thumb in their world, especially when Logan had regularly abandoned her to the social events in favour of his work.

'I'm glad we agree.' His eyes crinkled at the corners so she guessed he was smiling again. 'It should be plain sailing.' He glanced up as the anaesthetist finally wheeled their tiny patient into the room.

It was time to focus on work, on operating together for the first time. Telling herself that he was just another man, just another surgeon and that she owed him nothing beyond professional courtesy, Harper swallowed down her nerves.

'Which side of the bed do you prefer?' he asked, tilting his head in the direction of the operating table. 'From memory it's the left, but perhaps you *have* changed.'

Harper's face heated. Trust Logan to make some suggestive quip designed to remind her of their past.

'Oh, I've changed, plenty,' Harper shot back. 'But as you have seniority, *for now*,' she said pointedly, 'I defer to your preference. Of course, if I'm appointed as permanent clinical lead, that won't always be the case. So enjoy it while it lasts.'

His mask moved, his eyes smiling, and Harper looked away, relieved that she'd yet to see his mouth—the fullness of lips, the slanted curve of his smile, that dimple in his cheek. Wondering again at the wisdom of returning to the hospital where Logan worked, not that she'd had much choice—their chosen field was small, specialised and very competitive. She couldn't wait to be on the other side of this operation. To get away from him and gather herself. But with her eye on the prize of the job, Harper had no intention of being sidetracked by memories or friction with her ex-husband.

'Then let's do this,' he said with a decisive nod of his head that she recognised as a trait of the Logan of old. He positioned himself on the opposite side of the operating table from Harper so they could get to work, and Harper had never been more relieved to begin a complex surgery.

CHAPTER TWO

WITH BABY CONNOR'S surgery complete, and as the anaesthetist began to wake their tiny patient from the anaesthetic, Logan stretched out his back muscles and peeled off his gloves and mask, his glance drawn to Harper as it had been the very first time they'd met.

'Well, that went as smoothly as could be expected,' he said about the complex operation, surprised at how well they'd worked together, considering it was their first time and for all intents and purposes their divorce had made them enemies. But damn, she was a good surgeon, easily as good as him.

'Yes,' she said, tossing her garments into the laundry bin with the speedy efficiency that told him she planned to quickly make her escape. Now that the operation was over, the awkwardness from earlier had obviously returned.

But because of their history, it didn't feel right to let her simply walk away. If they were to be colleagues, surely they could be civil? After all, he'd never wished Harper any ill will, even after their divorce. In fact, he'd once loved this woman fiercely. Harper Dunn was the only woman he'd ever loved that deeply.

'Have you had a welcome tour of the hospital?' he

asked, adding his gown and hat to the dirty pile while his heart pounded the way it had when he'd first invited her on a date.

'No,' she said, fresh wariness creeping into her voice. She kept her eyes downcast as she bent over the sink to wash her hands. 'But I'm sure I'll figure it out. One hospital is much like the rest.'

Logan took a sick kind of satisfaction from her response. 'Afraid to be alone with me?' he asked, joining her at the sinks and quickly washing up. 'I know we're both pretending to be unaffected by each other, but are we really fooling anyone, given our history?'

It would be easier if they could pretend their marriage had never happened, but even after ten years apart, if he allowed himself, he could still remember their good times, not just the bad—the passion, the laughter, the feeling that he'd found his soulmate. Maybe Harper could remember the good times, too.

'Don't be ridiculous,' she said, snatching some paper towels from the dispenser and drying her hands. '*I'm* not pretending at all, Logan. And why would I be afraid when I can hardly remember us; it was so long ago.'

'Ouch…' he muttered, rinsing his hands; he didn't believe a word of her speech. But he shouldn't goad her, not when he was trying to clear the air.

'And if my presence bothers *you*, do you really want more of my company?' she asked, turning to face him. 'Are you that much of a glutton for punishment?'

His first full, unobstructed view of her face in ten years punched a disturbing slug of heat through his stomach. She was still gorgeous; he should have expected *that*. She'd always had some kind of bewitching hold over him.

Except her tied-back, long dark hair seemed richer than he remembered. Her golden-brown eyes with their thick lashes displayed all her emotions and sparked with predictable confrontation. And her lips... Full, soft looking with that pronounced cupid's bow, currently turned down in a frown. Why couldn't he for the life of him recall their taste?

Logan shrugged, acting casual while his heart raced. 'If we have to work together, who better than me, the department's acting lead clinician, to show you around? We need to find some way of working harmoniously together.'

But now he was regretting the offer. He didn't want to notice how physically, she still did it for him. Even with several weeks to prepare for her arrival at his hospital, she'd still somehow managed to throw him off balance. She *had* changed in some ways, as she kept reminding him. At thirty-seven, she was, of course, a little older, but she was still sharply intelligent and challenging and sexy as sin. Good thing he had work on which to focus.

'I guess we do need to be civil.' She smiled tightly. 'In that case, I'd love a tour. As long as it includes somewhere I can buy coffee.'

'That can be arranged,' he said, both relieved to have won her over and at the same time wishing he could simply ignore his ex-wife. Just because Harper was a beautiful woman he'd fancied the minute he'd seen her all those years ago, it didn't mean he was interested in making the same mistake twice. It had taken him a long time to get over her, after all.

'The hospital café is upstairs,' he said, holding open the door for her to pass through. His senses braced for that maddening light floral scent he'd immediately recognised even in the sterile environment of the operating room. It hit him anew, flooding his brain with memories. If he allowed himself to think about it, he could probably recall the name of that damned perfume. He'd bought it for her on more than one occasion during their relationship. But he'd spent ten years learning to forget his greatest failure in life: his divorce. He wasn't about to undo all that hard work in one morning.

Guiding her to the nearest flight of stairs, he forced his head to think about something other than how fantastic she looked and smelled. 'The fact that you have your goal set on a substantive post here must mean you're back in Manhattan for good?' He was fishing, but he'd always lived by the principle of *Know your enemy.*

While, after all these years, he still regularly met up for a beer with Charlie, Harper's dad, the two of them had made an unspoken agreement back at the start to rarely bring up Harper during their chats, which mainly centred on baseball and fishing. Charlie had of course, mentioned that Harper was returning from London, adding that she'd never managed to find love again after him, but Logan had breezed over it. Now he wondered if Charlie had ever told his daughter about his ongoing relationship with his ex-son-in-law.

'I'm afraid I am,' she said, shooting him another of those challenging looks that were both new and somehow also familiar. She certainly seemed more driven and ambitious, but still as self-sufficient as always. That aspect of her personality had given him the most grief when they were a couple.

'But surely you would never back down from a little healthy competition?' she added.

His pulse accelerated. Was she deliberately making this race for the job more exciting? She must remember his competitive streak. Dismissing the idea as irrelevant, he smiled. He wouldn't be flirting with his ex-wife, and when it came to competitions, he always won.

'Of course not,' he said. 'And the Harper I once knew was a great doctor. Whichever of us MMH appoints as clinical lead, they'll be getting a world-class surgeon.'

'I see your arrogance hasn't changed in the past ten years,' she said dryly, ignoring his compliment and entering the café on the hospital's ground floor.

'Like you, I've changed plenty, Harper,' he said, quietly, taking a deep, calming breath as they joined the queue. 'Clearly we're going to have to get to know each other all over again.'

After all, their work was intense and specialised, and just like this morning, often necessitated collaboration. The neonatal surgical team was tight-knit, the smaller congenital cardiac surgery team even more so.

'I'm not sure that's necessary,' she said primly as if horrified by the suggestion. 'I know all I need to know in order to effectively do my job, which is all I'm interested in.'

Logan huffed mirthlessly, his composure unravelling. 'There really is no need to keep beating me over the head with how uninterested you are in me as a person. I get it. It's loud and clear. But you know, if you want me to believe you're truly over me, no regrets whatsoever, you might want to consider dropping the hostile attitude, otherwise, it doesn't quite ring true.'

At his reminder of their past, her stare filled with momentary alarm, but she quickly composed herself. 'I knew you hadn't changed,' she challenged, somehow managing to look down her nose at him as she gave him the once-over. 'You're as egotistical as ever, always needing to win. No wonder there's no new wedding ring on your finger...'

His temperature spiked, half annoyance, half excitement. Despite her coolly indifferent act and her predictable jibes, she was just as curious about his personal life as he was about hers. 'It's like you said—one divorce is enough.' He shrugged, faking detachment, when really this woman had always had a knack of getting under his skin. That was one of the reasons their sex life had been so good. There was no fire without a spark.

'And you're right,' he added, 'I do intend to win this particular race. Just because you and I have history, did you really expect I'd simply roll over and allow you to steal a job I've worked my entire career for?'

She fisted her hands on her hips. 'I've worked my whole career for it, too.' Her pretty eyes narrowed. 'Perhaps harder than you, because I'm a woman and because I don't have the privilege of your family connections.'

'There it is...' he muttered, stunned that the deep-rooted source of all their marital disharmony—their differences—had shown itself so early. Fool that he was, he hadn't expected their past resentments, their inability to communicate without lashing out, to resurface so quickly, especially not in the workplace. But no matter how changed she claimed to be, no matter how altered he knew himself to be, no matter how many years had passed, it seemed neither of them had fully resolved the issues that had ultimately led to their divorce.

'I'm not sure I like your insinuation, Dr Dunn,' he said, calmly. 'If I get the permanent clinical lead position, I will have earned it every bit as much as you.' Clearly their ability to rile each other up was one thing that *hadn't* changed.

'Right,' she said with a knowing nod of her head and mocking smile. 'Because your last name has never opened any doors. There's even a Grant Wing in this very hospital.'

Logan clenched his jaw in frustration. 'That was my great-grandfather's name as you well know,' he pointed out, tired of battling a legacy he'd never asked for. Even when his refusal to join the family business had almost caused his parents to disown him, he'd been determined to forge his own path. That's why he'd chosen a career in medicine.

'I can't help the family I was born into,' he added. 'The family you married into, I might add.' Once, a long time ago, she'd loved him enough not to care that he was a Grant.

She turned to face him, glaring, one hand on her hip, accentuating the hourglass shape of her figure, all but daring his gaze to dip to her breasts, her waist, her hips. 'Because I wanted *you*, not your family, although it often felt as if I saw more of your parents than I did of you.'

For an unguarded second, her comment about wanting him stunned him into silence, transporting him back to the early years of their relationship when they'd been crazy for each other and barely able to keep their hands off one another. He'd once loved this woman so fiercely, he used to watch her sleep, marvelling that she was his. But it had soured quicker than either of them had foreseen. They'd rushed into marrying, and he'd neglected her one time too many, although Harper, too, had played her part.

'Did you want me?' he asked, despite the guilt clouding his judgement. 'You had a funny way of showing it. It didn't take long after our wedding for the cracks to start and it wasn't all my fault. You kept shutting me out emotionally.' Each of them had struggled with their own demons. She'd withdrawn every time she was reminded of the fact that her mother had walked out when she was a kid. And he, out of a warped sense of guilt that he'd abandoned his family's business, had thrown himself into his surgical career, neglecting Harper and failing to set robust boundaries for his parents, tolerating way too much of their interference.

'I wasn't solely to blame, either,' she snapped.

'I never said you were.' He scrubbed a hand over his face. The last thing he'd wanted was to publicly air his dirty laundry for the other café patrons to hear. And he couldn't allow their past to interfere with their work, not when it so clearly led down the same dead-end street.

'Your parents took every opportunity to show us both how much they disapproved of your choice of a wife,' she continued, ignoring his comment. 'A motherless nobody from Staten Island was in no way suitable daughter-in-law material. They never liked me.'

'And yet I, too, wanted *you*,' he said quietly, his sense of defeat reignited from the ashes he'd spent the past ten years smothering.

She blinked up at him, a frown cinching her brows. With his pulse whooshing in his ears, the café around them, the other patrons waiting in line disappeared as they faced each other angrily, breaths gusting, eyes clashing.

'Can I help you, Dr Grant?' the woman behind the register said, snapping him back to the present. 'The usual, is it?'

While he and Harper had been pointlessly rehashing old arguments, they'd reached the front of the coffee queue. Logan tried to smile, recalling himself.

'I'll get these,' he said to Harper, stepping forward. 'I have an account here.'

But she was obviously having none of that. 'I'll get my own coffee, thanks,' Harper said, smiling at the bewildered server sweetly.

Logan reluctantly conceded and moved aside, frustration tensing his muscles.

'Listen, Harper,' he patiently said as she joined him in the wait for their coffees. 'Us working together was always going to be an adjustment.' One he'd thought he could handle. Now he simply hoped they could find some way of sharing a workplace without a full-blown war.

'An adjustment…?' she said, scoffing. 'We can't make it half a day in each other's company without retracing well-worn paths paved with grudges and irritations.'

Logan pressed his lips together. She was right. Before he'd seen her again, he'd been confident he could leave the past in the past and work alongside his ex-wife as if she were any other colleague, but now he wasn't so sure.

'I think we should start again,' he went on. 'Our work is clearly important to us both. There's no place here for ego or one-upmanship. And how well we fit into a team environment will influence the admissions panel when it comes to appointing the clinical lead.'

'I agree,' she said haughtily, refusing to look his way. 'But this hospital tour was obviously a mistake. While we *have* to be colleagues, while we can put patients first and collaborate professionally, we clearly can't be *friends*.' She spoke the word with distaste, as if the idea of them ever getting along was unthinkable. 'There's too much history between us.' She looked up, her beautiful stare full of frustration and hurt, a flicker of vulnerability perhaps. Or maybe he imagined the latter.

'Maybe you're right,' he said with a sigh. 'After all, it wasn't friendship that brought us together.' That had been their mutual attraction, instantaneous, burning bright and hot.

'I suggest we simply focus on doing our jobs,' she said, her voice clipped. 'That's why *I'm* here. We cooperate when we must, but otherwise stay the hell away from each other. No more personal conversations. Because, when it comes to us, there really is nothing else left to say.'

Logan sighed again and bit his tongue. On some level, he had plenty he wanted to say. In the ten years he'd had to reflect on what had gone wrong in their marriage, he'd often wished he could go back in time and fix it. Instead, he'd lived with the guilt that he'd inadvertently neglected his marriage and hadn't stood up to his parents soon enough. He hadn't disabused them of all their fixed expectations, or fought against their pressures to conform and he hadn't protected Harper well enough. If he had, maybe, just maybe, he and Harper would still be together, because he'd never quite shaken the dissatisfaction of losing her.

'Maybe you should have thought about us having to

avoid each other before accepting a locum position here,' he muttered, deflated. 'There are other hospitals.' Although MMH was the biggest, the neonatal cardiac surgery department the top statewide. And while physically he could try and keep his distance, he had a bad feeling that mentally she would occupy many of his thoughts now that he'd seen her again. After all, it had taken him years to forget her the first time around.

'I had no choice, believe me,' she snapped. 'I'm an only child. My father has never remarried and he's—' She broke off, her voice strangled with emotion as she looked away.

But then she'd always struggled to rely on him emotionally, something he attributed to her mother's abandonment, something that had made him feel so helpless while they were married. She had even less reason to confide in him now.

'Is Charlie the reason you came back?' he pushed, stunned because he liked and respected Charlie, considered him a friend. The last time they met he'd seemed fine.

She swallowed and collected herself, her reply reluctant. 'He's not well. I need to be close to him.'

Logan's mind reeled, the past instantly forgotten. 'I'm sorry. I had no idea. What's wrong? Is it serious?' He frowned and fought the instinct to reach out and touch her for comfort. He'd last seen Charlie a month ago. The older man had ordered a soft drink rather than his usual beer, saying he needed to lose a little weight, but Logan hadn't thought much of it given that Charlie had been his usual cheerful self. They'd discussed the Yankees latest win and their vacation plans before Charlie had let slip that Harper was coming back. He hadn't mentioned a word about his health.

'I don't want to discuss it,' she said, leaving the unspoken *least of all with you* coiled between them like razor wire.

'Okay,' Logan bit out, frustrated that he had more questions than answers. But given he was just an ex-husband she struggled to be in the same room with, his curiosity where Harper was concerned seemed utterly futile. He would ask Charlie directly.

In that moment, her coffee arrived. She took it from the barista with another smile that left him irrationally jealous. Once, a long time ago, before he'd let her down and taken her for granted, she'd smiled at him that way.

She was about to turn away when he touched her arm, halting her escape. He hated feeling helpless and shut out. But damn, her skin *was* as soft as he remembered, and this close, her eyes were even more beautiful. 'I'm sorry about Charlie. If there's anything I can do...'

'Thank you,' she said automatically as she eyed his hand on her arm with suspicion, as if he were contagious. 'I need to go. I'm meeting my resident, Jess, on the NICU.'

'Right.' Logan released her and nodded, frustration an itch under his skin. 'Well, rest assured that unless it's patient or work related, I'll keep my distance, as requested.' He'd do his best to ignore her. After all, treating her as just another colleague was unlikely to be anywhere near as hard as getting over her had been, and he'd survived that.

She looked up. 'Great.' A moment of hesitation seemed to hover in her gaze, but she pushed her shoulders back, that polite, indifferent mask falling over her features. 'Have a good day.'

With a sigh, he watched her leave the café, her ponytail swinging. Working together was one thing. They'd proved this morning that they could successfully collaborate when they needed to, even though she was still sporting a massive chip on her shoulder and a whole heap of resentment directed Logan's way. But forgetting about Harper Dunn, when she was still sexy enough to scramble his mind? He hadn't managed to achieve that these past ten years, so what hope did he have now that she was back in his everyday life?

CHAPTER THREE

PREDICTABLY, HARPER HADN'T slept well on her first night back. Aside from the successful surgery, her reunion with Logan had been as disastrous as she'd imagined. No matter how hard she'd tried to stay immune to him, and despite his insistence that he'd changed, Logan had still managed to worm his way under her skin. Their fight in the café had unsettled her. His accusation that she'd kept him out emotionally when they'd been together had played on her mind as she'd lain awake for hours. Even now, the next morning, she couldn't help but ruminate on her struggles with her feelings of abandonment throughout her teens and twenties. But what had been the point of talking about something she'd had no power to change?

As Harper and her fifth-year neonatal surgical resident, Jess, arrived on the NICU for a ward round, Harper resolved to shove Logan from her mind. Pausing at the sinks to wash her hands, she scanned the ward, her stomach sinking when she spied Logan and his resident, Greg, talking to some parents. He looked good out of scrubs. Urbane and professional. If she were a parent with a sick baby, she would absolutely trust his judgement.

That didn't mean she trusted *him*.

'Where do you want to start?' Jess asked as Harper finished drying her hands.

'As Dr Grant is already here, why don't we start on the other side of the ward.' Today was a new day. Ignoring Logan unless they were discussing work seemed the only logical plan, and it would help her to manage the unexpected and surprisingly strong resurgence of attraction.

She and Jess were just about to begin their ward round when an ear-splitting alarm sounded. They rushed to the crowded bedside, along with Logan and Greg. The nurses drew the curtains and Harper reeled to see the baby in distress was Connor, the patient she and Logan had operated on the day before.

A sense of panic descended. All four of them, as well as the neonatal nurses, worked side by side to assess the baby, checking tubes and electrodes, measuring vital signs and taking blood for analysis.

'Oxygen saturations have dropped,' Greg told them, adjusting the flow of oxygen through the baby's ventilator. 'But he's been stable overnight.'

With her panicked pulse bounding and her mind filtering the possible causes for Connor's respiratory distress, Harper glanced at the monitors, noting that the baby's breathing was rapid and his heart rate slow, the amount of oxygen in his blood alarmingly low.

Logan had his stethoscope in his ears, the bell held to the baby's tiny chest. Harper reached for her own stethoscope, placing it next to Logan's. Their fingers brushed in the confined space of the incubator, but there was no time to worry about that. At twenty-four hours post-op, any setback in Connor's recovery was extremely alarming.

After a few seconds, Logan looked up, his stare meeting Harper's, his concern evident.

'I think he has reduced breath sounds on the left,' Harper said, relieved to see Logan nod in confirmation that he'd heard the same thing. 'Possible pneumothorax.'

'I agree.' Logan nodded. Where yesterday had been about their divisions, now that their shared patient was in danger, they seemed to be united. Logan turned to both residents. 'Call Radiology for an urgent chest X-ray.'

Jess nodded and pulled out her phone, stepping away to make the call.

'Any fever?' Logan asked Greg, snapping on a pair of gloves.

Greg shook his head. A post-op infection would also need to be excluded, but a pneumothorax was more immediately life-threatening. The baby's blood pressure dropped and another alarm sounded.

'We don't have time to wait for an X-ray,' Logan said.

'I agree. Let's try to aspirate.' Harper reached for a sterile needle and syringe from a nearby trolley and passed them to him before quickly pulling on her own gloves. While Logan opened the packaging of the syringe, she swabbed the skin of the baby's left chest wall with an alcohol wipe.

'Thanks,' Logan nodded in gratitude. There wasn't much space for them both to work, but every second counted.

With the needle inserted into Connor's chest cavity, Logan pulled back on the syringe and removed twenty CCs of air that had escaped the baby's lung. Almost immediately, Connor's oxygen saturations improved, his blood pressure stabilising.

'Good call.' Harper released a sigh of relief, seeing the same emotion in Logan's expression. At least clinically, they were on the same wavelength.

'It could be a ventilation pneumothorax,' Logan said to the residents. 'But let's get a repeat ECHO to check the heart.'

'Are you okay to insert a chest tube?' Harper asked Jess, her mind spinning through a list of possible post-op complications.

Jess nodded and Greg said, 'We can do it together.'

Just then the radiographer arrived with the portable X-ray machine and with the baby stabilised for now, everyone moved aside for the radiographer to take the X-ray.

'Let Connor's parents know about the incident,' Harper said to his NICU nurse. 'Reassure them that Dr Grant has treated Connor and he's stable now, but either myself or Dr Grant will speak to them and explain everything when they come in.'

Logan peeled off his gloves and headed for the sink to wash his hands and Harper followed.

'Are we missing anything?' she asked Logan as she washed up, her pulse still racing away. 'I checked on him last night before I left, and he was stable.' Their work came with a high burden of responsibility, and she wouldn't be human if she didn't feel it sometimes. When your patients were so tiny and vulnerable, those alarms, which usually indicated something serious, were terrifying.

'I checked him, too,' Logan said, glancing her way so she saw both reassurance and lingering worry in his stare. 'His observations have been stable overnight. We were both happy with how the surgery went.'

She nodded, grateful that, for this patient, the responsibility was shared. Even if their personal grudges were unresolved, they could at least be cooperative at work. She'd seen yesterday how Logan was indeed a world-class surgeon. She couldn't begrudge him her professional respect. And there was something about watching him interact with tiny babies that was…unsettling. Perhaps it was just that once, a long time ago, she'd imagined herself having *their* babies.

'Common things are common,' he went on, logically. 'Let's suspend our concerns until we have the test results back.'

'You're right.' Harper swallowed, only partly reassured. Logan was the last person she'd thought she'd look to for any kind of support. But just because she trusted his clinical judgement, didn't mean she'd changed her mind about them being friends. For one, their chemistry was still pretty potent, and secondly, they'd proved yesterday that they couldn't be trusted to have any kind of personal conversation without bickering.

Harper hesitated, also recalling how yesterday, when he'd touched her arm and offered to be there for Charlie, she'd almost embarrassed herself with the sting of tears in her eyes. It had been a long time since Harper had relied on anyone but herself emotionally. She'd learned the hard way, when her mother left and again when her marriage had fallen apart, that relying on others was a sure-fire way to be hurt and let down.

'Why don't we leave Jess and Greg to liaise over the test results,' Logan added as they dried their hands side by side, that prickly wariness between them building. Clearly their residents were used to working together, even if *they* weren't.

But what had she expected? She'd told him to leave her alone unless they were discussing a patient or operating together.

'One of us can review Connor again in light of any new findings,' he added. 'I'm happy to do that, unless you want to.' He met her stare. His was wary.

'I'm sure that neither of us will be satisfied unless we've reviewed him again. It doesn't really matter which of us gets around to it first.' Harper looked back to where their residents stood at Connor's bedside in close conversation. *Very* close conversation, their whispering and body language stating they were way more intimate than two colleagues in the same department.

'Are they a couple?' Harper asked Logan, her curiosity getting the better of her. Technically, talk about their residents' personal lives wasn't work related, so she was kind of breaking her own rules. But as the newest team member, she didn't want to be out of the loop.

Logan followed the direction of her stare with his own. 'Yes,' he said, that same gaze landing on Harper. 'Young love. Do you remember what it felt like?'

Harper stiffened and then before she could stop herself, scoffed. 'Vaguely...' she lied, returning her glance to the couple. 'I hope for their sakes they don't learn the hard way how fleeting love can be. How it's better to rely on yourself, make your own happiness.'

She looked up at him defiantly, needing to remind him and herself that yes, the love they'd shared in their twenties had been intense and optimistic, but she and Logan couldn't forget where they'd gone wrong, or how quickly that love had disintegrated.

'They seem pretty solid,' Logan countered, his eyes flashing with challenge. 'In fact, they're engaged.' His eyes dipped to her mouth and she self-consciously licked her lips. 'If you stick around MMH, you might even receive an invitation to the wedding in a few weeks.'

Stepping away, he balled his paper towels and aimed them at the bin.

Harper pursed her lips in annoyance, galled that he seemed more relaxed than her about discussing the past. 'I told you I'm sticking around, and I told you why.' They were veering back into personal territory, but she'd been the one to initiate this topic of conversation.

At her reminder, a small frown cinched his brows together. 'Is Charlie okay?' he asked again. 'I messaged him last night but I haven't heard back yet.'

Harper's jaw dropped in astonishment. 'You messaged my father?'

'Yes.' Logan shrugged, slinging his hands casually into the pockets of his pants. 'I was worried about him after what you said. Is that so hard to believe? Do you have such a low opinion of me?'

Harper frowned, shaking her head, reluctant to acknowledge that her ex was a decent human being. But of course he was. He was a doctor, and just like it had yesterday in the hospital café, his concern for Charlie seemed genuine. It would be churlish of her to keep Charlie's news from him, even if she and Logan couldn't be confidants.

'He's been diagnosed with type 2 diabetes,' she said, reluctantly. 'He has a glucose monitoring device and is on insulin, but it's proving quite difficult to manage. There's no need for you to worry.'

As she spoke, Harvey's frown deepened and he crossed his arms over his chest, one hand stroking his clean-shaven chin in that thoughtful way of his. 'I'm shocked to hear that,' he said, stepping closer and dropping his voice to a more intimate level. 'I saw him not long ago, and your father has always been so healthy and active.'

'My grandmother was diabetic,' she said confused that he seemed to know Charlie so well. 'Bad genes, I guess. Where did you see him?' She was supposed to be avoiding personal conversations, but if her father and her ex-husband had talked about her, she wanted to know.

Logan's expression remained calm and resolute, as if he had nothing to hide. 'I met up with him in Brooklyn. We went out for a beer, although he didn't drink alcohol. Now I understand why.'

Harper gaped, thrown off balance once more because the older Logan seemed full of surprises. 'You met my father for a beer?' she asked, incredulous. Why? Had they done that before? And did they talk about her?

Logan nodded, his expression perfectly relaxed. 'Yeah, we've been meeting up every month for the past ten years. Charlie and I have always got along,' he said simply, his stare boring into hers.

Suddenly, there didn't seem to be enough air. 'I can't believe this,' she muttered. 'You've stayed in touch with my father since the divorce?' What kind of man did that? She'd assumed that, like her, he'd want nothing more to do with her, her family or any reminders of what they'd once meant to each other after their split. Now it seemed she was wrong. While she'd run away to London to forget him, he'd carried on his relationship with her father as if they were still together.

'Yeah.' Logan nodded, staring at her in that intense way of his.

Harper reeled. Why had her father never told her? Perhaps because after the divorce, she'd needed a fresh start. She'd moved to London and refused to talk about her ex, even with Charlie. After all what was the point? It had been over.

'What do you talk about?' she asked in spite of her better judgement, her stomach twisting with a discomfort she couldn't name.

'I could tell you,' Logan said, 'but as it's not work related, you've forbidden it.'

She scowled up at him, bound by a rule of her own making.

Logan checked his watch. 'I'm sorry, I need to get on with the rest of my ward round.'

Harper nodded, more confused than ever. 'Of course. Me too.'

He paused beside her and leaned close so she was bathed in that cologne of his. 'Please send Charlie my regards.' He raised his hand to catch Greg's attention, then looked down at Harper. 'And if you ever decide that you want to talk about us after all, you know where to find me.'

He headed across to the other side of the NICU, where Greg was waiting. All Harper could do was watch him go and feel horribly confused. How had she once more been lured into a personal conversation when she'd insisted that they only speak to one another about work?

And how, when she was determined to come out on top in all her dealings with her ex-husband, did she feel as if he'd somehow gained the upper hand?

CHAPTER FOUR

TWO DAYS LATER, at the end of a long day, Logan was in the small room on the NICU designated for performing procedures on babies too unwell to leave the department, when Harper and Jess arrived.

'It is okay if Jess and I observe?' Harper asked, slipping on a mask from a box by the door. Her voice was wary but she didn't need to be there; she'd come by choice.

'Of course,' Logan replied, his gaze drawn to hers and his heart leaping excitedly. After the emergency on the NICU with baby Connor, they'd successfully steered clear of one another, only speaking when necessary about the patients in their joint care. That hadn't stopped Logan from constantly thinking about Harper or searching for a glimpse of her around the hospital. 'Why don't you scrub in,' Logan said to Harper, 'in case I need an extra pair of hands.'

Yes, things between them were...tense, but Logan trusted her as a surgeon.

'Okay,' she said as if eager to be involved. She donned a lead apron, washed her hands and slipped into a sterile gown and gloves.

Jess stood with Greg near the radiographer, where they

could see the monitor and the images of the cardiac cath-eterisation procedure but were away from the sterile zone. Harper stood opposite Logan, the patient between them.

'This is three-week-old Alex,' Logan said. 'He has a PDA.' Patent ductus arteriosus was a condition that allowed the redirection of too much blood to the lungs. The vessel was important in the foetus, as the mother was breathing for her baby. Normally, it closed soon after birth, but sometimes, as in Alex's case, it failed to shut.

'So far, it's been resistant to non-invasive treatments,' he went on. 'So I'm attempting a PDA occlusion, today.'

'It's resisted first and second line drugs?' Harper asked, studying the images from the baby's most recent ECHO on an overhead screen, which showed the abnormal blood flow from his heart and the size of the abnormal vessel connecting the two major arteries leaving his heart.

'Yes.' Logan nodded. 'He's currently a high-risk candidate for open-heart surgery, and he's showing signs of worsening lung function.' The transcatheter procedure was technically less invasive than surgery, but all procedures carried risk. And the most common side effect with this approach was bleeding.

'So will you be using an occluder or a vascular plug?' Harper asked about the device he would insert into the abnormal vessel between the baby's aorta and pulmonary artery.

'I prefer an occluder,' he replied, glancing at the anaesthetist, who gave the all-clear to begin the procedure. 'Right, if everyone is ready, let's get started.'

With the anaesthetist and the neonatal nurse monitoring the baby's vital signs—pulse, blood pressure, oxygen saturation and respiratory rate—Logan used the ECHO probe to locate the baby's femoral artery and vein in the groin. With the vessel located, he passed a guide wire into the vein, slowly feeding it along the vessels towards the heart.

He paused intermittently, and the radiographer displayed the position of the tip of the guide wire with real-time X-rays and the use of fluoroscópic dye that outlined the blood vessels.

'Right,' Logan said to the residents observing. 'I'm going to insert the occlusion device now.' Trying not to hold his breath, he slowly and carefully fed the device along the guide wire. With the occlusion device in the correct location lying across the abnormal connection, or ductus, he took one final X-ray to ensure he was happy with the position.

'Looks like a good placement,' Harper said, as she scrutinised the image and then glanced his way encouragingly.

Logan nodded, happy with the images. Slowly, he began to withdraw the guide wire. That was when the baby's heart rate shot up, triggering an ear-splitting alarm.

Logan froze, his eyes darting to the heart monitor, which showed an abnormally fast heart rate.

'Ventricular tachycardia,' the anaesthetist said, jerking to his feet. 'Blood pressure is falling.'

Adrenaline shot into Logan's system. The abnormal heart rhythm meant the heart was beating too fast to be effective. As both he and Harper tried to locate a pulse, her eyes met his.

'Nothing,' she said. 'You?'

Logan shook his head, his stomach sinking. 'He's in cardiac arrest.'

Shifting positions, Harper placed her hands around the baby's chest so her thumbs met over his sternum and commenced cardiac compressions. Logan quickly reached for the defibrillator, charging the device to deliver an electrical shock to the baby's heart.

'Clear,' he said, waiting for Harper to remove her hands. He placed the paddles on the baby's chest and delivered the shock.

With his pulse a deafening roar in his head, Logan stared at the heart monitor. It took a second or two, but then the heart returned to a normal, sinus rhythm. Logan all but sagged with relief. To check, he placed his fingertip in the baby's opposite groin, feeling the reassuring beat of the femoral pulse.

'Blood pressure recordable again,' the anaesthetist said, the tension around the room easing as everyone breathed normally once more.

Logan swallowed hard, the close call rattling him so his insides trembled from the adrenaline rush. Cardiac arrest were two of the most terrifying words when it came to their tiny and vulnerable patients. This procedure should have been relatively routine and less risky than open-heart surgery, but he knew from experience that he always needed to be ready for anything. Cardiac arrhythmias were more common in babies with congenital heart disease. And while this one might have been triggered by the procedure, Logan hadn't done anything wrong. That didn't stop the sudden flare of inadequacy the emergency had brought on.

'Well done,' Harper whispered as he looked up to see

his relief was mirrored in her eyes. Surgeon to surgeon, she was offering support, but because of their personal history, because she'd whispered her words as if for his ears only, her praise felt somehow intimate. And with things between them so...prickly, he wasn't prepared for that.

'Is everyone happy to proceed?' he asked, breathing through the feeling of responsibility. The buck *did* stop with him. This was his patient and he was the acting clinical lead in the department.

With the nod from the anaesthetist and catching the same from Harper, Logan continued to slowly withdraw the guide wire, completing the procedure without further incident.

'Let's run some blood tests,' he told Greg as he pulled off his gloves and mask, trying to hide how rattled he still felt. His resident nodded and set about taking a sample from the baby's central venous line.

'Can you order a repeat ECHO,' Harper asked Jess, who nodded and accessed the computer in the corner of the room.

'Keep an eye on Alex's urine output,' Logan told the neonatal nurse. 'And I want thirty-minute observations until further notice.'

As the nursing staff prepared baby Alex for a return to the NICU, Logan removed his gown and made a note of the procedure in Alex's file. Rationally, he knew that this could happen to anyone, including Harper, but for some reason, he couldn't look her way. He felt too raw. And instinct told him she would know exactly how he was feeling because of their history. Just like he knew her, she knew him. And with their past hurts unresolved, he didn't want her to see him when he was feeling so vulnerable.

'I'll go and speak to Mum and Dad,' he told Greg, before leaving the room and heading for the NICU family room. As he walked, he reasoned away his reaction. As his wife, Harper had once known him better than anyone. Would she still know that he struggled to tolerate failure, whether it was in his personal life or at work? He knew where that perfectionist trait came from: his parents' constant expectations while he'd been growing up. And when it came to Harper... He considered losing her his biggest failure of all. That was something he definitely didn't want her to know.

With baby Alex stable and recovering on the NICU after his procedure, Harper was thinking about leaving the hospital for the night, when her feet paused outside Logan's office. She loitered in the corridor, her heart thudding erratically and her stare fixed on his closed door. Was he still there or had he already gone home?

Because she'd once known him so well, and because he was still essentially the same person with the same values, she'd immediately recognised how shaken by the cardiac arrest he'd been earlier. She would have felt the same if she'd been the one performing the procedure. Everyone in that room had felt that sense of panic and urgency. Losing a baby was the worst part of their job.

She dragged in a breath, torn between keeping her word and staying away or making sure he was okay. Logan was a good surgeon, but he'd always been driven and uncompromising. No doubt he'd be meticulously analysing what he could have done differently right about now. But it was none of her business how he dealt with the tougher psychological aspects of their work. So why couldn't she just walk away?

Deciding it was best to show she was a team player, clear her conscience and check up on him she tapped on the door. Maybe she felt compelled because he'd offered her support over Charlie's diagnosis, or because he'd been constantly on her mind this week. Or maybe it was simply that their past history gave them a connection that was almost impossible to ignore and if she simply went home without ensuring he was okay, she'd only ruminate and worry her way through another sleepless night.

She held her breath, second-guessing the impulse. He wouldn't necessarily want her reassurance anyway, not when things between them were so…complicated. She was just about to walk away, deciding that he wasn't in his office after all, when the door opened.

He stood framed in the doorway, his tie removed, his top few shirt buttons undone and his dark gaze haunted.

'Hi…' she said, her throat tight. 'I just wanted to check you're okay before I left for the night.'

Memories of when he'd lost his beloved grandfather slammed into her. Back then, she'd held him throughout a long, sleepless night, silently making love to him in the pre-dawn, loving him so hard she could never have predicted that her feelings would end. Now the instinct to touch him was so strong she curled her fingers into fists. The thing that had been niggling at her for the entire week she'd been back nudged at her mind again. She didn't really know this older version of Logan even though she recognised traits of his similar to the man she'd once loved. He *had* changed. He was older and more confident, not that he'd ever had problems in that area. But he seemed more comfortable in his skin.

'Come in,' he said, inviting her into his office, which had a desk, a sofa and even a kitchenette with a sink and bar fridge.

Harper closed the door, her hands twisting together helplessly. Maybe this had been a mistake. She was supposed to be steering clear of him.

'It could have happened to anyone, Logan,' she said, sensing his doubts, knowing he'd be hard on himself because he hated to fail. 'We've all been there. I hope you're not blaming yourself.'

Logan winced, turning away from her. 'Would that knowledge make *you* feel any better if you'd been the one in charge of the procedure?' He took two bottles of water from the fridge and passed one to Harper, avoiding eye contact. 'Would it help when you had to explain to the frantically worried parents how their baby's heart had stopped under your care?'

Because her legs felt shaky, Harper sat on the edge of the sofa. 'I guess not,' she admitted in defeat. 'But you push yourself harder than most people. At least you used to…' The more she learned about this older Logan, the less certain she was that she'd ever known the smallest thing about him, other than how he'd made her feel cherished at first, and then later on in their relationship, lonely, abandoned, inadequate. Or maybe she'd made herself feel that final way, because of her mother…

'It's not that I push myself,' he said, wheeling his desk chair from behind the desk to sit opposite her. 'I just… hate to fail.'

Harper shrugged and smiled sadly. 'Same difference.'

His admission surprised her. They weren't able to be friends, only exes and colleagues. The Logan she'd been married to had often struggled to be vulnerable or express his feelings, thanks to his parents' expectations. Because of her abandonment issues, she'd been the same, so she hadn't pushed him too hard. Back then, they'd both locked part of themselves away.

'Anyway,' he said, unscrewing the lid of his bottle and taking a swallow, 'I thought we weren't allowed to discuss the past.' He was looking at her in a way that made her all too aware they were alone, late at night, the hospital around them quiet with only a skeleton staff on the night shift.

'We're not.' She looked down at her lap. 'I'm just checking up on a colleague after an alarming emergency. That's work related. And you'd do the same if it had been me running the procedure.'

'I would,' he said with a decisive nod. Something shifted between them as they stared at each other in awkward silence, the seconds ticking by. Harper fought the urge to squirm under his scrutiny while her heart galloped.

'Perhaps this was a mistake,' she said finally, placing her untouched bottle of water on the table and rising to her feet. 'I shouldn't have disturbed you. Sorry.'

She no longer knew this man, and because of the past, it wasn't her place to offer advice or comfort. Why would he want that from her, just like she wouldn't seek it from him? But his friendship with Charlie was...confusing.

He stood, too, their bodies closer than she'd have liked. 'I'm glad you stopped by,' he said, his glance shifting over her face. 'I've been wanting to talk to you. I don't think our agreement is working. I'd like to revise it.'

'Of course you would,' Harper said, unsurprised. 'What about it isn't working?' She raised her chin, looking up at him. His height and the cramped space meant he filled her vision, a perspective that left her jittery. It had been a long time since she'd been this close to him and alone.

'When I agreed to steer clear of you, I hadn't properly considered all the practicalities,' he said. 'With us seeing each other all the time around the hospital, with us working so closely together, things have been...playing on my mind.'

'What kind of things?' she asked cautiously, preparing for another disagreement.

'Well firstly,' he said, 'I'd like to clear the air and apologise for your first day.'

Harper started, blinking up at him, shocked into silence by his willingness to admit fallibility.

'I wasn't quite as prepared to see you again as I'd hoped I'd be,' he added, his eye contact unwavering despite him admitting he'd been nervous to see her. 'And obviously those past resentments are still there and need addressing. It certainly wasn't my intention to dredge up the past. It's like you said—ancient history. Like it or not, I had to get over you a long time ago.' His eyes bored into hers, as if he was forcing himself to prove the truth of his words.

Like it or not...?

Harper held her breath, more confused than ever. 'I got over you, too,' she said, unable to keep the challenge from her voice. But exactly how hard had it been for him to forget her? She'd assumed he'd moved on pretty quickly. After all, their entire relationship, their marriage certainly, had been brief. But now she'd not only discovered that he'd kept in touch with Charlie, but that he'd maybe struggled to let go of their relationship. These new revelations were messing with her head.

'And I did my fair share of dredging that first day,' she added. 'I'm a big girl. I can own up to my share of the blame, but I really didn't come here to talk about us.' Not when she was desperately trying to ignore the fact that they'd ever been a couple in order to manage her confusion at still finding him attractive, familiar but also foreign.

'I know,' he said, his eyes hardening. 'And I know we can't be friends. But that emergency earlier has proved that we can't simply operate as colleagues, either, separately going about our business. If you're staying on at MMH, we'll see a lot more of each other, whichever of us gets the job as clinical lead. I'd like to think we're mature enough to move past the fact that we used to be married, a long time ago.'

Harper hesitated, her brain snagging on how it had felt to be married to him. When times were good, they were amazing together, but she'd learned over the years not to torture herself with those particular memories. What was done, was done. She'd had to learn that when her mother left.

'So in the hopes of clearing the air between us,' he went on, 'I want to apologise, again.'

Harper frowned, her pulse whooshing in her ears. 'What for?' The old Logan had been uncompromising, bordering on arrogant, rarely admitting he was wrong.

For a second, doubt shifted over his expression. 'I let you down as a husband,' he said, holding her eye contact so her breath caught. 'I've always regretted that. Like I said, I hate to fail.' A ghost of a smile tugged at his mouth, and for an unguarded moment, Harper longed to see one of his genuine, full-blown smiles. Logan had an amazing smile.

'I...' She faltered. Stunned that he had regrets, and even more stunned that he'd admit them to her of all people, Harper blinked repeatedly, searching for the right words. 'You can't take all the blame,' she said, breathing hard. 'Our marital implosion was a joint effort. I didn't enjoy feeling second place to your career or being managed by your parents. It made me feel constantly inadequate. But my thirties have been all about learning that conflict isn't fatal. That I can hold my own, state my opinion calmly and decisively, rather than backing down, saying nothing and then feeling resentful.' Maybe they'd both do things differently now that they were older and wiser...

'I guess we were both dealing with things,' he said, tilting his head. 'Maybe we rushed into marrying because I had to start work while you were still a medical student.' He scrubbed a hand over his face so he heard the rasp of his facial hair, and she wondered how it would feel against her skin. 'Since you left, I've learned to take full ownership of my life and admit my flaws. Losing you certainly helped me to come to terms with the fact that I'm not ever going to be the perfectly moulded son my parents wanted.' He shrugged, his eyes hardening. 'Needless to say, they're still processing that reality. But it's no longer my problem.'

It came then, the smile she'd secretly craved, cautious at first, most likely because they had so much history and so much time had elapsed since they'd trusted each other. But just because this was the most honest conversation they'd ever had, she didn't need to trust him to work with him.

As his lips stretched wider, her stare snagged on his sexy mouth. That he'd changed, that he harboured regrets made no difference now. It was too late for them. And there was still a part of her desperate to cling to those past resentments. To let go of them fully would force her to acknowledge how little her attraction to this man had waned over the past ten years. Rationally, it made sense. Their insatiable chemistry, their healthy sex life had been the one area of their marriage that worked without effort. That didn't mean she had any desire to relive the past or fall back into old patterns.

'We don't have to talk about this,' she croaked out almost pleadingly. 'We're obviously both feeling emotional after the scare of the cardiac arrest, and it's late. It's been a long day in a busy week.' Emotional decisions were always open to regret and she couldn't afford to have regrets where Logan was concerned.

He nodded, his eyes glittering. 'I'm not denying that, but I think we need to talk sometime, Harper. About us. About what went wrong. Don't you ever think about it?'

Static buzzed in Harper's ears. How often did *he* think about it? 'Maybe...'

Maybe it wouldn't hurt to talk. Maybe it would help them both to lay the past to rest.

'But not tonight,' she finished.

That *he* had regrets, that he might be stuck in the past

added to her desperation to get away from the way he was making her feel, as if they could wipe the slate clean and start again. It would suit her better if they left their messy past *in* the past. Only there were elements of their relationship still very much rooted in the present, like their chemistry. No matter how hard she tried to ignore that, it constantly knocked her off balance.

'I should go,' she said, wrapping up the conversation as she glanced at the closed door. But her feet felt welded to the carpet.

'Thanks for checking on me.' He shifted his body, stepping closer still.

For a terrifying and exhilarating second, he looked like he might lean in and kiss her cheek. Acting on some kind of long-forgotten instinct, Harper responded, meeting him halfway, her conflicted thoughts finally falling silent as their lips touched.

Time sped up as exhilaration shot through her. His hands cupped her face and pulled her close. She rested her palms on his chest and surged up onto her toes, intercepting his passionate kiss as if it was the most natural thing in the world. To some extent it was. He might seem like a completely new man, but he was also achingly familiar. Just Logan. And he'd once been everything to her.

Harper's pulse bounded harder as his lips slid over hers, coaxing, chasing. His arms banded around her back so she was crushed against his hard chest. The well-known scent and heat of him washed over her like some sort of intoxicating love potion, drugging and entrancing, making her forget.

But she *didn't* love him any more. This was simply lust and poor judgement working hand in hand. Before her brain had a chance to snap out of its daze, his tongue surged against hers, turning her legs molten. As if acting on their own, her fingers tunnelled into his hair. She returned his kisses, losing herself for a moment in the good parts of their past. Moaning because it had been so long since she'd kissed anyone, and her body remembered this intense pleasure she'd only ever felt with Logan, craved it as if rebelling against the enforced abstinence she'd put it through in London, where she'd had only a couple of semi-serious relationships over the years.

But unlike those London men she'd optimistically dated off and on, she knew exactly where she stood with Logan. This meant nothing. They'd just done it so many times in the past their bodies remembered the moves. Muscle memory. And it was clearly a reaction to stress. A moment of madness that she'd put a stop to, any second. Unless he did first.

His hand found her breast and she gasped against his lips, darts of desire passing through her like lightning strikes. She needed to stop. She would, soon… His thumb brushed over her nipple through her clothes, and her body all but incinerated, liquid heat flooding her belly, her pelvis, her legs, leaving her unstable, so she clung to him.

'Harper…' he said after tearing his mouth away, her name and his eyes full of questions for which she had no logical answers. His fingers continued to stroke her nipple, driving her insane with need. His lips trailed down the side of her neck and she felt the hardness of him against her belly. Her mind spun, reason fighting its way to the surface for breath. What was she doing kissing her ex-husband? And at work? Just because it felt good didn't mean it was a good idea.

With an effort that felt superhuman, she finally shoved him away; her heart beating so fast she couldn't seem to catch her breath. They faced each other, panting hard. Dark desire made his eyes almost black. She looked away, blocking out the sight of him aroused and confused, reluctant to see how much he wanted her, because to witness it would be to admit she wanted him, too.

'That was stupid,' she said, choking back the surge of longing. Her body remembered the sublime pleasure of being touched by him, whether her mind wanted it to or not. A part of her knew giving in to that pleasure would be good. She and Logan had always just clicked in the bedroom. But that alone hadn't been enough to save their relationship.

Logan scrubbed a hand through his hair and then dragged it over his face. 'Probably,' he agreed, stepping back, putting some distance between them. 'You should go.'

Probably...?

What did he mean by that? Did he want to revisit the past? Part of Harper was tempted, too, because it would just be sex, really good sex. Nothing else could ever happen between them, not when they'd previously been there, bought the T-shirt *and* left a scathing one-star review.

'It's been an emotional day,' she reasoned, needing some logical explanation for why she'd behaved so recklessly with her ex-husband of all men.

He nodded and turned away, placing himself behind his desk, as if he needed the physical barrier. 'You're right. Goodnight, Harper.'

He clearly didn't want to discuss it any further, and maybe he was right to simply ignore that incredibly foolhardy kiss. After all, what else was there to say? It had been a mistake, and together they'd already made enough of those.

'Goodnight,' she croaked, reaching for the door handle with a trembling hand, desperate now to get away from him so she could shake some sense into her head.

But as she left the hospital and headed home on the subway, her footsteps automatic, her mind was free to wander. No matter how hard she tried, she couldn't forget that thirty seconds of easily accessed and effortless pleasure. Because Logan was the only man to ever make her burn that way.

CHAPTER FIVE

THAT SATURDAY LOGAN attended a gallery exhibition in SoHo that his charitable foundation was sponsoring. He'd started the Edgar Grant Foundation with the money left to him by his grandfather. As a single man of forty, Logan had all but given up thinking about having a family of his own, reasoning that even if he had found another woman he wanted to start a family with after Harper, the last thing he wanted to do was to follow in his parents' footsteps when it came to overbearing parenting. Setting up the foundation enabled him to do some good in his community, to give back to the city that had benefited his family so much.

But having met the Reece Gallery owner and purchased a piece of art from one of the up-and-coming artists, his work there was almost done. As soon as he could escape Elliot Reece, a talkative bohemian gent in his late fifties who seemed fond of flamboyant waistcoats…

As the gallery owner talked, Logan's mind wandered to Harper and that incendiary kiss in his office. What a stupid mistake. Things between them had been tense enough before they'd succumbed to temptation. Now he had fresh memories of kissing her to add to the long list of past ones, and that was enough to keep him awake at night.

Looking up from his conversation, which was growing a little tedious even if he had been paying full attention, he immediately spotted Harper at the other end of the cavernous room. His pulse leapt at the sight of her. The noises around him, the conversations and background music fell silent as she became Logan's sole focus. She looked fantastic, wearing a little black dress, her hair styled in soft waves that kissed her shoulders. But more invigorating than how she looked physically, was the fact that she was laughing and smiling with one of the artists, a tall guy in his thirties. But what was she doing there? Was she on a date...?

Vicious jealousy winded Logan. The foreign feeling was reminiscent of the possessiveness he'd experienced in the early days of their relationship, but perhaps it made sense in light of that seriously hot kiss in his office two nights earlier.

'Excuse me,' he said to Reece, cutting him off mid-sentence. 'I should probably mingle with some of the artists.' Having escaped, Logan made a beeline for Harper and her friend, his pulse accelerating with every step.

'I didn't know you were an art lover,' he said, as he joined them, and they both looked up.

Harper blinked, her cheeks flushing. Her lips, which were slicked with gloss, pursed as if she was annoyed to see him. 'Logan,' she said. 'What are you doing here?'

Her question dragged his mind from the inconvenient thought of how that one kiss had whet his appetite for more. A dangerous and pointless thought when she was standing there with another man. Not to mention that she was the last woman on earth Logan should be kissing, not that his body, his libido, seemed to give a damn.

'My foundation is sponsoring the exhibition,' he said, offering her friend his hand in greeting. 'I'm Logan Grant. Good to meet you.'

As he spoke, Harper made some hand gestures to the man and something tugged at Logan's memory.

'Logan, this is Jake Barrington,' Harper said, casting her friend an apologetic look and signing with her hands as she spoke. 'Jake is an old school friend of mine. You've actually met before, a long time ago.'

'Jake, of course,' Logan said with a smile, the pieces clicking into place. He *did* remember Jake, who was deaf and communicated by a combination of sign language and lip-reading. 'Congratulations on the exhibition,' Logan added to the other man, grateful to Harper for signing out his words. 'I love your work. I've actually purchased one of your pieces for my apartment.'

Jake signed thank you, and then they were interrupted by another man, who stole Jake away, leaving Logan and Harper finally alone. The air around them seemed to still.

'You started a foundation?' she asked, the scent she wore flooding his awareness so he noticed the shimmering make-up around her beautiful eyes. Damn, she looked good. *Too* good. Tempting.

'Yes. With the trust I inherited from my grandfather. I missed you at the hospital Friday,' he said, needing her to know that their kiss, the passion that they'd proved was just beneath the surface, had been constantly on his mind. 'Were you avoiding me?' he asked, noting how interested she seemed in the art lining the stark white walls all of a sudden.

'Don't be ridiculous,' she said, snagging a champagne flute from the tray of a passing server and taking a long swallow. 'Why would I need to avoid you? I spent most of Friday in clinic.' She swept a dismissive gaze over him, but he wasn't fooled. She wasn't as indifferent as she would have him believe, and the pulse in her neck was going crazy.

'Because we kissed,' he said, simply, his lips buzzing as he recalled the delicious taste of her, familiar but also foreign because it had been so long. But oh, how they'd slotted back into place, like two sides of the same coin.

She glanced around nervously and then glared up at him. 'I told you, that was a mistake. One I don't want to talk about.'

Logan pressed his lips together. He'd been expecting her denial. But he knew her too well for her to hide her body's reactions. 'Maybe, or maybe it was just unfinished business.' he said, gratified to see her stare widening in alarm.

If she hadn't stopped him Thursday, if he hadn't unearthed the strength to say goodnight and watch her walk away, he might have slept with her, right there in his office, because their chemistry didn't seem to care that they were divorced.

'Unfinished business?' she asked, her voice breaking.

Logan nodded, stepped closer, aware that they were surrounded by people admiring the paintings and enjoying delicious canapés. 'Was there no part of you that still yearned for me after we walked away from our marriage?' He was so close, he heard her soft gasp and pushed on. 'I let you go ten years ago, Harper, but just because I signed the papers, it didn't mean it was totally over for me.'

When he pulled back, her face was slack with shock, her eyes swimming with desire and confusion. 'Don't say that,' she whispered.

'Then don't look at me that way,' he replied, his gaze tracing her unique and beautiful features. 'There's obviously something left between us, otherwise you wouldn't have kissed me back as if we'd never been apart. Don't forget, I know you. I know your body's responses were honest the other night, even if you're now trying to deny it, perhaps to save face.'

Her lips pursed in disgust. 'Maybe we just momentarily slipped back onto old habits, ones that as far as I'm concerned are also *bad* habits.'

Logan sighed, reluctant to get into another argument, but even more reluctant to walk away for some reason, probably because their chemistry was simply too hard to ignore. He'd tried and failed.

'So you haven't once thought about me in ten years? Is that what you're saying?' he asked. 'I don't believe you. And I still think we should talk and clear the air, because avoiding each other is clearly impractical. Manhattan clearly isn't big enough.'

She shook her head in disbelief, but she looked away tellingly. 'Believe what you like. I kissed you, but I don't owe you any of my thoughts or confidences. That ship sailed when you showed me where I stood in your priorities and left me alone to fend for myself with your parents, time after time.'

Logan winced, hating that she was right. He *had* prioritised his career when they were together, missing social events for emergency surgeries, pulling long hours to prove to himself and his parents that he'd done the right thing in championing his choice of career. 'That wasn't conscious on my part,' he said. 'But I had my reasons. For one, I thought you would understand the demands of our profession. But you're evading the point.'

'And what is the point?'

'That since coming back to New York, since kissing me like there was no tomorrow, you must have wondered if our chemistry is still as hot as it used to be. At least I can be honest about it. Maybe it's *me* who shouldn't believe a word *you* say.'

She raised her chin and looked down her nose at him. 'Don't they say that the definition of stupidity is doing the same thing over and over again and expecting a different outcome?' Her eyes glittered with challenge. 'I'm not stupid, Logan. I told you, I'm here for Charlie and for work. Just because my body remembered the steps, doesn't mean I have any intention of dancing.'

So she *had* thought about it. She *did* remember how good they were physically, not that it really mattered. He wasn't stupid, either. 'Maybe you're right. Neither of us wants to go there, no matter how good it would feel,' he muttered, defeated. 'So are you seeing Jake?' He couldn't help asking. He almost hoped her answer would be yes, so he'd have a solid reason to totally back off.

She laughed, a mirthless sound. 'No, he's a friend. An old friend. I'm not looking for a relationship at the moment, not that it's any of *your* business.' She made a point of ignoring him and sweeping her gaze around the room as if looking for someone. 'What about *you*?

Where's your date? You don't want to be photographed for the society pages all alone.'

Now it was Logan's turn to scoff. 'If you're asking if I'm seeing anyone, the answer is no, but maybe you should have asked that before you kissed me.' In fact, it had been a while since he'd bothered with dating. Women his age expected a degree of time commitment that he couldn't often give because of his work. Of course, Harper now fully understood the demands of their job and shared his work ethic.

She shot him a venomous look.

'I'm here alone tonight,' he confirmed. 'And I don't care about social climbing. I never have.'

Hesitation clouded her gaze for a moment. Her eyes darted away once more, then her expression hardened, as if she were slipping on a mask of indifference. 'Maybe you don't care about appearances, but from what I remember, *they* do.' She tilted her chin, looking at someone behind him.

Logan turned and saw his parents, who had obviously just arrived at the exhibition. His stomach sank like a stone. He always kept his father abreast of the events supported by his charitable foundation, which after all, was named after Carter Grant's father. But his parents rarely attended, simply making a sizeable donation instead. He certainly hadn't expected them to turn up tonight, mainly because the Reece Gallery was small and situated on the wrong side of East Fifty-Ninth Street. But with perfect timing, here they were.

For a moment, Logan was transported back in time to other events, ones he and Harper had attended as a couple. In those days, Logan's parents had expected their attendance, as if they'd wanted to present a united Grant family front to the world. He'd known that Harper had felt out of her depth with his parents' snobby friends. She'd usually acted uncomfortable and withdrawn, and Logan had felt trapped in the middle, trying to appease both his wife and his parents, whom he'd left in the lurch by rejecting the family business. But the failure of his divorce had humbled him, sweeping away any need for pretence. Now, after losing the love of his life, he only pleased himself, even if it was too little too late for him and Harper.

Biddie and Carter scanned the room, spying him at once. They made their way over, their polite smiles faltering as they took in Harper, who had stiffened at his side. He half expected her to simply walk away from her ex-in-laws, but to her credit, Harper stood her ground.

'Mum, Dad… I wasn't sure if you'd make it.' He offered his parents a tight smile and shifted closer to Harper's side, fighting the temptation to put his hand at the small of her back in a clear and possessive demonstration of where his loyalties had always stood, even if he'd messed up and neglected to show Harper that in the past. 'I ran into Harper tonight,' he went on. 'She's recently returned from London and has joined us at Manhattan Memorial.'

Harper looked up at him sharply, as if surprised that he hadn't already told his parents she was back in the city. But, brought up with their emotionally distant style of parenting, Logan had never once confided in his parents about his divorce. And now, they needed to understand that he was only interested in rebuilding bridges with Harper, given they had to work together. He was determined that, one day, he and his ex-wife would also lay the past to rest.

Carter Grant recovered from his surprise first, swooping in to press a kiss to Harper's cheek. 'How are you, my dear?'

'I'm well, thank you. And you?' she asked, politely.

Carter Grant made some casual comment about getting older, to which Harper smiled. Logan's mother couldn't quite conceal her shock at finding Logan talking to his ex-wife, but she made a solid effort to cover it up.

'You look wonderful,' she told her ex-daughter-in-law. 'London obviously agreed with you. So are you back in Manhattan to stay?'

Trust his mother to cut straight to the point.

'I am.' Harper smiled, but that steely glint was back in her eye.

'Oh,' Biddie said, her eyes widening in surprise.

'Yes, MMH is very lucky to have her,' Logan added, his jaw clenched in frustration. The last thing he wanted while trying to forge a fresh start with Harper, both professionally and personally, was his parents spooking her off with some thoughtless or offhand comment. He had no idea what kind of relationship he and Harper might be able to salvage, he just knew he was struggling to ignore their chemistry and he wanted to clear the air.

'Why don't you look around,' he suggested to his parents, 'while Harper and I finish our conversation.' He stood at Harper's side, hoping his body language was clear. 'There are some very talented up-and-coming artists exhibiting. I particularly like Harper's friend Jake Barrington, so look out for his work. Might be worth an investment if you're in the market.'

'We will,' Carter said, accepting two glasses of champagne before passing one to his wife. With a final smile, they trailed off, leaving him and Harper alone once more.

'They looked *really* pleased to see me,' Harper said, glancing after them as they admired the art.

'Do you care either way?' he asked, because he'd stopped caring what his parents thought many years ago.

'*You* used to care,' she pointed out with a smirk.

Logan's jaw tightened. 'I'm not a kid any more. I no longer need their approval. And you're no longer their daughter-in-law, so you *definitely* shouldn't care what they think.' He held her stare, his heart pounding as his regrets resurfaced. 'As far as I'm concerned, Harper, you never needed their approval,' he said quietly, because he should have protected her from his parents' expectations back then, not abandoned her to deal with them alone.

'I don't care,' she said, her chin tilted up. 'And you didn't need to defend me, you know. Like you said, we're no longer a couple, so it's not your job. I can take care of myself, same as always.'

Logan sighed, his protective urges where this woman was concerned a hard habit to break. 'I know you've always valued your independent streak. But I also know how you felt our different upbringings mattered while we were together. For the record, for me, our differences were one of the things I liked most about you.'

Her shock gave him little pleasure, his regrets coming too late to avoid the damage he'd inflicted on their relationship with his carelessness. 'You didn't care about inconsequential things,' he went on. 'You stopped me from taking myself too seriously and showed me how privileged my life was.' He raised his glass. 'So cheers to that.'

Almost reluctantly, she touched her flute to his and took a sip, peering at him over the rim with caution that made him wonder with a sinking stomach if they'd ever be able to move past their history.

'Well… I'd…um…better look for Jake. I've neglected him for too long,' she said. 'Have a good evening.' And she wandered off.

Logan watched her go, his frustration building. When he'd seen her tonight, he'd felt as if he'd been given that chance to make things right. But it seemed that Harper hadn't changed as much as she'd made out, at least when it came to her emotional guarding and holding him at arm's length. He hadn't recognised it as such when they were together, but now it was obvious. She might have kissed him with the same passion he remembered; she might have thought about him and their unfinished business, but she clearly wasn't ready to forgive him, and he needed to find some way to be okay with that.

CHAPTER SIX

'HARPER,' SOMEONE CALLED after her as she left the gallery and headed for the subway. Of course she'd know Logan's voice anywhere. Her stomach fluttered as she stopped in her tracks and turned to find him hurrying after her.

'Let me give you a ride home,' he said, catching up in three easy strides.

'There's no need. I'm fine.' The last place she needed to be was trapped in another enclosed space with him, not when he looked so casually sexy in his shirt and sports jacket and smelled divine. She was confused enough after their kiss, after seeing him unexpectedly tonight, after his admission that he'd yearned for their relationship after the divorce. Not to mention his display of possessiveness and the way he'd protected her from his parents, not that she'd needed him to, of course. She'd always been self-sufficient and he'd been right. She no longer needed the Grants' approval.

'Please,' he said, his eyes pleading. 'It's late. I know you're independent, but if you get on the subway, I'll most likely be awake half the night worrying if you made it home safely. We don't have to talk. Just let me see you home.'

Harper watched him curiously, her heart pounding with confusion. She'd never denied that Logan was a considerate and caring person. It's what made him a great doctor, but she was no longer used to him caring about *her*. His words from earlier slid through her mind.

'As far as I'm concerned, Harper, you never needed their approval.'

Was that true? Had she created an unnecessary issue because of how she'd felt about herself? Somehow defective, her self-esteem damaged because her mother had been able to desert her and never look back?

'Shouldn't you stay at the exhibition?' she asked with a shiver, wishing she'd worn pants instead of a dress, because the temperatures had dropped.

Logan shrugged. 'I've done my duty as sponsor—paid for the event, spoken to the artists, purchased a painting.'

'Okay,' she finally conceded, her stomach knotting. 'But I'm probably not heading your way. I live on East Seventh Street, near Tompkins Square Park.'

He smiled and led the way. 'I live in the Village, too.'

Harper laughed. 'Yes, most likely the West Village,' she said about the city's most expensive neighbourhood.

'What can I say...' He shrugged. 'I like beautiful things, and I work hard for them.'

'Fair enough.' Harper laughed and let it go as they walked around the corner to an underground parking garage. These days, she was more secure about herself. She'd too worked hard, had a great career she loved and earned a comfortable income. Logan had been correct earlier. Where a twenty-something Harper had tried to fit in with her in-laws and never quite made the grade, the Harper who was almost forty, didn't need their approval or anyone else's.

His comments earlier, about how he'd liked her for their differences, had almost floored her. She certainly hadn't felt confident of that at the time. Or maybe she'd been too messed up when they were together to see things clearly. Now it added to the growing sense that maybe she hadn't really known Logan at all. With every day that passed, she learned something new about him. He *was* different. Inconveniently so.

'Nice car,' she said, as she slid into the passenger seat and was instantly cocooned in the heated leather upholstery. 'I see you're still a bit of a motorhead.'

Logan smiled and stroked the dash, lovingly. 'Another beautiful thing I can't deny myself. What do you drive these days?' he asked, scanning the street for traffic and then pulling out.

'I take the subway,' she said, laughing at him once more, but he seemed to take it in good humour. 'Your parents looked...well,' she added, magnanimously. It was the least she could do after Logan's friendship and support of Charlie. 'Are they?'

'Dad had a myocardial infarction three years ago,' he said, sobering. 'He has a coronary artery stent now, and Mum has developed rheumatoid arthritis, so she's had to give up a lot of things, including her beloved golf.'

'I'm sorry. I didn't know.' So Logan, too, had to deal with ageing parents.

Logan glanced her way. 'Why would you?'

'Is Carter still working?' she asked, keeping the conversation going because otherwise she might be tempted to analyse the way he was looking at her, the way he'd been looking at her all night: with hunger. The sexual tension between them at the gallery had been off the scale, mainly because Harper had spent the past two days reliving that steamy make-out session, wondering how good it would feel if they hadn't stopped. But they'd agreed it was a stupid mistake brought on by emotional stress.

'He's semi-retired,' Logan said, driving the way he operated—with wildly attractive confidence. 'My sister took over as CEO last year.'

Logan's sister, Sarah was the youngest of the Grants' three children, and the only one who'd followed in Carter's footsteps and joined the family business. 'And Sam? What's he up to now?'

'He's a paediatric plastic and reconstructive surgeon. He's just returned from two years in Uruguay and will soon be joining us at MMH.'

'Wow... I bet your parents are happy that at least one of you took an interest in the Grant Group.'

'How's Charlie doing?' he asked, changing the subject.

'He's good. He's joined a diabetes support group. I'm sure he'll tell you all about it the next time you two meet up.' She still found the fact that her ex-husband had stayed in touch with her father baffling, unless it was part of him struggling to let go...

'I popped into MMH this morning to check on baby Alex,' he said, dragging Harper from that inconvenient thought as the lights changed and slowed to a stop. 'The occluder seems to be working. His lung function is improved. He's put on a few grams. Hopefully we can get him off the ventilator soon.'

'That's really good news. Are you feeling better about the arrest now?' She'd heard from the NICU staff that

Alex's mother in particular had taken the news badly and yelled at Logan in the family room. Sometimes patients' relatives needed to express their fear out loud, not that it was easy to hear as a doctor.

He shrugged and looked straight ahead. 'I never want to acclimatise to losing patients, or almost losing them, as in this case.'

'No, but we're not dealing with healthy babies,' she pushed, because it could so easily have been her procedure. 'All of our patients are at risk. Arrhythmias are more common in babies with congenital heart defects. And if we didn't operate or intervene, most of them would have a greatly shortened life expectancy. You can't take the lashing out from a scared and emotional relative personally.'

'Thanks for saying that. I know we're not friends, but I appreciate your support, especially after...' His lips thinned. 'Well, you don't owe me any loyalty.'

He drove the final block in silence, and Harper joined him, too confused to risk further conversation. Were they forming a truce? Maybe he was right about clearing the air. Maybe it would help them both, especially as they couldn't avoid each other.

As he pulled up outside her building, he turned off the engine and turned to face her. 'Mind if I see you inside?' he asked, that determined look he'd worn outside the gallery back in his eyes.

'What...?' she said playfully. 'You don't like my neighbourhood?'

He smiled, but his stare hardened. 'Humour me, for old time's sake,' he said, falling serious, his hand still gripping the wheel tight enough to outline his knuckles.

'Okay, sure. Thanks.' She stepped out of the car and took her keys from her bag, her stomach swooping because they might not be friends, but his considerate gestures were adding to her confusion. 'I'm on the ground floor.'

She keyed in the code to unlock the door to the street and paused in the dimly lit corridor outside her apartment, her nerves shredded. Bad enough that she'd seen him tonight, without his displays of maturity, attentiveness and honesty, which highlighted how different he seemed. The things she'd learned about him since being back had left her almost second-guessing her past memories. And he'd been right earlier: the one thing that hadn't changed in the slightest was their intense chemistry.

'Well, thanks for the lovely warm ride,' she said, trying to think of anything but that kiss and how badly she wanted to do it again. 'I didn't plan the right outfit for the subway, I guess.'

Suddenly, she struggled to breathe deeply enough as she looked up at him. Perhaps they did have unfinished business. There'd been no switch to flick to turn off her feelings after the divorce. It had taken time to fall out of love when they hadn't worked out.

'You're welcome, Harper.' His look swept over her down to her toes, and her chest tightened. 'You look amazing, but then you always did, whatever you wore.'

She froze, her body flooded with heat as she recognised the hunger that was back in his stare. Why was he doing this? Reminding her that they'd once meant the world to each other? Reminding her that those bad habits she was terrified to indulge would feel, oh, so good?

'Logan...' she groaned pleadingly, her head telling her

to walk away. To enter her apartment and close the door on him. But no matter how foolish it was, she was still ensnared by their chemistry, by the changes in him, by their past connection and the knowledge that, on some level, she knew this man, who was decent and caring and incredibly sexy.

'Harper...?' he said, his glance shifting over her face and his breathing speeding up.

She parted her lips to say goodnight, to tell him to leave, but no sound emerged, only a resigned sigh she felt to the very tips of her toes.

'Go inside,' he urged, not moving a muscle. But his eyes blazed in the dim light, his voice almost an order, as if he was clinging to their last shred of sense by his fingernails.

She should obey. If she kissed him again, the way she wanted to, she wouldn't be able to stop this time. But maybe this was what they both needed, to tie up that loose end, the unfinished business, to move past their history and finally lay *them* to rest.

Her heart galloped as she stood there convincing herself, bargaining. She had no idea who moved first, but then it didn't matter. His mouth captured hers, roughly, almost reluctantly. Harper's legs trembled as his fingers tunnelled into her hair, holding her firm in that way she remembered, as if he couldn't bear the idea of their kiss ending. She moaned, parting her lips, melting into the kiss that she could no more fight than she could forget.

'Logan...' she gasped, as he trailed his mouth down the side of her neck, pressing every sensitised inch of her body hard against his. She gripped his jacket in her fists, holding him captive as his lips hit every erogenous zone on her neck.

'I know,' he groaned, shoving one thigh between her legs, parting them. The heat and firmness of him right where she craved him was incredible and made her eyes roll closed in bliss. Harper's knees buckled, her weight sagging against him, her lips seeking his once more. These kisses were way more dangerous than the ones in his office. Her bedroom was mere feet away. But she couldn't seem to find the energy to care, not when he seemed to still know her body so well, his touch lighting up her every nerve as if he remembered what she liked and how to turn her into a sobbing mess.

'Invite me in or kick me out,' he urged, his words whispered against her skin beneath her ear as his hand cupped her breast, the thumb rubbing her nipple into delicious awakening that left her gasping for breath and mentally incoherent.

Too turned-on to think, let alone speak or act in her own best interests, Harper spun in his arms and jammed her key into the lock. 'Hurry,' she said, spilling inside her darkened apartment. She didn't want to question this or think it through. She didn't have to forgive him to trust him with her body. She just wanted to feel, to relive the one thing about their relationship that had been so good, so easy. She wanted closure.

Behind her, Logan kicked the door closed and pressed his body to hers from behind, his lips once more finding that sensitive place on her neck, his hands gripping her hips, his erection pressed into her backside. 'Tell me you want this, same as me. I need to hear you say it, Harper. No more denials or pretending.'

His hot breath, his demands that she face up to wanting
him, sent shivers down her spine so she groaned silently.
'I want this,' she admitted, swallowing hard.

'So do I.' He spun her around, his mouth capturing
hers once more as he slid his hands under the hem of her
dress, caressing her stockinged thighs and the cheeks of
her backside as he ground his hard length into her belly.
Harper gasped into his kiss as his fingers delved between
her legs, stroking her through her underwear, zinging her
body to electrifying life. This man had once known her
body almost better than she had herself. He'd worshipped
every inch of her with his mouth, his hands, his greedy
stare and his words of love. But this wasn't about love.
Just sex.

Pulling back from his kiss, she took his hand and led
him across her tiny living room to the bedroom, praying that he had a condom on him, because she hadn't anticipated this. They collapsed on the bed together, lips
clashing, tongues surging, hands torn between caresses
and frantic tugs at each other's clothing.

It was fast and frantic, but Harper didn't want time
to think in case she changed her mind. Logan paused to
fish a condom from his wallet, placing it on the nightstand. Then he turned on the lamp, casting the bedroom
in a golden glow.

'I want to see you,' he said, undoing the last few buttons of his shirt, revealing his muscular and hairy chest.

Harper snagged her lower lip with her teeth and
watched him strip, marvelling at his mature physique
and how it could possibly be any sexier than it had been
ten years ago. But it was. When he was naked, he rejoined

her on the bed, impatiently divesting her of her dress, her bra, her underwear as if they were blocking his view.

'I'd forgotten how sexy you are,' he said, taking one of her nipples in his mouth and making her vision swim.

Harper moaned and reached for the condom. 'I want you, now.'

'Not yet,' he said, kissing her neck, her breasts, her stomach, lower and lower.

'Logan,' she gasped as he ended between her legs. Clearly he planned to reacquaint himself with all of her. Harper bit the back of her hand to hold in her moans. She wanted to hide from the intimacy of the act, something they'd of course, done many times before. But that was then, when she'd loved him and believed she could be vulnerable with him. But as pleasure swamped her, resistance fled. He knew her body too well, quickly transporting her to a place where she was suddenly desperate to go.

Logan paused to put on the condom and kissed his way back up her body, while her hands shifted restlessly over his arms, his shoulders, his back, as if she were re-learning his shape.

'You're sure?' he asked, pausing to peer down at her, braced over her on straight arms.

She nodded, gripping his biceps. Had she ever wanted him this badly? His gaze locked to hers, as if he'd waited ten years for this moment. Then he slowly pushed himself inside her.

Harper couldn't help the low moan she uttered as she closed her eyes. His observation was too intense, his possession of her body too thorough and too familiar. Her skin was covered in the scent of his cologne and the imprint of his lips. It was overwhelming.

'Kiss me,' she said, chasing his mouth with hers. She wanted oblivion not connection.

He obeyed, but not before he'd taken both her hands, entwined her fingers with his and pressed them into the pillow beside her head, the way he used to. Harper had forgotten how good Logan was at this. How he had a way of making her feel like the only woman on earth. How he handled sex the way he handled every other aspect of his life, with drive, determination, a desire to excel. But they'd been apart for ten years. There would have been many women since her just as there'd be more after her.

Wanting to cling to that idea in order to counter the flood of familiar feelings being intimate with him again had naturally brought up, she pushed her tongue into his mouth, kissing him for all she was worth, reminding them both that this was about desire and nothing more.

He moved inside her, his kisses deep, his grip on her hands unrelenting. She wrapped her legs around him and held on as he shunted them higher and higher, observing her as if daring her to deny the waves of almost suffocating pleasure. But it was too good to hold back. She surrendered herself to it, her orgasm striking as he tore his mouth from hers and watched her shatter, kissing up her cries, moving faster until he too succumbed to the fire they generated and climaxed with a low groan, his face buried in the side of her neck.

Dazed, Harper clung to his shoulders, desperately trying not to sniff the familiar scent of his hair as the last spasm of his hard body died. Panic replaced the euphoria, her mind scattered. What had she done? Why had she ever thought that sleeping with her ex-husband was a good idea? Where was the relief, the closure? Yes, it had been as amazing as always, but now she just wanted him to leave so she could fall apart and then pull herself together in private.

As if he too was stunned and waking up to the reality of what they'd done, Logan withdrew and sat on the side of the bed, his back to her while he caught his breath. Harper tugged at the sheet, pointlessly covering her nakedness. But there was no hiding the signs of his possession, the pink heat of her cheeks and lips and neck where he'd kissed her so much he'd grazed her skin with his facial hair. She swallowed, desperate to say something, anything but knowing whatever she produced would be wrong. Better to stay silent.

Logan collected himself first, tossing her a lifeline she grabbed with both hands. 'I'd better go,' he said, reaching for his clothes from the bedroom floor.

'Okay,' she said in a croaky voice that spoke of her mounting discomfort.

He took his clothes into the bathroom. Harper sprang out of bed and quickly donned her robe. When he emerged a few minutes later, he was fully dressed, his stare blank, as if he'd made a conscious effort to hide any trace of vulnerability left over from what they'd just done.

'Thanks for the lift home,' she said, walking towards the apartment's front door and pulling it open, sensing him behind her. She didn't want him to feel as if they needed to discuss what had just happened, in fact that was the last thing she wanted to encourage.

'I'll…um…see you Monday,' he said, scrubbing a hand through his messed-up hair as he stepped out into the lobby of her building.

'Enjoy the rest of your weekend,' she managed before

she closed the door, sagged back against the wood and buried her face in her hands.

What on earth had she done? How could she have been so stupid? She'd come home again to be close to Charlie, not to start things up again with Logan. They'd ended badly the first time around for a whole host of reasons that were still very much alive. The only consolation she could cling to was that the sex had been a one-time thing, and now that it was done, they could finally move on.

CHAPTER SEVEN

THE FOLLOWING MONDAY MORNING, after spending the remainder of the weekend futilely thinking about Harper and what had transpired Saturday night, Logan entered the emergency department of MMH.

'You've admitted a baby presenting with cyanosis and a heart murmur. Emily Walsh,' he said to the triage nurse on duty. 'Where might I find her?'

'Bay twelve,' the nurse answered, and Logan quickly made his way there.

He pulled open the curtains and saw that Harper was already with the patient and her parents. Their eyes met for a second, and that reignited awareness seemed to zap between them as if they were two magnets being held apart. But now wasn't the time to talk about the foolhardy decision they'd made to sleep together again.

'Dr Grant,' Harper said, 'this is baby Emily and her parents, Taylor and Chris. Dr Grant is a senior congenital heart surgeon here at MMH,' she told the concerned couple, who appeared to be in their late teens or early twenties, their faces pale with concern.

Logan's stomach clenched with empathy as he quickly greeted the parents and then washed his hands. 'Do you mind if I take a look at Emily, too?'

Mom and Dad nodded and Logan pulled on a face mask.

'Emily is two days old,' Harper went on, giving him a clinical summary. 'She was born at full term by vaginal delivery at home. Mom and Dad have noticed some blueness around the mouth, especially when Emily cries or is feeding, so they've brought her in today to be checked over.'

Logan nodded his thanks to Harper, and with the parents' permission examined the baby, noting her pulse, respiratory rate and the colour of her skin and the mucous membranes inside her mouth. He gently palpated her abdomen and then listened to her heart and lungs. With his examination complete, he gently passed the baby back to Mum, who dressed her and cuddled her close.

Washing his hands again, Logan glanced at Harper, seeing his clinical concerns reflected in her eyes. They were on the same wavelength. No doubt her mind was also working through the possible causes of Emily's cyanosis. Time to give this young couple some bad news, a part of their job that was never easy.

'The bluish colour around Emily's mouth is called cyanosis,' he explained quietly, his heart going out to the young couple, who weren't much older than kids themselves. 'What that means is that there's not enough oxygen in her blood. Now that can have many causes, but when we listen to Emily's heart and lungs—' he looked to Harper, who nodded in corroboration that she too had heard the heart murmur and the pulmonary oedema '—we can hear several things.'

Taylor's frown deepened as she glanced between him and Harper.

'We can hear a heart murmur,' Harper said, continuing to outline their findings and possible causes. 'That's usually a sign that the blood inside the heart is flowing in an abnormal way,' she said, her voice calm and reassuring. 'Sometimes that can mean that the heart hasn't developed properly while Emily was growing inside the womb.'

She paused and Logan nodded. 'There's also evidence,' he added, 'that there's some fluid on the lungs, which again, is a sign that something isn't quite right with Emily's heart.'

Taylor started to cry, and Chris put his arm around her shoulders.

'We'd like to organise some tests,' Harper said, passing over a box of tissues, her face full of compassion. 'Firstly a chest X-ray, and then a special ultrasound test called a cardiac ECHO and some blood tests.'

Logan allowed that to sink in, his mind working through the list of possible diagnoses, then added, 'If you agree, we'd like to admit Emily to the neonatal intensive care unit today, so we can treat her with some oxygen and other medicines to clear the fluid from her lungs while we run the tests. We'll also be able to monitor her growth and feeding. She's probably struggling to suck and tiring easily when she feeds at the moment. But we can put a small tube through her nose into her stomach that won't hurt her at all and feed her that way, because it's important that she puts on weight. Do you have any questions for either Dr Dunn or myself at this time?'

Chris frowned, clearly struggling every bit as much as Taylor. 'If the heart hasn't developed properly,' he asked, 'can you fix it?'

'Often babies born with what we call congenital heart

defects, require surgery,' Logan said, glancing at Harper, whose stare was encouraging, despite their personal issues. At least at work, they were a team again. 'That's our field of speciality,' he continued. 'But we don't want to go into too much detail about surgery until we've run the tests and know exactly what we're dealing with, okay? Do you have any friends or family members that can support you? We understand that this is a worrying time.'

The couple nodded and gripped each other's hand tighter, looking even more scared. Logan kept his expression stoic, wishing he could be more comforting. But until they had some of the test results back, they could only guess at what was going on.

'We'll leave you for now, to call your family,' Harper added, 'but we'll see you again soon up on the ward. You'll also meet our residents, doctors called Jess and Greg, who are on their way here to organise the tests and admit Emily to the NICU.'

With the action plan conveyed to the ED nursing staff caring for Emily, with some diuretics prescribed to help clear her tiny lungs of excess fluid, Logan and Harper left the emergency department. Together, they headed towards the Theatre, where they had a full morning of joint surgeries scheduled.

'I hate those difficult conversations,' Harper said, dragging in a deep breath. 'They're heartbreaking, and Emily's parents seem so young.'

'But at least they have each other.' Logan held open a door for her to pass through ahead of him, again fighting the urge to touch her. 'I didn't want to go into too much detail and overwhelm them, but we'll also need to refer them for some genetic testing to exclude chromosomal syndromes like DiGeorge and Down, although Emily's appearance wasn't obviously indicative of either of those.'

Harper's frown deepened as she glanced his way and nodded. She seemed distracted, and he could understand why. Their work sometimes came with a heavy toll, and after the weekend, after that reckless move of sleeping with her, the urge to support her, to pull her into his arms and comfort her the way he had when *they* were a couple, was scarily natural.

But he couldn't get used to that urge. They *weren't* a couple. He'd failed her once. He had no desire to relive that particular feeling of helplessness or hurt Harper all over again. With them having to work together, neither of them needed the complication. That being said, he'd left her place Saturday as if his tail was on fire. He needed to check she was okay and explain himself.

'Time for a quick coffee before we head into Theatre?' he asked, needing the caffeine, but also wanting to get the awkwardness over with.

'Sure,' she said, following him into the staff room, which was thankfully deserted.

Logan poured coffee into two mugs. 'Do you still take cream, no sugar?'

'Just milk please,' she said, clearly making an effort to sound *normal*. 'The Brits don't add cream to their coffee, so I had to break the habit.'

Logan handed her the coffee and they took a seat. He had to raise the elephant in the room even if she had no intention of mentioning Saturday. He knew her stubborn streak of old. 'How was the rest of your weekend,' he asked cautiously, the awkwardness they'd managed to shelve while they focussed on their patient building once more.

'Good, thanks.' She took a sip of coffee but he noticed the flush to her cheeks. 'Yours?'

Logan rested his gaze on hers, pausing to give her time to prepare. He wasn't going to simply swap pleasantries. 'I'm afraid it was not as productive as it normally would be. To say I was distracted Sunday would be an understatement.'

Harper froze, her eyes darting back to his. 'We don't have to talk about it,' she said, nervously glancing at the door. 'It happened. End of story.'

'I think we *should* talk about it.' His pulse accelerated. He too could be stubborn. 'As it was...unexpected.'

'What is there to say?' she asked in an impatient voice. 'It's like you said—unfinished business.' She seemed so pragmatic now, but Saturday night she'd wanted him as much as he'd wanted her. He'd made sure of that.

Logan waited, his pulse flying. If only it were as simple as unfinished business. If only he'd been able to sleep with her again and then switch off his thoughts. Instead, he'd spent all weekend reliving that night and thinking about her—wondering if she was okay, contemplating calling her, desperate for this morning to come around so he could see her again.

'And now it's definitely finished?' he asked at last, his chest tight, because in theory, things would be easier if she was right and he wrong. If they could have sex and just move on. But now that they'd slept together again, he knew he'd struggle to forget how good they were together and let it go. But just because he'd struggle, didn't make it impossible. He would have to try.

'Isn't it?' she asked, her stare holding his so he saw the merest hint of vulnerability in her beautiful brown eyes. 'I think it is for me.'

His heart sank. Perhaps she hadn't changed that much, after all. Maybe she was still emotionally guarded, at least with him, and he understood why. But sometimes, because of his regrets, he wondered if they would ever be truly over, at least for him. He didn't want to lie on his death bed suffocating under those regrets. Not that he was making any grand promises or suggesting they get back together. He hadn't made a serious commitment to a woman in ten years. He never wanted to hurt Harper or let her down again, and with her reluctance to rely on him or confide in him or to even hear him out about where they'd gone wrong, the reasons were still unresolved.

'Okay,' he said, his heart pounding. 'Thanks for being honest, at least. Unfortunately, for me, I'm not sure I'm quite there yet… You occupied my thoughts all day Sunday, no matter how hard I tried to think of something else. But I guess I'll get there, in time.'

Harper's expression grew more wary, steely glints in her eyes. 'I think it's best for us both. One time could be a blip, an error of judgement. More than that is just indulging old habits. Neither of us wants to go there. I'm not interested in relationships and obviously not with you, of all people…'

Logan winced, but he had asked for honesty. 'Neither am I, and likewise,' he said, his stomach griping. 'Of course, we're not getting back together.' He scoffed. The idea was laughable. But sadly, he feared he'd struggle to be around her all the time and not want her again.

'Obviously not,' she said, sounding inordinately re-lieved, as if desperate to convince herself and him.

It seemed as if they were back to pretending they were unaffected by each other once more.

Because he couldn't let it go, because he liked to win, he pushed. 'So we just pretend it didn't happen and move on?' For him, that would be no easy feat, but if that was what she wanted, he'd try, the same way he'd had to get over her after the divorce. After all, what was the alter-native? That they actually sat down and talked? Made themselves vulnerable in a way they hadn't been able to when they were married? With Harper's reluctance and his fear of failing, that seemed unlikely.

She shrugged. 'I'm really only here to focus on the promotion. My work is everything to me, as is yours, I'm sure.'

'Of course,' Logan said, looking up as another staff member entered the room. 'Sam.' He stood and greeted his younger brother, who'd recently returned from Uru-guay and joined the surgical team at MMH.

Sam hugged Logan and glanced at Harper. 'Harper, I heard you were back,' he said. She stood too, and Sam kissed both her cheeks, adding, 'You look fantastic.'

Harper flushed and smiled. 'So do you. You haven't changed at all.'

The three of them laughed and Logan's ribs pinched at the sense of nostalgia. With the memories of how ter-rifyingly good she'd felt in his arms Saturday still fresh, it was easy to imagine that the intervening ten years apart hadn't happened. Except they had. He'd taken her for granted and lost the most precious thing in his life. And she'd said it herself. She didn't owe him anything.

'So what's your situation?' Sam asked, as he filled a mug with coffee, clearly oblivious to the tension in the room. 'Are you remarried, this time to a keeper?' He flashed a playful smile at Logan, who waited on Harper's reply with bated breath. He knew she hadn't remarried, but she must have had other long-term relationships since him.

'No,' she said, shaking her head and glancing down. 'I've dated over the years, of course.' Her eyes darted to Logan's but she went on. 'But nothing serious. There was no point falling in love with an English guy when I always knew I'd want to come home.'

Logan heard the subtext she left unsaid. She'd probably held something back from her relationships with those English guys the way she'd held something back from him. Was she that changed? Or was she too stuck in the past? Was her fear of abandonment, her insistence on going it alone emotionally, still guiding her decisions, holding her back from being happy or finding love again? Maybe she didn't need love. He could relate to that. If it failed, it ripped you apart.

'What about you?' she asked his brother. 'Did you do any of that travelling you were so set upon?'

'I did.' Sam grinned. 'I spent two years in Uruguay with a medical relief organisation. In fact, I haven't been back that long myself.'

Just then Sam's pager sounded and he glanced down at the display. 'I need to go. It was great to see you Harper.'

'See you Sunday,' Logan said, reminding his brother of their squash session.

When they were alone again, Logan turned to Harper.

'What?' she said, looking up at him with a frown.

'Nothing…' Logan shrugged, curiosity getting the better of him. 'It just saddens me to think that you haven't come close to a serious relationship all these years?'

'Have you?' she countered, her stare defensive and accusing, any closeness he'd imagined Saturday, now long gone.

'No.' Maybe they were still as bad as each other… 'Clearly we're both emotionally guarded for our own reasons.'

'We've both been burned by rushing into marriage and ending up divorced,' she said defensively.

'I guess. But we both brought our issues into the marriage, too,' he added, because he couldn't seem to move on from Saturday as easily as Harper. 'You holding back was a definite theme in our relationship, too.' The comment was uttered before he'd had chance to censor it.

She looked up sharply. 'What do you mean? I'm not solely to blame for our divorce.'

'I'm not saying you were.' He didn't want them to argue again. 'I just mean there were some parts of your life you refused to discuss, even with me, your husband. Whenever I tried to talk to you about your mother, I always felt that you shut me out or that you never fully trusted me. It used to drive me crazy…'

'See,' she snapped, 'this is why what happened between us Saturday was a mistake. Now you feel as if you can say things like that, when it's none of your business any more. We're not together. We're *not* getting back together. My business, however I choose to manage it, is *my* business, Logan.'

Logan nodded but his frown deepened because her words hurt. 'You're right, it is. Just as the breakdown of *my* marriage, the biggest regret of my life, is *my* business.' He couldn't keep the cynicism from his voice. But did she think he had no feelings whatsoever? Yes, he'd made mistakes, but he wasn't the only one.

'That's not what I mean,' she hesitated, as if confused, her glance searching his.

'You can't diminish my experience because of your own, Harper. We hurt each other. We dealt with it in our own ways. And if we ever hope to reconcile our past, these are the kind of frank and honest discussions we'll need to have, in my opinion.'

Not that it seemed likely from the way she was staring at him as if he'd started speaking Mandarin. But she must know that a huge part of him, the part that always strived to be the best, would do anything to go back in time and fix them.

In that second, their pagers sounded in unison. They silenced them. It was Theatre.

'Look,' she said dismissively, tipping the last of her coffee down the sink. 'Let's just agree to put Saturday behind us and focus on work. Okay?'

'Okay,' Logan replied, placing his mug in the dishwasher. 'But before we go, let me say this. I know that you can't forgive me, because I let you down. But any time you're ready to hear my apology, any time you want to talk about us and where our relationship went wrong, I want you to know that I'm ready and willing.'

He left her gaping after him and made his way to the changing rooms, taking no satisfaction from the fact that for once, he seemed to have left her speechless.

CHAPTER EIGHT

AT THE END of that week, after diagnosing baby Emily Walsh with truncus arteriosus, or TA—a rare congenital heart defect where a single large vessel left the heart, instead of the normal two—Harper and Logan performed the complex surgery together.

'Okay. Let's reintroduce circulation,' Harper told the perfusionist in charge of the cardiopulmonary bypass machine, which had been doing the work of Emily's heart and lungs while she and Logan had completed the lengthy three-part surgery.

While the tense seconds ticked past, she glanced up at Logan, her stare meeting his over the top of their masks. She'd grown so used to seeing him opposite her while she operated. Seeking out his reassuring gaze at moments of high stress had become almost second nature. And there was no procedure more nerve-racking than restarting a patient's heart after open-heart surgery.

As the blood filled the tiny chambers of Emily's repaired heart and the organ once more began to beat, there was a collective sigh of relief from everyone around.

'Let's check the sutures one last time before we close up,' Harper said, examining her and Logan's handiwork. It was the end of a long week, but every surgery mattered. Fortunately, she and Logan shared a similar dedication to their work. And as long as they didn't discuss their personal life, their past or their recent slip-up when they'd slept together, they could get along perfectly well.

'Happy?' he asked, adjusting the angle of a retractor for a better view.

Harper nodded. 'Yes, you?'

'Looks good,' he said, with a decisive nod.

Harper sited a drain in place and then turned to Jess, who'd also been assisting. 'Would you like to close up, Jess?'

The younger doctor nodded, accepting a forceps and suture needle from the scrub nurse.

Harper supervised the closure of the pericardium, the sac around the baby's heart, and then seeing that the patient was stable and the anaesthetist happy, she removed her gloves and mask, her back protesting the long hours standing in Theatre.

Harper tossed her surgical gowns into the bin in the corner of the operating room. Outside the sterile zone was a row of computer terminals. Harper logged on and began to type up her operation notes into Emily's file while keeping one eye on Jess, aware of the fact she was due to meet Charlie for dinner in an hour.

Logan joined her doing the same thing at the terminal next to hers. She'd almost completed the operation notes when she sensed Logan stiffen at her side.

'What is it?' she asked, looking up. That damned intuition of hers was unavoidable. She knew Logan well enough to know when something was bothering him.

'The results of Emily's genetic testing came back.' He

met her glance, fatigue obvious around his eyes. 'She does have DiGeorge syndrome.'

Harper's stomach dropped. She clicked onto a new screen and pulled up the lab result, quickly scanning the letter from the geneticist. DiGeorge syndrome was caused by a deletion of part of one of the chromosomes. Along with congenital heart disease, common issues included learning disabilities and hearing problems. The extent to which baby Emily was affected would only become apparent as she grew. But it was more worrying news for her parents.

'I'll speak to Taylor and Chris,' Logan said, perhaps picking up on Harper's emotions. 'You have a dinner date with Charlie, and the surgery ran overtime. It's almost 7.00 p.m.'

Harper glanced at the clock and hesitated, not bothering to ask how he knew about her plans with her father. She could cancel dinner, but she liked to see her dad at least once a week in person. Charlie had a propensity to downplay how he was feeling over the phone, but face to face, he couldn't hide any symptoms from Harper.

'Are you sure?' she asked Logan, gratitude bubbling up. Informing Emily's parents of a test result wasn't really a two-person job, but nor would it be an easy conversation. 'I know we've both struggled with compassion fatigue in this particular case.' Sometimes, it was hard to stay detached and remember for them it was a job.

'Of course,' he said, a small smile tugging at his mouth. 'I'm Emily's lead clinician anyway. I'll head upstairs and speak to Taylor and Chris now. I'll take Greg with me. You head off to meet Charlie and give him my love.'

Before she could thank him or say another word, he left the operating room. All week, as if keeping his word, they'd avoided discussing last Saturday. Harper had avoided Logan as best she could, seeing him often, but never straying from patient-related conversations. If she tried really hard, she could almost convince herself that that night hadn't happened. But now the phrase *Be careful what you wish for* looped through her head. She'd wanted them to put the sex behind them. She'd shut down his suggestion they talk about the past and their relationship and he'd reluctantly let it go. And she'd never been more bewildered and uncertain. This was Logan. No matter how hard she tried, she couldn't forget how it had felt to sleep with him again. And even more worrying was how she'd felt when he'd said that their divorce was his greatest regret. It was as if she'd just discovered that, once upon a time, she'd made a huge mistake but hadn't even been aware of it.

'So how is your job going?' Charlie asked as they tucked into their meals. They were regulars at their favourite restaurant, Luca's, a family-run Italian place they'd been coming to for years.

'It's going well,' she said, trying to shove Logan and his offer of an apology from her mind. 'We're busy. My resident is getting married soon, so she'll be away on her honeymoon, so I'll probably get even busier while she's away. But you know me—I love my job.' Harper focused on her gnocchi, spearing a piece with her fork.

'How is working with Logan panning out?' Charlie asked, helping himself to some steamed vegetables, while staring at Harper's pasta longingly.

'It's fine, I think.' Harper looked up and met Charlie's eyes. 'You know, Dad, you could have told me that you two were in regular contact all these years. I wouldn't have minded.' Admittedly she might not have liked the idea at first, but she would never begrudge Charlie a friend, especially when she'd been out of the country and so far away.

'Could I?' he asked cautiously. 'You refused to discuss the split before you moved to London, so I figured you wanted nothing more to do with the guy, and I didn't want to upset you when we spoke on the phone, or during your visits home. Those were precious moments for me.'

'Me too,' she said, her eyes welling up. 'But I'm sorry if I made things awkward for you, Dad.' Harper ducked her head in shame. 'I didn't want that.' Logan was a decent man. He'd certainly been a better ex-son-in-law than she had been an ex-daughter-in-law...

'Not awkward,' Charlie said, reaching for her hand. 'I was just worried for you, that's all. You know you'll always have my loyalty, kiddo. Never doubt that. It's just that Logan was a good son-in-law to me while you two were together.'

She nodded, her throat hot as memories flooded her mind, and Charlie continued. 'When you told me it was over, I didn't like that he'd hurt you. But after you left for London, he came to me and explained everything... After that, it seemed rude to blank the man. You know me; that's not my style.'

'Of course not. I wouldn't have wanted you to do that for my sake.' She took a sip of water, her confusion growing. 'So what did he say? About us, I mean.' Had Logan blamed Harper for their split? That seemed unlikely.

Charlie wouldn't have stood by him all these years if all he'd had to say were criticisms. And Logan seemed willing to admit his part in their past mistakes. Again, it stunned her to think that while she'd been moving on in London, throwing herself into work and making new friends, Logan had been back here, stuck with his regrets. Her pulse vibrated in her fingertips. She shouldn't torture herself this way; it was in the past and irrelevant, but for some reason, she needed to know.

Charlie paused, looking uncomfortable. 'He was in a pretty bad way for a while, as I'm sure you were, too. He loved you. You'd loved each other. That was obvious to see. And it's hard to just switch off your feelings, isn't it?'

'It is...' Harper reached across the table and took his hand, knowing he was thinking about his own marriage breakdown. When Harper was old enough to understand, Charlie had once told her how Harper's mother had had an affair with a married work colleague and how they'd run off together, breaking many hearts in the process, not just hers and Charlie's.

And where Logan was concerned, falling out of love with him had been a gradual process for Harper, too. No quick fix.

'Then, in typical Logan style,' Charlie went on, 'he owned up to his mistakes. He said he'd let you down one time too many. He'd taken you for granted and thrown himself into his career. He'd allowed little things to grow into big issues instead of communicating effectively or squashing them and holding sight of what was important.'

Harper nodded, her appetite vanishing by the minute. It was only what Logan had hinted at to her, but to hear it from Charlie added extra weight somehow.

'I didn't know he felt as if he'd taken me for granted.' She had felt abandoned, lonely, a low priority. After her mother's desertion, that had cut deep, because she'd let her guard down with Logan. 'But the truth is we were both to blame for those communication issues,' she said, feeling sick. 'There was a part of me that never felt as if I fit in with his family so I withdrew instead of explaining why. I found his parents in particular suffocating and overbearing. Logan and I argued about that a lot.' Now she could see how she'd put Logan in an impossible position. You couldn't choose your family. She knew that better than anyone—otherwise she'd have chosen a mother who'd wanted a relationship with her daughter.

Charlie abandoned his cutlery and turned even more serious. 'Was I to blame for how you felt different? I tried to raise you to be confident and to know your worth, but I couldn't wholly make up for what your mother had done in abandoning you. I can forgive her for falling out of love and leaving me, but I'll never understand that.'

'No, Dad,' Harper cried, horrified. 'Absolutely not.' She gripped his hand tighter. 'You are the best father in the world. You gave me everything. If, as an adult, I allowed things to mess with my head, that's on me, not you. Maybe Logan and I rushed into marrying... Maybe if we'd been engaged for longer, we'd have worked through our individual issues together rather than apart... I don't know.' She sighed, deflated. Since sleeping with him again, she barely knew which way was up.

Maybe Logan was right—they *did* need to talk. She'd put it off because she'd wanted to focus on them being able to work together, because she was desperately trying to manage her complicated feelings for him, but maybe it *was* time she finally heard him out so they could both lay the past to rest.

'He said I held back from him emotionally,' she admitted in a small voice, 'and maybe I did. I never really liked to talk about my mother, then or now.' She met her father's saddened stare. 'To miss her, to even acknowledge how hurt I felt that she could just walk away like that seemed somehow disloyal to you, because *you* were always there for me.'

Charlie shrugged, his eyes shining. 'I'm your father. That's my job, one I love. And your feelings were valid, then *and* now. Try not to run away from them. Be the brave, intelligent mature woman you are and embrace them.'

Harper nodded. 'I love you, too, Dad.' She pushed away her cold gnocchi. 'And I'll try.' But being vulnerable with another person wasn't going to be easy, especially with Logan.

Charlie took a deep breath and caught the eye of their waitress. 'Dessert for you, I think,' he said to Harper, 'and more steamed vegetables for me.' He smiled and Harper loved him so hard, she knew that with him on her side, she could surely do anything, including face up to Logan and the mistakes of the past.

CHAPTER NINE

LATER THAT EVENING, after arriving home late from the hospital, Logan had just emerged from the shower when his apartment's buzzer sounded. Dressed only in a towel, he spoke into the intercom, addressing the building's doorman. 'Evening, Fred?'

'Good evening, Dr Grant.'

No matter how many times Logan insisted Fred use his first name, the older man was old school and preferred the formality of titles.

'I have a lovely young lady downstairs for you, sir,' Fred said. Logan could almost hear the smile in Fred's voice. 'Her name is Harper Dunn. Shall I send her up?'

Logan's pulse went nuts with excitement. Then a spike of adrenaline shot through him. Was she okay? Was something wrong with Charlie? 'Yes, thank you.'

Quickly unlocking the door to his apartment, Logan dashed back into his bedroom and hastily threw on some jeans and a T-shirt. It wasn't the right look to greet Harper in a towel, not when he was determined to act on his best behaviour. If she could forget last Saturday and move on as if it hadn't happened, he'd try his best to do the same. Even if it killed him, and it might.

As he made his way back through the apartment, he

cast a critical eye around his living space, which was very masculine in taste but usually pretty neat and tidy given that he spent so much time at the hospital. He'd just made in back into the foyer when Harper appeared in the doorway.

'Are you okay?' he asked, his stare sweeping over her from head to toe as if he would unearth some clue as to why she was there at 10.00 p.m. on a Friday. 'Is it Charlie?'

Rationally, he didn't know what would make Harper come to him for support. She didn't want to talk, after all. She obviously wasn't ready to forgive him or open up. But she was there for some reason.

'No, everything is fine.' She shook her head as she stepped inside and pushed the door closed. 'Sorry to call so late. I was on my way home from dinner with Dad and I just… I couldn't face another night of not being able to sleep.'

She looked up at him, her expression troubled. She clearly had had something she wanted to say. Would they finally have the long-overdue talk?

'Come in,' he said, heading for the kitchen. 'I haven't been back from MMH that long. I just stepped out of the shower. Do you want a glass of wine?'

Now that she'd come to him for something, he didn't want to jinx it so instead acted as if it was a perfectly normal occurrence. After a tense week, both professionally and personally, he'd had to constantly battle the urge to talk to her about them. So many times this week, he'd wanted to knock on her door after work. And every time he'd stopped himself, recalling the look on her face when she'd said that sleeping with him again had been a mistake. That for her it was over. That she would never want a relationship with him of all people. It shouldn't have stung quite so badly, given he agreed with her, but there was no denying his feelings.

She shrugged, looking uncomfortable, so he poured two glasses of red and passed her one.

'Why can't you sleep?' he asked, his pulse buzzing in his ears. It was time to cut to the chase. They weren't at work. There were no patients awaiting them. The sex was out of the way. He wanted to hear what she had to say, and maybe, just maybe, they could finally be honest.

She stared at the glass of wine, twirling the stem where it sat on the kitchen counter. Then she snatched it up and took a large swallow. When her eyes met his once more, she was breathing hard, her chest rising and falling with her rapid breaths in a very distracting way.

'I can't stop thinking about what you said last week,' she whispered, as if almost scared to say the words aloud. 'That our divorce was the biggest regret of your life.'

Logan's pulse ricocheted. He let her statement settle between them, keeping very still, weighing up how best to respond. But the time for caginess had been and gone. He'd never been one for games, and she must know how much he still wanted her, despite trying his damnedest to squash it.

'It is,' he said, his blood pounding in his veins. 'I deeply regret losing you, Harper. But I thought you didn't want to talk about it, about us. I thought you wanted to put that night behind us. Pretend it hadn't happened.'

And by God, he'd tried to forget. It had been hard, especially when they'd consulted on one patient or another every day. But then he'd always known that working with

Harper would be a challenge, one he'd complicated further still by sleeping with her again.

She winced and glanced down at her feet. 'I did want to do that, but… I've tried.' She looked up, her lips parted, emotions swimming in her eyes. 'And I can't forget. I don't know what's wrong with me. Maybe I've been too long without sex…'

He sucked air through his teeth at the sharp stab of jealousy under his ribs. 'I really don't want to know.'

'Or maybe it's being back in Manhattan,' she rushed on, ignoring his jealousy. 'Old memories resurfacing, or maybe it's just more unfinished business with you… I don't know,' she wailed, her stare anguished. 'I'm just so confused.'

She stepped closer and Logan curled his hands into fists to stop himself from reaching for her and dragging her into his arms, burying his face in her fragrant hair, feeling her heart beat against his.

'But I'm tired of fighting it, Logan, of tossing and turning at night. So… I thought the only sensible thing was to take you up on your offer to talk it through.'

'Okay,' he said, scared to move a muscle because the tension binding them together felt as fragile as spun sugar, one wrong move and it would crack. 'Do you want to sit down?' he choked out, tilting his head towards the darkened living room. 'I can light the fire.'

She glanced around his living space to the view beyond the large windows, which was dotted with city lights. When her gaze returned to his, he recognised the desire he saw there.

'Harper…' he said, her name filled with questions,

with warning. 'You can't come here and look at me like that and not expect me to want you. You said you were done. I've let it go, as you asked. But even I have limits. I'm human, not made of stone.' What was she trying to do to him? Torture him to death? Dangle herself in front of him and then snatch away temptation just as he reached for her?

Her eyes turned stormy with fury and accusation and fire. 'And you can't say you regret losing me and not expect me to—' She broke off, panting hard.

Logan froze, holding his breath. He was about to ask her to finish that sentence, when she closed the distance between them and threw her arms around his neck, her lips clashing into his.

At the touch of her lips, Logan's mind blanked. Every word he wanted to say, every question he had, ceased to exist like popped bubbles. He no longer wanted to talk; they'd done plenty of that this week and none of it had made as much sense as this. Her, in his arms, where she felt terrifyingly at home, where she made him believe he could earn her forgiveness. He hauled her body closer and parted her lips with his, his tongue meeting hers as their kiss deepened and he forgot all of the reasons that this was a bad idea. There would be time enough for reason. If he could only show her how much he'd changed, how much he regretted the past, maybe they could repair the damage.

'Logan,' she panted, leaning back against the kitchen island as he trailed kisses along her neck and slipped his hand under her sweater to caress her breast through her bra. 'I want you.' Her hands found the waist of his jeans, her fingers tugging at the button.

He cupped her face, his stare boring into hers while his fingers worked her nipple taut. 'Do you?' he asked, panting. 'I thought I was just an old habit. A bad habit. *I* can be honest about this, Harper. No matter how much easier it would be if it was dead between us—I want *you*. I wanted you that first day you walked into my OR. I wanted you even when I knew it was stupid. I wanted you when you said for you it was finished. Don't you think you owe me the same degree of honesty?'

She blinked up at him, doubt shifting over her expression. 'I'm trying. I'm just so confused, because logic tells me this, us, is still a stupid move, but I don't care. I haven't been able to get you off my mind all week. I haven't been able to stop thinking about what you said in the staff room, the way you looked. I can't stop thinking about last Saturday, the way it felt so right in a way that nothing else ever has, but then we never had any problems with that side of our relationship, did we?'

To hear her finally admit they'd done something right, and because he could relate to every word she'd said, he groaned and kissed her again, his own desires pummelling him like blows. 'This has always made sense. I haven't stopped thinking about you, either. This week has been hell.'

He popped the button of her jeans and slipped his hand into her underwear, stroking her, kissing her, groaning when she nodded and palmed his erection. He stroked the slickness between her thighs and pressed kisses over her face, her jaw, her neck.

'I don't want to talk any more,' she said, unbuttoning his fly and shoving his jeans over his hips. 'Hurry.'

Logan shook his head. 'If we're doing this again, first I want your promise that we will talk. And soon, Harper.'

'I promise.' She nodded and because he couldn't get close enough to her, because there were too many layers between them, he gripped her waist and sat her on the counter, one hand pushing up her sweater and the other hand popping her bra clasp so her breasts spilled free. He raised the sweater and took one nipple in his mouth and sucked.

'I've wanted you every day,' he said, inhaling the scent of her skin as he pressed kisses over her chest and breasts.

'Me too,' she sighed, impatiently shrugging off her sweater and bra and shifting restlessly in his arms.

When he captured the other nipple to lavish it with the same attention, she cried out, twisting his hair between her fingers as she held him close.

'Take this off,' she ordered tugging at his shirt. 'I want to see you.'

He obeyed, quickly dropping the T-shirt to the floor. Harper shimmied her jeans and underwear over her hips, and he tossed them aside and dropped to his knees on the kitchen tiles.

'Yes,' Harper gasped as he covered her with his mouth. She hooked her legs over his shoulders and fell back onto her elbows.

Resigned that his kitchen was officially ruined— every time he cooked in future he'd remember the way she looked right then—he looked up at her, triumph flooding his veins as she moaned his name over and over. He couldn't ever recall wanting a woman more. He already knew so much about this woman, who'd once meant everything to him. But this wasn't about for ever, just inescapable physical desire and old scores that needed settling.

Because he wanted her more than he wanted his next breath, he jerked to his feet and scooped his arms around her back, preparing to carry her to the bedroom. But she yanked his lips back to hers and kissed him deeply, shoving his jeans down.

'No condom out here,' he mumbled against her lips as she kissed him with mounting desperation and throaty little moans that drove him to distraction.

'I don't need it if you don't,' she said, kissing his chest, his neck, his jaw, while her hands grabbed his backside and urged him closer. 'On the pill.'

'Are you sure?' he asked, his resistance waning as he filled his hands with her breasts and she dropped her head back on a long sigh. They'd done this before, had sex wherever they'd found themselves. Another apartment, another time, but the memories added to the arousal he struggled to breathe against. The bedroom suddenly felt a long way away.

'Yes,' she cried, her hips bucking against his as she wrapped her legs around him and kissed him again.

'Harper,' he groaned, dragging her to the edge of the counter. She was hard enough to resist fully clothed and hostile, let alone like this, naked and begging.

'Logan,' she pleaded, biting into her lower lip.

He kissed her and pushed inside her, cupping her face

to hold her gaze to his while his heart thundered away behind his ribs.

'I've missed you,' he whispered, panting against her lips between her frantic kisses, while pleasure hijacked his body and mind. 'I've missed this, us.'

He hadn't been ready to say it the night of the Reece Gallery exhibition, but now that she'd come to him, opened up and let him in, he could no longer keep the words inside. It was true. Their connection was the deepest of his life. He might be scared of its potency, scared to make another mistake with her, but the part of him that had been hurt when they'd split up, needed to admit it.

'Me too.' She nodded, her hips writhing against his so he had to close his eyes and clench his teeth against the waves of desire making him dizzy.

Because he didn't want to think of how they'd ruined what they had, how there was no going back in time to fix it, he moved inside her, marvelling at how something so familiar could be so good. How could she get to him unlike any other woman? How could he want her this way, but have no idea what it meant for the future?

With their stares still locked together, all the things he'd wanted to say these past ten years seemed to cross the distance. Maybe he didn't need to say any of it aloud. Maybe she felt it too, this clamour of unresolved feelings they owed to themselves and to each other to air.

'I'm sorry I tried to deny this.' She bit her lip, her breathing laboured as she clung to his shoulders and crossed her ankles in the small of his back.

'It's too good,' he said. 'It always was.' He crushed her

close, kissed her deeply, held her as if he'd never again let her go. But just because they couldn't resist this, didn't mean she was his.

That was his last thought before her orgasm snatched one last cry from her throat. Groaning he came too, his body racked with spasms and engulfed in flames and his mind, the confusion he'd felt since she'd walked back into his life, somehow wiped clean.

CHAPTER TEN

HARPER OPENED HER eyes and blinked against the bright sunlight streaming into the room. Too much sunlight. *Her* bedroom had no window. Disoriented, she raised her head from the pillow and saw Logan, his head propped up on one bent elbow as he smiled down at her smugly.

'Good morning,' he said, gently brushing her hair back from her face as if she were...precious. 'How did you sleep?'

'Good,' she mumbled, gripping his sheet to her breasts as she sat up against the upholstered headboard. She hadn't intended to sleep over, but after having sex in the kitchen they'd showered together and then had sex again, this time slowly and lazily in his massive bed. Afterwards, she'd been so warm and satisfied that she'd snuggled into him and closed her eyes, just for a second. But now, in the cold light of day, she'd forgotten how to act around him.

'It's a little late for covering up,' he said, his eyes full of laughter and heat that told her he was reliving every erotic moment of last night. 'I've seen it all, hundreds of times. Kissed it all, too. I'll never be able to use my kitchen again without thinking of you.' He tapped the tip of his index finger to his temple to let her know the memories were stored away. Then he winked cheekily and leaned in to capture her lips in a kiss.

Harper couldn't help her smile, breathing through the full-body shudder as she lost herself for seconds, relaxing into his kiss as images from last night flooded her brain.

'I should go,' she said when he pulled back from their kiss. 'I didn't really mean to stay the night.' She hadn't even planned to knock on his door last night. But after leaving Charlie, after her heartfelt talk with her dad, and with her head full of all the things she'd learned about Logan since coming home, her feet had just led her to him.

'No need to rush off,' he said, relaxed. 'I made you coffee.'

Harper glanced at the nightstand where a steaming mug of white coffee sat. 'Thanks.' She took a sip, feeling ridiculously self-conscious. 'So what plans do you have for the weekend?' she asked, as if they were sitting in the Theatre staff room, passing the time between surgeries.

'I'm playing squash with my brother tomorrow, and I have a charity black tie thing this evening.'

'Another of your parents' galas that you must attend?' She spoke before thinking, wincing when she heard how bitter she sounded. 'Sorry...'

'It's an Edgar Grant Foundation event. I don't think they'll be there,' he said, breezing over it. 'What about your plans for the weekend?'

Harper gently released a sigh, awash with guilt that she'd judged him so harshly but also secretly relieved that he hadn't invited her along to the charity event that night. She had no label for whatever this was that they were doing, but it was definitely about sex and not dating.

She might be stupid enough to sleep with her ex-husband, but she was under no illusions that they could be more than casual. It hadn't worked the first time around for many reasons.

'I have some work to catch up on,' she said. 'I'm writing a review paper on pulmonary atresia treatment outcomes with Bill McIntyre.'

'Sounds interesting. I'd like to read that when you publish.'

Harper stared into his eyes the way she'd done thousands of times when they were a couple, her confusion returning. But no matter how weird this felt, lying in his bed on a Saturday morning, this man *wasn't* a stranger. She knew his core values, even if she was still discovering new things about him. And it was time to keep her side of the bargain.

'I've been thinking,' she said hesitantly, 'about what you said at the start of the week.' She ducked her head and stared down at the comforter, both Charlie's words and Logan's looping through her mind.

'About losing you being the biggest regret of my life?' he offered.

'Yes...that...' She looked up and nodded, still stunned by that confession, days later. 'But also about me holding back, not fully trusting you when we were together.' It was hard to look at him and admit the root of her part in their relationship breakdown at the same time, but she forced herself to keep eye contact. 'I'm sorry if that was how you saw it. It wasn't my intention to make you feel like that. I just... I guess when we were together, I was obviously still struggling with my abandonment issues. Charlie and I actually talked about it last night. He helped me to see that I was pretty messed up back then. It wasn't just you I kept out. I refused to discuss how I felt, even with Charlie. To say I was a sullen, withdrawn teenager at times, would be an understatement.'

He fell quiet, compassion in his eyes. Wordlessly, he reached for her hand and raised it to his lips, kissing her fingertips, one by one. 'It's okay, Harper. I understood it was a difficult subject for you. I tried to understand what it must have been like, but I had the opposite issue with my parents, as you know. I couldn't stop them from inserting themselves in my life. Into *our* lives, or so I thought at the time... I guess I just felt helpless with you. I wanted to be there for you, to help you through what was obviously a gaping wound, but I didn't know how. And everything I said just seemed to make it worse.'

Harper swallowed, regret a sour taste in her throat. 'You would have hated that feeling of helplessness, and I made it worse by just shutting you out. I'm sorry, Logan.'

He smiled sadly, neither denying nor confirming, but of course she was right.

'It was just that by the time I'd met you,' she went on, 'I'd spent so many years wondering what I'd done wrong to make my mother leave and how I could make her change her mind and come back, that a big part of me was sick of thinking about it. No one could have helped. I just needed to work through it on my own. I needed to realise that you can't make someone care about you or love you, no matter how fiercely you try. So it became easier to just block it out. Not to think about her. To just rely on myself and get on with things.'

'I'm sorry that she let you down so badly,' he said, squeezing her hand. 'You're an amazing woman. Strong and smart. I know it couldn't make up for what you'd lost, but for the record, *I* loved you.'

She blinked, glancing away, feeling as if she might burst into tears if he kept saying wonderful things. He'd complimented her like that in the past, but back when they'd been together she'd found it harder to believe. Now it just left her confused because it had been so long since she'd relied on him emotionally, and part of her didn't know how.

'Did you ever reach out to her the way you'd once contemplated?' he asked, keeping a hold of her hand.

She nodded her head, trying not to squirm at how foreign and intimate but also exhilarating the gesture felt. 'I did reach out to her from London. She lives in Ohio, or at least she used to. We swapped a few emails. She made some noises about coming to visit, but… I don't know, the contact kind of fizzled out.' And Harper had been devastated all over again. Too embarrassed to tell Charlie what she'd done, in case he was angry with her for being such a fool.

She shook her head and glanced at Logan, her pulse throbbing in her throat. 'I've never told anyone else that. Dad doesn't know, so please don't mention it, will you? I never want to hurt him.'

'Of course not.' He sucked in a breath and wrapped his arm around her shoulders, pressing his lips to her temple. 'I'm sorry.'

'She had another family, after me,' she whispered, the old familiar feelings of rejection hard to grapple with, even now. 'I have a half brother and sister I've never even met.'

Logan held her a little tighter, his fingers stroking her

arm. 'I'm so sorry. No one deserves to be so badly let down. I hope you know that none of it was your fault.'

Harper shrugged, her insides trembling. 'I do now. I finally made my peace with it in London. I realised that by trying to force the issue, trying to orchestrate a meeting that she clearly didn't want, I was just handing over the power for her to hurt me again. I don't need her for anything. I'm fine without her, so why bother? We don't even know each other any more. And I wouldn't want to upset Charlie in any way. *He's* my family.'

Logan smiled, his stare full of understanding. He pressed a kiss to her lips. 'He's a great guy, and he's always been there for you.'

Harper nodded, smiling. 'Always. And now I'm here for him.' She ducked her head and pushed on. 'I'm sorry, Logan, for my immaturity and emotional unavailability when we were together. I guess I did push you away, and then, when I'd decided it was over, I ran away to the UK. I'm embarrassed to think I might have inadvertently acted just like my mother, running when times were tough.'

Logan shifted, cupping her face between his palms. 'You're nothing like her. You would never walk away from your own child if you had one.'

The conviction of his statement stunned her, even though it was true that she wouldn't. But how could he still know her well enough to be so certain?

Because she felt caught at the centre of an emotional hurricane and couldn't see which way was up, she leaned in and kissed him. That they knew certain things about each other was inevitable. They'd lived together. Loved each other. But it didn't change anything. This was still about sex. Harper had spent too long living without love to ever trust it again, and clearly Logan was the same. Otherwise he wouldn't be single.

'I'd like to apologise, too,' Logan said softly when he pulled back. 'I also let you down. It wasn't intentional, but I neglected you and our relationship. I threw myself into becoming the best surgeon I could be, thinking you understood, thinking it was just temporary and you would always be there. But after I lost you, I realised I'd abandoned you one time too many. I cancelled dates and missed celebrations and left you to fend for yourself with my parents at all those functions they loved. They had far too much say over my life in those days.'

Harper watched him closely, her heart fluttering wildly. If only they'd been this mature when they were together. If only they'd communicated this effectively when they were married, maybe they would still be together. What might their lives now look like if they were? Would they have a family? Would they have found some way to work together and share childcare? Would their love have grown and matured as they did?

'When I met you,' he went on, 'I too was messed up. By the age of twenty-six, I'd already let my parents down so much, I carried a lot of guilt. I was their firstborn, their eldest son. They had all these grand plans for me to take over the Grant Group, and after growing up with the legacy hanging over me like a cloud, I didn't want it. It was as if I had a whole wardrobe of someone else's clothes ready and waiting for me to just step into them. It was suffocating. But by putting my foot down and insisting on my own career, I felt as if I had even more to prove. I was so fixated on being the best doctor I could be, on proving them wrong and me right, I lost sight of other things, like how my parents' expectations were still stifling. Like how those expectations spread beyond me to us, and affected you. I failed to protect what was truly important to me.' He paused and met her stare. 'You. *Us*. I'll always regret that.'

Harper froze, a silent gasp stuck in her throat. Her regrets multiplied and added to Logan's. She'd always known that in some ways they'd both messed up their relationship, but to hear confirmation of how pointless their divorce had been was sickening.

'I understand how growing up with your life mapped out for you would be hard,' Harper whispered, choked. 'You would have hated that.' Didn't his parents know him at all? Logan was the kind of person who simply tried harder when told something was impossible. 'But I'm so glad that you stuck to your guns with your career, for the sake of all the patients you've helped over the years. You're an amazing surgeon, Logan.'

'No one wants to feel they have no say in the direction of their own life,' he admitted, his eyes shining as his stare shifted over her face. 'Which was probably why both Sam and I rebelled in our different ways.'

Harper's heart thudded. 'Was I part of your rebellion?' she quietly asked. 'It's like you said—we probably rushed into getting married. For me, I think it was because part of me wanted the perfect, white picket fence future I'd missed out on as a child whose mother hadn't wanted her.' Maybe Logan had his own reasons, too.

'I've never thought of you that way,' he said, his stare shifting over her face. 'But maybe there was some part of me that was eager to prove to my parents that I had my life all figured out. But I fancied you the minute I saw you.' He grinned and she laughed, grateful for the lighter moment. 'One of the things I liked about you right off the bat was your feistiness and how you weren't remotely impressed by the privileged life I'd grown up with.'

Harper's smile widened, but she touched his cheek. 'You needed taking down a peg or two. And I too liked that we were different. You brought out my reckless side and you still do, it seems. Otherwise I wouldn't be in your bed naked this morning.'

Logan's smile stretched smugly. 'Hey, I don't see that as a negative.' He cupped her chin and tilted her lips up to his soft, lazy kiss that tasted like forgiveness.

Harper turned into his arms and tangled her fingers in his hair, her body swamped by languorous heat. He'd been right. It felt good to lay the past to rest, finally. Maybe now they could actually enjoy working together. Hopefully once the sex had run its course, they could have another of these mature conversations and part as friends.

Just as things turned more determined, the passion of their kisses growing, Harper's phone pinged with an incoming text.

Grabbing it up from the nightstand, she saw the message was from her father.

'It's Charlie.' She sat up, frantically scanning the text while her pulse flew. Her father normally called if he wanted to chat. 'He's at the hospital.' Her blood ran cold. 'He had a hypo this morning. I have to go.'

Harper leapt out of bed and walked naked through to Logan's kitchen, where her clothes from last night were still scattered on the floor.

By the time she'd pulled on her jeans and fastened her

bra, Logan had joined her, now fully dressed, that determined look back on his face. 'I'll drive you,' he said, handing over her sweater and scooping his car keys from a bowl near the door. His tone of voice brooked no argument, and she was too worried about Charlie to refuse the ride. Speed was of the essence.

Harper tugged on the sweater and slipped on her shoes, more grateful for Logan in that moment than she could possibly articulate. There was no time now to analyse why she'd come to *him* last night, no time to dissect their talk this morning, and little point pretending that she could fully keep Logan out of her life. As soon as she made sure Charlie was okay, then she could turn her attention to Logan and the consequences of what they'd done by being intimate again. She just hoped, for both their sakes, that she didn't come to regret her reckless impulse.

CHAPTER ELEVEN

LOGAN GRIPPED HARPER'S hand and marched into the emergency department of Staten Island Hospital at her side, his stomach knotted with concern. Harper was understandably worried and hadn't said much on the thirty-minute drive to hospital. Logan was just grateful that she'd allowed him to tag along. He too was concerned for Charlie, and after their renewed closeness following last night and their frank talk this morning, he absolutely wanted to be there to support Harper. He had no idea where this could go, but he wouldn't let her down if she needed him.

At the ED reception, Harper tugged her hand from his and gripped the edge of the desk, speaking to the woman behind the glass partition in a tight voice. 'I'm Harper Dunn. You have my father here. Charlie Dunn.'

The receptionist checked the computer. 'He's in bay fifteen. Through those double doors.'

Logan followed Harper, his pulse only slowing when they entered the bay and saw Charlie, pale but conscious, lying on a gurney.

'Dad,' Harper cried, going straight to her father and taking his hand. 'What happened?'

Charlie glanced at Logan, his expression surprised,

then he focussed on his daughter. 'I'm not really sure,' the older man said. 'I woke up this morning feeling fine, had breakfast as usual. Then I started to feel dizzy. I'd just managed to make it to Eric's house next door when I guess I must have passed out.'

Looking more closely now, Logan saw that Charlie had a graze on his forehead and along one forearm as if he'd tried to break his fall. Like Harper, he hated feeling helpless, but at least Charlie was making sense, moving all his limbs and by the looks of it hadn't needed stitches.

'Have you seen the doctor?' Harper asked, concern turning to practicalities. She stood a little taller, clearly switching between concerned daughter mode to fellow medical professional in search of answers.

'Yes, of course,' Charlie said. 'I'm just waiting for a CT scan. Hi, Logan,' Charlie added, sheepishly. 'Thanks for coming. Sorry to cause all this fuss.'

'It's no problem, Charlie. Harper and I just happened to be together, so we jumped in my car.'

Harper shot him a look that told him she probably didn't want her father to know they'd spent the night together, even though he'd kept his explanation vague. But how else could he explain his presence when they hadn't been at work?

'I'm going to find the doctor,' she said, turning back to Charlie.

'He's busy,' Charlie said. 'I'm fine now. Don't worry.'

Harper sighed in frustration. 'You're not fine, Dad. You're all beat up and you can't remember what happened.'

Charlie looked to Logan to back him up, but there

was no way Logan was stepping into the middle of that minefield.

'Why don't *I* find the doctor?' Logan said diplomatically, his eyes going to Harper. 'You stay with your dad.'

Harper nodded gratefully, and Logan ducked out of the bay and snagged the nearest ED nurse. As Logan was no longer a family member, no one would tell him anything, but he returned with the ED resident, a young guy in his twenties who looked as if he'd been up all night.

'Ms Dunn, I'm Dr Bates,' he introduced himself to Harper.

'It's Dr Dunn, actually,' she said. 'I'm a congenital heart surgeon at MMH.'

Dr Bates nodded. 'We've decided to admit your father for observation. As you can see, he took a bump to the head so I've ordered a CT scan. He suffered a hypoglycaemic attack with loss of consciousness. Fortunately his neighbour was present to put him in the recovery position and call for an ambulance.'

Charlie listened self-consciously. Logan fought the urge to touch Harper, who'd gone into full physician mode. 'His primary care physician has been struggling to manage his diabetes,' she explained.

Dr Bates nodded. 'Yes, we've seen that from his file. I've already made a referral to our endocrine specialist here and it might be worth considering a medical alarm to be installed at home.'

'Yes, of course.' Harper flushed, probably thinking she'd let Charlie down by not thinking of that sooner. 'I'll organise that today.'

The young doctor offered her and Charlie a reassuring smile. 'The admission is really just a precaution. I don't imagine Charlie will spend more than twenty-four hours with us. And I've told him to let us know if he suffers from any headaches or nausea or blurred vision.'

'Thanks, Dr Bates. I'll stay with him.' Harper glanced at Charlie, who was sensible enough not to argue with his daughter.

With a nod and smile for Logan, the doctor left.

Logan hesitated, uncertain what he should do. Now that Charlie was stable and in good hands, there was no reason for him to stay. He wouldn't have minded, but he doubted Harper would want him there. After all, just because they'd spent an incredible night together and had a highly cathartic conversation about their past, didn't mean they were a couple. Nor were they getting back together, even if they had been unable to fight their chemistry.

'I should leave you to it,' he said reluctantly, gripping Charlie's shoulder. 'Call me, any time, day or night, okay?'

Charlie nodded and Harper followed Logan out of the bay and out of earshot of her father. 'Thanks for the lift,' she said, clearly distracted. 'And thanks for coming in with me. I really appreciate it, Logan.'

'You can call me, too,' he said, wanting to drag her into his arms and hold her, to kiss away her concerns, but she obviously needed space and to be alone with her father. And he needed time to think about everything that had occurred over the past twenty-four hours.

'Thank you. I will.'

'What can I do to help?' he asked, that helpless feeling he detested so much, building. She didn't need him, but a part of him wanted her to rely on him the way she had last night when she'd come to his apartment. 'And don't say nothing. Let me help, please. I care about him as much as you do.'

Harper frowned, her stare flitting back to the curtained bay and her father. Then she surprised him by letting him in just a tiny bit more. 'Could you organise the alarm installation?' She pulled her keys from her purse and removed one, passing it over. 'This is the key to Charlie's house. I want to stay with him here, but I want the alarm installed by the time he's discharged.'

'Of course. Leave it with me.' Logan tried to steady his breathing while his heart thundered. This was a big step for Harper, who'd always been so self-sufficient, probably in response to her mother's rejection. After last night, after their heartfelt apologies this morning, he couldn't help but see it as a marker that maybe, just maybe she might be starting to trust him outside of work. Clearing the air between them had definitely been the right call.

'Thanks, Logan,' she breathed. 'That would be amazing.'

He nodded and reached for her hand, wishing he could kiss her. 'Try not to worry too much. He's in the right place, getting the right care and he seems fine now.'

'I guess…' she said, her teeth worrying at her lower lip.

Because he wanted to help as much as he could, he forced himself to press a kiss to her cheek and step away. 'I'll message you when the alarm is done, okay? Call me if you need anything else.'

She nodded. 'I'll keep you posted.' Then she disappeared back behind the curtains.

Logan left the hospital, the urgent call to the alarm company placed before he'd even reached his car. He'd offered them a sum they couldn't refuse for the rushed nature of the job, but if Harper wanted peace of mind, he'd make sure she got it. His next stop was the closest shopping mall. He might no longer be part of the Dunn family, but he could at least make Charlie and Harper's stay in the hospital more comfortable with everything they'd need for a night away from home: a change of clothes, toiletries, some magazines.

As he piled items into his shopping cart, it felt good to be able to help in some way. For a moment, back there in the hospital, he and Harper had felt like a proper team again, not just colleagues and exes who'd had sex again. He cared about Charlie. But more than that, he cared about Harper. Perhaps more than he should. As he headed back to the hospital to drop off the things he'd bought, he cautioned himself to be careful. Neither of them had been in a serious long-term relationship since they split up and they weren't in one now. He'd messed up once before. Hurt her and himself in the process. This time, whatever happened between them, he couldn't let her down again.

The following Monday, after a Sunday spent settling Charlie back at home after his hypoglycaemic attack, Harper met Jess on the NICU to review baby Emily, whose post-op recovery had, so far, been stable.

'Nothing to report overnight,' Jess said, bringing Harper up to speed on Emily's progress. 'She has good temperature regulation, healthy urine output and moderate weight gain, taking her up to the fiftieth percentile.'

'ECG and chest X-ray?' Harper asked, looping her stethoscope from around her neck and warming up the bell between her palms.

'Again normal, and both renal and liver function tests have normalised,' Jess added.

Harper gently listened to Emily's heart and lungs while she also palpated her peripheral pulses and abdomen. When she was happy with her examination, she removed her stethoscope. 'Good. If Dr Grant is also happy with her progress, I think we can begin to wean her off the ventilator. Can you speak to Greg and the neonatologists and make sure everyone is agreed.'

At least with Emily stable and improving there was one less concern. She'd had to shove her worries for Charlie from her mind when she arrived at work that morning, but his night in hospital had really shaken her.

Jess nodded and made a note in Emily's file. Before they left the NICU, they paused at the sinks to wash their hands.

'Dr Dunn,' Jess said, hesitantly, 'I don't know if you're aware, but Greg and I are getting married at the weekend.'

Harper smiled and nodded. 'I heard that you two were engaged from Dr Grant. Congratulations.' Mention of Logan sent her mind back to the weekend, a time of unexpected highs, when she'd spent the night in his bed, when they'd finally opened up about the past, and worrying lows with Charlie's admission to hospital. But as promised, Charlie had been discharged the following day, returning home to find the newly installed medical alarms, thanks to Logan.

Free to think about him now, her heart rate picked up. But just because they'd succumbed to their chemistry once more, just because she'd convinced herself it was harmless to sleep with him, it didn't mean anything serious. They weren't getting back together. Neither of them wanted that. And with the clinical lead position still to play for, with the interview next week, they each needed to remain focussed on work.

'I wondered if you would like to attend,' Jess continued, drawing Harper's thoughts away from Logan. 'I know it's short notice, and you don't have to if it's not convenient, but…well, Greg and I would love to see you there if you can make it.'

Slightly awkwardly, Jess pulled an envelope from the pocket of her white coat and passed it over with a shy smile.

'Thanks, Jess. Let me think about it. I'll let you know either way later today. And good luck with your preparations. Let me know if you need to leave early this week.'

As she made her way back to the surgical department, Harper opened the invitation. Jess and Greg's ceremony was being held in a rural setting overlooking the Hudson River, upstate in Westchester. Just thinking about attending brought back a rush of memories from her and Logan's wedding day. They'd opted to marry at a historic country estate in Staten Island, celebrating with an intimate party of close friends and relatives. Biddie Grant had been appalled they'd denied her the chance to host a lavish shindig at the Upper East Side's Brentwood Hotel, but for once, Harper had put her foot down.

Recalling how handsome Logan had looked in his wedding suit, she'd just let herself into her office, when there was a tap at the door and the man himself appeared. 'Hey, mind if I come in?'

'Of course.' Her stomach swooped at the sight of him, gratitude and longing catching her off guard.

Logan closed the door. 'How are you, and how's Charlie doing?' He frowned, worry in his dark eyes.

'I'm fine, a little tired,' she said. 'I didn't get much sleep at the hospital, obviously with just a chair to doze in. But Charlie seems back to his cheerful self. And his CT scan was all clear.'

'That's good news,' he sighed. 'I'm so relieved. That must have been quite the scare for you. What did the endocrinologist say?'

'They've adjusted his insulin and put him in touch with the community diabetic nurses.'

'So he'll have a bit more support.'

Harper nodded and stepped from behind her desk, making her way over to him. 'Thanks for organising the alarm installation and for the clothes and other things,' she said, her throat tight. She reached for his hand and squeezed his fingers. 'You didn't have to do that, but we both really appreciated it.' She'd been stunned when the bag of brand-new clothing and toiletries and reading material had arrived via the ward receptionist. Logan had thought of everything, including underwear and a toothbrush.

'You're welcome.' He shrugged, his stare lingering on hers. 'Your family used to be my family, so I wanted to help. Thanks for letting me.'

His reminders of what they'd once meant to each other left her desperate to step into his arms and bury her face over the thump of his heart, but she held back, still scared to rely on him emotionally, because she'd done that once before and been devastated when it was over, feeling as if she should have known better after learning from her mother. They weren't dating, they weren't simply picking up where they'd left off or getting back together. But she had no idea what it was that they were doing.

'Jess and I have just reviewed Emily Walsh,' she said. 'I think it's time to wean her off the ventilator, if you agree.'

Logan nodded. 'I'll pop in to see her before my clinic, but I'm sure that if you're happy, I will be, too.'

She shuddered. When had they started to professionally trust each other so much? It had been happening gradually since she'd come to MMH, maybe strengthened by the fact that she'd opened up to him emotionally, too.

'Is that an invitation to Jess and Greg's wedding?' Logan asked, glancing at the open envelope on her desk.

'Yes. Are you going?' Harper hadn't yet decided to accept the invitation. The idea of watching a young couple say 'I do' made her...nervous. If Logan was there, she'd be surrounded by reminders of their wedding day and by sleeping with him again she'd complicated everything. Not to mention that with Charlie's hospitalisation she'd barely had time to think about her and Logan and the risks they were talking by revisiting that side of their relationship.

'I am,' he said, hope shining in his dark eyes. 'What about you?'

'I'm undecided.' Harper glanced down at their hands. 'It's over an hour away and I'm not sure I want to leave Charlie alone in the city.'

Logan nodded, disappointment obvious in his eyes. 'It's easy enough to come back if he needs you. And he won't be completely alone. He has his brothers, the community nurses, his neighbour. He'd probably tell you not to worry if he was here.'

'He would,' she admitted, ducking her head, 'but it's not that simple. I'm his next of kin, his only child.'

Logan nodded and pulled her close, cupping her face to raise her stare to his. 'Well, if you decide to attend, I'm driving, so you're welcome to a ride.'

'Thanks, Logan. I might take you up on that. Although, I don't know. The last time you and I were together at a wedding, it was our own. Won't it be…awkward?' By awkward, she of course meant triggering, confusing, painful. So many reminders, missed chances and regrets. She wasn't sure she could face it.

'I know what you mean,' he said, tilting up her chin so their eyes met. 'But it's not about us. It's about Jess and Greg. If you want to go, there's no need to give it any more thought than that.'

She nodded, the tension between them pulling taut. She wished she didn't have to overthink it. But since the weekend, since she'd slept with him again, she couldn't help but feel confused, second-guessing her own judgement. After all, she felt powerless against their chemistry, but Logan was still the man she'd walked away from once before. He was still the rival doctor hoping to take the job she wanted. Was she still scared to trust him fully, because he had let her down before?

'What are we doing, Logan?' she whispered as he reached for her and she stepped close. 'I swing between wanting to rip your clothes off to thinking it's a really bad idea.' A part of her had hoped this need would have died down by now, but there seemed no end in sight.

'I'm not sure what it is, either,' he admitted, cupping her cheek. 'I just know that I want you. Does it need a label?'

Harper shook her head. She wanted him as much as he wanted her, but it felt beyond reckless to keep indulging in behaviour that could only end one way. Or maybe that was its appeal? She was so confused.

'Do you want to stop?' He frowned, his eyes stormy with desire and similar confusion.

'No.' Harper shook her head, stepping into his arms until their bodies met, their hearts banging together. 'Not yet.' Maybe she *was* overthinking it. Maybe she should just enjoy it while it lasted, live for the moment, because they both knew it couldn't be for ever.

Logan dipped his head, his lips grazing hers in the barest of teases, their gusting breaths mingling. 'Me neither. I missed you this weekend, even though I saw you Friday and Saturday.'

'Me too.' Harper tugged at his waist so their bodies collided, despite the flashing danger signs in her peripheral vision. Their lips met in a desperate clash, their kiss becoming deep and passionate in a way that was most definitely not suitable for work. But she couldn't become addicted to her ex-husband. Not when it was a dead end, when they were still rivals for the same job, when they'd hurt each other in the past.

'Can you come over tonight, after work?' he asked, pressing kisses over her face.

'I can't,' she sighed, her body melting into his. 'I'm going to Staten Island to check on Charlie.'

Logan groaned, looking up from nuzzling her neck, cupping her face and brushing her lips with his. 'Then when can I see you again away from here?'

Harper hesitated, her body shifting restlessly against

his. 'I don't know… I'm on call tomorrow. Maybe at the weekend, at the wedding.'

Logan groaned, kissed her determinedly and then stepped back, his breathing laboured. 'Okay. Then I'd better go. I have a packed clinic this afternoon and I can't be distracted by my gorgeous ex-wife.'

She laughed, shooing him out of the door, and he left with a cheeky wink that made her heart clench. But after he'd gone, she worried at her bottom lip with her teeth. Were they crazy? This could only end one way. She'd known that when she'd entered his building at the weekend. But she'd selfishly wanted him anyway.

Silently praying for the strength to keep whatever this was contained so they didn't wind up hurting each other again, she threw herself into work for the rest of the day.

CHAPTER TWELVE

THAT WEEKEND, FROM ACROSS the room, Logan's stare sought out Harper for what felt like the millionth time. The party around them in the cavernous stone barn with wooden beams laden with florals and twinkling lights, the dancing and the many conversations, faded to white noise as he watched her with fierce hunger and a strange ache in the centre of his chest.

She looked beautiful. She wore a simple green dress that skimmed her figure and made her dark eyes glow. Her styled hair cascaded in soft waves over one shoulder, her soft make-up accentuating her natural beauty. All day throughout Greg and Jess's ceremony and all night while they'd celebrated with a party, Logan had been forced to pretend that Harper was just his ex-wife and colleague, when, in reality, the emotions of the day had left him wanting to touch her and kiss her and hold her while they slow danced together.

But of course, today's wedding had also brought bittersweet memories of their own ceremony, where they'd promised to love each other until death. It sickened him how quickly those words he and Harper had said to each other had become meaningless. But then he'd always known that love came with conditions, and as well as being emotionally guarded with him maybe Harper had never loved Logan as deeply as Jess and Greg seemed to be in love.

Harper looked up from a conversation with one of Jess's aunts, her eyes meeting his from across the room. For a second, she froze, as if aware of the direction of his thoughts, which had been with her and only her since she'd walked into his apartment a week ago. He imagined he'd witnessed longing in her eyes, but it was hard to tell from so far away. Maybe that was just what he wanted to see, so he didn't feel so…alone. Because he ached and he was terrified.

The aunt touched Harper's arm as she spoke, before moving away. Done pretending to ignore her, Logan made his move, casually crossing the room to intercept Harper before she could become ensnared in another conversation.

'I've left you alone for as long as I can tolerate,' he said, slinging one hand in his pants pocket and feigning mild boredom as he forced himself to glance around the room, when in reality he burned for her touch. Maybe then, his conflicted feelings would settle.

'We don't want anyone, least of all our residents to think we're anything more than colleagues who can barely tolerate each other,' she said with a tight smile.

'How are you feeling after today?' he asked. Was she, like him, thinking of their own wedding, of their brief marriage and how they might have done things differently? She'd been right to hesitate about them attending this wedding together. To question what they were doing by indulging their chemistry, not that Logan had the answers, even now.

'I'm fine,' she said, finally glancing his way.

Logan caught the scent of her perfume and dragged in a breath. Then, because she seemed to be handling the emotions of the day better than him and because it had been on his mind all day, he blurted, 'Do you remember our wedding?' He winced at the vulnerability in his voice.

'Of course.' She watched him thoughtfully, a small smile curling her mouth. 'It's the only wedding I've had.' Then she looked away but continued to speak. 'I was so in love with you, I could hardly wait. I was so excited.'

Logan stared at her profile, an ache under his ribs. He'd spent so many years scared to trust that emotion, love, that her words made him restless. His parents' love had always seemed to come with conditions. Even Harper's love had been short-lived.

'Me too,' he said. 'Best day of my life.' He'd been so hopeful. He'd found *his* person. But now that he'd lived through their divorce, he couldn't help but wonder if she really had loved him then the way he'd loved her.

Harper looked up sharply. 'Really? Even though we messed up and it didn't last?

He shrugged sadly, desperate to touch her now that they were finally having this conversation. 'Sometimes, I wonder where we'd be now if we'd stayed together.' He should drop it; no sense dwelling in the past, but he couldn't help himself so he went on. 'Do you? Think about the future? Do you still want a family one day?'

Something in the stiffness of her posture left him unsettled. Of course they'd talked about having a family of their own when they'd been together. But since then, Logan had shoved the idea of being a father to the back of his mind. Maybe Harper, too, had a change of heart.

'I don't know,' she said, looking uncomfortable. 'I'm thirty-seven. My time is running out. Given that I'm single, it's not really something I've thought a lot about recently. What about you?' She looked up expectantly, although with the physical distance between them, as far as anyone knew, they could be talking about the weather or politics.

Logan glanced down, struggling to look at her because he wanted her so much, but he also felt strangely conflicted, maybe because of the emotions the wedding had unearthed. 'I think I've pretty much given up on the idea of becoming a father. I wouldn't want to turn into my parents after all.' It was a glib comment, designed to draw a line under this conversation that he'd started and now regretted.

'We could all say that.' Harper smiled as if reassuring him, but her own fear lingered in her eyes. If she ever became a mother, she wouldn't want to be like *her* mother, but at least she had Charlie, who was a great dad, to emulate.

'Can we leave yet?' he asked with a sigh, pretending to find his shoes fascinating, now desperate for them to be alone. 'It's gone 11.00 p.m.' But at least they'd booked separate rooms at the wedding venue.

After such an emotional day, and after missing her touch all week while they'd had to make do with fleeting glimpses of each other around the hospital, all he really wanted was to slowly strip Harper and lose himself in the fire of their chemistry.

'Yes.' Harper's lips twitched as she glanced around the room. 'But not together, obviously.'

'Okay.' Logan's pulse bounded, his desire easier to

manage than that restless feeling. 'You go first. I'll wait a suitably inconspicuous length of time and follow.' He looked over at her, scared by the power of his need for her. 'Your room or mine?' he asked, in a low voice, trying to smile to disguise the breath-catching urgency he felt.

'Mine,' she said with a flush. 'But wait at least twenty minutes before you follow me.'

Logan groaned silently but nodded. He should be used to playing it cool by now. All week at the hospital, he'd had to keep his feelings for her hidden and work as if he didn't ache for her. All week he'd analysed that conversation they'd had, where she'd voiced her confusion for what they were doing. She was right to be cautious. They'd been there before, tried to make a serious relationship work and failed, hurting each other in the process. Maybe this, the physical desire neither of them could deny, was all they could have of each other. The idea left him both relieved and yearning.

After Harper had hugged Jess goodnight and then discreetly slipped away from the party, Logan circled the room once more. When he came face to face with Greg, who was understandably a little merry, he shook the younger man's hand.

'Congratulations again,' he said with a genuine smile. 'I really do wish you and Jess every happiness.'

'Thank you,' Greg said. 'And thanks for coming. We both really appreciate it.' Greg glanced at his new wife, love shining from his eyes. 'I've asked all the men here this question, so now I'm asking you. I hope that's okay? Do you have any advice, man to man, for a newly married doctor?'

Logan smiled but hesitated. He wasn't sure someone

who'd been married for two years over a decade ago had any right offering advice, but he felt compelled suddenly to share some wisdom, at least on how *not* to do it.

'The intensity of love changes with time,' Logan shocked himself by saying. 'For everyone. But your connection strengthens. Take time to hug each other, every day. Not just a quick hug, but a deep, holding-each-other-for-twenty-or-thirty-seconds kind of hug. Studies have proved the health benefits: stress reduction, a boost to the immune system etc. But it also releases oxytocin, the love hormone and reminds you of that connection that today, on your wedding day, seems unbreakable.'

Greg nodded, earnestly. 'Hugs. I can do that. Anything else, boss?'

Logan smiled to himself. He wondered if Greg would regret asking his attending for personal advice once they were back at MMH. 'Yes,' he said, resolved to be honest to both himself and Greg. 'If you and Jess don't do it already, learn to communicate effectively. Hold hands when you talk, even if you're having a disagreement or an argument. It helps you to remember that you're a team, not only when times are good, but also when they're hard, which is perhaps even more important.'

As his voice trailed off, regret pressed on his lungs. If only Logan had heeded his own advice in his marriage to Harper. If only he'd asked all the men present on his wedding day for words of wisdom, maybe they might have stayed married. Who knew, maybe they'd have a family of their own by now if they had.

'Thanks, Dr Grant.' Greg leaned in for a man hug and Logan shrugged, self-consciously.

'I'm heading off soon, so goodnight,' he said. 'Thanks

for inviting me. Have a wonderful honeymoon and good luck with your marriage. May it be long and happy.'

With his words, ringing in his head, he left the party a short while later and wandered back to the accommodation and to Harper. He still had no answers about them, but he didn't want to live the rest of his life with regrets. He quickened his pace, shoving the doubts that day had brought up to the back of his mind.

Harper cinched the hotel's towelling robe around her waist with the belt and sat on the edge of the bed, waiting for Logan to join her. She'd been right to worry about attending a wedding with him. The day, while perfect for Jess and Greg, had been filled with emotional reminders for Harper. Throughout the ceremony, as she'd sat next to Logan while Jess and Greg had exchanged their vows, her mind had filled with the similar promises she and Logan had once made. She'd almost shed a tear, so acute were the memories. Her eyes had strayed to Logan so many times today, she was certain that their playing it cool act could be fooling no one.

But when he'd said their wedding had been the best day of his life, something at the centre of her chest had bloomed, making her wonder 'what if'.

The tap at the door sent Harper's pulse flying. Grateful that she had no more time to ruminate on their earlier conversation or answer that 'what if' question, she leapt off the bed and pulled open the door, hurriedly yanking Logan inside the room.

'What took you so long?' she said, surging up on tiptoes to press her lips to his in a desperate kiss that had been building all day, all week, since that one in her office. 'I've wanted to kiss you all day. You look so hot in this suit. Take it off.'

If she simply focussed on this desire, she could block out the confusion. Because if forced to examine it too closely, she might have to admit that it tasted suspiciously like regret. But regrets were pointless. There was no going back, and when it came to her and Logan, there was no future, either. They weren't making a commitment to each other, just exploring the passion that had always come so easily.

'I was killing time, like you said.' Logan laughed, his hands gripping her waist as he pulled her into his arms, where she wanted to be. 'And talking to Greg.'

'What about?' she asked, shoving his suit jacket over his shoulders, because she was already naked under the hotel's towelling robe after taking a shower, and he needed to catch up. 'I hope you weren't discussing work on the poor guy's wedding day,' she chided.

'Actually,' he said, draping his jacket over a chair, 'I was giving him marriage advice. He's a bit tipsy and he asked me for some pointers, man to man.' He snaked an arm around her waist and drew her close once more, chest to chest, his stare darkening with desire.

'Really?' Stunned, Harper leaned back and looked up at him, her hands sliding up and down his arms. 'What did you say?'

She was almost scared to ask and didn't really want to talk any more, not when as predicted, today had been fraught with emotions and reminders. But her curiosity won.

Logan shrugged, his intense stare latched to hers. 'Just things I wished some older and wiser man had said to me on our wedding day.' He placed his index finger under her chin and tilted her face up, brushing his lips over hers in a way that made her unable to breathe around the lump in her throat. 'The importance of communication and physical touch,' he said when he pulled back, 'that kind of thing.'

Harper swallowed, terrified to know if Logan had more regrets, especially when her own were beating at that door in her mind, the one she'd slammed shut when she'd moved to London.

'I want you,' she said instead, unable to fight the desire, in spite of those regrets.

His lips covered hers, and the endless waiting to be alone with him all week fuelled her desperation. She sagged against his hard body and met the surges of his tongue with her own, until she was trembling with need.

'This week has been torture,' he said, holding her face and sliding his lips along her jaw to her earlobe and the side of her neck. 'I didn't think it was possible to want you more after last weekend, but I thought I'd go out of my mind today, not being able to touch you and kiss you and hold your hand.'

'I know,' she said, closing her eyes and dropping her head back to give his lips better access. 'I kept forgetting myself, today. I almost touched you so many times.' Their enforced restraint had been the one thing, the only thing, that had helped her to contain her feelings. But where she wanted to speed things up, Logan slowed them down.

'When I was Greg's age,' he said, loosening the belt of her robe, allowing the garment to slide open against her sensitised skin, 'I was an idiot. I took you for granted, assumed that you would always be mine.' He glanced down at her naked body and then met her stare once more so she saw his emotions filter across his eyes.

'Logan…' she moaned, her voice pleading, for what she wasn't certain. That he'd say more. That he'd stop reminding her of their past mistakes. That he'd keep on touching her, so she could continue to pretend that this was real and going somewhere. 'It was so long ago,' she added, because a part of her needed to stay anchored in the present. There was no use imagining what might have been if they hadn't spent the past ten years apart.

'And yet here we are,' he said, his hands skimming her waist, her hips, cupping her backside and drawing her near-naked body flush to his fully clothed one. 'You're mine again, at least for tonight.' His stare searched hers, eyes alive with heat and possession as she dropped the robe to the floor.

'Yes, I am.' Because she didn't want to think beyond tonight, she wrapped her arms around his neck and kissed him, sliding her tongue against his and her fingers into his hair. He crushed her close as they stumbled towards the bed. Harper sat on the edge and pulled his shirt from the waist of his pants, unbuttoning it, exposing his toned abdomen and chest, pressing her lips to every inch of skin she revealed. Logan tossed the shirt away, kicked off his shoes and leaned over her, kissing her deeply as she collapsed back against the cool sheets.

'Logan,' she whispered when he pulled back and looked down at her, his eyes golden with desire. She held his handsome face between her palms. 'I'm sorry. I took you for granted, too.' At the time, she wasn't conscious of it, but now she saw that she'd almost set him a test. Holding him away to see how far she could push before he left her, just like her mother had done.

Logan took one of her hands and pressed a kiss, almost of forgiveness, to the centre of her palm. Then he held her hand to his chest. 'I hate that I let you down,' he choked out.

Harper shook her head, her throat tight with regret and shame and longing. 'It wasn't all your fault. We broke us together.'

With a groan of acknowledgement, his mouth covered hers once more, and Harper surrendered to the passion that was their norm, even after all these years. Logan removed the rest of his clothes and then set about kissing every inch of her body. With her skin sensitised from the brush of his lips and the scrape of his stubble, Harper did the same, kissing her way down his chest and abdomen and then taking his erection in her mouth. She moaned as his fingers tangled in her hair and he watched her pleasuring him. The power she held over him was heady, addictive, but short-lived.

He reached for her and rolled her under him, kissing her deeply, stroking her breasts and between her legs, driving her to the point of delirium. When he finally pushed inside her, they groaned together, gasping, smiling, kissing.

'I want you, Harper,' he said, moving inside her, staring down at her so there was nowhere left to hide. 'I can't lose you from my life again.'

'Logan,' she cried, overwhelmed by feelings and a sense of nostalgia for all the good parts of them. 'I want you, too.' She meant it. Somehow, they made more sense now. This was even better than it had been before, when they were younger. As scared as she was to label them, to imagine what the future might look like, she hoped they could be a part of each other's lives now that they'd reunited.

He dipped his head and captured her nipple in his mouth. Then he reached for her hand and pressed her palm over his chest, holding it flat over the thump of his heart as his thrusts grew more determined, faster, harder, his beautiful stare watching her fall apart. They shattered together, her cries mingling with his harsh groan, his arms crushing her so hard, the air left her lungs so all she could do was hold on tight.

Afterwards, he drew the sheet over them, his body wrapped around hers from behind, their legs tangled together like the creeping ivy on the stonework outside. Lulled by the steady thump of his heart against her back, Harper's eyes wanted to drift closed. Part of her felt more content than she'd been in years, but something niggled at her mind. There was no need to panic, not when this physical part of their relationship was just temporary, when she and Logan were older and wiser and had surely learned from their past mistakes.

Logan's arm gripped her tighter, his breath hot against her ear. 'I can't help but think we could make this work this time,' he whispered. 'We've both changed so much.'

Harper's pulse became frantic. She held her breath, scared to move a muscle. She understood where he was coming from; her imagination had pictured similar scenarios. But now that he'd voiced it, the contentment she'd felt only seconds ago drained away, to be replaced by the sudden chill of doubt and confusion. Could she really trust his words and her own feelings? Or was this simply moving too fast? Even when they were in love and married, they hadn't been able to make it work, for many reasons and on both sides. They'd been apart for more years than they'd actually been a couple. Had they changed enough, and could they put all their past hurts and resentments behind them to make it work now? Was there any reason to believe that this time would be different?

'Maybe,' she replied, her voice so soft and low she wasn't certain that he'd have heard.

For a long time after Logan fell asleep, Harper lay wide awake in his arms. She was desperately trying not to panic, but she wasn't certain that she was ready to be that vulnerable again. To let him in and trust not only her judgement, which had been wrong before where Logan was concerned, but also trust that they wouldn't hurt each other again. The last time she'd fallen in love, it had failed, as she'd almost expected it would. She was older now, but had she really changed enough that she was willing to risk it and with Logan of all men?

Try as she might to find the answers, those questions, the dilemmas and doubts kept her awake for half the night.

CHAPTER THIRTEEN

THE MONDAY FOLLOWING Jess and Greg's wedding, Logan arrived on the NICU to review a three-week-old patient with Down syndrome, or Trisomy 21. He and Harper had agreed to collaborate on the baby's surgery to repair a large heart defect. Given that their residents were both away on their honeymoon, Harper was already discussing the case with the neonatal resident, Tom. Logan smiled as he joined them, his glance briefly meeting Harper's.

The thrill of excitement her presence always brought zapped through him, but after the weekend, he had more questions than answers. She'd been vague and dismissive when he'd, in the heat of the moment Saturday night, suggested that they might have a better shot at making them work second time around. She'd been quiet on the drive home, Sunday, withdrawn. She'd blamed it on her concern for Charlie, and Logan had accepted that, because he hadn't wanted to push her.

But now wasn't the time to discuss their relationship. He set aside his doubts and focussed on the clinical presentation of the patient.

'Benjamin Davies,' Tom said, 'is a three-week-old boy born at thirty-eight weeks gestation by vaginal delivery.

As you're already aware, he has a large atrioventricular septal defect, which was diagnosed on the antenatal scan.'

The defect allowed blood from all four chambers of the heart to mix, and untreated, led to heart failure, lung damage and failure to thrive.

Harper handed Logan a ward tablet, displaying the baby's notes as Tom continued. 'Medical management so far has consisted of diuretics and vasodilators. Here's his most recent ECHO and cardiac catheterisation results,' Tom said, bringing up the scans on the computer in the NICU office.

'A complete defect,' Harper said, pointing out the large hole between the two sides of the heart, due to a failure of development in utero. 'Has he had a cardiac MRI?'

'That's booked for this afternoon,' Tom confirmed as Logan handed over the tablet.

'Shall we go and meet Benjamin?' Logan said to Harper, who followed him from the office. She was quiet and thoughtful as they washed their hands, perhaps like him, already planning what would be a complex surgery.

Together, he and Harper introduced themselves to the boy's parents and then examined the baby, who had a loud heart murmur, an enlarged liver and signs of fluid on the lungs, or pulmonary oedema.

'We know you've had Benjamin's heart defect explained to you before,' Logan said to the couple, 'but we're here to review him today because the medicines can only help so much. We've held off the surgery until now to allow your little man to grow and to optimise his heart and lung function as best we can with the medicines. But the longer we leave the surgical repair, the greater the risk that the increased pressure on the lungs leads to permanent damage.'

'Dr Grant and I are keen to operate on Benjamin's heart as soon as possible,' Harper continued, 'but obviously, no surgery is risk free, so we just want you to be aware of the complications.'

Benjamin's father nodded and slipped his arm around his wife. 'The young doctors, Jess and Greg have explained all the risks to us. We simply want the best chance at a normal life for Benjamin, so we're happy to go ahead.'

'Of course,' Logan said, compassion he knew Harper would share building like a lump in his chest. 'And given the size of the hole in Benjamin's heart, surgery is the best option, because it's not going to close on its own, as sometimes happens with small defects.'

He paused, and the parents nodded. They were clearly well informed, which made his and Harper's job a little easier. He glanced over at her and continued. 'Dr Dunn and I will discuss the best type of surgery, as we'll be collaborating on the operation. When we have a plan and the results of this afternoon's MRI scan, we'll come back and explain the procedure to you both in more detail. Okay?'

The couple seemed happy, so Logan and Harper left the NICU, continuing the conversation as they walked towards the stairs.

'I prefer a two-patch closure over one,' Harper said about the defect between the two sides of Benjamin's heart, which allowed blood meant for the lungs to mix with that meant for the rest of the body. 'Is that what you'd do in this situation?'

'Yes.' He nodded and pulled open the door to the

nearby stairwell. 'A two-patch closure has the advantage of fewer potential post-op complications. And we'll have to pay special attention to the atrioventricular valve repair to try and minimise post-op regurgitation.'

As the door closed behind them, Harper paused on the landing, indicating to him that she was headed upstairs, whereas he was going down. She still seemed withdrawn, but perhaps she was tired after the weekend.

'So when do you want to book the operation?' Harper asked with a frown he wanted to kiss away. 'Sometime in the next two weeks?'

Logan nodded, considering the timing, glad that they'd be doing this surgery together, because he'd come to rely on her skill and experience. 'Yes, or we could stretch it a bit further out, maybe a month. See if we can optimise the medical treatments and clear the lungs.'

Harper looked down at her feet and then met his stare, chewing at her lip. 'I might not be here if we leave it longer,' she said, catching him off guard. 'The interview for the clinical lead is on Friday. If you're appointed to the permanent post and not me, I'll have to look elsewhere for a job. My locum contract was only for four weeks.'

'Of course...' Logan's stomach swooped sickeningly, his mind racing. 'I'd almost forgotten. Why didn't you remind me?'

'I just did,' she said tightly, leaving him even more frustrated.

He'd thought they'd moved past their emotional barriers. How had it slipped his mind that Harper was only temporarily working at MMH, that they'd started off as rivals? He'd grown so used to working with her, collaborating on complex surgeries and discussing tricky cases, relying on each other's expertise and emotional support, it was hard to imagine *not* working alongside her. Because he'd blurred those lines even further by rekindling their physical relationship. By voicing his regrets for the past and indulging the fantasy that they might, this time, be able to make their partnership work. Not that Harper had raised the subject again the day after the wedding on the drive back to Manhattan. Maybe her withdrawal then had been more than a desire to get back to the city to check on Charlie. Maybe she still wasn't ready to forgive Logan.

A sense of déjà vu struck him. They'd been there before, Harper clamming up when she was upset and Logan feeling helpless and pushing for her to talk.

'Unless you get the job,' he said, playing devil's advocate, torn, because while he'd worked his entire career for the position of clinical lead and he was already acting in the role, a big part of him didn't want Harper to leave MMH. He loved working with her.

'Where would you go if not here?' he asked, his stomach rolling and his throat dry as he tried to swallow. What if he'd allowed his feelings to get the better of him the night of the wedding, when he'd suggested that they might have a future? What if Harper just wasn't feeling it? Maybe she was being cautious, holding back emotionally, the way she'd done even when they were a couple.

Harper shrugged, not quite meeting his eye. 'Manhattan Children's Hospital have a vacancy for a locum that I've applied for, just in case.'

Logan frowned, wishing they were somewhere private so he could touch her or kiss her, or sound out her feelings to see if they matched his own. 'But you'll be over-qualified for a general surgical post,' he pointed out instead, fingers of doubt creeping up his spine. Was he rushing into this again the way he had with their marriage? Was he alone developing feelings, risking being hurt again, where Harper was already withdrawing to stay safe?

She gave another shrug. 'Beggars can't be choosers. I still want to be near Charlie, so I don't want to move out of state. I'll have to do what I have to do.'

She sounded resigned. Detached. Self-sufficient, same as always. Leaving him to wonder what it would mean for him, for their relationship, if he was appointed as permanent clinical lead. Unless of course, there was no relationship.

'Of course,' Logan said, feeling sick. He couldn't withdraw his application for the position, just to ensure Harper stayed at MMH. But if he got the position over her, he would not only miss working with her, there would be a part of him that would feel as if he was letting her down all over again.

Needing to touch her, to connect the way they had at the weekend, he stepped closer and reached for her hand. 'Can we talk about this later, away from work?' He wanted to know her plans and discuss options, together, as a team. But more than that he also wanted to talk about them. Surely she felt the trust and renewed connection between them the way he did? Surely she wanted to explore it further, irrespective of if they worked together?

Harper nodded, her fingers curling around his as she gave him a small smile. 'Although with Jess away and me picking up some of her duties, I'm not sure what time I'll get out of here. But I'll message you later.' She glanced at her watch and stepped back, clearly distracted by her workload. 'I have to go. I'm due in clinic and with no resident, it's going to be an extra busy one.'

Logan too had a busy day ahead with Greg away, and with limited cover, so he let it go. 'I'll see you tonight,' he said, watching her walk away, up the stairs.

As he made his way down to the ED, the helpless feeling he detested almost as much as failure, grew. He understood that she was planning for disappointment if she wasn't appointed for the role. He'd do the same. But because of their broken trust, because he'd seen her withdraw in the past, her hesitancy made him nervous. Was he ready to put everything on the line again with Harper? After all, they'd failed at their relationship once. He didn't want to back himself into a corner. The last time he'd loved Harper he'd felt as if she wasn't quite as committed to him as he'd been to her. The last thing he wanted was to be in that horrible position again.

Later that evening, after a busy day, Harper had just emerged from the shower when her apartment's buzzer sounded.

'It's me.' Logan's voice came through the intercom, leaving her heart pounding excitedly but her stomach tight with nerves.

'Come in.' Harper unlocked the street door and pulled open the door to her apartment, willing herself to calm down. Ever since the night of the wedding, she'd relived their conversations, over and over, telling herself that maybe Logan was right, maybe they could make a go of it this time around. But every time she tried to imagine allowing herself to fall back in love with Logan, she got scared. There'd been a part of her, all those years ago, a secret, hidden part traumatised by her mother's abandonment that had wanted him to fight harder for her, but he hadn't. What if that happened again? What if the pain she experienced was bigger this time, because she couldn't run away, not when Charlie needed her to stay in Manhattan?

'Hi,' she said as he appeared, pulling him inside and closing the door.

His smile was full of relief, as if he'd been equally desperate to see her. Without speaking he stepped close, cupped her face and kissed her, slowly and thoroughly. 'I missed you.'

'Me too.' Harper sighed, gripping his arms. 'But you saw me a few hours ago.' They were clearly frantic for each other, this unstoppable passion burning out of their control.

'I know,' he said. 'But I couldn't kiss you then.' As if to prove his point, he dragged her close once more, wrapped his arms around her and pressed his lips to hers.

When they pulled back feeling shaky with longing, she wrapped her arms around his waist and rested her head against his chest. 'Do you want a glass of wine or some tea?'

He pressed a kiss to the top of her head and nodded. 'I'll have what you're having,' he said, shrugging off his coat. 'Can we talk, too?'

'Of course.' Harper made tea and sat beside him on her sofa, her stomach in knots. 'What do you want to talk about?' she asked cagily, because the weekend had left her more confused than ever.

'I feel terrible about the job,' he said, reaching for

her hand. 'For some reason, I'd lost track of the fact that you're only a locum, that MMH might not employ you permanently once the position of lead clinician is filled. Probably because you're so sexy, you've scrambled my mind.' He cupped her face and swept his thumb over her cheekbone, sending shivers of delight down her spine.

'I know what you mean,' she said, glancing away from his doubt-filled stare. 'But we can't both win, Logan. We always knew that.'

She couldn't deny that with every day she spent with Logan, their connection built, stronger and stronger. She trusted him at work, implicitly. She even trusted him outside of work. But her old habits, her self-sufficiency and emotional guarding were hard to break. Being fully open with him wasn't going to happen overnight. Because they'd hurt each other before.

'There's only one clinical lead,' she went on, 'and since I've been working with you, since I've learned your surgical style and seen what an amazing doctor you are, I can't think of any reason why they wouldn't give you the permanent role. That's what I'd do, if it were down to me.'

Logan frowned, clearly troubled. 'Don't say that… I'll miss you if you leave MMH. You're an amazing surgeon, too.'

'I know I am.' She smiled, although a part of her felt irrationally close to tears. What was wrong with her? She wasn't normally this emotional. It was only a job and he was only a man.

Logan joined her in smiling but quickly sobered. 'Maybe, if they do appoint me, I could persuade the powers that be to keep you on. It would be a shame for MMH to lose a surgeon with your skills. We clearly need you. There's enough work for us both.'

'You don't have to fix it for me, Logan. I'm a big girl. Plus, the job isn't yours. Don't count me out just yet.

He smiled and nodded, then pressed his lips to hers. 'There's something else.' He paused and Harper felt herself tense. 'I wanted to invite you on a date Saturday.'

'A date?' Harper swallowed, her pulse fluttering excitedly but her stomach hollow. *A date* sounded more serious than sex, and after what he'd said the night of Jess and Greg's wedding she was terrified that this was moving too fast, that she'd get swept away by feelings because of their past relationship and find herself hurt again.

'Yes,' he said with a hopeful smile. 'My foundation is having its annual fundraising gala this weekend. I'd like you to come, as my guest? What do you say?'

Harper's breathing stilled, her insides twisting with fear. 'I don't know, Logan… That sounds lovely, but—'

'But you're not sure you're ready for a date with me,' he finished, flatly, doing his best to hide his disappointment.

Harper squeezed his hand. 'I just think we need to be careful. Maybe we should slow down a bit. The past few weeks have been intense—reuniting after so many years, working together, getting to know each other all over again, the job interview…'

Logan nodded and Harper leaned in and kissed him to lessen the sting of her words. 'Don't forget, we rushed into it last time. I'm sure neither of wants to do that again.'

'No.' He ducked his head. 'You're right. We should slow down.'

'It's not that I don't want to go on a date with you,'

she rushed on, 'it's just that… I guess I'm scared.' She sagged, feeling drained.

'Me too.' Logan nodded, raising her hand to his lips. 'Neither of us expected to find ourselves here.' He didn't say *back together*, and for that Harper was so relieved.

She watched his emotions shift over his eyes as he went on. 'I'm scared that we've been here before and messed up. I'm scared that I'll hurt you or let you down again. But… I don't know, I'm more scared to walk away, at least until I've fully explored what this might be.'

Harper nodded along with his every word, her fears matching his and her hopes soaring with his. 'I don't want this to be over, either,' she said, trying to set the worst of her fears aside, because Logan deserved to know how she was feeling. 'It feels different this time. Maybe because we're both older and we know ourselves better.'

'I agree.' Logan nodded, too, hope shining from his stare. 'It's like we know what we want and what we won't tolerate. You're right. There is no rush. Maybe I got a little carried away because… I don't know. Being with you just feels so easy.'

Harper nodded and kissed him again because the threat of tears was back.

'So will you come to the gala?' he asked when she pulled away. 'No pressure. If you don't want it to be a date, it won't be. I won't pick you up, or tell you how beautiful you look or seduce you at the end of the night.'

Harper laughed and leaned into him, resting her head on his shoulder. He was wonderful sometimes, not that the reminder was particularly helpful when she was feeling so conflicted.

'No one knows we're seeing each other again,' he

added, 'and I won't touch you in public, unless you want me to, that is. I'd just really like to show you some of the work my foundation does. I'm proud of it, and you were kind of the inspiration behind the idea.'

'Me?' She looked up at him, stunned.

He nodded. 'Yes. When we were together, you always teased me for the privileged lifestyle I'd grown up with. I could have simply spent my inheritance from my grandfather on fast cars, a bigger apartment, art and racehorses. But when I thought about it, I realised that I don't need those things. I wanted to give something back to the city that made my family wealthy. So I had the idea to start the foundation.' He shrugged, tailing off.

Harper gripped his face, holding his stare to hers. 'That's amazing, Logan... But don't make it harder for me to remember why I let you go before.'

He smiled sadly. 'I'm right here now.'

Because she couldn't stay away a second longer, Harper straddled his lap and kissed him, pushing him back against the sofa cushions. A date sounded harmless enough, especially now that he understood she wanted to slow things down. And how could she refuse this caring, compassionate, good guy Logan anything?

'Come to bed,' she whispered when she pulled back from their deep and passionate kiss.

'Come to my gala,' he countered, desire darkening his irises to almost black. But his hands slipped along her thighs, under her robe to her backside and he ground down her hips and pressed his erection between her legs.

'You don't play fair,' she said on a strangled moan, kissing him again. 'Okay, I'll come.'

'Brilliant.' He beamed and she couldn't help but laugh. 'Then hold tight.'

She wrapped her arms around his neck and squealed as he carried her to the bedroom. Maybe everything would be fine after all.

CHAPTER FOURTEEN

ON THE FRIDAY before the fundraising gala, Logan had just arrived in Theatre for his routine surgical list when he ducked into the staff room to grab a coffee. Finding Harper there, his heart kicked at his ribs. They'd been so busy that week with their residents away that they hadn't seen as much of each other. He'd barely spoken a personal word to her since leaving her apartment Tuesday morning after she'd agreed to attend the gala, given he'd been on call at the hospital. And that morning they'd also had their interviews for the clinical lead role.

Harper glanced up and smiled. Logan stilled, his stomach sinking when he realised that she hadn't yet been informed of the result of the interviews.

She took in the look on his face, her shoulders sagging. 'You were appointed, weren't you?'

Logan winced and stepped close, wishing he could drag her into his arms and reassure her that it would be okay, that they'd figure something out, but he didn't want to patronise her or move too fast.

'Yes,' he said, flatly. 'Didn't they call you to tell you?'

She shrugged. 'There's a message on my voice mail but I haven't had a chance to listen to it yet. I'm on call today and with Jess away, it's already turning into one of those days.'

She looked tired and a little pale and now that he'd delivered the bad news personally, wouldn't quite meet his eye.

'I'm sorry,' he said, feeling that it was somehow his fault.

'No need for that.' She smiled, but the expression didn't quite reach her eyes. 'I'm really happy for you. You deserve it. Congratulations, Logan.'

'Thank you,' he said, hating the enforced distance between them. But the competition for the role was always going to cast them as rivals. 'Look, we can't talk now, but before you go applying for a permanent post at a different hospital, let me talk to the hospital administrators. We might be able to work something out.'

She nodded and looked away, blinking rapidly as if she were close to tears. 'Don't do that,' she said, looking down and shaking her head. 'I'm a big girl, I can take care of myself. I don't need you to fix it for me.'

Logan scowled, his stomach tight. Of course she didn't need him, he just wanted her to want him the way he wanted her. 'I'm not trying to fix it, Harper. It's just that, as clinical lead, it is my responsibility to see to it that we have sufficient surgeons to meet the demands of the service. There's no reason that your locum position couldn't become substantive. All I'm saying is don't rush into anything.'

Maybe because his words matched hers from the other night, when they'd both admitted how scared they felt, she nodded but looked unconvinced. 'But I don't want to get my hopes up and then be disappointed. And, I don't

161

know, a change of scene might be a good idea, anyway.'
She held his eye contact and he sensed her slamming
up another wall. 'Maybe it wouldn't be such a bad thing
for us to work at different hospitals. But as you said, we
can't discuss it now.'

With perfect timing, her phone rang. She pulled it from
her pocket and connected the call. 'Dr Dunn speaking.'

While Logan's frustration built—he didn't particularly want to postpone their conversation, but he had no
choice—he watched Harper's expression turn to alarm
as she listened to the other person speak.

'What are her bloods doing?' Harper asked, her glance,
when it did land on his, full of concern and urgency. She
listened, pacing the room impatiently. 'Okay. Continue
the broad-spectrum antibiotics and I'll come and see her
as soon as I can.' With that she hung up the phone and
looked up. 'Emily Walsh has a wound infection,' she
said, worry dimming her eyes. 'They started antibiotics
overnight, and the locum neonatologist forgot to take
blood cultures first, so now we're simply guessing the
causative bacteria.'

Logan frowned, his own concerns building as his mind
raced. 'How is she doing?'

Harper gripped her phone, her knuckles showing. 'Not
good. She has a fever and tachycardia. I know I said I'd
assist you in Theatre today, but with Jess and Greg away,
I think one of us should go and see her right now, before
it turns into septicaemia.'

'Yes, I agree.' Logan nodded, glad they could still set
aside their personal stuff when it counted. A postopera-
tive infection was worrying in such a vulnerable neonate
and the risk of life-threatening septicaemia was real. 'Do

you mind going? My first patient is on their way down to Theatre from the NICU. I don't want to postpone unless I have to.'

'Of course not,' she said, already headed for the door. 'I'll keep you posted and join you in Theatre when I can.'

Logan watched her go, a sense of unease growing. Not just for their patient, baby Emily, but also when it came to Harper. He had a horrible feeling that she was holding something back. He didn't know what, but he recognised her emotional withdrawal, because they'd been there before. Was it just the fear that they were moving too fast or something else?

As he headed into surgery to scrub up, he pushed the thoughts and feelings from his mind, preparing for a long day.

The Edgar Grant Foundation annual charity gala on Saturday was a glamorous and glittering black tie affair fit for Manhattan's wealthiest socialites. Harper had been on call the night before and she'd stayed at MMH most of today, trying to stabilise Emily Walsh. That meant, as promised, Logan hadn't picked her up for their date. Instead, she'd arrived alone. A good thing because she'd needed the time to steel herself before she saw him.

She glanced around the ballroom at the Gainsborough Hotel, nerves twisting her stomach. The place was packed with Manhattan's elite, who were dressed to the nines. Harper couldn't help but feel a little out of place, as she always did at events like this, where the goal was to part attendees from as much of their eyewatering disposable income as possible in the name of a good cause. No doubt her insecurities were made worse by the fact that, as predicted, Logan had been appointed as the permanent clinical lead for congenital heart surgery at MMH leaving Harper temporarily unemployed. But the main reason she was out of sorts, was that that afternoon, after realising her period was a day or two late, she'd taken a pregnancy test, and it was positive.

Her breath caught anew, the news that she and Logan had made a baby still sinking in. She was going to be a mother. That of course, explained why she was so emotionally labile and quick to tears. Why she no longer felt in control of her own life and felt constantly confused. And she already felt fiercely protective of their child. But Logan's words from the night of the wedding, kept looping through her head.

'I've pretty much given up on the idea of becoming a father. I wouldn't want to turn into my parents after all.'

Whatever his feelings were about the baby, she would have to tell him, tonight, maybe after the gala. Spying Logan in conversation with his parents and some other guests, her pulse fluttered. He was so handsome in his black tux, looking perfectly at home and relaxed in the company. But then, why shouldn't he be? This was his world and she'd never really belonged.

Rolling back her shoulders in preparation, Harper made her way over to him, weaving her way past lavishly decorated banquet tables and groups of people socialising and drinking champagne. As she arrived at their group, Biddie Carter's eyes widened with surprise and then swooped the length of Harper's simple black gown to her toes before bouncing back up. No doubt her ex-mother-in-law was wondering what on earth Harper was doing there, and Harper wished she knew.

'Harper,' Logan said, his eyes lighting up. 'I'm so glad you made it.' He leaned in and pressed his cheek to hers, one warm hand resting on her bare shoulder so she shuddered from his touch. Clearly Logan's mother had her own concerns about how close her son and his ex-wife really were, not that Harper cared what the Grants thought of her any longer. But their alarm was understandable. They wouldn't want Logan to make the same mistake twice.

'Hello again,' Harper greeted them with a tense smile. The last thing she needed tonight was any probing questions from her in-laws, who were no doubt as confused as Harper was about what was going on between her and Logan. Only Harper's confusion was amplified by the fact that stupidly, crazily, she'd realised when she saw that positive test that she'd fallen back in love with her ex-husband and she was terrified.

Logan introduced her to the man with her parents, who even Harper recognised as a local, world-famous billionaire. She managed a smile for the man, her trepidation building. Now that she'd seen Logan, the full force of her feelings for him squashed her lungs. She wasn't going to make it through an entire evening of making small talk with the city's wealthy. She already felt claustrophobic.

'Would you like a drink?' Logan asked, signalling for a waiter with a loaded tray of champagne flutes before she could even answer.

'I'm fine, thanks.' She understood that tonight was about having a good time while donating to charity, but she felt sick to her stomach with nerves and almost regretted that she'd come. But she'd promised Logan, and the minute those two pink lines had appeared, she knew she needed to tell him her news, as soon as she could get him alone.

Perhaps sensing something was wrong, Logan finished up his conversation and excused himself. With his hand in the small of her back, he steered her to a quiet area beside the stage.

'What's wrong?' he asked with a frown. 'You look pale. Is it Emily?' He dropped his voice to a discreet whisper, glancing around to ensure they were out of earshot of the other guests while he enquired after their patient.

Harper shook her head. 'No, Emily's stable. I'm just tired.'

He rested his hand on her shoulder once more, his stare sympathetic.

'The on call last night was busy,' she rushed on, 'and I stayed on the NICU most of today with Emily. I'm obviously concerned.' Emily's condition, the infection was worrying, but since she'd texted Logan with an update that morning, there was nothing new to report.

Logan nodded, his hand resting on her upper arm. 'Me too. I planned to pop in and check on her tonight, after the gala, before I head home.'

Harper blinked up at him, her eyes stinging. He was such a great doctor. Would he be a good father, too, even though it wasn't a part of his plan. How would they navigate parenthood together and how would she see him all the time, interacting with their baby, and not fall deeper and deeper in love? But her feelings were dangerous. She couldn't rely on his vague and confusing words whispered in the dark the night of the wedding. She and Logan had been in love before, committed, married, and it still hadn't worked out. As always, Harper could only truly, one hundred percent, rely on herself. And unlike when they were a couple, now there was a child to consider. She needed to protect not only her own heart, but also to protect the baby, because she didn't want her child to grow up without knowing one parent the way she had.

With a lurch of her heart, she realised the precariousness of her situation. Ten years ago she'd had to fall out of love with him, because it hadn't worked out, a feat that had been harder than she could ever have imagined when she'd left him. And now, here she was again. Desperate to avoid the rejection that would come if they tried and failed to have a relationship, but this time, she would be unable to run away from it all. She'd have to see him, to share their child with him. The pain would be so much worse.

'What is it, Harper? You're worrying me,' he said frowning.

'I need to tell you something,' she said, her stare flicking over his shoulder, where she spied Logan's mother covertly watching them talk. She hated to do this here and now, but she had no choice.

'Okay,' he said looking a little distracted. No doubt he had guests to greet and official duties. Her timing was terrible. But surely he would want to know as soon as possible, and now that she'd faced him, here of all places, she couldn't wait to leave and fall apart in private.

'I'm pregnant,' she said, blinking up at him.

He frowned, clearly shocked and confused, so she rushed on. 'I know now isn't the best time to tell you this. I was going to wait until the end of the night. But I don't think I can stay after all.'

His frown deepened. 'I… I don't know what to say. Are you certain? It can't be very far along… It's only been a few weeks.'

Harper nodded, feeling sick. 'I took a test this afternoon, and yes, obviously it's very early. But it's okay, Logan. You can be as involved as you want. I'll be fine doing this alone. I just wanted you to know.'

'I'm stunned.' His hands gripped her upper arms and he drew her close, his lips pressed to her forehead. 'But I guess I shouldn't be.'

Harper closed her eyes and breathed in the scent of him, imagining for a moment that the three of them, him, her and the baby, could be a proper family. But she'd learned long ago, waiting for her own mother to come back for her, that wishes never came true. Time to put on her big girl pants once more and be strong, for their child.

'How are you feeling?' he asked, pulling back to look down at her, his eyes understandably full of questions.

'Tired. Sick. The usual.' Harper glanced over at her former in-laws. Biddie Grant looked like she'd swallowed something bitter. But of course they were probably thinking Harper and Logan were getting back together and were rightly horrified.

'I can't believe this,' he said, his hesitant smile breaking her heart.

'I know you didn't want to be a father—'

'Only because I'd never met the right woman,' he interjected, 'and I was worried that I might be overbearing and emotionally cold like my own parents. But this…this changes everything.'

'Not really…' Harper dragged in a deep breath as tiny flickers of hope built in her chest, but just like she had as a child and the last time she'd loved this man, she did her best to extinguish them.

Logan looked confused. 'What do you mean?'

Harper stepped back out of his arms. She didn't want to make a scene or cause gossip. 'I mean, obviously *my* life is about to change, but yours only has to if you want it to.'

'Of course I want it to,' he said, his expression mildly hurt. 'You won't be doing this alone. I'm going to be a father to my own child, Harper, and we'll be together, raising him or her. We can be a couple again. It makes sense.'

Harper shook her head, too scared to trust his words. 'Is that the best idea?' He wasn't in love with her, he just wanted her in his life. She didn't want to be a couple only because they'd made a baby together. Not when *she'd* stupidly fallen back in love with Logan. She would die inside, knowing that he didn't love her back, that there was probably something unlovable about her after all. She was better off alone, as she'd always been.

'What do you mean?' he asked with a scowl. 'You don't want me?'

Forcing herself to think about the baby's needs and not her own, she raised her chin. 'I think we've inadvertently rushed into this again, Logan. That's what I was scared of. I think it's best for all of us if you and I focus on being the best parents we can be. We both want that, right?'

She knew this man. He liked to excel at everything he did. He wouldn't tolerate any hint of failure when it came to fatherhood.

'Of course I want to be the best father I can be, that goes without saying.'

Harper rushed on. 'So we have to put the baby first and

find a way to be there for our child. Because we tried to be a couple before and it didn't work out. So I think it's best if we put us aside now. After all, we have something more important to focus on—our baby.'

'But what about us?' His stare darkened. She was hurting him again, but she needed to be strong so she didn't get hurt herself, only worse because she loved him, desperately and even more deeply than before. 'I thought you'd started to forgive me?' he said. 'Is this because of the job?'

'Of course it's not about the job.' Harper shook her head, her heart cracking open a little more. She didn't care one hoot for the job. At the age of thirty-seven, she'd be considered a geriatric mother. She wanted to do everything in her power to ensure her baby was healthy. 'I just don't want us to hurt each other again,' she said, pleadingly, 'like we did before. And if it goes wrong again, we will hurt each other, Logan. We'll turn into two people who resent each other and can't be in the same room as each other, with their child caught in the middle. I don't want that for our baby. I want what you said at the wedding. You and I a part of each other's lives, especially now, for the sake of the baby. I want us to be civilised and mature and respectful. Isn't that what you want too? Isn't that more important?'

He nodded, his mouth turned down but his stare hardening. 'Of course it's important. I'll always be there for you and our child.'

Harper nodded, relieved and devastated at the same time. She tried to smile, her eyes stinging with unshed tears. She'd been right to protect herself. Last time they'd split up, a secret part of her had wanted Logan to fight for her, but he hadn't. And now history was repeating itself, only this time, all that mattered was that he kept his promise to their child. Her heart would heal.

'That's all I want,' she whispered, her throat aching. 'Because I've been that child, Logan, abandoned by a parent and wondering what I did wrong or if there was something wrong with me. I never want *our* child to go through that.'

'It won't,' he said, glancing up and gesturing impatiently to someone who obviously needed his attention.

'I'm going to go,' she said, relieved to have a genuine excuse to sneak out. 'You have host commitments, and I'm not really in a party kind of place.' Bravely, she surged onto her tiptoes and pressed a kiss to his cheek, trying not to inhale the scent of him. 'Have a good evening and we'll talk again soon.'

Clearly frustrated, he clenched his jaw and nodded once. Harper left the ballroom the way she'd entered, her head held high. She couldn't have everything she wanted, but she didn't need it all. She'd have a cordial relationship with Logan, but their child would have two parents and as much love as it needed. That would be enough for Harper.

CHAPTER FIFTEEN

WITH HIS HOST duties almost over for the evening, Logan checked his watch for what felt like the millionth time, counting down the minutes until he too could leave the Gainsborough Hotel and chase after Harper. Fear and nausea tussled for dominance inside him. He couldn't quite believe how she'd dropped the bombshell about the baby, killed their relationship and then run. And he'd simply let her leave…

A hand landed on his shoulder, making him start. He looked up to see his brother, Sam, grinning at him.

'Congratulations on a great night,' Sam said. 'I hope you've successfully filled the foundation's coffers for another year.'

Logan nodded distractedly, the success of the evening the last thing on his mind. All he could think about was how Harper was having his child, but didn't want to be with him. She clearly had no feelings for him. She was still keeping him out emotionally. Whereas he…he'd let down his guard and started to see their future together.

'What's wrong?' Sam asked, as if sensing his older brother's turmoil.

Logan swallowed and rubbed a hand over his face, debating how much to tell Sam. He didn't want news of the baby getting back to his parents, not until he'd figured out a way to convince Harper to give them another chance and was ready to tell them they were going to be grandparents himself.

'This is just between me and you, but Harper is pregnant. I'm going to have a baby,' he said, reliving how stunned he'd been by her news. She'd said she was taking the pill, so he'd assumed a pregnancy was unlikely. But with time to get used to the idea, his mind had filled with happy family images—him, Harper and their child together, a dream he could never have imagined when she'd first come back into his life.

Then she'd dealt the fatal blow and declared she didn't want the future he saw so clearly. She didn't want *him*.

'Wow!' Sam said, his eyes wide with shock. 'I didn't even know you two were back together. Double congratulations.' He hugged Logan, who winced and shook his head, weighed down by defeat.

'We're not back together.'

'Oh… I see.' Sam's excitement dimmed. He looked as confused as Logan felt. 'So…how do you feel? About the baby?'

'I'm excited, of course,' Logan said automatically. He still couldn't quite believe the wonderful news. Then he swallowed hard, because his other feelings of devastation and failure that he and Harper weren't going to try and be together were overwhelming his joy. 'Obviously I'm a bit worried that I'm too old to be a dad,' he went on, needing to fill the silence with words so he couldn't hear Harper's rejection again and again. 'That I'll mess it up or get it wrong, but apart from that, I can't wait.'

Sam frowned, looking concerned. 'Why would you

mess it up? You've never in your life messed anything up. You're such an overachiever.'

Logan snorted a mirthless laugh. 'Except when it comes to Harper.' He'd messed that up. Twice. That's why he let her leave earlier. Having lost her before, he knew she'd been right: it was better to have some part of her in his life, than have none of her at all. And he would never tolerate being absent from his child's life.

'So if you feel that way about her, why can't you make a go of it?' Sam asked hesitantly. 'Especially now you two are having a kid together.'

Of course Sam would ask the million-dollar question.

Logan shrugged, wishing he had the answer. 'Because she doesn't want to.' She didn't want him. She'd convinced herself they couldn't work and hadn't even given him a chance. She'd pushed him away again.

'I'm sorry,' Sam said, shaking his head sadly. 'I still don't really understand where you two went wrong. You're so perfect for each other, and neither of you ever found anyone else to come close to what you had together.'

Logan's stomach rolled with helplessness. 'What can I say? Last time we were both a bit messed up, and this time... I guess we're both scared that history will repeat itself.'

Sam stayed silent for a few seconds, then said, 'Exactly how scared are you?'

Logan looked up sharply. 'What do you mean?'

'I mean how scared are you?' Sam pushed in that way a younger brother could. 'Are you scared enough to just walk away from her again? Or do you want to be with this woman? Because it seems to me that you're still crazy for each other. The minute she comes back to Manhattan, you both pick up where you left off and make a baby together.'

'I'm not walking away.' Logan gritted his teeth. He wasn't letting Harper go, not this time. 'But I can't make her want me if she doesn't.'

His skin began to crawl. Forced to analyse exactly what she'd said earlier, a greater sense of clarity developed. Harper had been the one to push him away. *Again*. And he'd allowed it out of some kind of fear to fail. He'd meekly accepted her depressing solution for them to abandon what they'd rediscovered with each other since she'd returned to Manhattan and set it aside to focus on being parents. But what he really wanted to do was fight for them. To fight for her, the only woman he'd ever loved.

He dropped his head into his hand and breathed through the panic flooding his body with adrenaline. Had he failed her again because he too was scared? He didn't want to hurt her again. He didn't want to let her down. He certainly never wanted to let down their child. But Sam was right—that fear wasn't a good enough reason to stop him from fighting for Harper, the way he should have done the last time she tried to make him leave her. Why couldn't he have everything he wanted? A relationship with Harper *and* his baby. The three of them could be a family, but only if he could convince Harper that what they had was worth being terrified for, worth fighting for. He loved her. He'd never stopped. It wasn't over until he'd told her that and showed her what they might have in the future.

Logan gripped his brother's shoulder, fierce urgency in control of his nervous system. 'Can you do me a favour? Can you stand in for me? Shake hands and thank people for coming as they leave?'

'Of course,' Sam said. 'I take it you're going to Harper's place?'

'I am.' Logan nodded. 'I'm not giving up on us this time. I'm not going to let her push me away.'

'Then get out of here,' Sam said with an encouraging smile.

Logan sneaked out the back and jumped into his car.

Needing to flee the city, to outrun her confusion and pain and to think straight, Harper had gone home to Charlie's place in Staten Island after she'd left Logan's gala. As she'd known he wouldn't, Charlie hadn't asked any questions when he'd found her on his doorstep. He'd taken one look at her expression and tucked her into her childhood bed with a mug of hot chocolate and told her that he loved her. Of course, she'd cried half the night. But when she'd opened her eyes in the morning, she'd pulled herself together, dressed and taken Charlie out for breakfast at their favourite diner, followed by a walk along South Beach in the sun.

'I didn't push you last night, but you're still quiet today,' Charlie said as they walked side by side. 'Do you want to talk about it with your old man?'

Harper tried to put on a brave face, to smile reassuringly, but her heart was too sore. She hadn't anticipated that ending things with Logan would hurt this much. She'd done it to protect herself and the baby from possible pain. But somehow, she'd ended up back there, in love with Logan and alone again. She dragged in some deep breaths and prayed that this feeling of desolation would pass quickly this time. After all, she'd got over him once before, she could do it again. She'd have to, for the baby's sake.

'I'm okay,' she said, plucking up the courage to tell Charlie her news. 'I actually have something to tell you. It's very early days, so don't get too excited just yet, but I'm pregnant, Dad. You're going to be a grandpa.'

Charlie stopped walking and pulled Harper into a hug, saying nothing. Her throat burned as she clung to him, sucked in the reassuring scent of the cologne he'd always worn and the clean linen smell of his sweater, somehow more overcome by his steady, silent approval than if he'd praised her to the heavens. But then Charlie had always been her port in the storm.

'Well, fancy that,' he said, smiling broadly as he brushed her windblown hair back from her face the way he had a thousand times when she was a little girl. 'A grandpa. I like the sound of that.'

'Me too.' Harper laughed, brushing away the tears that had escaped as they resumed their stroll. But the moment of peace was short-lived.

'Is it Logan's baby, too?' he asked keeping his eyes straight ahead.

'Yes,' she said with a sigh, not bothering to deny it. 'How did you know?' Had Logan told him? No. He wouldn't do that.

Charlie shrugged, turning wise eyes on his daughter. 'I know you both quite well. He actually called last night after you'd gone to bed, looking for you. It was late and I didn't want to wake you.'

Harper paused again. 'He did?' What did he want? Just to check up on her probably. She'd need to get used to seeing him and speaking to him without touching him, kissing him, or throwing herself into his arms and begging him to love her.

Charlie nodded, looking out to sea. 'He didn't tell me about the baby, of course, but I knew from the tone of his voice that something was up. So are you two getting back together? Is that it?'

Harper sighed, the nausea returning, even though it was too early to be due to morning sickness. 'I don't think so, Dad. It's too risky. There's too much history between us, and now that there's a baby to think about, we can't afford to mess up our relationship again. I'd rather he was in my life, mine and the baby's, than not. So we have to make the best of the situation.'

It sounded sensible enough, but her reassuring words didn't seem to have any impact on the ache in her chest, which only throbbed harder.

'The best of the situation…?' Charlie asked, sounding disappointed with her. 'Of course you want him in your life, but what's stopping the two of you from making a real go of it? For keeps this time.'

Harper looked away, the horizon blurring out of focus as she tried to hold herself together and not sob. 'So many things,' she admitted, hoping that eventually, with each time she spoke the words aloud, they would start to come true. 'It didn't work out for us last time, for one. We hurt each other. There's nothing to say that this time would be any different.'

Charlie nodded, considering her argument in his quiet way. 'But you've both changed. You're older now. And you are going to have a baby together. If ever there was a reason to make something work, that's it, right there.'

She smiled sadly at her dad. 'That's not enough of a reason to keep two people together. You know that, better than anyone. I don't want him to just be with me because of our child. I'm better off alone.'

'Are you really?' Charlie observed her sadly. 'You can't compare our situations. Don't forget that your mother fell out of love with me, whereas I don't think Logan ever stopped loving you, even after the divorce.'

Harper swallowed hard, fighting tears. 'I think you're wrong there, Dad. He hasn't said he's in love with me.' But why would Charlie say that if he didn't believe it to be true?

'Am I?' Charlie said, patiently staring like she was a little girl with tricky maths problem he knew she'd be able to figure out as long as she believed in herself. 'Are you sure about that, kiddo? He might not have said the words but I know him.'

Harper opened her mouth to reply and then closed it again, completely lost for words. She knew Logan, too. She knew he hated to fail. She knew he would be scared to hurt her or let her down again. She knew she too had been scared, terrified, so she'd shut down her heart to keep herself safe. Could Logan love her the way she loved him? Was it possible that she'd pushed him away again out of fear that no one could love her?

'I've seen you two together,' Charlie went on, 'both then and now, and if I was a betting man, I'd say he's head over heels. And your face is telling me that you're the same for him.'

Harper ducked her head, trying not to cry. 'I don't know how he feels...' she said in a quiet voice. Not that she'd given him a chance to tell her. She'd sprung her news on him at a charity function he was hosting, told him she didn't want to be in a relationship with him, even though that was a lie and then fled, just like the last time. Had she been testing him again? Sabotaging what they'd had before she'd let him too close, before she could get hurt or abandoned once more?

'Maybe he's scared, too,' Charlie said. 'Scared to tell you how he feels in case you can't love him back. He once told me that he'd been brought up in a house where love felt conditional. Maybe he doesn't feel worthy of your love, having blamed himself for letting you down once before.'

Harper stared at her father, willing his words to be untrue. If Logan loved her but was scared, that would mean that she'd pushed away the very thing she wanted: a second chance at loving him. She loved him, harder than before, and if he could ever love her again one day, she would grab him with both hands and hold on tight and never let him go.

'What did you tell him?' she asked urgently, 'last night when he called?' She stepped close to Charlie, stopping just short of gripping his arms and demanding an answer.

'I told him you were asleep in your old bed. Why?'

'I need to go to him. I need to find out if what you said is true.' With icy panic in her veins, Harper turned and headed back towards Charlie's car, praying it wasn't too late.

CHAPTER SIXTEEN

THE MINUTE LOGAN spied Charlie's car pulling into the street, he stepped from his own vehicle, sheepishly scanning the neighbour's house, because he'd banged so hard on Charlie's door ten minutes ago that he wondered if someone might call the police. His heart stuttered with relief as he saw Harper in the passenger's seat.

Charlie pulled into the driveway and got out. 'Hi, Logan. I, um…just need to check on my neighbour, Eric.' He shuffled off next door, and Logan went to Harper, as she climbed from the car.

'Can we talk?' he asked, the lump in his throat so big, he could barely breathe.

'Of course.' She eyed him nervously, leading the way onto the porch, where there were two garden seats. She took one and Logan the other, although fear and urgency left him too jittery to sit still.

'Harper. I came to your apartment last night, after the gala, but obviously you weren't home.'

She shook her head. 'I couldn't face being alone with myself so I came home to Charlie.' Her eyes shone with emotion and he wished he'd dragged her into his arms the moment he'd faced her. 'Logan, I'm so sorry for last night. I should have waited to tell you about the baby.

And I shouldn't have pushed you away. I just let my old insecurities, my fear of rejection, get in the way.'

'That's why I'm here, Harper,' he said, resolute, reaching for her hand. 'I'm not going to let you push me away this time. I know I failed the test when we were married. I regret that I didn't fight for us then, for you. But I won't fail you again or let you down.' He raised her hand to his lips, pressing a kiss over her knuckles. 'I love you, Harper. I always have. You are the only woman I've ever loved. I never stopped loving you in fact, not even for the ten years we were apart.'

'Logan…' she whispered, pleading, as tears spilled over her lashes.

'I want you, not just in my life, but as my life partner,' he rushed on, needing to say all the things he should have said last night. 'I want us to work together and raise our child together and grow old together. So you can push and doubt and believe that you're better off without me, but I'll never stop trying to convince you. I'll never stop loving you. I'll love you until the day I die, just like I promised when we made those marriage vows.'

She covered her mouth with her hand, crying freely now. Logan scooted closer and gripped her hand tight as if he could make her love him back. 'I know you're scared,' he whispered. 'We both are. And you were right last night. There is more at stake now, because we're going to be parents. But I'm not giving up on us, on me, you and the baby. We're a family, Harper. I'll be there for you both, every day until you believe that I won't let you down again. Until you forgive me and believe that I love you. Until you let me love you the way you deserve.'

'Logan,' she groaned, surging forward and silencing

him with a kiss that was salty with her tears. 'I love you, too,' she cried. 'I believe you *now*, today, and I've already forgiven you and myself for messing up last time. I just got scared because this time, I think I love you more than before. It feels so much stronger I can hardly breathe.'

He gripped her face, his heart banging against his ribs, her amazing words turning his fear to joy. 'You do?'

She nodded, laughing through the tears still falling. 'I want all the things you just said. I want us to be a family, always. No giving up on us this time. We stay together and we communicate and we work at our relationship and we love each other hard. Because we owe it not only to our baby but also to ourselves. We both deserve this love.'

Because he couldn't be so far away from her, he tugged her hand and pulled her into his lap. He cupped her face and drew her lips to his, kissing her the way he'd wanted to every day since she walked back into his life. The way he wanted to every day for the rest of their lives.

'I love you, Harper,' he said when he finally pulled back. 'I won't let anything come between us again, not even ourselves. It's me and you and the baby against the world from now on, understand?'

She gazed down at him with love, nodded and laughed. 'Yes. Us against the world.'

Logan's heart soared, and he kissed her again, holding her so close their hearts thudded together.

When she pulled back, he wiped the tears from her cheeks, his own eyes burning. 'Did you tell Charlie, about the baby?' he asked, his excitement for fatherhood finally bubbling over now that Harper was his again.

'Yes. Did you tell your parents?' She looked hesitant, so he brushed her lips with his and shook his head.

'No. I was so focussed on winning you back. I did tell Sam, though. He helped me to see that I'd allowed old habits, old ways of thinking to mess with my head. And I almost lost you for a second time. I can't believe I'm that stupid.'

Harper cupped his face. 'I'm yours,' she said. 'But I don't think your parents are going to like us getting back together. They had a hard enough time with us talking last night.'

He grinned. 'Do you care? Because I don't. It's their choice if they want to be a part of their first grandchild's life or not. I told you, I only care about us.' His arms tightened around her and she breathed a kiss over his lips.

'You do know that I love you back, right?' she whispered, her feelings shining from her beautiful eyes. 'My love isn't conditional or something you have to earn. It's something that's just there, because of who you are. And it's not going anywhere. Not even I could fight it, and you know how stubborn I can be.'

Logan nodded, smiling as he captured her lips once more. 'And you do know that I'll never leave you again, right? This is it now. You're stuck with me for ever.'

Harper wrapped her arms around his neck and snuggled into his chest, sighing with what sounded like contentment. 'So where will we live? Your apartment is bigger with better views.'

'I don't care where we live,' he said, kissing the top of her head, 'as long as it's together. And first thing tomorrow, my first job as clinical lead for congenital heart surgery at Manhattan Memorial Hospital will be to offer you a permanent job.'

'You can't do that,' she said, outraged but smiling up

at him. 'Employing the woman you're sleeping with is the ultimate in nepotism.'

Logan shrugged, uncaring. 'The woman I love,' he said, tilting up her chin. 'The woman I hope to one day reinstate as my wife, if she'll have me.'

Harper's stunning smile curled her mouth. 'I'm sure she will.'

'See,' he said, nuzzling the side of her neck as he breathed in her scent. 'I always win.'

EPILOGUE

'IT'S A GIRL!' Logan cried, staring down at his tiny daughter and then turning back to Harper, kissing her, brushing wisps of damp hair back from her face. 'You made us a daughter. I love you, so much.'

'I love you, too,' Harper said, both laughing and crying as she reached for their newborn, drawing her onto her chest and peering down at her with wonder that filled her heart to bursting. 'She's so beautiful.' She couldn't take her eyes off her daughter, but nor could she stop looking at Logan, who she loved a bit harder every day.

In that moment, the baby opened her eyes. She and Logan held their breath. Their daughter stared up at Harper and then closed her eyes again, instantly falling asleep.

Harper's delighted grin matched Logan's. They laughed softly together as if every move their baby made was magical and extraordinary.

'She looks just like you,' Logan said, his arm around Harper's shoulders and his face pressed to hers as they both watched their daughter take her first nap out in the world. 'I didn't think it was possible for me to love you any more,' he whispered for Harper's ears only. 'But I do.'

She looked up at him and blinked back her tears.

'You are amazing,' he said, pressing his lips to hers once more. 'And you're going to be the best mother in the world. I just know it.'

Harper smiled, her stare torn between Logan, who wore a look of love and adoration and respect, and their miraculous baby girl. 'I think I will,' she said, feeling the certainty to the marrow of her bones. 'I'm her mother.'

'Yes, you are, my love.' He breathed into her hair, his lips pressed to her temple.

With the baby's delivery complete, their midwife carefully wrapped their precious sleeping bundle in a clean towel. 'When you're ready to take a shower, perhaps Dad could hold her. And there are three very eager grandparents outside in the waiting room.'

Logan's parents had come around to the fact they were back together, and Charlie had been their number one supporter. Harper had gone back to work part-time at MMH. She felt confident that she and Logan would find a work-life balance that suited all three of them.

'Not yet,' Harper said, still marvelling at her tiny daughter, loving their skin-to-skin contact and wondering how she would ever again put her down.

'They can wait a bit longer,' Logan added, inching onto the bed beside Harper. With one arm around Harper's shoulders and the other around the baby in her arms, the three of them formed a tight circle of love that Harper felt certain would be unbreakable.

'What shall we call her?' Harper asked, looking up at Logan to see the same wonder she was feeling on his handsome face.

'Perfection.' He said with an indulgent smile. 'Beloved.

Ours,' he offered with a straight face, because of course, baby girl Grant was all of those things.

Harper nodded. 'We'll think of something. There's no rush.'

They each went back to staring at their sleeping daughter. After a few minutes, Logan said, 'Perhaps the more important question is one for you.'

'What's that?' Harper said, distracted by the length of her baby's tiny eyelashes and her miniscule finger nails. She looked up to see Logan was no longer looking at the baby, but at her, wearing the same expression of love.

'Will you marry me again, Harper?' he said, his voice choked with emotion. 'I want us to be a family and I want *you*. Please say you'll be my wife again, because I want nothing more than to be her father.' He tilted his head in the baby's direction. 'And your husband.'

Fresh tears stung Harper's eyes. 'Yes. I will marry you again. I'm yours and you're mine.'

Logan's smile, the elation in his stare was almost as beautiful as their daughter. Almost.

'I'm going to spend the rest of my life making sure you don't regret that,' he said, kissing her with such soft tenderness, her heart almost burst with love.

'I could never regret us,' she said. 'I love you. I love our life and now I love our family.' She kissed him and smiled. 'Now who's the winner?'

They celebrated their love with another kiss.

* * * * *

Look out for the next story in the
Sexy Surgeons in the City duet
New York Nights with Mr Right
by Tina Beckett

And if you enjoyed this story,
check out these other great reads
from JC Harroway

Forbidden Fiji Nights with Her Rival
Secretly Dating the Baby Doc
Nurse's Secret Royal Fling

All available now!

NEW YORK NIGHTS
WITH MR RIGHT

TINA BECKETT

MILLS & BOON

To my family, as always. I love you!

PROLOGUE

SAMUEL GRANT SWALLOWED as the heavy metallic clang of a door sliding shut came from somewhere beyond his line of sight. He knew what was coming, if not now, then soon enough. Skipping school to attend that protest march had probably not been the smartest move, but his closest friends had done the same thing. Then fists started flying and the same friends who'd urged him to come with them ditched him the second the police pulled up in their cruisers.

Sam blew out a breath. He would have fled too, if not for the elderly man who'd fallen after being jostled by the crowd. Sam had reached down to help him up and waited with him until he was steady on his feet, a photo he'd dropped now clutched in his weathered hand. As soon as the man started walking away, though, Sam had felt a hand on his arm. He knew instinctively that it wasn't to help him but to restrain him from leaving.

Voices traveled down the gray hallway, reaching him. The one he recognized made him close his eyes for a moment. It looked like the inevitable was going to happen right now.

He braced himself, tilting his chin in a belligerent

move that belied the pounding of his heart. Then his dad appeared on the other side of the bars.

Carter Grant stared at him for a long time without saying a word, and for an instant he wondered if his dad was just going to leave him in there. His way of teaching his rebellious son a lesson, maybe. Just like so many other lessons he'd had over the years. People who said money could buy happiness were wrong. So very wrong.

Because Sam wasn't happy. And from looking at his dad's face, those steely eyes and tight set of his jaw which contained a mixture of anger and exasperation, he doubted his father was happy either.

Maybe that was partly Sam's doing. But certainly not all of it.

"Go ahead and open the door." His dad's voice was steady…the low tones gave nothing away. Not a good sign.

The guard murmured something into the device he held in his hand. A second later, the door slid open with a grinding of gears that made his teeth hurt. Sam was pretty sure he was going to hear that sound in his dreams. It was also a wake-up call. There had to be a better way to assert his ideas than constantly going head-to-head with his father. But he had no idea what that might be. Or how to go about it.

His dad motioned him out but said nothing as they walked down the hallway. He said nothing as the officer at a desk handed Sam his cell phone and wallet and a few other belongings. And he said nothing on the long ride home. But as their driver pulled up in front of the huge, exorbitant home Sam had grown up in in Manhattan, his dad held up a finger, telling him to wait.

And so he did, although the urge to burst from the car and sprint to his room was strong. But no. He was going to face the music this time.

The man who'd raised him turned to face him. "Anything to say for yourself?"

Sam had a lot to say, actually, but nothing that would do him any good, nor did he want it to, so he just shrugged.

His dad pinched the bridge of his nose between his thumb and fingers and sighed. "So be it. But you're not to come out of your room for the next week, except to go to school and come home. And I will check with the school to make sure you are where you're supposed to be."

A week was nothing. Sam was surprised his punishment wasn't longer, seeing as he'd been arrested, but because he was only fifteen, he'd been sent to juvenile hall rather than placed in a holding cell with adults. "I will be."

The truth was Sam didn't want to wind up in jail. He could help no one from there. So he'd better figure out another way to go about things before he did something that might cost him more than a mere week of restriction.

"See that you are." His dad sighed before adding, "And I'd rather you don't tell your brother and sister and especially not your mother what kind of trouble you've gone and gotten yourself into this time. You make straight A's, for God's sake. So why do you always feel the need to buck my authority?"

It wasn't like Sam had ever done anything like this before. He didn't "buck authority." At least not his teachers or coaches. If he was honest, it was just his dad. And it was usually just stuff that he knew would irritate the hell out of him.

Sam had no idea why he did it, so all he could do was just give his father another shrug.

"Are you at least going to keep quiet about it to your mom?"

"I won't say anything to anyone." Not to his mom, sister or his older brother or his teachers. But what he was going to do was find another way to make a difference in this world. Something that wouldn't get him sent to juvie or get him into hot water like it had today. Or at least he hoped that it wouldn't.

"Good. Now, let's get you inside. I'm sure Theresa has set something aside for your dinner." The family's housekeeper had been a godsend for Sam and was used to his parents' absence, since they had obligations almost every single day. Running a mega corporation and being the head of a large charitable organization took a lot of time and energy. Energy that left the Grant kids with a lot of time on their hands.

Sam got out of the car, aware that his father had also exited and was following close behind. He had expected more berating and accusations than what had happened. But that didn't mean that this was going to blow over like the rest of his stunts had. No, he was pretty sure this was going to come back and bite him in the butt when he least expected it to.

But he deserved it. He'd done what he'd done and couldn't expect there to be no consequences. So for the next week, he was going to do what he could to stay out of trouble. But one thing was for sure—in three years, when he turned eighteen, he was getting out. Out of the house, out of Manhattan and maybe even out of the United States.

He didn't know what that would look like yet, but anything was better than being the richest kid at a school filled with other rich kids. Soon he would be out from under that cloud and on his own. Then he could start helping people who couldn't help themselves. How he would do that without money was yet to be seen. But he'd find a way.

Or at least he hoped that he would.

CHAPTER ONE

LUCINDA GALEANO ENTERED the small conference room, her nerves on edge. She and a handful of other people at the hospital were being given the opportunity to join a groundbreaking team that combined microsurgery, physical therapy, plastic surgery and a few other specialties that would help people with facial paralysis. It was funded by a grant from some big corporation that she'd never heard of and would be called the Manhattan Memorial Hospital Pediatric Microsurgery and Facial-Reanimation Department. They had brought in some outside doctor to head up the project, and everyone would be meeting him. He'd evidently been at the hospital for a few weeks already, but since she'd only recently been asked to join the team, she had no idea who he was. Lucy thought she'd read the name somewhere—in a flyer, maybe it had been mentioned when she'd been called in to talk with the hospital administrator—but hell if she could remember it now. The name hadn't mattered. The opportunity had. And it had come at the perfect time.

Her gaze swept the room before frowning. Except for a man with his back to her who seemed to be perusing some sort of pamphlet, she was the first one there. She glanced at her watch…hmmm…there were still twenty minutes until the meeting actually started. Lucy's foot collided with something—a chair?—and a mad scramble to maintain her grip on the coffee in her hand ensued. The coffee won as the cup flew a few feet and landed on the table in front of her, the lid popping off and sloshing scalding liquid everywhere, including the front of her new scrubs, the ones with bright blue parrots all over them.

Before she could stop herself, she swore long and loud, the stream of words in her mother tongue spewing through the room in a fury every bit as hot as her coffee. She stared at the mess she'd made. It had already been a chaotic day, and to add this…

At least no one had been sitting at that table. She glanced around to see if there were any paper towels at the nearby refreshment table.

"Dejame ayudarte con eso."

The soft words murmured in accented Spanish made her head jerk to the side. The man who'd been at the front of the room now stood next to her, a handful of the paper towels she'd been looking for gripped in his strong hand. And his eyes… She swallowed. They were bluer than anything she could remember seeing and held an amusement that should have made her anger go up another notch. But instead it defused all of her irritation, and she shut her own eyes, mentally switching her language to English. Then she peered up at him, nose crinkling as she finally saw the humor in the situation.

"Tell me you didn't understand a thing I said a second ago."

"Every single word of it, and let me tell you… I'm shocked."

Except he wasn't, and that made her laugh. And that

surprised her as much as his words had. "I'm sorry. Not everyone understands Spanish, so it's been a habit to confine my more—er, colorful language—to something other than English."

"Colorful language. It definitely contained a few hues I recognized. And some that are new to me." A smile cracked the right side of his face, fascinating her and sending a flare of heat through her midsection. What would it look like if he fully embraced that smile? She bit her lip. Better not to even think about that.

She smirked. "I guess I should sort out those colors before letting them leave my mouth."

The heat in her belly grew, and she studied him under her lashes, liking everything that she saw. What was wrong with her?

Remember the last time you let a stranger affect you that way?

It ended with a note left on her pillow a month before her wedding day.

So she counted from one to twenty. In Spanish. Non-colorful Spanish.

One of his brows went up. "Great strategy. I'll have to remember that."

For a split second, she thought she'd counted out loud rather than in her head, then realized he was talking about what she'd said about her cursing. *¡Dios!* She was going to have to watch herself around this one. She wondered which department he worked in.

She tried to take the paper towels from him to clean up the coffee, but he did it for her, sweeping up the liquid with a speed that was impressive. As was just about everything about the man, from the straight sandy hair that fell over his forehead to the tanned forearms revealed by the rolled sleeves of his blue button-down shirt. Lord have mercy, she was treading on dangerous ground here.

But at least it had jolted her from any painful memories. At least for the moment. So she could forgive herself for noticing something…anything…that didn't have to do with her fiancé's sudden change of heart. *Ex*-fiancé.

He finished cleaning up and then threw the towels into a nearby trash can before coming back over to her, right hand outstretched. "Sam Grant, and you are?"

The name rang a bell, and right now that bell was clanging an alarm that she couldn't ignore. But neither could she avoid shaking the man's hand, so she put her fingers in his and introduced herself. "I'm Lucy Galeano."

Wait. There was a Logan Grant here at the hospital who was the head of the neonatal surgical unit. He'd just gotten back together with his ex-wife, from what she'd heard. Could they be related? Not likely. Grant was a fairly common surname here in the States. Kind of like Suarez in Paraguay, where her parents were from. And if Logan's brother was working here at the hospital, surely she would have heard about it. Or their paths would have crossed.

"Ah, you must be our pediatric physical therapist. Welcome."

The authority with which he said that made her release his hand in a hurry and take a step back. But now there were other people filing into the room and taking seats. With a nod, he went back to the front of the room where MMH's administrator joined him, shaking Sam's hand.

But she'd bet Todd Wells's palm wouldn't tingle the way hers was still doing.

She rolled the name around in her head over and over, trying to figure it out as she took one of the few seats that were now left. It looked like there were fifteen people who would be on the team.

Todd went to where the U-shaped configuration of tables opened up. He welcomed them to the exciting new team that was one of only a few medical centers embarking in this new field. "And it was the only way we could lure one of our medical school alumni, back from Uruguay, where he's just opened a clinic specializing in some of the things we hope to do. Everyone, please welcome the head of our team, Sam Grant," Todd said. "He arrived a few weeks ago, so some of you may have met him at our fundraising gala. Most of you know of his family, who funded a wing of this hospital. And of course, he is the brother of our own Logan Grant over in the neonatal department."

Dios Santo. He *was* related to Logan. And Sam was the new head of the team? Her mind zeroed in on the name, and yes, now she remembered it had been on that flyer. In bold print.

What on earth would he think of her? All that stuff about swearing in Spanish and sloshing her coffee all over the table? Was he wondering how on earth he could trust her with children who required precise, delicate care?

She hoped not. This was her dream job. She loved working with kids but longed to do something beyond physical therapy for broken wrists or sprained ankles. And to work with complex facial muscles was the chance of a lifetime. Would he now have her thrown off the team and replaced?

As soon as this was over, Lucy was going to go up to him and apologize. One for not recognizing his name. And two for letting her temper get the best of her. She never ever lost her cool with her young patients. But from now on, every interaction she had with this man was going to be schooled. Every smile, every frown, every word was going to be analyzed before she let it happen.

At least she hoped it would. In reality, if she couldn't keep her emotions in check, then maybe she didn't deserve to be on this team.

The hell she didn't! And to even let herself think along those lines was to invite disaster. One she was going to do everything in her power to avoid. Because she did deserve to be here. She'd worked her butt off to prove to herself and everyone else that she was good at her job. And to be invited to join this group of top professionals was something she'd only dreamed of. So she was going to prove to Sam Grant and everyone else that they'd picked the exact right person for this exact right job. No matter what it took.

Sam tensed the second Todd Wells mentioned his family and the grant his father had given to the hospital. He'd been so careful to make sure the offer from Manhattan Memorial hadn't been orchestrated by his father. He'd even called Logan to ask his advice and see if he'd heard anything. He hadn't, and Carter Grant hadn't said anything to him about trying to get Sam back to New York.

And Todd Wells had confirmed that they'd gotten his

name from a colleague who'd heard of his work at the clinic in Uruguay.

Fortunately their sister was poised to take up the reins of the corporation, since neither Sam nor Logan were interested in running their father's business. And Sam actually hadn't heard from his dad once in the two years he'd been in Uruguay, other than in the perfunctory birthday text messages his mom sent him. They'd always said that his father sent his love. He didn't believe it—after all his dad had never used those words with him and probably never would.

He knew at some point he'd run into at least his mom here at the hospital since one of her charity works had her doing a weekly story reading to the children in the oncology department. And he'd asked Logan not to say anything to them until he at least got situated. But then Todd had asked him to go to the fundraiser which had happened not long after he'd arrived back in the States, and of course his mom and dad had been there. He'd been forced to say hello, but his parents had been called to greet someone else almost immediately, and that had been that.

He shook his family from his thoughts as he tried to remember why he was here. It was far too soon to be having second thoughts about leaving Uruguay. Even though it had come at the perfect time. He'd broken up with Priscilla, the woman he'd lived with for the last five years.

She'd been the reason he'd gone to Uruguay in the first place, since her family was all there. But then he'd overheard a quiet conversation between her and her mother about the money he'd inherited from his grandfather, and something in his gut had curdled. And when he decided to donate it all to start a clinic specializing in children who needed facial surgery, she'd balked and tried to talk him out of it. And even though she now worked at that very same clinic, it had been the beginning of the end. There'd been many arguments before he finally moved out of their shared apartment and got on a plane heading back to the States a year and a half after the clinic opened.

But to return to Manhattan? It hadn't even been on his radar, until that offer had come in.

His eyes landed on Lucy Galeano. Lucy had to be short for something. At least he thought it might be. Lucinda? Luciana? And although she spoke Spanish, her accent was different from what he'd heard in Uruguay.

It didn't matter where she was from. She was on his team—thanks to him—and he'd be working with her. The less curious he was about her as a person, the better it would be for both of them.

He'd already tried having a romance with someone he worked with…someone he'd lived and breathed hospital life with. In the end, it hadn't worked out—and probably wouldn't have even if he hadn't overheard that conversation. Because although he'd cared for Priscilla, he'd discovered his parents' influence on him as a child had been more powerful than he'd imagined. He had a hard time investing himself emotionally because he'd never experienced much of that. Except with people like coaches and teachers. Priscilla had seemed to give it her all, but even she hadn't been able to make up for his deficit. In the end, his family's money had tainted what he'd believed about their relationship. And it cemented the idea that keeping his distance emotionally—even when it came to romantic partners—was the right thing to do. At least for him. That way no one got hurt.

He'd do well to remember that.

Sam didn't remember much about what he said in his speech to the group, but thankfully he'd had notes to rely on as he explained what he hoped to accomplish as a team. He was glad he'd opted to keep things short and to the point and was happy to hand the meeting back over to Todd, keeping his attention firmly on the man this time. The administrator was much more eloquent than Sam had been as he gave his closing remarks. Then again it was the man's job to be persuasive, just as it had been his dad's job when it came to running a company.

But Sam wasn't running an empire or even a clinic anymore. All he wanted to do was help people. He just hoped he didn't come to regret working in a place where his dad had waved his magic wand and made a hospital wing appear out of thin air. All it had taken was money. A whole lot of money.

"Are there any questions for Dr. Grant?" The administrator's question made him tense all over again. He hadn't really expected a question-and-answer session, since he wasn't exactly sure how things were going to work at this point. He much preferred to call people into his office one at a time and discuss expectations on both sides. Sam didn't shrink from hard conversations, but he preferred that those happen in private.

And any future meetings with Lucy Galeano?

His jaw tightened. They would be exactly the same as all of his other meetings. Professional and to the point.

Just like his speech. None of the people in this room had officially signed a written contract yet. That wouldn't happen until he could feel them out—he wanted to hand-pick his own team and had made that clear to Todd, who'd agreed. The administrator had simply offered to be a filter, bringing in people he thought would be a good fit. And Lucy's bio seemed to be perfect. But if she didn't fit the bill for what he was looking for, he needed to be objective enough to say so. And right now, he was not at all objective. Because all he could hear in his head was the sexy huskiness of her voice as she'd let those words tumble from her lips. Very pink lips with very...

Get a grip! He was just months out from his relationship with Pri, and he did not need to be thinking of anyone like that.

Surprisingly, there were no questions, and the meeting was soon dismissed. Several people came up to shake his hand and express their excitement about the hospital's newest program, but his attention was on Lucy, who was hanging out at the back of the room, looking very much like she was waiting to have a word with him but preferred not to do that in front of everyone else.

Why?

That innocent back-and-forth banter they'd had before the meeting came to mind. He hoped she hadn't taken things out of context and was hoping he'd ask her out. Maybe he needed to set the record straight. And Todd had mentioned his family's money and its contribution to the hospital. But Sam had let that portion of his life go when he'd opened the clinic. So if, like Priscilla, she had dollar signs in her eyes she'd be sorely disappointed when she found out the truth.

The last person left, and Lucy made her way up to him, picking her steps with care this time. He had no idea what he was going to say if she really did think he was attracted to her. Because, hell, he had been, and she'd probably been able to see it immediately.

"Um… Dr. Grant…about earlier…" Her words faded away, but the fact that she'd addressed him by his title made a few of his muscles relax.

"What about it?" The words came out a little more curt than he'd meant them to, but then he felt out of his element right now.

"I hope it won't affect the way you see me as a physical therapist. I don't normally go around cussing."

It wasn't what he'd expected her to say, and he couldn't stop his smile, a sense of relief washing over him. So this was what she was worried about?

"At least not in English." He went on, "It's fine. I've read about your work with children and have to say I was very impressed. I asked that you be added to the team. Although we won't make that official until I meet with you one-on-one."

"You asked for me? I wondered why I'd been added to the roster just two weeks ago."

He had, but he normally wasn't great with names. The fact that he'd known who she was the second she'd introduced herself was strange. If it were anyone else who'd been in the room, would he have? Probably not just from reading their bio.

"We'll need someone whose patience can be tested

and who isn't easily rattled. At least unless there's coffee involved." His smile switched back on, which wasn't like him. But there was something about this woman that made him want to tease her into some kind of reaction.

The type of reaction he was after was the only thing in question.

"Hot coffee is my weakness. I needed that shot of caffeine, you know."

"Afraid I'd put you to sleep?"

Her teeth came down on her lip before she said, "That wasn't what I meant. I actually needed something to distract me from…"

She'd been about to add something before stopping. He'd never know what unless he asked her, and he wasn't about to do that.

He decided to put her mind at ease. "Don't worry about it. Things are fine, if that's what you're worried about."

"I kind of was. I thought maybe an apology was in order."

"Not at all. I think it was just what I needed—the reminder that we all are human, that we all have our weaknesses."

Her brows went up. "Even you?"

"Especially me." The longer he was around her, the more he realized that just because he'd ended one relationship, it didn't mean he was immune to all women. He wasn't. Lucy was proving that to be true, and he wasn't sure why. It was time to cut this conversation short until he could figure that out. "So if there's nothing else…?"

She blinked once, twice before her brows came together. "Um…no. Nothing else. I assume you'll let us know exactly what you need?"

He didn't want to look too closely at those words.

"Yep, I'll be getting together with everyone soon and hashing out roles and making formal offers."

"Within our particular specialties, right?"

"Can you think of another way to do it?"

She shook her head. "No. Not at this moment, but if I do, I'll let you know."

Damn. He realized he was smiling again. Lucy was too much for him to deal with right now. Maybe in a few days after he'd talked to some other people on the team, his head would be clearer. The only thing he was sure of was that the longer he stood there, the more he'd be smiling, and that was not what he wanted to do. With anyone.

"You do that. I'll set up a meeting with you in a few days, if that's okay, and get your thoughts on the new department." In case she got the wrong idea, he quickly added, "I plan on doing the same thing with all the folks who were here today."

"Understood. Let me know if you need me to do anything before then."

That was another sentence he wasn't going to touch with a ten-foot pole. So with one last smile—one of the fake smiles that he hated so much—he bid her farewell. "I'm sure I'll see you around."

How stupid was that as a get-me-out-of-here tactic? But it was evidently effective, since she gave a nod of her head and spun on her heel leaving the room. It was then that he realized the printing all over her scrubs had been parrots with tiny conversation bubbles over their heads that read *Repeat after me* inscribed in black ink. Prophetic, no? Because he was about to find himself saying that over and over in his dealings with her.

Which he did, the moment she left the room. "Repeat after me—no more getting involved with anyone from work." He was going to be saying that a lot over the next couple of days, until it was emblazoned on his brain in as many languages as he could muster. Until he actually believed it was true.

CHAPTER TWO

IT HAD BEEN three days since the team introductions, and Lucy hadn't heard from Sam yet, but then again he'd said he would be meeting with them over the next few days, so it hadn't been that long. She couldn't help wondering where she fell on that list and whether or not it was significant that she hadn't been one of the first names he'd picked out of his proverbial hat. Or that she'd been notified of her place on the team much later than most of the other folks. But he said he'd asked for her specifically, so there was that.

Being notified at the last minute seemed to be a normal part of her life. Like not having any idea her fiancé was having second thoughts about marrying her until almost the last minute. Did she matter so little to people? Or was it that her cheerful manner made them think that she could handle anything and everything? Because she couldn't. And his actions had made her insecure about who she was. She now found herself having to give herself pep talks more frequently than she should have.

Like she was doing right now?

Her next patient was a five-year-old child who had fallen in kindergarten a few days ago and had complained of pain in his right hand and forearm. X-rays had shown no fractures, and so the consensus was that he had a soft-tissue injury. The recommendation was physical therapy since the pain was ongoing. It was hard in a patient this young because the tendency was to protect the injured area to avoid pain, and so at times those little guys could make the problem worse and affect their range of motion. And the mom said it was affecting his fine motor skills.

While the boy's mom watched from a nearby chair, Devon hunched in front of Lucy, a blank coloring book on the table in front of him. Although he wasn't engaging in the activity in a physical way, he was very interested in the pictures. She decided to take a different tack.

"Okay, Devon, we're going to play some different games, okay?" She frowned at the long-sleeved shirt and glanced at the boy's mother. "Do you mind if we take his shirt off? I want to watch how his arm moves as we do some exercises."

"Anything. I just want him to feel better."

She turned her attention back to the child. "Are you okay if we do that?"

He nodded but didn't say anything.

"Can you show me where it hurts, so I can be careful with it?"

Devon moved his left hand over an area that encompassed his wrist and about halfway up his forearm. "Here."

The wrist explained why he was hesitant to color, since his mom said he normally loved art and coloring. They were doing scissor work in school, and the teacher relayed that Devon cried every time he had to cut something, which was another reason he was here.

"All right. Can you lift your arms straight over your head so I can slide your shirt up?" She demonstrated the movement for him, and Devon copied it without a hitch. Another reason why she'd wanted to take the shirt off. So, there was no shoulder involvement that she could see.

She eased the shirt over his head, taking care with his injured wrist and hand. "There, that should make it easier for you." Lucy smiled at him as she folded his shirt and handed it to his mom. "Okay, let's start our games."

She pulled two sock puppets out of a drawer. One was a dog with long droopy ears and brown-and-white spots; the other was a duck, complete with beak and soft feathers. "Which one would you like?"

The boy smiled for the first time since he arrived. "The dog. He's funny."

"He is. Do you want to name him?"

Devon tilted his head. "Spot." He pointed at the puppet using his left hand. "Because he has spots."

"Good choice."

It was telling that he was using his nondominant hand. Getting him to do anything with his right hand might be tricky. She picked up her puppet. "I think I'll call my duck Quack."

"That's silly."

"It is, because Quack is a silly guy. Now, we'll use the puppets in a minute, but I want you to do some things with this hand." She put her fingers on the boy's wrist, using a bit of pressure and watching closely. He didn't flinch. So the pain must've come from movement rather than pressure.

"I—I don't want to." His voice quivered a bit, showing his anxiety.

"I know. It hurts, doesn't it?"

He nodded.

"But I want to try to help it feel better. Will you let me help you?" Lucy pulled out a chart of faces, represented by yellow circles. The circles ranged from a large smile and traveled to a face that was crying. "You can tell me how much each activity hurts, okay?"

She'd normally be able to tell through his reactions, but some children were more stoic than others. Plus Lucy wanted Devon to be able to express his own pain level regardless of how much she could tell as they went through the exercises.

He nodded. "But you won't hurt it."

"I won't touch your hand unless I tell you I'm going to, okay?" She smiled again to reassure him.

"Okay."

"I want you to copy what I do. First I want you to hold out both hands in front of you, then we're going to close our hands like this." She made both of her hands into loose fists. "Can you do this?"

Devon did the left one effortlessly, but he was slower with the right one. But he was able to curl his fingers and get them to close.

She then had him point to the chart to say how much that had hurt. Not too much, judging from the face he chose. It was a closed-mouth smile.

"Very good. Now we're both going to put our hands on the table like this." She put her hands flat on the table, fingers splayed apart. Devon copied her. "Okay, this might be a little harder, but try to do what I do. Let's lift our pinkies."

Lucy raised both little fingers, keeping the rest of her digits where they were.

Devon had no problem doing this, raising his fingers. He did the same with the rest of them as she slowly worked her way to where she suspected the pain was. When she lifted her index fingers Devon only did it with his left hand.

"Can you do it with your other hand too?"

"It'll hurt." That quavery in his voice returned.

"How much do you think it will hurt?"

He pointed to the crying face on the chart, again using his left hand.

"That bad, huh?"

He nodded.

She thought for a minute. If his index finger hurt to lift, it stood to reason that the ligament that controlled the movement was inflamed, since it traveled part way up the forearm. "Can I touch your finger?"

Devon shook his head to say no.

"How about Quack. Can he touch it?" She slid the puppet onto her hand, glancing up as a movement at the door caught her eye. Her heart seized for a minute before starting up again. Sam Grant was standing just inside the physical therapy room, his gaze catching and holding hers as he leaned against the wall and crossed his arms over his chest. Was he checking up on her? Well, she wasn't going to let him rattle her. She was going to do her job the same way she always did it.

"Maybe. He won't hurt it, will he?"

"No, he won't hurt it." If what she suspected was true, his finger wouldn't hurt if someone else made it go up, it would only hurt if Devon tried to initiate the movement himself. If that was the case, some anti-inflammatories and icing it could take down the swelling and help it heal.

"Okay, Quack, you heard Devon. You can touch his finger, but be very, very careful." She was hyperaware of Sam not twenty yards away. And although the room tended to be noisy with an array of different patients and therapists, she had no doubt that he could hear every word she said.

Lucy had the puppet touch the boy's finger, running his beak up the digit and following the path she knew the ligament traveled. "Is this where it hurts?"

"It doesn't hurt now."

"I know. But is this where it would hurt if you lifted your finger?"

He nodded.

This was a boy of few words. But that was okay. He was actually doing great. Some children really disliked the process, which was how she'd discovered that the puppets could often do what she as a person couldn't.

She took the puppet off. "Do you think Spot could keep Quack company for a minute while I get something?"

Lucy was tempted to go over to see what Sam wanted, but her patient came first. She helped the boy put the duck puppet on, not batting an eye when he took his own puppet off first rather than letting her put it on his right hand. That was okay. She just wanted to get a ruler to see if he would let Quack lift that finger using a flat object.

She went over to where the equipment was kept and

grabbed a small plastic school-type ruler. She'd chosen yellow to match her puppet. As she was walking back to the table where Devon sat with his back to her, she could hear Spot "talking" to Quack. Then she frowned as something caught her eye. What was that on his lower back? A mark of some kind.

She got closer and squatted down to get a better look. Devon's skin was mottled with red over his lumbar spine. Midline, actually. "I'm right behind you, Devon. Does your back hurt at all?"

"No."

She slid on an exam glove from a nearby drawer and touched the area, using gentle pressure to assess it. It was completely flat, looking almost rash-like but having no raised edges. She glanced at his mom. "Has he always had this red patch on his back?"

"Yes. We always just thought it was a birthmark. Why?"

"No particular reason." Staying where she was, she went on, "How did Devon hurt his hand—do you know?"

"They said he was running and his feet seemed to get tangled together, and he fell." His mother shook her head. "He actually falls quite a bit when he's not paying attention to what he's doing."

A chill went over her. "Devon, do your legs or feet ever hurt?"

He shrugged.

It wasn't a no. But it also wasn't a yes. She bit her lip, hesitating.

Her glance went back to his mother. "How often would you say he falls?"

"I don't know exactly. Every couple of days. He's an active kid. Is it important?"

"Not necessarily." She stood and caught Sam's eye and motioned him over. She knew he was a plastic surgeon and not a neurologist, but she could use another set of eyes right now. Hopefully he would tell her she was overreacting. But she'd had some very personal experience with childhood spinal issues. Her older sister, Bella, had been born with a neural tube defect that had needed to be corrected. It was why they'd come to the States from Paraguay.

And Lucy had been deeply involved in helping her sister work on her PT exercises even as a child, idolizing the people who came to the house to help with therapy. It was one of the reasons she'd become a physical therapist herself.

So yes, she was probably seeing things that weren't there. But if she wasn't... And if Devon fell or moved just the wrong way and her gut feeling was right, it could have devastating consequences.

Sam came over immediately. When she knelt back down beside Devon, he followed suit. "What do you make of this?"

Devon's mom stood and came over to look at what they were doing. "Is something wrong?"

Thankfully the boy was still playing with the puppets and wasn't paying much attention to what they were doing.

She forced herself to smile at Devon's mom. "This is Dr. Grant. I just wanted him to look at this mark. You said he's had it since birth?"

"Well, I always thought so. I didn't actually notice it until he was a month old. He was a preemie and stayed in the hospital for three weeks. I pointed it out to his pediatrician—in Arkansas, where we moved from—and he thought it was just a birthmark too, since all of Devon's scores were within normal ranges."

"I'm only pointing it out now because of where the mark is located and the mention of frequent falls. It might be nothing."

Sam glanced at her and nodded as if saying he understood what she was thinking. He stood and turned toward Devon's mom. "Would you mind if I have one of my colleagues come down and take a look, if he's available? Your son has never had an MRI of his spine?"

"His spine? No. He's never complained of back pain to me. But if you think that mark might mean something, then yes, please let anyone you want look at it."

"Thanks," he said. "I'll be back in just a moment."

Lucy put her hand on the mom's shoulder and gave a gentle squeeze. "Let's not worry until there's something to worry about."

"Okay." But the woman didn't look convinced. She couldn't blame her. If Devon were her child, she'd be plenty worried. Lucy was concerned, and the boy wasn't even hers.

"Let's get back to the session." Lucy sat down with Devon. "See this little ruler I have here?"

"Yes."

"If I can have Quack back, I'm going to have him slide it under this finger." She touched his index finger. "He won't do anything with it unless I tell him to. And I'll tell you and Spot first."

"Will it hurt?"

"I don't think so, but if it does you can tell me to stop, okay?"

"Okay."

She helped Devon put Spot back on his hand, then she donned the duck puppet.

Then she put the ruler between the duck's beak as if he were holding it. "Devon, I don't want you to move your hand or fingers while Quack does this. Just let them rest."

"Can I keep Spot with me?"

"Yes, of course. He can help you. And he can help Quack." She had the puppet carefully slide the ruler beneath the boy's index finger, turning it so that only that particular digit was lying on the thin plastic. She leaned down as if whispering something to Quack and nodding as if the puppet had answered her. "Quack wants to lift the ruler just a little. Your finger will go up too. Are you ready?"

His face became anxious again. "It's gonna hurt!"

"I don't think it will," she said again. "But if it does we'll stop."

His mom slid closer and put her arm around his thin shoulders. "You can do this, Dev. I'm right here with you."

He didn't say anything else, so using the puppet, Lucy lifted his finger about a centimeter off the table. "Does that hurt?"

Devon shook his head. "Good." When Lucy lifted it

a little higher, repeating the question, Devon again indicated it didn't hurt.

"Very good." She lowered the ruler and slid it out from under the boy's hand.

She did a few more exercises with Devon and found that his wrist didn't hurt unless his index finger was in use. It looked to be a much simpler injury than the report or her exam indicated. She would check with his pediatrician, but she would bet that he jammed the finger when he fell and the ligament used when the digit was raised was inflamed. It could be almost as painful as a fracture. Especially to a child who didn't understand why something in his body hurt.

"I think it's just in his index finger. I'm going to call his pediatrician and ask about taking an anti-inflammatory and using ice on the area."

His mom hugged him and then looked at her. "That's great news. But what about his back?"

Lucy glanced up to see that Sam was heading their way. When he arrived, he said, "Dr. Asbury is with a patient and can't come down at the moment, but we can put you in an exam room and he'll take a look as soon as he has a minute. Are you in a rush to get anywhere?"

"He would normally be going to his T-ball practice, but since his hand still hurts a lot, we decided to skip it today. So we have time."

T-ball. Lucy tried to contain her shudder. One of those games that could very well cause a lot of damage if that mark indicated what she thought it might.

"I think that's a good call," Sam said. "I'll take you up there."

He glanced at Lucy, who shook her head, although there was nowhere she'd rather be right now than in that room with her patient. "I have another appointment in fifteen minutes." She smiled at Devon and thought for a minute. "But hopefully I'll see you next week. Do you want to take Spot with you until then?"

"Could I?" The boy's words were filled with excitement, and he held the puppet close to his chest as if cradling a real puppy.

"Of course you can." She turned to her own puppet. "Tell them bye, Quack."

"Quack. Quack." Lucy made the noises as duck-like as she could muster.

When she glanced at Sam, she saw he was trying not to smile. So she added another *"Quack!"* for good measure.

This time the man did smile. "You did that on purpose," he murmured for her ears only.

"*I* didn't do it. Quack did."

Sam rolled his eyes. "I'd like to talk to you a little bit later. Let me know when you have an opening in your schedule."

"Okay."

The trio left the therapy area, and all of her anxieties rose to the surface again. An opening in her schedule? Was that why he'd come down here? Was he having second thoughts about her being on the team?

Surely not. That wouldn't make any sense. But she didn't have time to worry about it right now. She had another patient to get ready for.

Lucy cleared her desk and sanitized the space Devon had occupied before opening the big drawer at the bottom of her desk where she kept about ten puppets. They almost always put her more nervous patients at ease. And she did a lot of role-play with them on injuries, having the child sometimes act out how he or she had been hurt. She started to stuff Quack in there with the rest of them but paused, giving the puppet a stern look. "If you hurt my chances for being on that team, you and I are going to have a long talk."

The puppet didn't make a sound. But Lucy could have sworn the thing looked at her with a sly grin before she dropped him into the drawer and quickly slammed it shut.

Greg Asbury saw them almost immediately. Sam had stayed because he was curious about what the mark might mean. He'd already deduced what Lucy thought it could indicate: tethered cord syndrome.

Tethered cord syndrome was a close relative of spina bifida—also known as neural tube defect—but rather than having a portion of the spinal cord that hadn't closed during gestation, a tethered cord occurred when part of the spinal cord attached to another structure, in this case the skin of the lower back. It was a fairly rare finding. But the discoloration was one of a cluster of symptoms that could occur with the syndrome, like an anomaly of the skin, whether a dimpling or a hemangioma. There were even cases where patches of hair grew in the spot where the cord was tethered. Falling or leg weakness or pain were also symptoms. Some people lived with a tethered cord their whole lives without knowing it. But if it were taut, a quick move or injury could cause the cord to stretch past its capacity, sometimes causing irreparable damage to the nerves. Then leg weakness could become paralysis.

There was only one way to know for sure. An MRI.

Dr. Asbury did a careful examination after hearing from both Sam and Devon's mom. When he looked at the boy's back, he frowned and asked some more pointed questions about muscle weakness.

"I don't know, really. He does fall—like kids do—but other than that and sometimes having trouble keeping up with his classmates when he's running the bases in T-ball, I haven't really noticed anything. And his teachers haven't mentioned anything either."

The pediatric neurologist, who was also on Sam's team, talked about the possibility of the cord being stuck in the area where the birthmark was and asking if he could try and get Devon cleared for an MRI in the next week or so. "He can't play sports until we know for sure, so if he's involved in any…"

"Just T-ball, but I can explain to the coaches that he can't play until the test is done. If it is what you mentioned, can it be fixed?"

"Depending on how much of the cord is tethered, we can normally go in and free that portion of the tissue."

"You mean surgery."

"Yes. But it's not as involved as some of the other surgeries involving the spinal cord. We just want to make sure the vertebrae are all there and shaped the way they should be. We'll know more after the MRI."

"I take it we can't just leave it alone."

Greg took a seat next to Devon's mom, who'd introduced herself as Rachel. "I wouldn't recommend it. If he gets struck in the back by, say, a baseball or if he slides into home, for example, it could jerk the cord and not only cause a lot of pain but actually damage the cord itself. That is something we don't want happening under any circumstances."

"I see. So the sooner we have the MRI, the better. Will someone Devon's age even hold still for it to be done? He's not the most cooperative child in the world. You can ask Lucy, his physical therapist."

The mention of her name made Sam's jaw tense before he forced it to relax as Greg answered the question.

"We can sometimes give them a light sedative, if there's a lot of anxiety. We can also put children's music onto a set of headphones and let him listen to that and put a sleep mask on him to help with any claustrophobia he might feel. There are all kinds of ways to help with anxiety."

"Okay. So until then, we just wait?" Rachel asked.

"Yes." Greg put a hand on Devon's head. "His hand injury might be a blessing in disguise. From what you said he doesn't want to use it."

"No, he doesn't."

"Well, that might work to our advantage. So try to just keep him calm. I imagine by next Monday we'll have our answer."

"Okay. Is there anything else?" she asked.

Greg smiled. "Yes. Go home and try not to worry. If it's a tethered cord, we've caught it fairly early. That's a good thing."

Her lips twisted. "I'll take your word for it. But thank

you for seeing us. Devon, can you tell Dr. Grant and Dr. Asbury goodbye?"

The boy held up his puppet, and like Lucy had done, he had it bark a goodbye.

Once they were out of the room, Greg clapped Sam on the shoulder. "That was a good catch. Not everyone would have seen that mark or realized what it could mean."

"It actually wasn't me. It was the physical therapist who'll be on our pediatric microsurgery team."

"Ah… Lucy Galeano. She is extremely good at her job. They send all of the tough PT cases her way."

Something about the way the man said that made Sam look a little bit closer, but he saw nothing but sincerity in the neurosurgeon's face. Besides, there was a ring on the other doctor's left hand.

And if there was something more there? It was none of his business as long as it didn't affect either's professionalism while on the job. He didn't want any kind of messy publicity damaging the new program before it even got off the ground.

Since when did he worry about things like that? He thought his parents' hypersensitivity about the media would have burned that out of him long ago. Maybe there was a little bit of them in him after all. Logan seemed to have made his peace with their father, and their sister had embraced the company and all it stood for. But as long as Carter Grant stayed out of Sam's way and didn't try to interfere with his work at the hospital, they would stick with whatever uneasy truce they'd had over these last several years. They weren't friends, nor were they ever likely to be. But he could deal with the way things were.

At least for now.

CHAPTER THREE

LUCY TRIED TO rein in her curiosity, but it finally got the better of her. She hadn't heard from Sam about Devon, and she really didn't want to wait another day to hear if they'd found something or not. Or maybe they hadn't even scheduled an MRI. Maybe the neurologist had brushed off her fears as unfounded.

But still. A simple phone call or text to update her would have been nice.

Except she didn't think she had Sam's personal cell phone number, and he probably didn't have hers either. And did she really want to go through the hospital directory or a personal assistant, if the man even had one? Not really. Especially if it turned out her fears were unfounded. It might be reason enough for him to wonder about her qualifications for the new position.

And he'd never told her exactly why he'd come down to the PT department in the first place.

It was driving her crazy, and she could only think of one way to quiet her thoughts.

Lucy could venture up to the fourth floor and see if he was in his office. She could always use the pretext of wanting to give him that date he'd asked for.

Well, not a date as in going out to dinner, but he'd

asked her for some openings in her schedule. Which she now had after looking at it for what seemed like hours and then screwing up the courage to actually enter some dates and times into her phone.

She wasn't sure about seeing him face-to-face, although if she was going to work with the man, she was going to have to get over her reservations. The smile he'd given her after she'd made those silly duck sounds had thrown her for a loop. She'd wanted to see a full smile ever since he'd cranked up that one side of his mouth during the initial team meeting. Well, she'd finally gotten that smile, and the combination of white teeth and tiny lines beside his eyes had made her mouth go dry. She couldn't have quacked again if her life depended on it.

She left her puppet in the drawer this time and went to the elevator, taking a deep breath and forcing herself to push the button to go up. She'd never actually had a need to go to the plastic surgery department. And although she'd heard that Sam didn't deal with adult surgeries and only specialized in pediatric corrective procedures, she still wondered if he would dissect someone's looks and find them lacking in areas. How many before-and-after pictures had he seen during his training? And how many insecurities had driven people to seek out surgery?

Lucy had her own insecurities. Especially now.

That was ridiculous. People chose to straighten or whiten their teeth all the time. Or tattooed and pierced their bodies. And she never thought anything of it. Her own ears were pierced, and she had a tiny bunny tattoo on her left shoulder representing her sister, Bella. Why should anyone be given grief for getting tummy tucks or other elective surgeries? Just because Sam looked pretty perfect in every way didn't mean he judged other people on how they looked.

Like she was judging him?

Yes. She was being a hypocrite for even thinking along those lines.

Ugh. Once she arrived at the fourth floor, she found that those thoughts melted away the moment she spotted Sam in the large waiting room to the left. He was cradling a baby in his arms while he talked to a woman who was probably the mother. Even from here, she could see the baby's lip had been sutured in what looked to be a repair of some sort.

He hadn't notice her yet, and an army of butterflies gathered in her stomach, their soft wings brushing her insides in a way that felt vaguely warm...inviting. Not what butterflies normally did in these circumstances. Ugh. That had better not be her ovaries sitting up and taking notice of the scene, because she was not in the market for babies or significant others. Not after what had happened with Matt. But before that? She'd always hoped they'd have a couple of children of their own. Had looked forward to it, actually.

And then she'd found that horrible note. She'd never heard from him again. He'd left her to cancel all of the wedding plans and return gifts from the shower. It had been a singularly humiliating experience. Thank heavens her sister had been there to help her.

But the worst thing of all were the whys that kept swirling around in her head. Even now. Had he found someone else? Found something in her that was lacking...

or too irritating to stand? So many questions remained unanswered. He'd never been the type of person who'd worn his heart on his sleeve, and his *I love you*s had been few and far between. But Lucy had been demonstrative enough for the both of them. Or at least she'd thought so. Maybe that had been part of the problem. But for her to have had no idea that he'd changed his mind about marrying her had been singularly crushing.

And seeing a baby just reminded her of all the hopes that had been—

Just then Sam's head turned, and he saw her. "Lucy. Hi. Are you waiting to see me?"

All she could do was nod.

She realized she was still staring when the mother's head cocked as if wondering why Lucy was just standing there. *Dios.* Every time she was around the man she seemed to make some kind of mess. Whether with her coffee or her words…or just her presence. "I can come back."

"No, just go on to my office. I'll be there shortly."

"Okay." She had no idea where the man's office even was, which was ludicrous, since that was where she'd been headed in the first place. The urge to run back to her own department came, and she had to force herself not to act on that impulse. She somehow needed to get herself under control, or she needed to just resign from the team here and now. And she didn't want to do that.

Especially after seeing that baby and knowing that his or her life had just been changed. And Sam had played a big role in that.

This was Lucy's chance to do something big too. To

help kids who might not be able to speak or smile or even chew without great difficulty. And heaven help her, she wanted to be in on that. She'd seen what could be done in Bella's case. Her sister was now a wedding planner. She was graceful and elegant, and other than her cane and a slight hitch to her gait, no one would ever know that there had been some question over whether she would ever walk. But she had. And her family owed it all to a gifted neurosurgeon who had just recently retired from his practice. Her mom still sent him a card every single year on the anniversary of Bella's surgery, thanking him for the miracle that was her daughter.

Lucy had cried on her sister's shoulder after she'd gotten that note from Matt. But Bella had walked with her through every step of undoing all the work they'd done on planning the wedding. In the end they had gone on that honeymoon cruise themselves and had laughed and drank and enjoyed life. If Matt had been that unhappy, then he'd done them both a favor by backing out. He just should have talked to her face-to-face and told her the truth rather than taking a coward's way out. But what was done was done. No matter how much she wanted to change the way it had played out, she couldn't. That was on Matt and no one else.

Lucy stopped at the nurses' desk. When one of them smiled at her and commented on her scrubs—the same ones she'd spilled coffee on a week ago—she relaxed. "Thank you. I work down in the PT department. Could you tell me where Dr. Grant's office is?"

"Which Dr. Grant? Sam or Logan? Or Harper, although she's gone by Dunn for years."

Harper? That threw her for a moment until she remembered Sam and Logan were both Grants. Maybe Harper
was related to them somehow? "Sorry. *Sam* Grant."

"Got it," the woman said. "Go right down that hallway,
and it'll be the third door on your left."

"Thanks."

She turned and followed the directions, finding his
office right where the nurse said it would be. But she
balked at going in there on her own, so she found a little
waiting room a few steps away and went to sit in there.
Right now it was empty. It would give her a chance to
stop and collect her thoughts.

What was it about Sam that was messing with her
head so much? Was it his looks? The man was undeni-
ably gorgeous. But there were other good-looking guys
at the hospital, and she'd never gotten flustered around
them. Maybe the breakup was affecting how she inter-
acted with the opposite sex more than she'd realized.

She sat and took a couple of deep, calming breaths,
just like she did in yoga class. Or maybe it was that Lucy
hadn't expected to see Sam holding an infant. Or to look
so comfortable doing so. Even though Lucy worked with
kids each and every day, none of them were babies. Even
holding a friend's infant a few days ago had made her
tense up, resulting in the child crying. Lucy had quickly
handed the baby back. So for him to look so natural…
A lump rose in her throat. He would make a great dad.

And why had that even come to mind?

Just then, the man in question rounded the corner
walking right past the waiting room before backtrack-
ing and looking at her. "Why are you out here?"

She shrugged and stood. "I didn't want you to think I was ransacking your office."

Ransacking...really, Lucy?

His brow went up as he motioned her to follow him. "There's not much in there to ransack, and since I don't see a cup of coffee in your hand, there's nothing to worry about."

"Coffee?" She remembered and heat flooded her face. "Oh...*coffee.*"

He grinned and opened the door. "Come on in."

And there was that smile again. *Santa Maria*, she was in trouble.

"Sorry. I didn't realize you'd be with a patient." She sat in one of the chairs that was in front of his desk. The office was large and could be quite opulent with the right decor, but right at the moment it seemed spartan. She wasn't sure if that was surprising or not based on what she'd seen of the man. Then again, he hadn't been at the hospital that long, had he?

"Not a problem. It was just a follow-up appointment."

"I didn't realize you were already doing surgeries."

"I'm not, at least not the kinds of surgeries I hope the team will be doing. Marcus—the baby—was actually my first surgical repair at Manhattan Memorial. Now, what can I do for you? Are you here for our meeting?" He frowned. "Did we even set that up?"

"No." She felt a little more foolish for just showing up on his proverbial doorstep and decided to be honest. "I actually came to see if you'd heard anything about Devon."

"Devon?" His face cleared. "Oh, your patient from the other day. Sorry—I thought maybe Greg would have called you and let you know about the outcome. You were right. He has a tethered cord. They've already scheduled surgery to repair it. If you hadn't caught it… Well, you know what could have happened."

"I do. I have a sister who was born with spina bifida. So even though it's not the same thing, I've done quite a lot of research on spinal cord defects."

"I'm sorry. Is she okay?"

"She is, actually. She's kind and beautiful." Lucy laughed. "None of that has anything to do with her condition. Or maybe it does. She was fortunate that it could be corrected when she was still a baby. My parents made the trip to NYC after her surgeon came to Paraguay on a medical mission and arranged for them to come back to the States with him. They decided to stay in the New York area afterward. My dad was a radiologist in Paraguay and was able to get his certification to work in his field here."

"That's great. I'm glad your sister's cord defect could be corrected."

"Me too. It was a complicated surgery, but it all worked out. And I'm glad that Devon's condition can be fixed as well."

"Thanks to you."

"Thanks to Greg." She shook her head. "I just happened to notice the odd coloration. If I hadn't needed him to take his shirt off, I never would have guessed."

"He's lucky you did." Sam's eyes met hers. "I assumed you already knew the outcome of the MRI. Sorry about that. I should have checked to make sure."

"It's okay. I would have called or texted but realized I

didn't know your number. Or Dr. Asbury's. And I wasn't sure about calling his office. He probably doesn't even know my name."

"Oh, he knows your name." He gave another smile, although this one didn't quite reach his eyes.

She tilted her head. "What do you mean?"

"Nothing. He just recognized that you were on our team. Greg is on it as well."

"He is? I didn't realize that. I didn't see him at the meeting." She thought for a moment. "But it makes sense that a neurosurgeon would be included. Hopefully I'll be able to really get to know the other members of the group. That initial meeting was kind of crazy and overwhelming. Actually, it was very much so."

"Yes, it was. For me as well. I still don't know a lot of people at the hospital."

Really? He'd seemed so cool and calm. "At least you know your brother. What's it like working at the same hospital as a member of your family? Is Harper your sister? One of the nurses mentioned her when I asked where Dr. Grant's office was."

"Harper is—*was*—my sister-in-law." Sam didn't say anything else for a minute, but his smile faded. "As for Logan, it's good working with him. We're close."

That was kind of a strange thing to say, especially since she didn't think she'd implied that they weren't. But then again, it seemed like his whole family was pretty involved with the hospital since the administrator had mentioned something about a wing carrying their name. Which meant they had to be pretty well off too. Not that it meant anything.

"That's good. Does Logan know Spanish as well?"

"No."

The answer was short, almost curt, and she decided that maybe she'd already outworn her welcome. "Well, I just wanted to check on Devon. Thanks for letting me know."

She got up to leave.

"Wait. Why don't we go ahead and set the time for our meeting? You're actually the last one on my list, so can you let me know when you're free?"

That was right. She'd come to give him those dates as well. But somehow it stung that she was the last one to meet with him, as if she were somehow the weakest link in the chain. Hadn't she wondered about that? Or were there more gaps in her self-confidence—thanks to Matt—than she'd realized?

Hell, you're reading too much into his words, Lucy.

She opened her phone and found the calendar app, where she'd marked the dates. "I have Friday of this week open and Tuesday of next week." She glanced up. "Do you need me to continue?"

He was looking at his phone as well. "Friday afternoon works for me. Do you want to meet here in my office?"

It was probably the best place, but then again, maybe it was better to meet on neutral ground, since being closed up in here with him was making her rather squirmy, even though he'd done nothing to make her feel that way. It was those damned butterflies. "How about the hospital café instead?"

"That's on the first floor, isn't it?"

"It is. You haven't been there yet?" There were plenty

of people who frequented the place. Maybe she wouldn't feel so out of sorts there. Because here in his office with his attention focused solely on her... Maybe it was still tied to the way he'd held that infant, his big hand cradling that tiny head in a way that said he'd done the same thing many, many times before.

The man could be the father of three for all she knew. But somehow she didn't think so. He didn't wear a ring and hadn't mentioned a wife or kids, but then again they hadn't talked much about their personal lives. He knew she had a sister, and she knew he had a brother and an ex-sister-in-law. And she certainly hadn't mentioned her broken engagement. Nor was she planning on it. But it was a good reminder that she shouldn't go daydreaming about anyone right now. Maybe in a year or two when the sting of rejection wasn't quite so strong. Actually she was feeling that same sting in being the last member of the team chosen and the last one contacted for that individual meeting.

"I haven't," Sam said. "It seems rather loud and noisy and—"

A knock at the door interrupted whatever he'd been about to say.

"Come in."

The door opened, and a slender woman with well-manicured nails and an elegant air about her stood in the entry.

The woman's perfect brows arched. "So it is true. Why didn't you tell us you were back for good? I had to hear it from one of the nurses in Oncology. Not even Logan mentioned it. I thought your appearance at the gala was

just a fluke or maybe you'd come to the city on business."
Her attention swung to Lucy, and cool eyes very much
like Sam's perused her from head to toe, taking in her
scrubs and messy bun before she seemed to dismiss her.
Lucy suddenly felt unkempt.

The woman's attention turned back to Sam. "I'm sorry.
I didn't realize you were in a meeting."

"It's okay." He got up from the desk and went over and
kissed the woman on the cheek, the act coming across
as very strained. "The offer to work at the hospital came
pretty suddenly. I would have gotten around to calling
you, Mom. The fundraiser was just not the place for that
kind of conversation."

Mom. This was Sam and Logan's mom? Her face was
more youthful than Lucy would have expected.

And he hadn't "gotten around" to calling her? Lucy
was in constant contact with both her parents and her
sister, so it seemed totally alien to be in the same city as
they were and not notify them. In fact, Lucy lived in the
same Brooklyn neighborhood as her parents. And Bella
still lived at home.

Whatever was between Sam and his mother wasn't
something she wanted to witness so she stood. "Well,
I'll let you two talk. I need to get back to my department anyway."

The woman looked at her again, peering closer as if
trying to figure something out. "Aren't you going to introduce us, Samuel? Is this the friend you traveled to
Uruguay with?"

There was a pause that stretched beyond the awkward
stage. "No, Mom, Priscilla stayed in Uruguay. This is just

someone I work with. Lucy Galeano, this is my mother, Biddie Grant."

"Nice to meet you." Lucy went over and clasped his mom's hand briefly, suddenly feeling an urgent need to get out of there. Even though she knew his words were true, being introduced as *just someone he worked with* had struck her oddly. Which meant whoever this Priscilla was, she'd been more than that. Or maybe she still was?

"You as well, Lucy. Are you a doctor too?"

"No, I'm a physical therapist."

"Ah… When I saw Logan after I did my reading in the children's wing and asked if it was true that you were actually back to stay, he mentioned it might be nice if we all met for dinner."

"Again, I'm sorry I didn't call you."

They were blocking the door and Lucy couldn't get out, but standing this close to them was about as uncomfortable as it got. She should have stayed in her seat, where there was at least some breathing room. These two were being so stilted with each other—as if they were total strangers. Not at all like her family, where hugging and laughing…or whatever the emotion du jour happened to be was the name of the game.

As if she sensed Lucy's discomfort, Biddie Grant said, "Well, Samuel, I'll let you get back to your meeting. Dinner on Friday, maybe?"

"Uh. I can't that day." He glanced Lucy's way.

She realized it was because he was supposed to meet with her. "Oh, that's okay. We can get together another time. Just let me know when you want to."

"Bring her with you, Samuel. You know Theresa always makes plenty of food."

"I don't think so," Sam said. "But we'll do it another time soon, Mom."

She's just someone I work with. For some reason tears pricked at the backs of Lucy's eyes, and she blinked rapidly to send them back to wherever they'd come from.

"Well, okay. But please do. Your father will want to visit with you too."

"I will. I'll call you."

Biddie sent her a smile that was as cool and elegant as the rest of her. "Well, it was nice meeting you, Lucy."

"You too."

With that, the woman turned, her low pumps clicking on the polished floor as she walked away.

What had she just witnessed? She tried again. "We really can meet another time. Your family should come first."

"Should it?" He seemed to realize how that sounded and continued. "No, it's fine. I'm sorry you had to witness that."

So he *was* aware of how awkward that had been.

"It's okay."

He smiled, looking world-weary all of a sudden. "It's really not. Let's not meet at the hospital. Do you mind if we go to a restaurant instead?"

"No, that's fine." But there was the matter of whoever Priscilla was. "But will it make it awkward for you and your…er, girlfriend?"

"My girlfriend? Oh, Priscilla. No. She was someone I was seeing, but that's over."

The image of a note on her pillow appeared in her mind's eye. She hoped he'd picked a better way of ending things than Matt had.

Lucy probably should not be going out to eat with him, especially with how she seemed to react whenever she was within ten feet of him. He obviously had no such problem. But if she tried to wiggle out of it now, he might wonder why. Or change his mind about her being on the team.

So she said, "Okay, dinner will be fine."

He nodded. "Pick a place and let me know where. I'm not as familiar with Manhattan as I used to be."

How long had he been in Uruguay? Long enough to have a relationship and travel there with whoever it was. Was that why he'd come back here? Because the relationship had failed? It also explained why he spoke Spanish well enough to know all of those curse words.

She couldn't ever imagine leaving her family or Brooklyn. She had a whole lifetime's worth of memories there. But Sam's personal life was none of her business. That was driven further home by the encounter with his mom. Had he been trying to emphasize that their meeting would be business only? No mixing of personal lives with work? Not that she would ever think otherwise.

So why was there a voice in the back of her head whispering something completely different? And why was it throwing out names of places that were quiet and intimate?

"All right. I'll do some searching and let you know what I come up with." And it would not be quiet or intimate.

"Sounds good." But the man was already back at his

desk, sifting through papers and making it obvious that he was very busy. So she slid away on silent feet and wondered what the hell she'd gotten herself into.

The moment the door to his office closed, Sam tossed the papers aside and leaned back in his chair. His mom had picked a hell of a time to come say hi. He had a feeling he hadn't handled the introductions between her and Lucy very well, but he absolutely did not want his parents getting any ideas. Especially not after what Logan had gone through with Harper in the early days of their marriage.

Although Logan had never come out and said it, Sam was pretty sure his mom and dad had caused the rift that had resulted in their divorcing. It was one reason he was glad he and Priscilla had happened outside of the reach of their influence. That way he knew the breakup had been completely due to their own personalities and not for any other reason. In the end, they'd wanted different things out of life.

Priscilla, although she was a PA and still worked at the clinic, had gotten a side gig as a model once they'd moved to Uruguay. It was just before he'd overheard the conversation between her and her mother about how rich the Grant family was. She evidently wanted the swanky cars, posh life and media spotlight and realized she'd never get that in the medical field. Maybe it was why she'd started looking for modeling jobs.

Sam didn't care about his family's money. Not only didn't he care, he didn't want it—which was why he'd gotten rid of as much of it as he could. Actually his parents probably would have approved of his ex.

And Lucy? Would they have approved of her?

The thought of subjecting Lucy or any other woman to his parents made him cringe. Not that he and the physical therapist would ever be more than colleagues. Hopefully he'd learned his lesson as far as that went.

So why had he waited so long to have their meeting? He'd met with all of the other prospective teammates within days of that initial meeting, but he kept putting off Lucy's. Maybe because his mind kept playing over that spilled coffee and the amusing back-and-forth conversation they'd had? Maybe it had been that kick-to-the-gut attraction the second he heard that husky voice.

It was why he'd gone down to the physical therapy department the other day. He thought he could just wait until she was done with her patient and then go in and quickly give her the timeline he and the administrator had come up with for accepting patients. Except he'd gotten caught up in watching her use those puppets to reach a child who was scared and in pain. It had been heartwarming and very clever. It made him more sure than ever that she belonged on their team.

So he'd stood there and told himself he was observing, when it had gone far beyond that. And then she'd called him over, and he'd had to pry himself from that wall. Once she'd pointed out the mottling on her patient's back, the atmosphere had changed and he was no longer thinking about what she was doing and he was totally caught up in what needed to happen.

After that, he'd put off contacting her again. And again. Until she'd appeared in his office and asked how Devon was. And then there was no more getting out of it. The easy path would be to not include her on the team. But then he'd have to explain why, and the least professional thing he could do was exclude someone because he was worried about the way his body reacted when she was near.

If anything, watching her work should make him even more determined to include her, since she was obviously qualified and his observations had told him that she was willing to go above and beyond for her patients.

He should have just handed her the formal contract and sheaf of papers with the new department's information on it and been done with it, but that wasn't fair to her. And if he was going to head this thing, he needed to keep his personal feelings out of the arena when it came to his team. Something he'd never done very well when it came to his parents. They hated it when emotions took center stage, so he'd gone out of his way as a teen to make sure they did exactly that.

If his parents ever argued, Sam hadn't witnessed it. Nor did they show open affection to each other and only rarely to their kids. He had no idea how his sister was able to work for the family business. He knew he couldn't do it. Logan evidently couldn't either.

His mind came back to Lucy. Sam could admit there was an attraction there. He was pretty sure she'd felt it too in that conference room, although she'd never been anything but professional with him. And he had no idea why he'd suggested dinner out. Maybe because he'd been so relieved to get out of eating with his parents that he'd felt like celebrating. And she'd been sitting right there.

Or maybe he just hadn't wanted another accidental meeting with his mom by meeting in the hospital cafeteria.

But whatever it was, he was going to have to make sure it didn't go beyond dinner. And it wouldn't. He had enough Grant blood in him to be able to appear cool, calm and collected when the situation called for it.

And this one did. Of that he had no doubt.

CHAPTER FOUR

THERE WAS A slip of paper on the desk in her cubicle written in what appeared to be a masculine scrawl. Lucy tensed, a sense of doom coming over her, before realizing there was no way her ex would have been anywhere near this place. He didn't like needles...or hospitals. Actually she'd met Matt through her sister, who'd been planning a wedding for one of his brothers. They'd gone out once and sprinted straight to bed. It had all happened so fast. Too fast, if she were honest with herself. But happen it had. The end of their relationship had happened with the same speed. As if he had problems with impulse control. Evidently so did she, since she'd been just as quick to jump into a relationship without weighing things first. It made her doubt her instincts. And normally she was pretty damned good at reading people.

But she wasn't going to go blindly into something like that ever again.

And the note? It was stupid to still react to them this way. But who wouldn't?

Well, obviously not her. Because a second ago, she'd been certain that note was going to be life-altering. She picked it up.

Just verifying tonight. Want to meet in the parking lot

around seven? I don't know which restaurant you chose. Or if you've been too busy to think about it, I made a tentative reservation at Milo's, which came highly recommended from Logan. Text me if you already have a spot in mind, and I'll cancel the reservation.

It was from Sam and included his phone number this time, and she realized they hadn't exchanged them in his office the day his mom had come in. Which explained the note and why he'd had to come down to the PT department.

Damn. She'd completely forgotten he'd tasked her with choosing where they would eat tonight. Quiet and intimate? Wasn't that what she *hadn't* wanted? Well, Milo's had both of those things in spades.

She and Matt had been there several times, since as an architect he often met prospective clients there. And he'd even proposed to her on one of those dinner dates. Something else that seemed to come at lightning speed. Not something she liked to remember. But unless she wanted to lie and say she'd already picked out another place, it looked like she was stuck with it.

And she'd probably better at least acknowledge that she'd seen the note. So she typed his contact information into her phone and then answered him.

Seven is fine, as is Milo's. See you then.

Her thumb hovered over the Send button for several seconds before she finally pushed it. She then realized she'd forgotten to say who she was. But it should be pretty obvious right? Unless he was planning on taking other women to Milo's on other nights.

Who knew. He might be.

Her phone pinged seconds later. She swallowed and held it up to look. It was from Sam, but all that was there was a thumbs-up sign. Rather anticlimactic. But better than *Who is this?*

She could have simply responded, *Just someone you work with.*

That made her laugh. Maybe she shouldn't be glad that Sam and his ex had ended their relationship. But no matter how hard she tried to whisper those words to her brain, her heart kept kicking them right back out as untruths. And it was right. Because it wasn't true.

But even if she was, in fact, glad, it didn't mean that anything could come of them working together. Or that it should. She had hopefully learned her lesson about jumping into things sight unseen. And Sam had made it pretty plain that he wasn't interested, and that should've brought her a sense of relief. And it would, once she put any and all thoughts of office romances out of her head. She and Sam would be work colleagues. To hope for anything else was to invite disaster and ruin her chances of staying on the team.

Her next patient was here, so she threw herself into work and hoped beyond hope that everything went well tonight. And wasn't as awkward as she was imagining it was going to be.

Why had he thought this was going to be weird? Lucy was talking a mile a minute, and every other thing she said was as funny as hell. She'd just finished telling him a story about her dad calling the rest of their family to let them know he'd arrived at the restaurant where they were supposed to meet. But when he tried to follow the directions they gave him to their table, there was an elderly couple sitting there instead. It turned out that Gilberto Galeano had driven to a restaurant of the same name in a different neighborhood.

Sam couldn't think of a single funny story involving his mom and dad. Nor would they have found the humor in it if they'd found themselves in different restaurants in neighboring towns.

Priscilla had been beautiful and sexy, but her sense of humor was dark and often made him cringe when it was aimed at others. Whereas Lucy found humor in the lighter things in life and could laugh at herself with ease.

"So, did your dad drive back to Brooklyn?"

"No, we met him halfway at a different restaurant. So it all worked out in the end."

He pulled into a paid parking area a half block from Milo's, thankful his brother had warned him of the parking issues in this part of town. In fact, Sam didn't drive nearly as much as he had in Uruguay. Public transportation in NYC was great with subways, trains and even taxis all getting people where they needed to be.

"We'll need to walk a little bit to get there. Sorry about that."

Lucy kicked off the slides she'd paired with her dark-washed denim and tan short-sleeved jacket. "Not a problem."

She was going to walk barefoot? Why did that surprise him? It was the first time he'd actually seen her in clothes that weren't scrubs. She climbed out of the car before he could come around to let her out, looking perfectly at home with bare feet, her pink glittery polish winking at him in the sunlight that, even at seven, was still out. Spring in New York was pleasant for the most part. But there were hints of the heat that would soon attack the city when midsummer came.

They walked down the sidewalk with her swinging her shoes beside her. "So when is Devon's surgery?"

"It's actually on Saturday."

"Wow, surgery on a Saturday?"

"Greg wants to get this done and feels it's important enough that he's coming in on his day off."

"I am off, so I could come and observe. Will you be there?" As if thinking maybe that last question wasn't appropriate, she quickly added, "Not that it matters. And Greg might wonder if I suddenly show up."

"I was planning on being there, but even if I weren't, I have no doubt he would just think you were interested in it, since Devon is your patient too."

She smiled. "You remembered his name this time."

"I felt pretty silly not knowing who he was when you came to my office earlier in the week."

"I'm sure you have so many patients it's hard to keep them all straight."

"You seem to be able to."

"Not always. I do sometimes forget. I guess I have a little of my dad in me."

How easily she said that, as if being like her dad were of no consequence. If someone had told him he had some of his father in him, he would have probably been ready to throw down and fight. Because his dad and Lucy's were nothing alike.

But he also knew he probably had more of his dad in him than he liked to admit.

She turned so that she was walking backward when she asked, "Is there a timeline for when we accept that first patient?"

"You mean in the reanimation department?"

"Yes."

"Not yet. Todd wants to have a press release announcing the name of the new department. I think he hopes to garner additional funding to help with any unforeseen costs or price hikes. Microsurgery equipment is not cheap."

Lucy spun back to the front so that she was walking with him again. "Doesn't the hospital already do some microsurgery? I'm almost sure that they do. They could save costs by sharing equipment."

"Yes, but trying to manage equipment between two different floors could get dicey."

"I can see that. Do you think your father will help, like your family did the other hospital wing?" She stopped and bit her lip as if regretting her words. "I'm sorry. That's none of my business."

"It's okay. And no, he won't. I'm almost sure of it."

Her head jerked to the side to look at him, and Sam realized how that had sounded. "Let's just say my dad and I don't always see eye to eye."

She didn't say anything for a minute. "I kind of got that idea when your mom was in your office. I'm sorry.

I can't imagine not having a good relationship with my mom and dad…or my sister, for that matter."

"You're lucky."

"I know I am." She glanced at him. "Do you think things with your parents will ever get better?" She added almost immediately, "Sorry *again*."

That made him laugh. "It's okay *again*. And I can't say that things will *never* get better, because obviously our new department is built on technology that no one thought would exist twenty years ago. So anything's possible."

"True. I guess there's always hope."

"There is. But there's a lot of bad water under that particular bridge."

Including his parents destroying his brother's marriage and his dad objecting to Sam leaving the country, even telling him not to bother coming back or expect any inheritance from him, that his grandfather's money would be all he would ever get.

Little had his father known that he neither wanted nor expected an inheritance. From anyone. If his dad was smart, he would leave his money to their sister, who was a shrewd businesswoman in her own right. Or to Logan, who would also do right by the money.

Was it wise to wish away any help his dad might want to give to the fledgling department?

Probably not, but gifts from Carter Grant normally came with strings attached. After he'd hired a lawyer to defend Sam after his arrest, his dad had then used that to try to strong-arm him into working for his company. Sam had refused. And things had been strained—to say the least—ever since then. Sam had put himself through medical school with scholarships and some student loans and had paid off those loans all on his own. He didn't want to be beholden to anyone, especially not his father. And when the time came to practice medicine, he'd chosen to work in Rochester rather than at Manhattan Memorial, although they'd wanted to keep him. At thirty-eight, Sam was pretty sure he was now as set in his ways as his father was. He didn't see either of them budging.

Lucy glanced again at him just as they reached the front entrance to Milo's. "Maybe it's time to clean up that water, then?"

Sam didn't have time to think about what that meant as someone from inside the restaurant opened the door and ushered them inside. He gave the hostess his name when she asked if he had a reservation. Within a minute they were being led through the dim recesses of the place.

He frowned. Maybe he should have asked Logan for a little more information when he'd given him the name of the restaurant. The fanciness of the place didn't faze him, but warm wood, leather and candlelight weren't what he'd expected either. "Have you been here before?"

"I have."

Lucy didn't expand on that statement, and he didn't press her for more information. But he was surprised that she'd want to come here with a work colleague, since it seemed more a place for romantic getaways.

He wasn't worried about the cost. At least not in terms of money. But he'd been feeling pretty damned good about this outing up until about a minute ago. Now all of those warm fuzzies that he'd allowed himself to feel were coming back to nip him in some places that were especially uncomfortable. Because he could easily get caught up in this atmosphere—in *her*—if he wasn't careful. She made being with her light and effortless. Just like her personality. No drama. No angst. She had a free-spirited air to her that made him want to stay close.

Priscilla had been serious and moody, always open with her feelings and emotions, and that had drawn him to her immediately. They were things he hadn't gotten at home, and their relationship had worked very well for a number of years. Until she seemed to want him to be more ambitious and to be more open to spending on luxurious living. She'd often hinted that he could easily be a hospital administrator or CEO with his people skills.

People skills? He had no idea what she was talking about because he was not an administrative type of person. He didn't see himself as having those talents or even wanting them. And money… Because he spent very little, he'd ended up with a bank account that was pretty padded even without the inheritance. Pri seemed to instinctively know that. And she sure as hell had found out that his grandfather had left him money.

So what had initially drawn him to her had ended up being the very things that drove them apart five years later. He'd needed someone more like he was—guarded and able to live a pretty independent existence without heavy displays of emotion. Priscilla had not been that.

Neither was *free-spirited and wildly funny*, the things that he liked about Lucy. And while neither woman was like the other one, the thing they had in common was that they were both in touch with their emotions and neither one of them was afraid of expressing them.

Well, Sam was. No, he took that back. He wasn't afraid of emotions in and of themselves. He just didn't let himself give in to them. Priscilla had wanted to hear the words, had wanted him to tell her he loved her on a regular basis, not realizing how much effort it took him to even say it once, let alone multiple times a day like she seemed to be able to do.

He really was like his parents. Damn.

He realized Lucy was staring at him in a strange way. "What? I'm sorry—did you say something?"

She bobbed her head to the right, and he glanced over and realized a waiter was standing there pen and paper in hand. Oh, hell. How long had the man been waiting? And had he asked for drink orders, food orders…what?

"Sorry about that." He addressed Lucy, "What are you getting?"

"Water." She said it completely deadpan.

"Okay, thanks for all your help." He smiled. "I'll take a water and a whiskey. Preferably mixed."

Lucy laughed.

Yes, it was easy being with her. A little too easy. He was going to need to watch himself.

"Any appetizers?" The waiter still stood at the ready.

The problem was Sam hadn't even looked at a menu, which wasn't the case for Lucy, since hers was open in front of her. He couldn't believe he'd sat there staring into space for what probably seemed an eternity.

He glanced across the table. She shook her head.

"I think we're good," he said to the man. "But if you

could give me a few more minutes to look at the menu I would appreciate it."

"Not a problem. I'll bring your drinks."

The man left, and Sam said, "Why didn't you say something?"

"I thought you'd eventually realize he was there."

"I normally would have." He didn't offer any more than that. Instead he changed the subject. "You said you've been here before. Any suggestions on what to order?"

"I like the eggplant."

Eggplant. Okay.

He'd never quite been able to get over the way that particular vegetable looked, although he did like the baba ghanoush he'd been tricked into trying at a dinner party in Uruguay. It was supposedly made of eggplant, and the dip had become one of his favorite dishes while he was there. Maybe he should give it a chance. "You mean as in eggplant parmesan?"

"You really haven't been here before, have you? Their specialty is risotto with eggplant and a special cheese. One that's not parmesan."

"Is that what you're getting?"

"I think so, yes. Although I've liked everything I've tried at Milo's."

The waiter came back about that time with their drinks and asked if they were ready. Sam nodded. "I think we are."

He waited for Lucy to place her order. She opted for a salad with her main dish, whereas when he ordered, he asked for a gnocchi soup with his risotto.

The waiter left, and Sam waited a minute or two before he said, "Do you want to wait and talk about the position after we eat, or are you happy to start now and continue on afterward?"

"Why don't we go ahead?"

"Okay. I don't have the official contract here in the restaurant, but I have a copy of it in the car. Even if you think the job is a good fit, make sure you look at the pay structure. HR will want to go over it with you."

She stared at him for a minute. "Um…will there be a cut in pay?"

"What? No, that's not what I meant. There will be an increase. I just meant it might not be as much as you were expecting."

"I actually didn't expect a pay increase at all, so that surprises me."

Sam smiled. "Are you saying you would have accepted the position even if there were a pay cut involved?"

"No. So don't get any bright ideas." She grinned at him.

He couldn't help but smile back. How did she do that, turn a serious conversation into something that was less weighty? "I wasn't thinking anything."

"That was pretty obvious a few minutes ago. You looked completely lost."

"Sorry."

"Don't worry about it. Thinking about the new department?"

His head tilted to the right. "You could put it that way. More like hoping we have the resources to do our patients justice."

"We will. You already have the talent in place. From

what you said, all that is lacking is some specialized equipment. If necessary, we could even get that from a hospital that might be upgrading and be looking to get rid of its old stuff."

He wasn't sure how he felt about that. He was hoping to be cutting edge, but he saw her point. "Hopefully it will work out."

"And if it doesn't all come together as soon as you hope it will, what will you do? Leave?"

There was an expression on her face that he couldn't decipher.

He hadn't even thought about what he'd do. He'd assumed the hospital had already given a lot of thought to the needs of opening a new department. After all, they'd done it several times before. And his dad's money hadn't been necessary in all of those cases. In fact, contrary to Lucy's assertion, his father was probably less likely to donate to a department that the son who'd given him so much grief was heading. Even though Sam would never admit that to anyone. Not even Lucy.

"I'm pretty sure the hospital has a plan in place for dealing with financing," he said. "I think that's why Todd has waited before announcing that change is coming. He probably wanted to be able to publicize the names of the team, hoping some of those names will generate some revenue for the new work."

"Okay. But don't expect my name to do that. I'm pretty much an unknown."

Sam didn't like the way she said that—as if what she brought to the table didn't amount to much—but the waiter had arrived, bringing Lucy's salad and Sam's soup and carefully placing them in front of them. He also brought an additional glass of water for Sam, who hadn't yet touched his glass of whiskey.

He did so now, bringing the tumbler to his lips and swallowing a healthy amount. It was the only drink he'd have tonight, and he wanted to savor it, since he probably wouldn't have more than that taste. He was driving, and he was no longer young and stupid. He'd done a lot of growing up since graduating from high school and medical school. His dad might even like the man he'd become if given the chance.

Sam just didn't want to give him that chance. He wasn't sure why, but right now wasn't the place to untangle the crazy web of his childhood.

"So what kinds of kids are you hoping for?"

"Excuse me?"

Her eyes widened. "I—I meant what kinds of kids are you hoping will come to the new department for help."

The words were said with care, and he realized he'd taken her question the wrong way. "I don't ever see the demand for these specialized surgeries taking the place of my regular practice, but you never know. The surgeries I've done until now have centered around the mouth. Cleft lips and palates and traumatic injuries to the tissues of those areas. I've performed surgeries at a clinic in Uruguay where more specialized procedures are done. Like grafting thigh muscles into the cheek as a way to repair impaired movement to areas damaged by other procedures or due to birth defects." He didn't know why, but he didn't want to mention that the clinic was one that had been part funded by his grandfather's inheritance.

"How about Moebius syndrome?"

He sat back in his seat, unable to hide his surprise. "Not many people know about Moebius."

"I actually worked with a patient with Moebius syndrome when I was a student. She was a sixteen-year-old girl. They were doing speech therapy with her, and there was talk of trying to do just what you spoke of. Microsurgery and grafting muscles and nerves to help repair the areas that had been damaged in utero."

"The so-called smile surgery?" Moebius developed in the womb and was due to damage to the sixth and sometimes seventh cranial nerve. The cause was thought to be an interruption in the supply of oxygen or due to drug use, although a genetic component couldn't be totally ruled out. Eye movement could be affected as well as parts of the face that helped relay emotion. The resultant paralysis of those muscles affected so many areas of a person's life. Whether it was nursing, eating, swallowing or speech. Part of Manhattan Memorial's new department would help those kinds of patients and others like them.

"Yes."

"Where was this?"

"Actually," she said, "it was here. The patient was having trouble getting cleared by her insurance company for the specialized surgery. And we didn't offer it here at the time."

"I know Mayo does it and a few of the other healthcare giants. But if MMH's hopes are realized it means it will be within reach of other large teaching hospitals."

He picked up his spoon and ate a few bites of soup as Lucy did the same with her salad. The soup was wonderfully balanced with a creaminess that made him want more. But from what she'd said, their entree was going to be just as good.

Lucy paused and looked at him. "I think the program is going to be a success. As soon as I heard about it, I thought about that patient. I just never dreamed I'd be able to take part in something as important as this."

He smiled. "So I haven't scared you off yet?"

"No. I think it would take something huge to do that." She shrugged. "So if I'm hearing you correctly, I'll keep seeing my patients as per usual but will just jump in whenever a facial paralysis case comes in?"

"Yes. That's what all of us will agree to do. So we won't be dedicated entirely to the new department but will come together as a team whenever a new case comes in. We'll meet as a group and decide the best course of treatment that will encompass the patient as a whole, from pre-op preparation to the surgery to the aftercare and physical therapy. You will probably be their first and last stop," he said, "because you'll see the patient before we come up with a treatment plan and give us a baseline assessment. And then after the surgery you'll do their physical therapy and let us know how much change you see from where they started."

"Wow, I'm kind of surprised. I saw myself as handling the post-op physical therapy more than anything. But I really like your thinking as far as using PT as a measuring tool. I often think we're underutilized."

"I agree."

The waiter came with their entrees and set them in

front of them, clearing away some of the other plates. "Would you like another whiskey, sir?"

"No, you can take the glass. I'd just like another water, please."

"Of course," the man said.

After he'd left she glanced at Sam. "You didn't finish your drink."

He gave a half shrug. "I'm driving."

"I'm sorry. I could have driven. Or we could have taken public transport."

"It's okay. I don't drink a whole lot anyway." That was one good thing that his dad had instilled in him. Sam had never seen his dad drunk, although he and his mom did drink during social events. But they were both very disciplined and knew their limits. During his rebellious years, Sam had been reckless and had been lucky. But hopefully he was older and wiser nowadays.

Something touched his leg, and he blinked. Had Lucy just put her foot on him?

It had to be his damned imagination. There was no way she would do that, no matter how much of a free spirit she was.

But when it happened again, her foot sliding a bit higher, a spark of electricity went up his thigh and headed straight for his pleasure center. One that needed to stay asleep for the duration of this dinner. He moved his leg.

A few seconds later, her face turned blood red and she glanced under the table. "Oh, *Dios*! Was that your... your...?"

"My...leg? Why, yes. Yes, it was." He couldn't stop his slow smile when she couldn't seem to get the word out. And what could have become a very uncomfortable moment turned humorous. Especially when the horrified expression on her face made it clear she'd not done it on purpose. "I can put my leg back where it was, if you want, though."

"I swear I thought it was the table leg. Not a human leg. I hope you know I never would have—"

"I know. It's good to know, though, that you prefer table legs to real legs."

"I don't. I mean, I do…"

He had to rescue her. "I'm kidding, Luce. Don't think anything of it."

Because he would be doing enough thinking about it for the both of them. And not only about the smooth slide of her foot along his leg, but about his reasons for suddenly using the shortened version of her name.

Wasn't that how his relationship with Priscilla had begun? He'd shortened her name to Pri, and within a few days they were in bed together.

That couldn't happen here, though. He and Lucy could not wind up anywhere but in an exam room together.

Hell, that wasn't any better, because the images running through his head were now of them doing X-rated things in one of those rooms. Things where her foot on his leg was the least of his worries.

A half hour later, they found themselves back in Sam's car, and Lucy still couldn't believe she'd run her foot up his leg. *¡Dios!* Why was she becoming an absolute idiot when it came to Sam? Because the moment she reached for what she thought was the table leg a third time to find that it was no longer there, she'd taken a split second to process the possibilities and come up with the only probable explanation. And she'd wanted to die and slide under the table. Only he'd joked about it and given her that quirky smile and quickly put her at ease.

And then he'd called her Luce in that low silky voice of his, and it set all of her nerve endings on fire. They were still burning. Because she'd liked it. A little too much. The problem was she was pretty sure he had no idea he'd even done it. Kind of like the fact that she'd had no idea the "table" leg was actually his leg, probably because her shoe was on and she hadn't felt that it was denim rather than metal. She'd been about to do some very inappropriate things like run her foot all the way to the top of the table leg, something that had become a habit. It allowed her to stretch her leg in a way that no one could see.

But if she'd done it that third time, she was pretty sure she'd have discovered that the "table leg" gave way to something else entirely. And that was something there would be no coming back from.

"Anywhere you want to stop?" Sam put the keys in the ignition and paused before starting the vehicle.

Maybe the nearest fire hydrant so she could cool herself off? If she were with any of her friends she wouldn't have hesitated to make that joke. But suddenly it didn't seem very funny. Because she really was having some weird and scorching thoughts, and she didn't know how to make them stop.

But she also didn't want what had happened in there to be the last memory he had of her: of her shoed foot climbing his leg in search of his...

No. She absolutely hadn't been in search of that.

"There's a little park around the corner. Do you have time to walk for a few minutes? I'm stuffed after that meal. And it's cool outside."

"I was just thinking along those lines myself."

She blinked. "You were?"

"Is that okay?"

"Yes. Yes, of course." Her nerves were stretched tighter than a violin right now. And doing anything with him, including walking, probably wasn't the smartest idea. But she really did want to get out of the car before she broke out in a sweat that might give her away.

He took the keys back out of the ignition and turned toward her. "Are you sure?"

Lucy mustered all the sincerity she could muster. "I am. I really could use some fresh air."

"Are you okay going to the park on foot so we don't have to go searching for another parking place?"

"Yes." She smiled for the first time since the debacle in the restaurant. "I was just thinking the same thing."

CHAPTER FIVE

IT WAS JUST after nine, and the temperatures were blessedly cool. Since it was Friday night, Manhattan was still teeming with people who were either out eating dinner or bar hopping, or just hanging out with friends. None of which described his current situation.

He was glad she'd suggested going for a walk, because he found he liked her company, even her funny way of apologizing for playing footsie with him.

"Which way is the park?"

When he'd lived in Manhattan with his parents, his life had been a whirlwind of school, sports and other activities. It was rare that Sam actually walked in a park. And as far as he knew, his parents never had.

"We'll turn right at the next corner."

This area looked vaguely familiar. He didn't think Milo's had been in existence when he was a kid, though. So it must have opened up after he'd left for Uruguay.

They turned right, and he saw a sign that sparked a memory. It was advertising an auto-repair shop with the funny slogan *Bad Wreckered? We can fix that.* He'd seen a sign very similar to that one on the day...

Then the park name came into view: Pirius Park. It was named after a figure in New York's history.

Hell. This was the park where the protest had been held when he was fifteen. The protest that had made him set a different course for his life and get his act together.

Rather than dread seeing it or it bringing up terrible memories, he saw it as a place of epiphanies. Walking through the arched iron gateway, he saw it for what it currently was, without the angry students who were protesting too much homework. He'd almost forgotten what they'd been there for.

But now it was full of clipped hedges and groomed wood-chipped pathways, well lit and beautiful. In this section of the park swagged rows of twinkle lights hung over their heads and trees were draped in the same kind of lights. Not like Christmas decorations—it didn't have that vibe. It was more like a make-believe world where anything could happen. Like the changes in his life he'd made after his arrest? It was hard to believe that was over twenty years ago.

"I don't think I've ever been here at night," Sam said. "It's beautiful. And it's quieter than I would have expected it to be." Almost silent. Unlike it had been the day of the protest.

"Yes, it is."

They walked in silence for a few minutes, passing only one person as they moved deeper into the park. At the center of it, if he remembered right, would be a cleared square with some benches and an abstract fountain of some sort. The older man who'd fallen during the protest had been there to remember his wife who'd died the previous year. Pirius Park had been her favorite in all of Manhattan.

The memory rose unbidden and almost forgotten, but it was part of the reason why Sam had stopped to help him. He'd been looking for the picture of his wife that he'd dropped after being jostled. They'd found it, and Sam had walked the man a few feet to where the crowds had thinned out. That was when the police had stopped him.

So many years ago.

Lucy put a hand on his arm, stopping him. When he looked down at her there was a haunted sheen to her eyes. "I just want to say…this program is going to make a difference in so many lives, Sam."

"I hope so."

"I know it will." Her lips pressed tightly together as if holding back some strong emotion. "Remember the Moebius patient I told you about?"

He nodded, a sense of foreboding stealing over him. "You said you wished you knew whether or not she got the surgery." Was that what this was about? That it bothered her that she didn't know? Maybe that was why she'd been so anxious to know what happened with Devon. It was hard not knowing.

"Yes. I was talking to her one day, and she had this little dry-erase board that she would write messages on because it was hard to understand her most of the time. She turned her head to look around the room and then wrote *surgery?* with quick jerky movements. She pointed to it and then erased with a swipe of her hand. I got the feeling she didn't want anyone else to see." Lucy pressed her lips tightly together. "I was just a student and didn't know anything about whether or not she was going to be able to get it, so I told her to ask her doctor. But she shook her head and wrote the word again.

"I had to tell her I didn't know if she would get the surgery or not, that I didn't make those decisions. I felt like a cad to even have to say it. And her eyes… *Dios*. Her face might not have been able to show emotion, but I saw what I thought was a pain so, so deep in those green eyes."

"I'm sorry, Luce." He brushed a strand of hair out of her eyes, feeling every bit of what she was saying.

"Do you know what she did then? She erased that word and wrote something else. She drew two circles. In the first one she wrote *surgery*. In the other circle she wrote *life*. She slowly drew a diagonal line through the first circle and then stared at the board for a long time. Then she put a line through the circle with the word *life*. I've never forgotten it, and I never want another patient to feel like that."

"I can't imagine. But we can't always give patients the outcome they want. Or that we want. Even in plastic surgery."

"I know. But I kept thinking it would be easier if that particular surgery were available at hospitals other than just the mega ones." She swallowed. "I've never told anyone about that experience before. I hope she found the help she needed."

"I do too. For what it's worth, I'm glad you told me." And he was. Not just because it would help him be more sensitive toward patients facing tough choices or who were fighting insurance companies or crippled with personal finance issues, but because it helped him understand Lucy even more. As if he hadn't already seen her concern when she'd dealt with Devon. He was positive that her Moebius patient had written those words to Lucy and Lucy alone because she'd seen what Sam saw in her. What probably a hundred other patients and their families saw in her: a compassion so deep that it gave them hope, made them want to trust.

His parents didn't have that. Neither did Priscilla. Not really. And it had Sam wanting to make confessions that were every bit as weighty as the one she'd just made about her patient. He struggled to keep bottled up how his upbringing had affected him or how much the sight of that old man searching for the picture of his dead wife had touched him.

He was able to bite back the words, but what he couldn't do was resist touching her cheek or saying, "You're pretty incredible—do you know that?"

"I'm not really."

"I'm not the only one who sees it. Devon's mom told me that he had another physical therapist at first who couldn't get him to cooperate. But you got through to him."

"It wasn't me. It was Quack."

Sam chuckled. "Okay, then. You *and* Quack are pretty incredible."

"Thank you." Their eyes met and held for several long seconds, and his thumb strayed from its perch and slowly traced the path from her cheek to her ear. Lucy made a soft sound deep in her throat before whispering his name.

His hands cupped her face. "So incredible."

Then his face lowered and his lips covered hers.

* * *

Dios. Lucy had been looking for relief from the heat that had been building inside of her, and she'd found it. Sam's lips were cool and soothing, and they touched hers like the softest snow. All of her cares melted away: The sadness over the patient she hadn't been able to comfort. The worries over not being good enough to be on Sam's team. All washed away by the press of his mouth to hers.

She couldn't stop herself from going up on tiptoe and winding her arms around his neck. *Santa Maria.* How had she not noticed how tall the man was? Lucy was not short by any means, but she had to stretch to reach him properly. And to kiss him properly.

And she loved it.

Loved that he'd known just what to say to make her feel better about herself. He hadn't given her some canned speech about how doctors were not responsible for what their patients felt or didn't feel. She knew that, though hearing it never helped.

What did help was that he knew that she did as much as she could for her patients. Not everyone recognized that, and he certainly hadn't gotten it from her bio. That only happened by getting to know a person on a level that went beyond team lead and team member. And yet they hadn't even started working together. How could that even be?

Her fingertips eased into his short hair, finding it oh, so soft, the strands shifting over her skin in a way that made it come to life. And oh, she never wanted this to end, wanted to stand here in the dark with him forever.

The sound of voices slid through her mind, and at

first she thought it was just her inner monologue asking what she thought she was doing, until one of those voices laughed knowingly and then the sounds moved away.

Dios. Someone had seen them.

She pulled away, her arms slowly unwinding and falling back to her sides. "Someone was here," she whispered.

"Where?" His face was still close, his breath brushing over her cheeks in a way that made her close her eyes for a second. Then she forced them back open. No! They shouldn't be doing this. She'd already lectured herself on falling for someone again. Someone she barely knew.

She swallowed and took a step away, moving out from whatever spell he had cast over her. "It doesn't matter. They're gone now. But this isn't something we should be doing. We have to work together."

As if he, too, had come to his senses, he said nothing as she turned away, focusing her gaze on the lights behind them. They were still pretty, but they no longer held the magic that they had a few moments earlier.

Sam touched her shoulder, but she didn't turn around. "You're right, Lucy. I'm sorry. I never planned for that to happen."

"I know." She turned around. "Neither of us did. But I... I can't get involved with anyone right now. I'm just getting over a broken engagement, and things have been weird for the last five months since he left me."

There was a pause. "I'm sorry. I didn't know. Priscilla and I ended a few months ago as well. Only I was the one who did the leaving."

"I bet you told her in person, though." She knew there was a bitter note to the words, but she couldn't help it.

"I did. I take it your ex didn't?"

"Nope. Left me a note that I found when I got home. Said he couldn't do it. All his things were gone, and I never saw him again. I even contacted the firm where he worked only to find he'd given notice, effective immediately."

Sam's brows came together. "Hell, I'm sorry, Lucy. But you're right. This is the wrong place and the wrong time…for both of us, it sounds like. I want to be honest, though. I don't think there will be a right place or time for me. It's not something I see myself doing again."

"I get it." For some reason, his admission made her feel better. She didn't have to worry about him wanting something more. Something she was too afraid to give at this point in her life. And it was the out she needed. And strangely enough, it helped her save face. He hadn't rejected her, specifically, and she hadn't rejected him. They'd rejected the idea of relationships.

And she was okay with that.

He tipped her chin up. "So we're good? I'd hate to lose you from the team just because of my stupidity."

"You weren't stupid. Neither of us were. And no, I have no plans of withdrawing from the team. If you even tried to get rid of me, I might have to fight you."

"You would, would you?"

"Definitely."

He smiled and let his hand drop. "Then I'd better get you home before you change your mind."

She glanced at her watch, surprised to find it was after

ten. "It's the witching hour for me, actually. I'm normally in bed by now."

"I didn't realize you had a curfew."

"That's the price of getting old."

He laughed. "I don't think you're quite there yet. But the last thing I want to do is keep a woman from her bed."

If they hadn't been interrupted, she might have asked him to share that bed with her. And that would have been an even bigger mistake. Because Lucy had always had a hard time separating sex from emotions. For her they tended to go hand in hand.

It was one thing to kiss the man. But go to bed with him? Look at what had happened with Matt. First to bed...then to living together. She couldn't do that again. And to let herself fall in love with someone who was about to lead the team she'd soon be involved with? That would be the biggest mistake she could imagine making. She made a pact with herself that she was going to stay out of Sam's arms. And whatever else she did, she was definitely going to stay out of his bed.

The press release went out four days after that kiss, and Todd sent a text to the team saying to get ready because the phones had been ringing nonstop ever since. With everyone from reporters to doctors from other hospitals who wanted to move to Manhattan Memorial to patients who wanted to be seen, there had been little time to think about anything but what was going on with the hospital.

Not that it didn't stop Sam from dissecting that kiss— every earth-shattering second of it. It was crazy and stupid, but he found it hard to not think about it at least once an hour.

He might've been thinking about it, but he hadn't talked to Lucy once since that walk in the park. He'd talked with most other members of the team, whose excitement was growing in the face of the media storm that was going on right now. Especially since it came almost on the heels of the hospital gala that'd happened right after he'd returned from Uruguay.

A knock sounded at his door. For a second he thought it might be Lucy, but the face that peered around the corner was definitely not feminine.

"Logan, come in."

His brother dropped into a chair. "Are you the reason why this place has gone crazy all of a sudden?"

Sam's brows lifted. "Would it surprise you?"

"Not at all." His brother laughed. "You always did like to stir the pot. Why should it be any different at MMH? Seriously, though, congratulations. I think this is going to be a great step for our hospital to take. I'm a little bummed not to be on the team. Not that we could ever work together without killing each other."

"If I remember right, you used to cover for me plenty of times with Mom and Dad."

"Speaking of Mom and Dad…"

Sam sank back in his chair. "Don't tell me she's now getting you to do her dirty work. I told her we'd have dinner soon. I just didn't commit. I'm not sure I'm up for seeing Dad yet."

"Not even for your niece or nephew?"

"You mean…" His eyes widened.

"We haven't told them yet."

Sam made a face. "I don't envy you that discussion."

"I'm not looking forward to it either. But Harper's about to the second trimester, and we can't put it off much longer. They don't even know we're officially back together."

"That's a tough one." He tried to imagine what would happen if he had to tell them that he and Lucy were a couple. Not that they ever would be. Right now that gave him a sense of relief that was larger than it should have been. And maybe he should be thanking Logan for keeping him grounded and making him even more certain of keeping his relationship status firmly in the *single and not ready to mingle* category.

"We are thinking of having a dinner in order to give them the news, and I wouldn't mind having a buffer there when we do. They made it pretty hard for Harper in the past. I'm not sure if Mom realizes just how terrible she was toward her. But we both agreed that we'll never let anyone step between us again."

"I'm happy for you. Really. I will say that what happened between you and Harper was one of the reasons I never brought Priscilla home to meet them. I didn't want them jinxing things. Moving to Uruguay seemed like a godsend at the time. But it turns out that sometimes things aren't meant to be, even when there's no one meddling."

Logan glanced at his face. "I'm sorry about that. I don't think I realized it was completely over. Are you sure? I mean, Harper and I thought we were done too, then…" His brother made a curving gesture over his midsection.

"I'm sure. It turned out Pri and I want completely different things out of life."

And yet sometimes even when people wanted the same things, they shouldn't be together. Like him and Lucy? Yes. Because it didn't change the fact that he couldn't— no, he didn't *want to*—tie himself emotionally to anyone other than his patients. And maybe he could with them because he knew it was for a limited time frame. After all, you could pretend to be someone you weren't for a short period of time. But for a lifetime? Well, it wouldn't work. At least not for him. He and Priscilla had tried that, but in the end, they just couldn't make themselves into something they weren't.

"I get it. But I'm still sorry. She seemed like a nice person."

"She is. And I only want good things for her."

Logan gave him an earnest look. "So…my real reason for coming. Do you think you can face Mom and Dad for a couple of hours while we tell them about the pregnancy? You can bring someone if you want, as kind of your own buffer."

"I don't think I'd want to put anyone through that, honestly. But I will come if it'll help."

"It will. I'll owe you big time."

"No, you won't. Consider it payback for all of those times we talked about that you covered for me. Do you have a day in mind?"

"Next week sometime? Maybe Tuesday or Wednesday?"

"At their place?"

Logan frowned at him. "You mean at our *childhood home*?"

That had come out wrong, and Sam hadn't meant it to

sound like he resented his whole childhood. He didn't. He'd come to see that there were parts of it that were good and parts of it that were horrible. But one thing would never change. He loved Logan and Sarah, and he would always be in their corner. Sarah was already proving that she would run the company her way and refused to be a carbon copy of their dad. Sam bet Carter *loved* that.

"That's what I meant," he said.

"I'll see what Harper wants to do. Since it's our idea, she may want it at my place. I'm good with anything."

"I'll be happy to be there with you. Just let me know when. Maybe they'll turn out to be good grandparents. Stranger things have happened."

He didn't hold out a ton of hope for that, but diagnoses that looked hopeless sometimes found a way to turn themselves around.

"Thanks, Sam. Harper and I both appreciate it." He opened the door and turned to look back at him. "If it's worth anything, I really am glad you're home."

Sam smiled. "As strange as it sounds, I'm glad I'm home too."

Lucy's phone pinged as a text came through. She glanced up from the notes she'd been writing on a patient and looked at her phone which was on the far side of the desk in her cubicle.

Devon's surgery moved to tomorrow instead of Saturday due to pain in his back. Do you still want to observe?

Sam hadn't contacted her in almost a week, and she'd begun to wonder if he'd had second thoughts about her being on the team despite what he'd said after that kiss. The ride home had been a little awkward that night, but they'd seemed to part on good terms. But things could always change.

Just like people could always change, as she'd seen in her relationship with Matt. One minute he'd been a loving fiancé, then almost overnight, he'd wanted out of the relationship. So it stood to reason that Sam might have felt that kiss was a good enough reason to drop her from the team. And ultimately, it was his choice. Todd had made that clear when he'd spoken to the group, that just because their name appeared on a list didn't mean that list was written in stone and no one should take it personally if they were no longer included.

Lucy checked her schedule. She had a couple of appointments in the afternoon. It was a school day, so most of her work happened after the kids finished for the day. It was why she worked until six or seven when most of the other physical therapists got off at five.

She texted back.

a.m. or p.m.?

The little text box squiggled, letting her know he was writing a reply.

Eight a.m.

Okay, that was earlier than she normally got to work, but for Devon she would make it happen.

Yes, that works.

He replied with the number of the surgical suite, and that was that. There was no indication of whether or not he would be there too or if she'd be alone up there. It didn't matter. She was going either way, although if she were honest, it might be easier if he wasn't there. She would feel a little more comfortable, and her mind would be less on that damned kiss.

It always came down to that. Lucy somehow couldn't think about the man without that moment filtering back in. A moment that had lasted less than five minutes. She smiled. Actually that kiss had started way before their lips ever met. It had probably even begun when she'd mistaken his leg for part of the table. The seed had been planted then. It had germinated when they were joking about it. And the first blooms had opened when she'd talked about the heartache of her Moebius patient.

And then his lips had touched hers. And it had been wonderful and sweet and sexy and all the good things you associated with a kiss like that. Maybe it was even good that it had happened. Maybe they had gotten something out of their system that had been festering under the surface.

Festering. Ha! That was one way of looking at it. In reality, it hadn't *needed* to happen. But she couldn't quite make herself sorry that it had. Lucy had semi-fantasized about him from the day of that first meeting in the conference room when he spoke to her in Spanish. So now that she'd kissed him and she no longer needed to wonder what it would be like, she should be over it. It was a most excellent kiss. And she would no longer have to mull over the possibilities in her head.

So if Sam was at that surgery, she would be fine. So would he. And hopefully Devon would come out of the procedure with the assurance that he could run and play like other kids without ever having to worry that doing so would endanger his mobility. It would be a win for everyone. And as long as she kept thinking like that, everything would be great.

Just great.

CHAPTER SIX

HE'D INVITED HER, so why was Sam surprised to see her at eight o'clock sharp the next morning? Maybe because she'd only arrived five seconds before the procedure had started while he'd been there since Devon had gotten to the hospital.

Greg Asbury was very good at what he did, so Sam had no doubt that things would run well, unless something unforeseen came along. And he didn't see that happening.

There were several medical students already here, so while he nodded to Lucy, he didn't motion for her to come down to the front and join him. But she did anyway. He sensed her presence even before she actually sat in the chair, and he wasn't sure how he felt about that.

"Sorry I'm late," she murmured. "The commuter train was running behind."

Interesting. Why didn't he know she took the train? He couldn't remember if she'd actually told him where she lived.

He wasn't sure what that said about him that he could kiss a woman without knowing much about her.

Except he did. He'd read her eyes when she told him about her patient and those word bubbles on the white board, just like she'd read that young woman's eyes when she wrote them.

And that kiss had been…

Well, he hadn't quite found an adjective that would describe it. Or maybe he was just afraid to look for one.

No, that wasn't it at all.

So why hadn't *he* heard the people she said were there when he'd been kissing her? Had he been that caught up in what was going on that he'd blocked everything else out? Or had Lucy made them up as a way of getting out of telling him the truth—that she hadn't liked kissing him?

The hell she hadn't. Those fingertips pressed against his scalp told a different story. The way she'd held him against her as if afraid he would simply disappear. Those were the acts of someone who liked what was happening.

But it wasn't going to happen here. Or anywhere else for that matter. And he needed to keep his mind on Devon's surgery, or he would miss that too.

Greg kept up a running commentary as he went through each step. Opening the skin, going through the muscles, checking the vertebrae with methodical accuracy.

It looked to be intact and capable of protecting the cord once they were able to separate it from the structures holding it in place. That was getting ready to happen.

The neurosurgeon had told the family the mottling should subside once the spinal cord was no longer attached, although Devon would now have a scar in its place.

"Getting ready to free the cord."

Everyone held their breath as complete silence enveloped the room. Greg didn't play music while operating, unlike Sam, who liked to have the soft sounds of instrumental jazz in his surgical suite. Five seconds went by. Ten. Then Greg stood up straight and glanced up at the observation room and gave a thumbs-up. "It's free. And it looks good. This boy will be able to go back to playing T-ball and should have a normal life."

Excited murmurs went through the room as Greg went back to work finishing up the surgery. Sam felt a hand squeeze his for a single second, and then it was gone. Almost before he'd had a chance to register its presence. And when he looked down at Lucy, she acted like nothing had happened. Had he just imagined it?

No way. He knew her touch, although he had no idea how or why. But he liked that even after what had happened, she wasn't afraid to squeeze his hand in a friendly way. Maybe because that was what they had become. Friends? Or if they weren't exactly there yet, they were hopefully circling around that point looking for a place to land. Because friendship with her would be…better than the alternative, which was aloof colleagues who were there for the job and not much else.

Although hopefully the team would become close enough to be able to bat around ideas without involving egos or a sense of turf. They all needed to work together as one unit.

Kind of like that kiss? Where he and Lucy had become fused into one being?

Oh, hell.

He needed to stop this. Lucy stood, and he followed her up.

"I can't believe it was that simple. Not that it was really. But it was so fast. All that worry and now it's almost over. Once he heals, he'll be able to go on with his life." She sucked in a breath. "I'm hoping that for any and all patients who come through the facial-reanimation program too."

"There are a lot of us who think the same thing. Do you want to go talk to Greg?"

"I do. You?"

"I'd planned on it."

They went down and met Greg as he was coming out of the room. He'd already stripped off his gloves and hat, but his booties were still on his feet.

"Nice work," Sam said.

"Thanks. It's always good when it turns out to be pretty much as you imagined it would be. Nothing complicated. Thankfully the cord itself wasn't tangled up with the skin cells. We just need to let him heal and hope there are no post-op complications."

"You'll keep us updated?"

Greg glanced from him to Lucy. Sam gave a silent curse. He hadn't meant to make him and Lucy sound like a unit, but evidently the neurosurgeon had heard differently.

Fused. Wasn't that the term Sam had just used in his head?

Lucy smiled. "Thankfully Sam was down in PT the day Devon's shirt came off, revealing the mark."

Good save, Luce.

"Well, I'm glad you both saw it. Because even though the nerve cells hadn't grown through the skin, the skin could have become a stricture that could have later tightened or pulled against the cord, causing a tremendous amount of damage. The pain he felt in his back this last week gave evidence to that, as did the fact that the nerves in his feet were being affected."

"Which is why his mom noticed him tripping?"

"Exactly." Greg smiled at both of them. "I'd better head for the waiting room and let Mom know that things went well. See you both around. I'm hoping that our new department will start hopping soon."

"I have no doubt it will."

Greg stopped and turned to Lucy. "Oh, are you responsible for the dog puppet that Devon brought with him to the hospital?"

"You mean Spot?"

"Yes. That's the one."

Lucy looked a little unsure. "Yes, but I always sanitize them between patients, so…"

"No, it's not about that. He almost refused to have the surgery if Spot couldn't be there with him. I had to reassure him that the puppy would be right beside him when he woke up."

"Yikes. Sorry."

"Don't be. I think it's nice. And I already read the recovery team the riot act and told them to make sure the hound is there when he wakes up. I don't want a child calling me a liar." He laughed. "Okay, see you two later."

Greg left to do what he needed to do, leaving the two of them standing there. Sam smiled. "You and those puppets."

"What? The kids love them."

"That part is obvious." He paused. "You don't have patients this morning?"

"Not until after school. But it's not worth traveling back to Brooklyn only to have to turn around and come back in a few hours."

He frowned. "I'm sorry. I didn't realize you came in specifically for the surgery."

"Don't be sorry. I wouldn't have it any other way. I'll just grab some breakfast."

He thought for a minute. "Are you interested in making your breakfast a working one? I have a patient I'd like you to see, and then I could use some help running through a mock case file. When we do actually start getting more patients, I'd like to have a step-by-step chart that starts with the patient's referral and follows them all the way through to completion. It's hard to get all of us together, since we all work different schedules. I'll still get the other team members' input on it, but if you have time and wouldn't mind being a sounding board…"

And if she didn't want to? Then he'd have to respect her decision and would handle it on his own. Todd couldn't help him because he wasn't actually a doctor and some of the logistics would be out of his realm of expertise.

"Sure. It'll keep me from twiddling my thumbs down in my cubicle."

His brows went up. He wasn't sure how he felt about barely making it above the level of twiddling thumbs, but at this point he'd take what he could get. "Are you good seeing the patient first?"

"Yep."

Together they walked down the hallway. Abby Garner

needed one of the surgeries that would soon be done on a regular basis at the hospital. So as they walked he gave Lucy a rundown on what they were looking at. "How much do you know about nerve transplantation?"

"Some, from my studies in kinesiology."

"This patient is an adult, but she fits the bill of what we are looking to do in kids. Her facial nerve was damaged during surgery for a tumor on one of her salivary glands a few months ago. While the surgeon was hoping the function would come back as she healed, that's not been the case. And there's a window of about two years for us to do a masseter nerve–to–facial nerve transfer."

"Masseter nerve involves chewing, correct?"

"It does. With Abby, we're hoping to take one branch of the masseter nerve and graft it onto the part of the facial nerve that involves smiling."

"Ah, the smile surgery that we talked about earlier."

They stopped in front of the door. "Yes, exactly. I know you deal with children, but I'd like her to go through PT with you once she's a few weeks out of surgery, since you're on the team. It takes six months or so for us to really get a good picture of how successful the surgery will be. We'll be getting some advice from a sister hospital along the way."

"I'm excited to get started."

They went into the room. The patient was a twenty-one-year-old woman. Sam introduced them and then watched as Lucy talked to her and asked to examine her facial muscles.

Abby gave her permission, and Lucy went through a wide range of exercises designed to see where she stood as far as her facial muscles went. In fact, he was surprised at the way she deftly identified the muscles for each facial movement and decided which ones worked normally and which ones showed signs of impairment.

"Will you be able to fix it?" Abby spoke very slowly, each word seeming to take an enormous effort.

Lucy glanced at Sam, as if waiting for him to talk. He explained the procedure and what he hoped it would accomplish. "It'll require some patience on your part because nerves take a long time to heal and start firing again."

The patient nodded and pointed at Lucy rather than trying to talk again.

"Yes, I can help do your physical therapy, if you think we'd be a good match."

"Y-yes."

Sam gave the patient's shoulder a soft squeeze. "We'll need to go through your insurance company and get the surgery approved. Once that's done, we can schedule you and hopefully restore most of the function you've lost."

Abby nodded, but when he glanced at Lucy he saw she was frowning. Did she disagree with something he'd said?

Once they finished here, he'd ask her.

They spent a few more minutes with Sam explaining the procedure in more detail, using a video demonstration of how the transplant would be done. And then they said goodbye.

"I hope to see you in PT in the not-so-distant future." Lucy gave her a soft smile that made his stomach clench. She was good with her patients in a way that he never would be. He was much more direct, much more matter of fact. But Lucy dealt in hope. In hard work and effort. And in the PT world, all of that probably did make a difference. Hopefully it would for Abby and all of their future patients.

As they left the room, he glanced at her. "What's on your mind?"

She didn't ask what he was talking about. "What if insurance denies her the surgery?"

"There's always that chance. But we won't know if we don't try."

She shook her head. "She needs this surgery. I've never understood how anyone can say no. Isn't there a way around it?"

Was she thinking about the patient she'd mentioned from years earlier?

"There's always the ability to pay out of pocket, but most people can't afford it. But MMH is hoping to have grant money that will help fill in some of those gaps. And I'll be donating some of my time on some of these cases where we know finances are an issue."

She seemed to relax. "That makes me feel better."

"Let's just take it one step at a time and see where things go." He glanced at her. "Are you still up for helping me on the project? You can see from meeting Abby that we need to have a set of guidelines in place...and dealing with insurance companies is part of that process."

"Yes. I'd love to have a say in it. But can I run by the cafeteria first and grab a bite to eat?"

"Of course. Sorry—I should have thought of that."

She smiled, her nose crinkling. "Not a problem. Do you want me to bring you something from the cafeteria?"

"Maybe just a coffee?"

"Okay." She started to walk away before turning back to him. "Cream? Sugar?"

"One of each, if they have it."

"Got it. See you in a few." She walked away, and the gentle sway of her hips brought his attention to the pattern of her scrub top. It was the same parrot one she'd worn a couple of times. She must've really liked it.

He should too, because it bore the reminder to *repeat after me*. Something he'd been doing for the last week. Repeating over and over that he shouldn't kiss her again. No matter how much he might want to.

Lucy asked for her food to be put into a bag to make it easier to carry upstairs. Shoving their coffees into a drink carrier, she managed to balance the bagged breakfast on top of it and headed to the elevators.

Sam's brother, Logan, happened to be there as well and smiled when he saw her, glancing at her hands. "You must really like coffee."

"Actually one of them is for… Sam." She hesitated before adding his name. Then hurried to explain. "He's trying to make a protocol for our eventual facial-reanimation patients and asked for some input on it."

"I see."

Had her explanation made things better or worse? She wasn't sure, but if she kept trying to explain over and over she was going to come across as being in too much of a hurry to explain away something that had very little significance. Unless she made it seem like it did.

And that was the last thing she wanted to do. So she

just let it stand. Thankfully the door opened, and they both got on.

He pushed the button for the fourth floor, even though the neonatal department was housed within the maternity ward. But when she reached to push the floor for him, he shook his head. "I'm headed to Sam's office too. But I just need to tell him something quick, then I'll be on my way."

"Oh, don't hurry on account of me, okay? Sam and I can always do this later."

"Nope. He doesn't even know I was coming. I just wanted to give him the details on our dinner with our parents."

Oh, so he was going to have dinner with them after all? Sam had made it seem like he and his parents didn't get along all that well. Actually, she'd gotten that impression when his mom was at his office trying to get him to commit to coming over for dinner. Something he'd never actually done while she was standing there. Instead he'd put her off, saying she would call him.

"I'm glad to hear they were able to nail down a date."

Logan blinked. "A date?"

Ugh, he had no idea what she was talking about, and Lucy didn't really want to explain that this wasn't the first time that she'd been in Sam's office. Or make it sound like they'd discussed his personal life. They hadn't. Not really. She'd simply happened to be there during a very uncomfortable encounter between the two.

"Your mom happened to come by while Sam and I were discussing the new department."

That was the closest she wanted to come to admitting

that she knew anything about them. But the fact that she kept calling him Sam rather than Dr. Grant might be something he looked askance at too.

"Ahh, yes, he told me about that."

He had? What exactly had he said?

She couldn't think of anything to say, so chose to say nothing at all.

Logan glanced at her and then said, "He said she wanted him to come over for dinner and he hadn't given her a date. So Harper and I invited Sam to come over when our parents are going to be there. We figured it would make things easier on everyone. Harper is expecting a baby. And we really could use Sam there as a buffer. Or as a witness." He grinned in a way that looked very much like his brother's smile.

"Oh! Congratulations on the baby. I didn't know."

"Not everyone does. Thankfully Sam was gracious enough to agree to come. I just need to confirm the date and time. It'll only take a minute."

The elevator doors opened, and she stepped off, juggling the coffees and the bag as she pulled one of the hot drinks from the carrier. "I'll let you go in there first. This is his coffee, if you don't mind giving it to him."

"You don't have to wait outside."

"It's okay. I'd prefer it that way."

Logan looked a little bit confused, but he took the proffered cup. Lucy couldn't blame him. She was turning this into something weird, but she couldn't figure out a way to go back and undo anything she'd said. Not that she'd actually said anything that made it sound like they were meeting for personal reasons.

They weren't.

But he doubted that Sam had told his brother about that kiss either. So the last thing she wanted to do was be the one who let the cat out of the bag. Talk about making a big deal out of nothing. She was pretty sure she'd used those exact words with Sam and told him it was *not* a big deal.

Without saying anything else, she found the little waiting room that she'd sat in the day she'd exited the elevator and seen Sam cradling that baby.

Lucy dropped into a chair and put her breakfast on the seat next to her and bent over to cradle her own head in her hands. *Dios.* Why was she acting guilty about meeting him in his office?

Was it that she *felt* guilty? Because of that kiss?

She hoped not, because he'd made it clear that he wanted to put that behind them. And the fact that he'd asked her to help him to construct a template for future patients said he'd been able to do just that: put the kiss behind him. So why was she having a heck of a time doing the same? She had no idea, but she'd better put things back on a normal track, or Sam was going to figure it out and things would become super awkward between them. And she didn't want that.

A few seconds later, Logan went by and gave her a wave. "See? Done. He's all yours."

Lucy knew the man had no idea how that had just sounded. At least to her. All because of those crazy thoughts she kept having.

So she stood and went to his door, which was thankfully standing open, because she wasn't sure how she was going to knock on his door with her hands full.

Poking her head in, she saw he was looking at something on his phone. "Are you ready for me?"

He shut whatever app it was and held up his coffee. "Thanks for this. But you didn't have to stay in the waiting area. Logan didn't stay long."

"I know, but I kind of…" She crinkled her nose. "I kind of gave it away that your mom was here and that you hadn't given her a date for dinner."

He smiled. "Logan already knew about that. I told him. No big deal. Harper is expecting a baby, and he wanted me there when they told my parents."

"That's what he said. So you're going to be an uncle. Congratulations."

"Thanks. Better him than me, though."

She tilted her head. "You don't mean that. I saw you holding that baby the first day I came up here. You looked like a natural."

"That's only because I could hand her back over to her real mom."

"But surely someday…" Why was she interrogating him? Hadn't she gotten a kind of sick feeling in the pit of her stomach about babies after Matt had left? Maybe it was the same with Sam, since he'd broken up with his girlfriend.

"I think my dad will be a lot happier that Logan and Harper are the ones making them grandparents than the alternative."

"I'm sure he would be just as happy if it were you."

He looked at her for a minute. "You don't know my father. Well, anyway, shall we get started?"

"Yes. Of course."

She found her seat and saw that he had a big blank pad of paper on his desk with a permanent marker laid across the top of it.

Then he stood and picked up his coffee. "This will be easier if we're on the same side of the desk, so is it okay if I join you?"

"Of course." Lucy obviously hadn't thought this out clearly. Somehow she'd been picturing constructing a PowerPoint presentation, with him sitting on one side of the desk and her on the other.

As he sat in the chair next to her, the same warm scent of timber and earthy forest floors enveloped her, just as it had when they'd been in the observation room watching Devon's surgery. It was the same scent that had also curled around her senses when they'd kissed in that park a week ago.

And as it had this morning, it brought back memories that she'd been trying so hard to bury. Trying so hard to put behind her, like she had Matt. But for some reason this was proving much harder to do. But she needed to keep working at it. Maybe this meeting would give her a chance to do exactly that.

She tried to make a light moment of it. "Somehow I thought this was going to be a little more high-tech than pad and paper."

His head tilted. "Does that bother you? I always work better when I can actually write the words out rather than typing them on an app."

"I was thinking more along the lines of a PowerPoint."

He smiled. "I'm not quite that computer literate."

"Really?" She did presentations all the time. It was

a good teaching tool for her patients, and several times she'd sent parents home with a flash drive of instructions and suggestions for exercises. "I can write one up later, if you want."

"Are you serious? That would be great for when the team meets next. If you don't mind manning the computer as I talk my way through it."

She shrugged. "I would be happy to."

"I think it'll make Todd happy too. He's been after me to get him something in computer form. I was afraid I was going to end up sending him a big piece of paper with a graph drawn on it with lines leading here, there and everywhere."

Lucy crossed her legs, and her foot accidentally bumped against his shin. Memories of her foot trailing up his leg at the restaurant made her stutter out an apology. "Sorry. That was an accident, I swear."

A laugh came from the man next to her. "You have your share of accidents, don't you?"

She bit her lip. "Evidently I'm a magnet for them. Good thing I didn't go into neurosurgery."

His hand covered hers for a second. "I was kidding, Luce. I have no doubt that if you'd gone into neurosurgery, you would be as successful at that as you are at physical therapy."

A sense of relief went over her. She had had a lot of little slip ups when he was around. It had to be nerves. But at least he wasn't taking it as some kind of shortcoming on her part. "Thanks."

They got down to business, with both of them throwing out ideas and trying to decide where each step would fit on their chart. The insurance part of it was the most complicated because they had no doubt that some of those companies would automatically throw the procedures out, citing them as experimental, even though almost all of them had been around for a while in some form or another. So additional steps for the appeals process would need to be taken into account.

"Okay." Sam tore off the sheet they'd been working on. It was a mess of writing and scratch outs by now, and he set it on the desk next to a new clean sheet of paper. There were three other discards that were beneath that one. "Let's try to make some sense out of this."

"You're right. I have no idea how we would get this onto a PowerPoint without graphing it out on paper first."

He looked at her as if feigning surprise. "I think you're the first person who has ever spotted the genius behind my madness."

"I never used the word *genius*."

"But you know it's true, right?"

She bumped shoulders with him. "It's true that I never used the word *genius*."

The bump was returned. "Just give it time. You will."

This was really nice. Now that her nerves had settled down, they'd actually gotten quite a bit done. And she was surprised to find that they worked well together, even though they both saw things from a different point of view. Sam was definitely more task-oriented and was all about getting the job done, while Lucy took into account a patient's emotional state and was more about giving them time to process things. Of course, a lot of Sam's patients needed things to happen quickly, while her job saw recovery as more of a process that took time. But maybe that's what made it work so well. They complemented each other.

They hashed through the process one more time, and this time the sheet of paper only had one thing scratched through and one arrow that moved something to a different location.

Lucy glanced at her watch, surprised to find that it was almost one o'clock. "I have a patient coming in about an hour, so I probably need to get ready for her."

Sam stretched his arms up and over his head, giving a groan. "And I probably need to get out of this chair before I become glued to it." He glanced at the paper. "But I'm happy with this. You?"

"I think it's good. But I do think it would be good to have some more input on it."

He nodded. "Were you serious about putting it into PowerPoint form? Or can you not even figure out how to organize it?"

"I think we've done a good job of doing that. All that's needed is to plug it into the program. It's not that hard. I can work on it later this evening."

"No, don't. Give yourself a break. If you could get it to me by next Friday that would be soon enough. I can let Todd know it's coming."

"I'll definitely get it to you before then. How about Tuesday afternoon? We can go over it together, and you can make sure it looks how you expect it to."

"I am tied up the rest of the week with meetings. And Tuesday…" He seemed to think for a minute. "Well, that's the night Logan asked me to come over for dinner while they tell my parents. So maybe afterward…? I've been racking my brain for a way to get out of there within a two-hour time frame."

He sighed again. "But then that would mean that you'd have to sit around and twiddle your thumbs until I'm done. And we both know how much you like doing that."

She laughed, remembering their early conversation.

"I could wait in the car and serve as the getaway driver." A thought occurred to her. "Or I could come with you, if you don't think Logan and Harper would mind. But then again, that's kind of a personal time for them, and as an outsider—"

"I'm pretty damned sure they wouldn't mind." Sam seemed to leap on her idea with lightning speed. Had he already been thinking along these lines?

But whatever it was, it was too late for her to take back the idea. "Are you sure?"

"If you really don't mind? It would lend weight to the idea that I really do have a project that has a deadline. And I really don't want to get into a heated discussion with my dad, which seems to always happen when we're together."

"That bad, huh?" She'd never had to be someone's exit excuse before.

"It could be, although it's been a long time since I've had any kind of lengthy discussion with him. Then again, it might be fine. But I'd rather dip my toes into the water and then wade a little deeper each time I see him."

Ooh, she was no longer so sure her idea was a good one. Hadn't his mom already asked if Lucy was the one he'd gone to Uruguay with? But she saw that really he was struggling with going, and she'd been the one to suggest that he work on cleaning up the "bad water" that had gone under their bridge. So to renege on her offer didn't feel right either, since it was obvious he wanted to support Logan and Harper. "We don't have to pretend to be a couple, right?"

He seemed taken aback. "I would never ask you to do that."

"Sorry—I think I phrased that badly. I just don't want them to get the wrong idea about us."

"Logan knows we're just colleagues, and I'll let him know ahead of time. He said he wanted to use me as a buffer between them and Dad and even suggested I take a plus-one as a buffer for myself. I didn't think I needed one, but…maybe having an 'outsider' isn't such a bad idea. My parents are all about public image. And this is important to Logan and Harper. They've been through a lot. And I…"

"And you don't want to leave things with your dad for longer than necessary."

"How did you know?"

"It was more a suggestion than guessing your motives behind going." She shrugged. "None of us knows how much time we have on this earth, and I believe we should be at peace with everyone we can be. Unless there's been abuse or some other reason."

"No, nothing like that. As much as I hate to admit it, I do want to make my peace with him. If it's possible. And if it's not, I want to walk away knowing that I tried."

She smiled. "Exactly, Sam. What time are you supposed to be there?"

"Seven. They'll have dinner. Nothing fancy. No catering or employees."

Her eyes widened. "Why am I thinking that the opposite is the norm when it comes to your parents?"

"Because it is. But Harper wants to set a new tone with them and wants some boundaries set firmly in place when it comes to protecting her and Logan's relationship and for when the baby comes. But they'll do that after I leave. I already told Logan I probably wouldn't stay longer than dinner, and that works out for them as well. If things fall apart, then my parents will probably be leaving early as well."

"Oh, wow. I hope that's not the case."

"I hope not either. Thanks for offering to come. I'll try to make sure you're not subjected to anything that makes you uncomfortable. Just nudge me under the table."

"Do you want me to do that with my foot or…"

Sam laughed right on cue, and she was glad that she could make him feel a little bit better about something that was obviously hard for him. "It depends whether it's *my* leg or the table leg."

"Why, your leg, of course."

With that, they wound things up, and Sam pulled the sheet of paper off of the block and folded it before handing it to her. "Don't you want a copy of that first?" she asked.

"I trust you."

She sure hoped he wasn't misguided in that trust. And she hoped that when they were at Logan's house that she wasn't tempted to step in and play a part she had no business playing: that of Sam's *significant* other.

Because that wasn't what she was. And it wasn't what either of them wanted.

So why was she suddenly so very tempted to do exactly that?

CHAPTER SEVEN

OH, HELL, WHY ON earth had he agreed to go to Logan's tonight? And why was Lucy letting him drag her along with him? It really wasn't fair of him to expect her to come, even though she'd been the one to offer. But he couldn't imagine she was looking forward to it any more than he was. Although she'd texted him this morning and said that she'd finished the presentation and they could go over it after leaving the party.

Party? He doubted very much that tonight would be very festive, although he genuinely hoped that his mom and dad didn't make Harper sorry that she and Logan invited them into this part of their lives.

At least he could look forward to seeing what Lucy had accomplished with all their chicken scratch and know that the next big hurdle toward the official opening of the new department was going to be behind them. Todd had shared that they already had a couple of grants lined up that would pay for most of the new pieces of equipment that they would need. And they had arranged for a huge teaching hospital to fly over a few members of their own facial-reanimation team to come have a Q&A. Thankfully the center didn't see them as competition but rather a way to relieve their own workload that found patients stuck with hefty wait times.

Another few months and they should be where they needed to be. They might even be able to take a patient or two before that if the stars lined up right.

He glanced in the bathroom mirror, giving his hair a quick comb-through, trying to see what his dad would see when he looked at him. They'd barely spoken at the gala.

Sam already had some gray showing through his hair, and there were lines in his face that hadn't been there when he'd left for Uruguay two years ago. He'd also let some scruff grow on his face, which his dad had never been a fan of. On anyone.

But regardless of whether or not his dad approved of the way he looked or lived his life, Lucy was right. It was time. If things could be made right, he wanted to do so now before it was too late. Their sister couldn't make it tonight—she was working late—but promised to try to get together with the siblings another time. Sam wasn't worried about Sarah. They'd always gotten along.

He set the comb down and shrugged his way into the blue button-down shirt he'd planned on wearing with his jeans.

Lucy expected to meet him at the hospital at six thirty; she'd arranged to have her last patient come in a little earlier than normal so that she'd be done in time. He halfway hoped she'd be dressed in her parrot scrub top. It was his favorite.

And why did he even have a favorite piece of clothing for her?

It didn't matter. He'd already figured out how to introduce her. She was a colleague on his team, and they were working on a presentation that needed to be done by tomorrow morning. They'd decided to kill two birds with one stone, and Logan inviting him to dinner had been perfect timing. He didn't really care if they bought the explanation or not. It was true enough, and if they chose to believe something else? Not his problem.

But then again, he'd promised Lucy that he'd make sure no one thought they were a couple, so he needed to smack down any stray questions or comments that his mom or dad made that looked like they were leaning in that direction. There was no need to put her in the middle of anything.

He went out to where he'd parked his car and was able to make it to the hospital by six thirty sharp. Lucy was already waiting out front and slid into the passenger seat. She wasn't wearing her parrot scrubs but rather was dressed in a white ribbed tank top over a flared black skirt. She looked cool and comfortable yet elegant. She glanced at him, her lips twisting as if needing to tell him something but not sure how. Maybe she was going to back out on him.

"Second thoughts?" he asked.

"Not about coming tonight, but there's been a slight hiccup. I know you wanted to work on the presentation tonight. But after I got to MMH tonight, I remembered that I need to move my car. The street sweepers will be there in the morning, and if I leave it too long, there won't be a spot available. Would you mind taking me home after we leave Logan's?" She took a breath. "We can work on the finalization at my house, since it probably won't take too long. I just want you to make sure I haven't forgotten anything."

That was what she was worried about? That was an easy one. "That's fine. It'll even play into our reason for needing to leave early. You're in Brooklyn, right?"

Sam knew that the street sweepers were a big thing in a lot of the neighborhoods with cars needing to be moved in anticipation of them coming. They were programmed for different days, and it was always a hassle for everyone—the city workers included.

"Yes. Thank you. I really appreciate it."

"If you want you can just send me the presentation, if you don't feel like working that late."

"I'd rather you look it over before I send it to you, since you don't know how to work the program. That way it's done and dusted, and you can just forward it to Todd."

"Are you sure?"

"I am. You'll be doing me a favor anyway because I won't need to catch the train back to Brooklyn tonight."

"As if it'll be any faster to drive." He sent her a smile to let her know that he was kidding, although not about the traffic. "You're doing me an even bigger favor in coming to dinner. Are you sure you don't want to back out?"

"I'm sure. How about you?"

"Hell, I never wanted to go in the first place. But I love my brother, so I'll see it through." He held up a bottle that sat between their seats. "I did bring wine, though. I figured we all might need it."

Lucy bit her lip.

"What?" he asked.

"Harper probably can't drink any of it. With the pregnancy and all."

"Damn. Of course she can't."

"It's not a big deal. They might want to serve it to your parents, or they can save it for a later date."

He shook his head. "I think maybe we'll just have a glass at your house while we're working on the presentation. Unless you don't drink either."

"Oh, I drink, all right." She laughed. "Okay, so that came out a little too enthusiastic, so let me try again. I only drink in moderation."

"Such a sensible answer. But since I'm driving, I'm the one who'll be watching what I drink."

They pulled up to Logan and Harper's place right at seven. Which was good because they wouldn't need to sit around trying to think of small talk, since his parents would undoubtedly already be there. They were always fashionably early to everything. Not too early, though. No one wanted to seem too eager.

He found a spot to park and glanced over at Lucy. "It's not too late to back out."

"Yes, it is. Even if it weren't, though, we'd still go in. This will be good, Sam. Hopefully it'll be a new start for you and your dad."

"Always the optimist. It's what I like about you." He squeezed her hand, more for his own sake than hers. "Let's go."

Lucy was not at all nervous, surprisingly, as Harper opened the door and greeted them. "So glad you guys could come." She chuckled. "And I mean *really* glad."

"They're already here?"

"Yep. Arrived about a half hour ago. We've sat around mainly sizing each other up and trying to find small talk topics that haven't already been covered. I didn't think this would be so hard. Although Logan has been wonderful. He hasn't left my side. Well, at least until the doorbell rang."

She ushered them inside.

"Congratulations again, by the way," Lucy whispered.

Harper took her hand and gave it a squeeze, much like Sam had done a few minutes ago. "Thanks. Wish us luck when we share the news."

"Consider it wished."

Sam hadn't said anything so far, but when she glanced up at him she saw that his jaw was so tight it looked ready to break.

She pressed her arm to his. "It's going to be okay, Sam. It's only one point in time. Just remember that. No matter how uncomfortable things might get, it's only a small blip in a lifetime of experiences."

He visibly relaxed. "Thanks, Luce. I needed to hear that."

They went into the room. The woman who'd come by Sam's office a month ago stood and came over to them, kissing Sam on the cheek and then giving her a perfunctory hug. "Nice to see you again."

The embrace might have been stiff, but her words were not as chilly as they'd been the last time they'd met. Or maybe it was Lucy's imagination. Sam had pegged her right when he'd said she was an optimist. She always tried to see the best in people. And although Matt had sent her into a tailspin and made everything dark and hopeless looking, her sister had been the one to give her the advice about this only being one point in time and that it wasn't forever. That had meant so much to her that she'd felt she needed to tell Sam the same thing.

It seemed to work.

Biddie went back over to sit with her husband, and Lucy whispered up to Sam, "Consider this nudge number one. Take me over there and introduce me to him."

He took a visible breath before heading toward the man who was sitting on the sofa, his back ramrod straight, although he was thinner than Lucy had somehow pictured him. But the aura he gave off was one of power. She imagined he cowed a whole lot of people. But Lucy wasn't one of them. Ah... Sam wasn't either, which was why they'd probably butted heads over the years. The realization came to her in a flash.

Sam stopped in front of his father, who didn't stand to greet them. Lucy instinctively lifted her chin and prepared for battle. Then belatedly, the man did actually rise from his seat. "How was Uruguay? I didn't get a chance to ask you at the fundraiser."

"It was fine, Dad." He nodded toward her. "This is a coworker from the hospital, Lucy Galeano. We're working on the planning for a new department. Lucy, this is my dad, Carter Grant."

Carter held out his hand, and his grip was firm but not a death squeeze, which she'd been halfway expecting.

"Nice to meet you," she murmured. "I met your wife a few weeks ago at the hospital."

Logan appeared from the kitchen and came over. "Dinner is ready. Everything is in the kitchen, we're doing this buffet style—as in everyone will serve themselves."

If Biddie or Carter seemed surprised by that, they hid it well. And suddenly she realized that was how they were. Even if they hated something, she doubted anyone would realize it. At least not right away. Those cuts would, instead, come in a million subtle ways. And that had to have made it hard on their kids. Carter had made no effort to shake Sam's hand or fold him into an embrace the way her own father would have done if he'd had a son. That didn't make him necessarily a bad man but maybe one who felt a need to protect himself.

Sam did that too, even though he probably didn't realize it.

They followed Logan and Harper into a large kitchen area. "It smells wonderful in here," Lucy said.

Harper came over and looped her arm through hers. "I knew I was going to like you. I'm just now starting to like the smell of food again." Her voice was soft—only meant for Lucy. "The last time I saw Sam, he told me how much you were helping with the new program."

Lucy smiled. "I really haven't done all that much. But we are trying to get a presentation ready for tomorrow. So I'm sorry we have to run out on you early."

She slid that in, lifting the level of her voice enough for Biddie and Carter to hopefully hear the apology.

Harper nodded. "Sam told us. We do appreciate you coming anyway, though."

Then she went to the head of what looked to be a long line of food to join Logan.

He named the dishes and motioned to the plates and

cutlery near the front. He then smiled. "There are no as-signed seats at the table, so sit anywhere you want."

Lucy heard Sam chuckle under his breath, and she glanced over and whispered, "I take it that's not the way things were done when you were kids."

"Nope. But I'm glad Logan is setting the standard, and I know him well enough to know he'll stick to it, whether Dad likes it or not."

"Mom and Dad, why don't you go first." Logan came back and led the pair to the front of the line. And there was no way you would have known that Biddie and Carter hadn't done this a million times before. Although they probably had, since they undoubtedly attended a lot of charitable functions, some of them probably serving buf-fet dinners much like this one.

They made it through the line, and then Harper mo-tioned for her and Sam to go ahead. As Lucy picked up her plate, she murmured to her, "Is there anything I can do to help?"

Harper smiled. "Just be you. That's what will help."

That surprised her. Lucy knew of Harper, but she didn't really *know* her. And since the couple both worked with neonates, they didn't really deal with the population segment that frequented Lucy's cubicle over in PT. But hospitals were huge gossip mills, so maybe they'd heard things about her. Hopefully good things.

Once everyone had their plates, they started eating. Carter turned to Sam and said, "Tell me about this new venture you're heading at the hospital."

As soon as she heard the words, Lucy knew they would set the wrong tone with Sam. He would not see this as a venture but as a mission. She used her knee to nudge him under the table. One side of his mouth went up, saying he'd felt the slight pressure and it had struck him as humorous.

"We're hoping to help people who are unable to show emotion."

¡Dios! Lucy had just taken a drink of water and it went down the wrong pipe, and she started coughing into her elbow. Loudly. When she glanced at Harper, horrified and trying to stop the spasms before they came to the surface, she found that the other woman was dabbing her mouth with a napkin, trying to hide her own smile.

Had Sam said that on purpose?

Lucy gained control of herself and added, "It's kind of a fascinating field. It's for people who've had something affect some of the nerves of their face, leaving those muscles paralyzed. Some are unable to smile or even move their eyes. Sam will be heading a department that will transplant muscles and nerves that will help change that."

Biddie smiled, maybe trying to show that her own muscles weren't actually impaired. "That does sound fascinating. I never knew such a thing existed."

Sam seemed to catch on to what he should be doing and expanded on the field, trying to use terms that laymen could understand. "We're hoping it will be up and running a few months from now."

"Are you looking for grant money?" Carter asked the question, and no one said anything for several long seconds. Sam had hinted that Carter probably wouldn't want to fund a program that he was involved with. But Lucy wasn't getting that vibe. Still, she was pretty sure that Sam would be leery of any money that came from Carter's own coffers.

"We've already gotten quite a bit of funding with more being pledged daily."

Parry and feint. A decent strategy on Sam's part. He wasn't saying that they couldn't use the funding while at the same time making sure that Carter knew he hadn't come here to ask for money.

The man nodded. "I saw the press release. I always thought Todd Wells was the right man to lead Manhattan Memorial."

Lucy was pretty sure that was a roundabout way of paying the hospital a compliment for being forward thinking. She crossed her fingers under the table.

"I love the pediatric oncology department. Those kids are the sweetest." Biddie seemed to follow Carter's lead. And the woman probably really did love those kids, since Sam said she went once a week to do a book reading for them. She could always find other charities that had fewer heartbreaking stories. For her to keep going week after week was a testament to an inner strength that Lucy wondered if her son saw.

They talked for a few more minutes about the new department as everyone finished their meal, and then Logan got up and brought in dessert. "I know how much Mom likes flan, so we made this especially for her."

"Oh!" Biddie's smile seemed to widen. "I do love it. Thank you."

Logan served wedges of the dessert onto small plates and served Harper last, bending down to kiss her on the mouth. Then he looked at the group. "Before we start eating, and because I know that Sam and Lucy have to leave soon to finish a project, I have some news to share with all of you." He motioned Harper to stand with him. She did, looping her arms around his waist and gazing up at him. He glanced down at her. "Actually, I'm going to let Harper tell you."

"Okay." Harper lifted up her dessert plate and untaped something from beneath it. When she unfolded it and held it up for everyone to see, there was another period of silence at the table as everyone looked at the unmistakable image on the sheet of paper.

"Do you mean…" Biddie's tentative voice faded away, and her hand went to her mouth.

Harper nodded. "Logan and I are expecting a baby."

"I'm going to be a grandmother?"

"You are."

Biddie threw her napkin onto the table and got up from her spot, coming around to hug Harper, squeezing tight. When Lucy glanced over at Logan, she saw his mouth was open as if he couldn't quite believe what he was seeing.

Evidently this hadn't been a normal mode of expressing joy in their household. Harper glanced over at Logan, then her arms went around the older woman, a sheen of what looked like tears in her eyes. Lucy had heard that babies could be a source of healing, and she believed it. When she'd seen Sam cradling the infant he'd operated on a few weeks ago, it had done something to Lucy's insides. It had basically turned them to mush.

Not wanting to let on that she and Sam already knew the news, Lucy got up and went over to hug first Logan and then Harper. Sam followed suit, and there were a lot of words of congratulations. The only one who hadn't said anything was Carter, and when she glanced at him, he seemed perfectly stoic, sitting all alone like a statue that was cemented in place.

Then the man with whom Sam had had such conflict over the years suddenly looked over at his wife and his eyes rolled back in his head before falling sideways out of his chair, landing on the floor with a loud thud.

Sam was the first to his father's side, taking his pulse. Lucy came over with her phone turned to the flashlight function, and he had her flick it back and forth across the man's pupils as Sam pushed his lids open.

"Pulse is good, if just a little bit fast, and pupils are equal and reactive. I think we should call a squad because of his cardiac history, but I think... I think maybe he just fainted."

"Fainted? Carter has never fainted in his life." Biddie's voice shook.

"I know. Logan is already calling the squad. He'll get great care."

Two hours later, dessert forgotten, everyone—including Sarah, who'd rushed over from her office at the family firm—was gathered in a waiting area at the hospital, hoping for some news. Greg Asbury happened to be there late winding up some paperwork and came down to examine him. He appeared in the doorway, and the family all stood up. Biddie was twisting her fingers and kept pressing tissues to her eyes although she'd never actually sobbed out loud. Still, Sam sensed she was worried in a way he'd never known her to be.

Greg slid into a chair and waited for everyone to sit back down. Hell, had his dad died? He remembered Lucy's words about no one knowing how much time anyone had left and that he should work on clearing the air.

Had he actually succeeded in doing that at all?

Logan finally broke the silence. "How is he?"

The neurosurgeon actually smiled. "You mean besides being angry as hell about us poking and prodding him? Not that you can tell much of anything from his stony silence."

Sarah actually laughed. "Sounds like Dad."

Yes, it did. Sam had no doubt death would only take his dad by dragging him bodily into the other realm.

"Seriously, though. As far as I can tell he's fine. His MRI came back clean, as did his other tests. The stents are holding. And his gray matter looks good. No signs of a transient ischemic attack."

"So what happened to him?" Sarah asked.

"I think Sam was right—he simply fainted when you told him the news." Greg smiled again. "Congratulations again, by the way. I'd like to keep him overnight for observation, but I doubt very much that he'll let us, so if you'll agree to keep an eye on him and call us at the first sign of trouble, I'll get his discharge papers started."

"Thank God." The words were soft but unmistakable. His mom continued. "I'll take him home. Between me and our housekeeper, we'll keep watch over him tonight."

"I'll spend the night too, if that's okay, Mom." Sarah went over and put an arm around her mother's shoulders, giving her a gentle squeeze. "I'll let everyone know how he is in the morning."

Greg slapped his palms on his knees and stood. "That sounds like a good plan to me. We'll have him out as soon as we can. Be ready for some general grumpiness."

"Truer words were never spoken," said Logan, hugging Harper. "Are you okay?"

"Yes. I'm just glad he's okay. And you know what? I think everything else will be as well."

Logan glanced over at them. "Damn, you two needed to leave, didn't you?"

"It's okay." Lucy sat in a chair, where she'd been ever since they arrived at the hospital. She hadn't said much, but this had to be awkward for her. She hadn't signed up for being roped into a family emergency.

Sam stood. It was after ten. Again. He seemed to be making a habit of getting her home late. "Let's get you back to Brooklyn. We can work on the project tomorrow. I know you've got to move your car."

When all eyes turned to her, Lucy gave a half grin. "Street-sweeper day tomorrow."

There were a couple of groans, saying people knew exactly what she was talking about. "How hard is it going to be for you to find a parking place?" Harper asked.

She shrugged. "It'll be okay."

Or maybe it wouldn't. He thought of something but decided to wait until they got in the car to share it with her.

A few minutes later they were on their way.

"How about if we get your car and bring it back to my place?"

Shock rolled through Lucy's system. "What?" She had to have misunderstood his words.

"Just hear me out. It's going to be almost impossible for you to park at this time of night. By the time we get there it'll be almost eleven. I have two bedrooms. We can pick up some of your things, and you can follow me back."

"I can't put you out like that." But even as she said it, she had to admit it sounded better than circling the block for hours or having to double park, which was always an iffy prospect. This was what she got for having a place that only had street parking. And her parents didn't have any extra spots in front of theirs, since Bella shared the space with them and had a car of her own.

"You won't be putting me out. Besides, I was the one who asked you to come tonight. It's the least I can do."

It sounded harmless enough, and she was pretty exhausted. "You have an extra parking space?"

"My apartment is assigned two spots, so yes. It'll be fine. The place came furnished, so there's actually a bed in the second bedroom, which I couldn't promise if I'd had to furnish it."

"Okay. But only if you're sure."

"I am. If you don't have to be at work right away, we can get up in the morning and go over the presentation and send it off to Todd. No one will ever know that you spent the night. Not even my family."

Relief washed over her. She really hadn't wanted his family to get the wrong idea, and telling them that she was spending the night was sure to send a couple of stray thoughts winging through their synapses. It was human nature.

"Thanks. And I'm so glad your dad is going to be okay."

"Me too." He glanced over as they made their way to

Brooklyn. "Thank you for everything tonight. For the advice and for coming with me."

"Not a problem."

The next half hour was spent in silence, and when they pulled up in front of her house, she noted that hers was one of the only vehicles still on this side of the road. Most people had been smart enough to move theirs hours ago. "That'll teach me not to leave a spare key with my family. I'll just be a minute."

She ran in and gathered a few necessities and her computer, putting an extra flash drive in the bag she carried the device in. Then she ran back out the door and got into her car, texting her mom really quick and letting her know she'd be spending the night in Manhattan with a friend. Otherwise she would worry.

I'll send another text when I get there.

Her mom sent a text back.

Okay. Have fun.

She didn't even ask if it was a male friend or a female friend. Maybe because she'd been so devastated over the breakup with Matt that she would have never guessed that Lucy had actually kissed another man.

And liked it.

She then texted Sam.

I'm ready whenever you are.

He answered by flicking his brights on and off and then pulled into the street, waiting until she was behind him before setting off and heading back to Manhattan.

CHAPTER EIGHT

IT WAS AFTER midnight when they finally arrived back at his apartment complex. He'd texted Lucy his address before they left in case he lost her, but she'd stuck to him like glue, pulling several almost crazy moves to keep up with him. He eased his vehicle into the 2101 A parking place and waited for her to take the 2101 B spot. He'd never actually thought he'd need the second one, but he'd wanted an extra bedroom just in case he had a guest or wanted to convert it into an office or workout space. But the truth was he wasn't actually here enough to do that, pretty much just coming home to sleep and going back to work the next day.

And as for having company? He never had. He wasn't even sure if the bed had sheets on it, although the apartment had come with several sets of linens.

He got out of the car and waited for Lucy, taking her two bags, one a gym bag that probably held a change of clothes and the other a computer case. "I have a laptop, you know."

"I figured, but I know mine's quirks and the Power-Point version that I like the best is on it." She yawned. "I have to admit I was having trouble staying awake the last several miles."

"I'm sorry. I should have thought to send you home on a train rather than dragging you with me to the hospital."

"No. I wanted to be there. I'm just so glad he's okay. It was worth a little loss of sleep."

"I can't believe he fainted. I've never known my dad to show any weakness outside of his infarction a few years back. Even then, Logan had a hell of a time trying to convince him that he needed to get stents."

"I'm sure he's mad that he did. That's probably what Greg was seeing. Anger at himself rather than at anyone at the hospital. And that was a pretty big piece of news. If he was trying to contain his emotions by holding his breath, it could have slowed his heart rate enough to send him into bradycardia. Kind of like a child who holds his breath, then faints and then starts breathing normally again."

"Greg knows my dad pretty well and pulled me aside after talking to the family. That was his hunch as well—that temporary bradycardia caused him to faint."

"I can't help but think your parents are ecstatic about the baby. Hopefully it will soften your dad's heart a little bit. Raising kids is stressful and not everyone gets it right all the time. But grandkids? From what I've heard, that's when people have the most fun because they can enjoy those little ones without the strain of discipline and all of the things that go with parenting."

"Not disciplining? That sounds like torture for my dad." But he laughed as he said it.

They reached his apartment, and he used a keypad to let himself in. His place wasn't super fancy, but it did what he needed it to do. Sam had never had a need for the things that wealth brought. He lived for his work. It was where he was the happiest. Priscilla would probably never understand that. And since living the way the other preferred to would only lead to a life of misery for one or both of them, he'd broken things off. The cursing she'd done in Spanish when he had hadn't been nearly as cute as Lucy's had been that day in the conference room. But then again, it hadn't been aimed at him either. She would be fine. From what it looked like, her modeling career would soon eclipse her career in medicine. And it would bring her everything she wanted out of life.

Lucy, on the other hand, seemed to love what she did for a living. And from her comments about the contract, she wasn't worried about the money aspect of it any more than he was.

And that was something he didn't want to look too closely at.

She was right about being tired. He was feeling the effects of the long day and the stress of spending time with his parents. Anything he might've been thinking right now was the result of that. So he needed to save things that needed methodical and rational consideration for morning.

"I think you're probably right about the grandkids. But as for softening my dad? I guess time will tell. He'll have to learn a whole new way of dealing with people and kids for it to work, though. After everything Logan and Harper have been through, I know my brother isn't going to take any crap from him this time around. And I don't blame him."

"And are you going to take any crap from him?"

"I think I got most of that out of my system when I was fifteen." He took her stuff to the second bedroom and set it on the bed. "I sure hope there are sheets on this thing."

Lucy pulled the covers away from the pillows and revealed pillowcases and sheets that looked clean and crisp. "They probably changed these right before you moved in."

"If you say so." He glanced at a closet in the hallway. "Looks like there are some spares in here if you want me to change them out."

"It's fine. It's not like you've lived here that long." She glanced at him before sitting on the edge of the bed. "You were saying something about getting it out of your system when you were fifteen?"

He shook his head. "It doesn't matter." The last thing she needed to hear when she was tired was the stupid stuff he'd done when he was younger.

"No, really. I want to know what you did. Go to wild parties? Get someone pregnant?"

What would have happened if Priscilla had wound up pregnant when they were together? Not something he wanted to even contemplate.

"Nothing like that." He paused. "I actually got arrested while at a protest march."

"Arrested. Seriously? When you were fifteen?" She actually looked shocked. "What kind of march was it?"

He made a clicking sound with his tongue. "Yeah…it was about real weighty stuff."

Her eyes widened. "World peace? Wars? Politics?"

"Homework."

There wasn't a sound for about fifteen seconds, and

then she started laughing. The sound started low and grew until she was gasping for breath. He was afraid for a second that she might pass out herself. He sat down beside her.

"You're lying." Her breathing was still ragged.

He held up a hand, three fingers raised. "I swear. A bunch of schools participated, skipping class and going to a park—Pirius Park, actually—to protest the homework load we were getting. Of course, several schools being there meant that rival football teams eventually met up and some fights ensued, and well…the police showed up and handcuffed anyone they could catch. Me included. My dad was not happy. At all. But you know what? He never raised his voice to me and only grounded me for a week. But he did turn the screws and try to guilt me into coming to work for his company."

"Okay, wow. You've got me beat on the teenage rebellion. I never got arrested. Mine was much milder, and I was seventeen at the time."

This he had to hear. "What did you do, Lucy?"

"I got this." She twisted on the bed and pulled the top of her tank top aside and revealed ink.

His brows went up, and he leaned in to get a closer look. It was a black line tattoo on her left shoulder. About an inch and a half square, it was the image of a tiny bunny sitting up on its haunches holding a piece of clover. His finger touched it. "Cute. Was there an occasion?"

"I got it for my sister." She shrugged the shoulder. "I'm not even sure why. She never asked me to. But there was just this sense of need inside of me when I saw it in the window of a tattoo parlor. I couldn't resist. And I love it. I don't regret getting it done."

"I like your rebellion a hell of a lot better than mine." He could definitely relate to the sense of need that couldn't be resisted. "Did you get in trouble?"

"No. My dad is against tattoos, but he never said anything. And my mom said she liked it. But not to do it again." Lucy laughed and looked up at him, her eyes soft and dreamy. "Have you ever done anything you liked but shouldn't do again?"

He swallowed before answering. "I have. Not too long ago, actually."

"Mmm… Yeah. Me too."

His eyes swept over her tattoo again. She might have been telling the truth about her reasons for getting it, but when he looked at the tattoo, he saw her in the figure. The bunny was cute and perky and full of vibrant hope. Just like Lucy. He envied her for being able to be like that. Sam had always felt like he had a dark undercurrent that never quite went away no matter what he did.

"I like this." His fingers brushed across it again. "It fits you."

Before he could stop himself he leaned over and kissed it. He'd meant to touch it and leave, but her skin was soft and clean, and the scent coming off of her was like the freshest of meadows. Just like the place the bunny in her tattoo might inhabit.

Her head tilted forward and she moved her long hair to the side as if opening the site up for his exploration. But he didn't dare. Because if he did, he might not stop.

"Luce." The word was muttered an inch away from

her skin, helpless to move, as if he were tethered there by an unseen string.

She lifted her hand, her palm cradling the back of his head. "I like *that*."

There was no question about what she meant. "Are you sure?"

She gave a husky laugh. "It isn't just teenagers who rebel. Sometimes adults need to visit dangerous places too."

Nerve endings all across his body prickled to life.

"Is this a dangerous place?" He kissed the tattoo again.

"Not even warm."

God, her voice. How could a simple change in tone drive him crazy? But it did.

"How about here?" He kissed the nape of her neck, letting his lips trail to a shadowed spot behind her ear.

"Warmer. So, so warm."

He bit the edge of her ear, nibbling his way to the lobe, taking it and the small glittering diamond that sat on it into his mouth.

"Ahh…" The sound was thick, and he recognized the need in it because he was feeling it too.

"Warmer?"

"Much."

He moved to the edge of her mouth and kissed the corner of it. "And here. Is this warmer?"

"No, Sam, that is hot. And I want it now." She turned her head, and this time it was her kissing him with a fervor that drove his body into high gear, and they'd barely even begun to explore each other. But they would. He just had to hold on long enough to get the job done.

Job? Oh, hell no. This wasn't work. This was pure un-adulterated pleasure.

Or maybe it was adulterated. No. Wrong word. He was looking for the word *adultery*. No, that was wrong too. Neither of them was married. Neither of them had any entanglements. They were both free to do whatever they wanted. For however long they desired.

And damn if Sam didn't want to do it for a long, long time.

He pressed her back onto the mattress and pulled the stretchy material of her top away from her shoulder, pressing his mouth to the side of her neck and applying gentle suction. What was a little rebellion? He needed it.

As if answering him, she arched her back and pressed into his mouth. "Yes!"

Sam sucked harder, and she gasped, hands coming up and holding him against her neck, sending a tremendous need over him.

He rose up and grabbed his shirt, going to haul it over his head, only to realize it was buttoned and not his normal polo shirt. "Damn!"

Her eyes opened, and she looked at what he was doing before pushing his hands away. "Let me." She sat up, his thighs straddling her hips, and reached up, undoing his buttons one at a time.

He touched her neck, realizing the redness there was caused by him. "I left a mark."

"Yes. You did." Her smile was the sexiest thing he had ever seen.

Then her hands were pushing the shirt down his arms and helping him shrug out of it. She might not care about the mark now, but she would when they eventually had to leave this room. But he could worry about that later.

Any hint of tiredness had vanished, and in its place was a need he'd never felt before. Lucy was gorgeous and sexy and everything that was good in a person, and for tonight, she was his.

And if you want more than tonight?

He swiped the thought away, admonishing himself to stay in the here and now.

Here and now was exactly where he wanted to be. Here with this woman and now, in this moment.

It was good enough. It would have to be because he couldn't ask for any more than that.

Her fingers traced over his pecs and across his nipples, sending a shudder over him. But she didn't pause, just went down his sides, her short nails adding an extra layer of texture to the already heady sensation. She hit a ticklish spot on his ribs and his skin rippled, but he'd never felt less like laughing than he did right now because the tickle was mixed with a sensuality that swept everything else to the side.

His hands went to her sides and gripped her, even though he was pretty sure she wasn't going to slip away into the night, but he needed to touch her—to hold her—to make himself believe that she was really here with him.

He took hold of the bottom of her white tank top, marveling in the contrast between it and the deep tan of her skin, and slid it up, missing the feel of her hands on his skin as she helped him get the garment over her head. He tossed it to where his crumpled shirt lay on the floor.

Her nude bra, lacy enough to show glimpses of her

breasts, drew his hands, and he curved his palms over the soft flesh. Lucy's nipples were tight and pushed into his flesh, and the need to get her bra off came fast and hard. He undid the hooks in back and then flung the undergarment away.

This woman had everything a man could want, and he took a moment to gaze at her before smoothing her hair back from her face and looking into her eyes. "You are so beautiful. Do you know that?"

She smiled. "So are you. You're a walking advertisement for plastic surgery."

That scraped across a raw spot no one could see. His dad had ridiculed him for going into his field.

Lucy sat up straighter and peered at him. "What?"

"Nothing."

She cupped his face. "Hey. I didn't mean that in a bad way. You're just gorgeous. And I can't think of a way to say it that will adequately get that across."

He relaxed. "Same here." He leaned over and kissed her forehead and then pressed his brow against it. Why was he picking apart her words rather than making love to her?

He didn't know, but that stopped now. He stood, and then as she watched, he undid his jeans and slid out of them, taking his briefs down with them. Then his shoes and socks followed.

"Wow." She blinked, but her eyes were not on his face but on his…

That made him laugh. "Want to play footsie with me again?"

She licked her lips. "I just might. But I wouldn't be using my foot."

His flesh jerked and she moved closer, but he shook his head. "Not this time." Then he scooped her off the bed and pivoted so that the back of his knees were against the mattress. He lowered himself onto it. "I have other ideas."

Sam settled her onto him so that she was doing what he'd done earlier, straddling his thighs. He bunched her skirt and settled her on him so that his erection was tight against her. It was heaven on earth. "Can you reach my nightstand drawer?"

Her head twisted to look. "I think so." She leaned over, needing to go back up on her knees to get to the pull. She slid it open and reached inside. "Looking for these?"

"Yes." He held his hand out for the unopened box of condoms, but she shook her head.

"I don't think you've earned the right to these yet."

He laughed. "Earned the right?"

"You heard me." She set the box on the bed and then, still up on her knees, she came back in front of him and looked down at him, her fingers tracing his temples, his nose and then trailing down to his mouth.

Her breasts were right in front of him, and he realized what she wanted. And he was more than happy to oblige. Splaying his hands on her back, he used gentle pressure to move her forward, kissing between the soft mounds and working his way over the top of the first one, without ever touching her nipple. When he started to do the same with her other breast, she made a sound.

"What?" he said. "I'm earning my keep."

Her fingers buried themselves in his hair. "You're really not."

"Then show me." His brows went up in challenge.

She drew his head to her body in a way that left no doubt as to what she wanted. Finally. He took her nipple in his mouth and used his tongue to slide over the tight skin before suckling it, holding her in place with light pressure from his teeth.

"Dios. ¡Sí! ¡Así!"

The Spanish words telling him to do it "just like that" crashed into him like a wave—big and powerful and stripping any willpower he had left.

He reached for the box and made quick work out of opening it and sheathing himself. When she went to climb off of him as if to finish undressing, he grabbed her hips. "No. Just come here."

She settled back on top of him while he kissed her neck, her chin, her eyes and finally took her mouth, his tongue thrusting deep and mimicking what his body was about to do. His arm went around her hips and jerked them forward until he was gripped between his stomach and hers, reveling in the pressure and knowing better things were soon to come. He kept kissing her, even as his hands on her hips guided her up until he found the elastic of her panties and slid them aside, finding a moist heat that drove his mind into a frenzy of want and need. Pulling her back to him, he drew her down, found her in a single attempt and thrust upward, even as he settled her fully onto him.

He closed his eyes and absorbed the sensation, not daring to move, and holding her in place so she didn't either.

"Damn. It's so good. So, so good." His muttered words against her mouth were all he could manage as they poised precariously on the edge of a cliff. A cliff of firsts that, once fallen off of, could never be revisited. He never wanted to forget this moment.

"Yes, it is." Her mouth reached for his. "But I want more, Sam. I *need* more."

The words tickled at a place in his subconscious, but he ignored it, knowing she hadn't meant her words that way.

He gave her what she wanted, easing his grip on her hips and helping her move on him. The ripples of pleasure were indescribable as her body slid up and away from him before returning time and time again as if sating a deep need. Each pump brought a greater craving that he soon would be powerless to resist.

Up and down. Engulfing him fully and then up until only the tip had contact. God. It was the portals of heaven coming down to where he was.

Lucy's arms wrapped around his neck and head as she rose and fell, her tempo increasing, raising the level of his insanity. She muttered words in Spanish that he no longer tried to translate. He was powerless to. Powerless to do anything else but hang on and let her do what she wanted, to let her get what she needed from him and to give it back in spades.

The rhythm changed, becoming one of utter desperation, until she gave a long keening cry, her head thrown back as she continued to rise and fall in quick staccato movements of her hips. And in an instant, he was gone, tumbling over that cliff he'd imagined earlier and falling all the way to the bottom. The crash on impact, when it came, overwhelmed him and brought a coarse shout that he couldn't have contained if he'd tried.

Sam couldn't think, couldn't breathe, couldn't move as Lucy slowed her pace, the fingers that had gripped his shoulders easing and becoming soothing touches that helped him transition from tornado-like furor to a calm sea that cradled and comforted. His arms went around her and held her against him as all movements stopped.

He didn't want to get up. Didn't want this moment to end, because when it did...

No. He didn't want to think beyond the feel of her skin against his.

"Sam?" Her low voice pulled him from whatever dreamland he'd been in, and he took a deep breath, hoping she wasn't going to say anything profound or weighty. Or talk about needing more from him. He didn't think he could handle it right now.

"Yep?" It took everything in him to get that one word out. And he braced himself for whatever she was about to say.

She leaned back and looked at him. "I think you earned it."

His mind scrambled, trying to figure out what she was talking about, then her fingers walked across the mattress until she reached the box that was still beside her hip. She tapped it, and her eyebrows gave a sexy wiggle.

All of a sudden he laughed and laid back, dragging her with him. He shut his eyes. It was going to be okay. Everything would be okay.

CHAPTER NINE

LUCY WOKE UP feeling a little stiff and out of sorts. And very, very tired. Where was she?

She glanced to the side and saw an end table, the drawer still halfway open. Oh, God. They really had…

She sat up in an instant and listened, trying to figure out where Sam was. He wasn't in the room or in the adjoining bathroom, since that door was open and the lights were out.

How many times had they made love last night?

Too many. She should've been stretching her arms up and relishing what had happened. But in the way that it always was with her, her emotions were cramped and small and hiding in a corner because they knew she was not going to be happy to see them.

Why? It was just sex. Great, uninhibited sex like she'd never had before in her life.

Still listening for Sam, her mind crouched, looking at the bundle of feelings that were shrinking away as if trying very hard to protect her from the truth. Again, why? People had sex all the time. It was no big deal. It wasn't like it was her first time. And she'd wanted this to happen almost from the moment she laid eyes on him. All of that had happened in less than a month.

Remember Matt? Things happened fast with him too. So, so fast.

She frowned, a sliver of anger coming over her. Sam wasn't Matt. And they weren't committed. Or engaged.

But it's what you're hoping for. All in under a month. Just like with Matt.

"It's not the same!" Her words were low, and she glanced at the door to make sure Sam wasn't standing there listening. He wasn't.

Her thoughts strayed again to that dark corner, and slowly her feelings crept out into the open where she could see them. *Oh, God, no.* She closed her eyes as a truth—a truth that was every bit as catastrophic to her senses as last night had been—revealed itself.

She'd done the unthinkable. Done exactly what she'd warned herself over and over not to do.

She'd fallen in love with Sam.

And it hadn't happened last night either. It had been there for the past couple of weeks—she just hadn't recognized it. Which made it even worse.

What had he told her? That he didn't want to be involved with anyone. That he probably would *never* want to be involved with anyone ever again. He'd never lied to her or promised her anything. They'd wanted each other and had acted on it. It wasn't his fault. And it really wasn't hers either. As long as she didn't press him to give her something more than he already had.

He couldn't know. She was going to have to work very hard to not let him see what had happened. The bunny on her shoulder burned with a fire that seared her conscience. She was horrible at hiding her feelings. The worst.

Maybe it was why Matt had left her a note instead of facing her.

Well, she was going to have to learn quick or ruin everything she'd worked so hard for. She doubted he'd throw her off the team, but she might not be able to stay on it if she couldn't keep her feelings in check. If she couldn't make him believe that last night would never happen again, that it had meant nothing.

It was a lie. It had meant everything. But no matter how she looked at it, she couldn't see a way in which this would work out, unless he'd fallen in love with her too.

And that seemed improbable if not impossible, given everything he'd told her.

Where was he? Maybe he was cooking a gourmet breakfast for her, waiting to tell her how much last night meant to him.

Lucy wrinkled her nose as if sniffing the air. Nothing. And there wasn't a sound coming from anywhere. No sounds of toilets flushing or water running or of bare feet walking across the hardwood floors of his little apartment.

Gingerly she got out of bed and thanked God that she'd brought a change of clothing with her. Her clothes were still on the floor, but Sam's were not. He'd evidently picked them up. She swallowed. The box of condoms was gone as well, and she didn't see it in the drawer of the side table either. She pushed the drawer shut and caught sight of something else. It wasn't the missing box.

A sense of horror came over her. There was a slip of paper on one of the pillows at the head of the bed. The pillows that neither one of them had used last night.

She slowly walked over to it, her feet feeling as if they were encased in blocks of concrete, getting heavier with every step. The note was folded, and she wasn't going to be able to read it without touching it. And she didn't want to touch it. She knew exactly what that paper would feel like against her skin.

It would feel like heartbreak. All over again.

She forced her hand to move forward and pick it up, fingers opening the folded portion of it.

Emergency at MMH. Talk later.

He hadn't even signed the note, and she couldn't remember hearing the sound of a phone going off. Which could mean nothing. His phone could have been on vibrate or on the table in the foyer. Or it could mean that he'd simply been looking for an excuse to get out of his own apartment before she woke up and he had to face her.

And talk later? The last thing Lucy wanted to do was talk. Not until she'd had a chance to stop and think about the ramifications of everything that had happened.

Whichever scenario was the case, thank God she had her own car and didn't have to be at work until later this afternoon. Because she was going to get dressed—she glanced down, realizing she was still completely naked—drive home and figure out a way to get past this. One that didn't involve leaving her job or quitting the team. She wouldn't have to leave her job, since they worked in completely different parts of the hospital and she would rarely have to see him. But leaving the team?

Even the thought of meeting with him and finishing the work on that presentation filled her with a sense of nausea. And the idea of talking things through with him?

When his eyes met hers, she had visions of him shrinking away after seeing the truth written all over her face.

No, he wouldn't. Because she was about to become the best damned actress MMH had ever seen. No one would guess. Not Logan, not Harper and definitely not Sam. She'd taken a chance with Matt and had come out on the losing end. She was not about to do that a second time.

Nor was she going to face Sam over the keyboard of a computer and work on that project. She couldn't. Not today.

Yanking on her clothes, she went out to the dining room table, hoping he had just left and wouldn't be home for a while. Then she pulled her computer out of its bag and opened it, sitting in one of his chairs and getting to work.

In a half hour, she'd done everything she needed to do and put the extra flash drive into the slot and loaded her work onto it. Then, retrieving the note from the pillow, she brought it to where her computer sat on the table. She pulled an ink pen from her bag and sat down again, staring at the note for a long time. Then she added a reply onto it.

No need to talk. Project ready for Todd. See copy on flash drive.

She didn't sign her name either, just folded the note back up and dropped the tiny device on top of it. Then she gathered all of her stuff and left the apartment.

Lucy glanced at her phone and saw that she'd missed a call from him. Swallowing, she didn't try to return it. Right now, she just wanted to get out.

When she got to the parking lot, she was grateful to

see that the space next her car's was empty. Maybe her feelings were just an overflow of giddiness from what had happened last night. Except the discovery of those emotions had not had the slightest resemblance to anything she'd felt last night. They were somber and sad and knew exactly what would happen once she recognized them.

She threw her stuff into the back seat and drove home as fast as she could. Fortunately the street sweeper had already come and gone and she was able to park fairly close to her little house. But when she got out, her sister was evidently waiting for her and came down the sidewalk toward her. She took Lucy's computer bag without a word, looking into her face and then a little bit lower, her cane leaning against her thigh.

"What happened?"

Dios. She couldn't even hide the truth for five seconds without someone guessing it. How on earth was she going to keep it from Sam?

She dropped her overnight bag onto the sidewalk and covered her face with her hands, silent tears streaming down her face.

"Oh, Luce…tell me. Tell me, please."

"I—I… Oh, God, I fell in love."

Bella evidently guessed that this was not good news because she held her as Lucy sobbed onto her shoulder. "I'm so sorry, honey. So, so sorry. Is there no chance?"

"None." Even as she said it, she knew it was true. Because she wasn't willing to take a chance on being rejected again. She wasn't going to tell Sam. Or her mom or dad. Or anyone else. "You can't say anything, Bell. Promise me."

"I promise. But promise me you won't give up."

"I can't. But what I can promise you is that it's not going to keep me from doing what I love doing."

"Good. You know I'm here for you, right?"

Lucy leaned back and gave her sister a watery smile. "I do. And thank you for that." She gave a shrug. "At least there are no wedding plans to cancel this time."

With that, Bella walked her up to her front porch and came inside the house. "You may not want it right now, but I'm going to make you some strong coffee. But not before you lie down and get some sleep."

"How did you guess?"

"I just know. But there's also this." She touched a spot on Lucy's neck.

She put a hand up, remembering the second that mark had happened. A shudder went through her. Oh, God!

She hoped she had something to cover that up with.

Bella kissed her cheek. "Now, go get cleaned up. I'll wake you up before you need to go to work."

She would have asked her sister how she knew what time that would be, but she didn't. Because like her sister had said—she knew. Just like she always did.

Sam was exhausted. A half hour after he'd finally fallen asleep last night, he'd gotten a call that a child had fallen off a step and caught her upper lip on a piece of fencing. It had ripped through all the layers, laying the flesh wide open. Anyone in the ER could have sutured it up, but those doctors also knew that getting the lip margins to perfectly meet was tricky business. It could look right now, but later on any deviation in those edges would be visible as the child grew. So they'd called Sam.

He'd only had time to write a quick note to Lucy and drive to the hospital. Once he'd finished the repair, he checked his phone and saw no messages from Lucy, so he tried to call her and got no response. Either she was still asleep, which was understandable, or she was dreading seeing him again.

He wanted to believe that last night was a mistake, but he couldn't quite bring himself to that point. Sex with her had been like nothing he'd ever experienced before. But the fact that he already wanted it again was a wake-up call. He'd told her the truth. He was not good at relationships. Not with his parents, not with Priscilla. Hell, he didn't even get along with his siblings sometimes. He hated having his emotions exposed and examined... even by his own mind.

And yet Lucy was so good. So kind. And so giving, whether in bed or in life.

He swallowed, thinking about what she'd said about her ex. She'd been hurt in the worst possible way by someone she'd loved. Could he risk hurting her if things crashed and burned like they had with Priscilla?

Maybe she didn't even want anything from him. It could be that he was making a crisis out of something that simply wasn't there.

I want more, Sam. I need more.

She'd said it in the heat of passion, but even then the words had scraped at something inside of him. Because while he might have been able to give her more in a physical sense, he wasn't sure he had it in him to give her more emotionally.

Plus, he'd gotten a text from Todd asking if they could host the team from New York's Grayson Specialty Hospital sooner than they'd anticipated. They could come next week if Sam could pull the team together for the Q&A. Todd had also asked about the work he and Lucy had done on the protocol. He told the man he'd have it by the end of the day, but the thought of texting Lucy again made his chest hurt. He was going to have to face her sometime, but it was kind of like his dad. Sam's comfort meter was dialed to avoidance right now.

The fact that she hadn't called him back made him think she felt pretty much the same way, that she was in no hurry to try to figure this thing out. Maybe he could just text her and ask her to forward the presentation file to Todd. But he wasn't going to do that right now, not when exhaustion was pulling at every cell of his body.

So he went back to his office and stretched out on the very uncomfortable futon that the last occupant had left in there and did his best to shut off his mind even as he shut his eyes.

Sam kicked back to consciousness, reaching for something that wasn't there and almost falling off the bed in the process. His eyes popped open.

It wasn't a bed, it was a narrow couch, and the thing he'd been reaching for...

Wasn't there. And probably never would be.

Great. He glanced at his watch and saw that it was a little after one. He'd been asleep for almost four hours.

He sat up and scrubbed a hand across his face. It was going to be a long day.

Checking his phone and scrolling through several messages, he noted there was still nothing from Lucy. No word on the project or if she'd even driven home. Surely she wasn't waiting at his apartment for him?

No. That didn't sound like something she would do. But what she would do…

He dragged his hands through his hair and decided to head down to the first floor. Catching the elevator and leaning his head against the wall of the empty car, he tried to run over what he was going to say to her. Nothing sounded appropriate for work.

Or really anywhere, since most everything that popped into his head started off with, *I'm sorry.*

He exited into the main lobby of the hospital and took a right, heading down the corridor that led to the PT department, the big sign overhead stating that he was entering the Manhattan Memorial Hospital Physical Therapy and Wellness Center. He paused at the door before pushing through it with a sense of determination. The sooner they cleared the air, the better for both of them.

Then he heard a familiar sound. A quacking sound that came from his left. There sat Lucy as cheerful as ever, as if nothing had happened to change her world. So why was she able to bounce back so quickly while he felt he was being sucked down into a pit of quicksand? The more he struggled against it, the greater the suction. He stood and watched her for a second, as fascinated by what she did as he had been the last time he visited this department. This child wasn't Devon but was instead a little girl who was actually sitting on top of one of those exercise balls. The child had a puppet of her own, and she and Lucy were carrying on a conversation through the pretend animals. On top of her desk was a spotted dog.

Where had he seen that before?

Spot. That was its name. And Devon. Their tethered-cord patient. He must have visited if the dog was there. Or maybe she'd bought one to replace the one she'd given the boy.

Just then she glanced over, catching sight of him. There was a moment's hesitation, then a brilliant smile lit her face. He frowned. What was she so cheerful about?

Wasn't that just who Lucy was? She was the most optimistic, chipper person he'd ever met. He was glad to see that what happened hadn't seemed to squashed that part of her. She held up a finger to tell him to wait.

Somehow the fact that she seemed so unruffled bothered him. He'd sat and stewed and worried for what seemed like hours before he'd fallen asleep. Or maybe she thought what happened wouldn't change their relationship.

That should've been good news. Except her apparent happiness was making him feel even more miserable. As well it should've. He'd known from the beginning that sleeping with her would bring unintended consequences. But had that stopped him?

No. Because he was too stupid to open his eyes and acknowledge that actions *always* had consequences. Like getting arrested when he was fifteen. Only he was a grown man now. And able to think through things before he did them. Or at least he'd thought he could.

He was tempted to just scribble a note and leave it for her at the information desk, but that wasn't going to solve the problem. They needed to at least have a quick conversation and make sure that they were both good to go on from here. Because if they weren't...

Well, he hadn't thought that far ahead. Would she want to quit the team? Even the thought of that made his gut churn. Maybe it would be easier. But was it what he wanted? He was no longer sure of anything.

Lucy stood up and held the ball while the girl did the same, taking the puppet off her hand. Then a woman, who was probably the child's mom, smiled and said something to Lucy and her daughter before taking the girl's hand and leading her toward the entrance. The girl was limping. He couldn't tell if it was from an injury or if there was some other problem, but that was not why he was here.

Lucy motioned him over. Sam took a deep breath and started toward her.

Her eyes sparkled, and she pointed toward the exercise ball. "Want to have a seat?"

There was no sign of anything on her neck. He could have sworn he'd kissed her hard enough to...

Evidently nothing he'd done last night had left a mark. Except on him.

And her perky words just made his sense of irritation grow. "No, thank you."

"Well, if you insist, there's also a chair."

He sat in it, knowing he was being grumpy and probably was going to act like a jerk pretty soon, but he'd been trying to figure out all morning what he was going to say to her when he finally saw her, but it looked like he needn't have worried.

She went on: "I ended up leaving a flash drive of the presentation on your dining room table, but I have another copy here if you need it for Todd right away. I hope everything with your emergency went well."

"It did—thanks." She was totally not bothered by last night?

Sam was finding that hard to believe. So he decided to come right out with it. "About last night…" The words choked to a halt.

"Yes?" She still had that half smile on her face. Was she hoping for an admission of love? No. He didn't see anything like that in her expression.

He tried again. "I think we were both…"

She was still smiling. "Let me stop you right there. I'm not worried about it if you're not. But I think we can both agree that it's something that shouldn't happen again."

Not exactly what he'd been going to say, but the fact that she'd had no problem getting her words out in a way that was so…unflappable was grating.

His eyes narrowed, and he decided to up his bid to match hers. "I agree."

She slipped her duck puppet on. "Do we need to sign a contract agreeing to that? *Quack-quack.*"

He went very still, the flippant tone sending a shard that went straight to his heart. "I'm glad you find all of this so amusing."

As if she realized she'd gone too far, she set the puppet down. "No, it's not amusing. But I'm also not going to lose sleep over it. I knew where we stood before last night happened, so unless you have something you're dying to say, I suggest we forget it. Getting angsty about it isn't going to help either of us, and we still have to work together on the team." Her brows went up. "Unless you have something to say about that matter as well?"

What could he say? Nothing really, although the idea of working beside her had lost all of its attraction because she might agree to signing a hands-off contract—even in jest—but he wasn't so sure that he could stick to those terms. Because even watching her work with that little girl had warmed his chest. He cared about her. He could admit to that. But the alternative was for one of them to step down, and that held no appeal either. Could he avoid working with her as an individual and keep it strictly to things that were happening within the group as a whole?

Maybe.

"Nope, I have nothing to say. I'm glad things are okay between us."

But were they? Sam wasn't so sure. At least on his side.

"Good," she said. Her smile was back in place. "I have another patient coming in a few minutes, so unless there's something else…"

"No. Nothing else." He stood and looked down at her, still searching for any sign of that kissing mark on her neck. "Thanks for the flash drive. If you have an extra one here, could I borrow it? I promised Todd I'd get it to him today, and it looks like the Q&A with the other hospital is going to take place next week."

"Wow, was that you? Or Todd?"

"Neither. Their hospital decided they wanted to do it

earlier than scheduled, so we'll have some scrambling to do to get ready."

"Then I'd better let you go so you can start scrambling." She opened the drawer to her desk. "And here's the flash drive. You can have it. I have the presentation saved on my computer as well, so if you need it, I can make more copies."

"This should be good. Thanks, though."

With that he headed back the way he came, feeling no better about things than when he'd entered the room. He should've been glad that he'd gotten off easy, but the whole idea of that made him feel slightly queasy, as if he were coming down with something.

And he couldn't afford to come down with anything. Not when so many things were riding on his shoulders and counting on him to hold them up. For the first time since he'd been back, he missed Uruguay. But he knew better than most that you couldn't always go back and expect things to be the way they'd been before. Not with Uruguay. And probably not with Lucy either. He couldn't undo what had happened between them. So all he could do was try to make things work the best he could and go on from where they currently stood.

As he was making his way across the lobby, he was shocked to see his dad striding through the big double doors. As always, he was a man on a mission. But he really shouldn't even be out. Not after his fainting episode last night.

Sam moved to intercept him, coming up behind his father. "Dad. What are you doing here?"

Carter Grant stopped in his tracks and stood there for

a minute before turning to face him. "I'm looking for my son."

A bitter taste washed up his throat, but he clenched his teeth and willed it away. "Logan is probably in his office."

"No. He's not. And I'm not looking for that son."

For a second he didn't understand what his father was saying, and then he blinked. "You came to see me?"

"Is there somewhere we can go that is a little more private?"

"Are you having a problem? I can page Dr. Asbury and get him down here."

He shook his head. "It's not my health. But last night was a wake-up call."

Hell, he hoped his dad didn't want to talk about making out his will or money because Sam wasn't in the mood.

"Let's go up to my office."

As soon as they got off the elevator and he opened the door to his space, he realized it was a mistake. His sofa was still pulled into a bed and a blanket was haphazardly thrown over it. But he motioned his father into the room and quickly tossed the blanket aside and righted the sofa. "Have a seat."

"I'll stand, if that's okay. I won't take up a lot of your time."

He tried again. "You really should be at home resting."

His dad shook his head. "Logan came by the house this morning to see how I was doing, and I…" He cleared his throat. "And I decided to come see you."

Sam swallowed. His dad hadn't been the one on his

mind this morning. A faint sense of guilt washed over him. "Can't this wait until after you've recovered?"

Carter grunted. "If I'm going to have a heart attack, where better to have it than at the hospital?"

How could he argue with that? He couldn't. And the sooner his father had his say, the sooner Sam could take him home. "Let's sit. Both of us."

This time, his dad lowered himself onto the couch while Sam spun one of the chairs in front of the desk to face him.

"I know Logan thinks your mother and I played a part in the breakup of their marriage, and maybe he's right. I told him I want to do things differently this time, especially since Harper is expecting."

Sam still didn't see what that had to do with him, so he just sat and waited.

"I was hard on you when you were growing up. If I had it to do over again…well, there's no going back, so let's just say, I regret some things. And when you went away to Uruguay, I wasn't sure I'd ever see you again."

And yet his dad had never contacted him. Not once. But maybe that was pride. Sam, more than anyone, could understand about letting pride get in the way of real conversations. Something he wasn't going to think about right now.

He forced a smile. "Well, you won't have to worry about that anymore."

"I'm sorry?"

Realizing his dad might think he was leaving again, he hurried to set him straight. "I'm here to stay. This new program means a lot to me."

"And the woman from last night? Does she play more of a role than you're letting on?"

"Her name is Lucy." If his father thought he was going to break down and make some big confession, he was sorely mistaken. But Sam could at least extend an olive branch. After all, for his dad to say any of this was something of a miracle. And Sam was smart enough to know that he'd also played a part in their rift over the years. "I don't think so. But I promise to try to communicate more."

Lucy's words about time and trying to make things right while he still could rang in his ears. Maybe his father had come to the same conclusion. But whatever it was, he had to see this as a peace offering. Why else would he have come to see him?

"Thank you, son."

There was that word again. He couldn't remember his dad ever actually calling him that. Maybe there was hope. Or at least a slight glimmer of something that resembled hope.

His dad stood. "Well, I won't take any more of your time. Thanks for letting me say my piece." He held out his hand, and Sam took it and gave a gentle squeeze and looked into his father's face, seeing the aging process for maybe the first time. "I'll take you home."

"No need. My driver is waiting for me at the front."

Of course he was. "Let's get together for lunch sometime, then."

"I'll contact you."

That made Sam smile. Some things would never

change. Well…maybe they would, but it would be in small increments.

As Carter made his way out of the door with a backhanded wave, some of the weight lifted from Sam's shoulders. All might not be right with his world, but at least it wasn't all wrong either. And he might need to learn to be content with that.

CHAPTER TEN

LUCY SLID INTO the conference room feeling a weird sense of déjà vu. This was how her entry into the facial-reanimation team had started. Only it hadn't carried the heartache that it did today. She hadn't seen Sam since the day he'd appeared in her department and asked for that flash drive. And he'd given no indication that he noticed anything different about her, other than that curt question about whether she found the whole situation amusing. She guessed her acting job had been a little too convincing.

But while she might've appeared fine on the outside, on the inside she was dealing with a pain that just would not quit. Had she felt this horrible after Matt had broken up with her?

She and Sam hadn't even been a couple. They'd slept together. One. Time.

So why was she having trouble sleeping and eating? But most of all why was she now considering giving up something she'd wanted so badly a month ago?

Because even the thought of seeing Sam, much less talking to him, caused a kind of anxiety she'd never ex-perienced before. Todd had called her into his office and thanked her for all of the work on the protocol presentation and said it had been sent around to the rest of the team, who'd been unanimous in their approval of it.

Even talking about the project made her shrink away. She'd debated on not coming today. But this was the big Q&A that everyone had been looking forward to. And she was hoping for a sign that would send her in one direction or the other.

She found an empty seat and slid into it, noting that the panel was already in place on the podium, a microphone in front of each of the players, although one spot was empty. She swallowed, spotting Sam talking to one of the people at the front. He smiled at something the other man said, and it made her squirm.

She didn't think she could do this.

Lucy had been hoping her feelings would fade away, kind of in the same way they had when Matt had left. But these were still as strong as they'd been that day she discovered she loved Sam.

She still loved him. And she knew he was real and authentic in a way that Matthew had not been. He hadn't tried to play games with her or vaguely say things that weren't true. He'd had no problem agreeing with her that sleeping together had been a mistake.

Of course, she'd been pretty blithe in the way she'd presented it. But her reasons for thinking it was a mistake were probably very different from his.

Sam turned around and started to come down the steps. As he reached the floor, his eyes met hers for a minute. He stopped and held her gaze steady for a minute before his lips thinned and he glanced away. The move wasn't a fluke. He was telling her in no uncertain terms where they stood.

And it was not on good ground.

She'd done okay holed up in her own department over the last week, except for that day he'd come down to see her. She was confident she could still work in the PT department. But Sam *was* the facial-reanimation department. He wasn't some minor player on the team. Everything revolved around him, and as such he would oversee every part of it. Which meant multiple conversations every time a new patient came through MMH's doors.

She'd actually gone to Human Resources and asked if there was someone who could take her place on the team if it turned out she had to step down.

Melissa had pressed her, telling Lucy she could trust her with whatever she needed to say. Lucy had simply said some personal things had come up and she was rethinking her involvement. Her friend had told her to think long and hard about her decision, that opportunities like this didn't come along every day. She even offered to lighten her load in PT if that was the problem.

Lightening her load would only give her more time to think…to dread and probably avoid any interaction with Sam, which she knew meant she couldn't give the job what it needed. It needed someone who was there wholeheartedly for the patients no matter what conflicts she might have with any of the other team members. And there were no conflicts. Other than the one raging inside of her own heart.

To stay or to go. That was the question, and one she still couldn't answer.

What she needed right now was some air. Lucy glanced at her watch. She still had five more minutes until the event started. She grabbed a water bottle on her way through the door and unscrewed the cap, taking a long drink of the cool liquid as she headed to a nearby wall, leaning against it.

She needed to at least stay for this, no matter how she felt about Sam. She wanted to hear what these experts had to say, and there was a physical therapist listed as one of the speakers. There was a short bio on each person, but she really didn't recognize any of the names.

Leaning her head against the wall, she closed her eyes and took another drink, the cool liquid soothing her heated emotions in a way that helped, surprisingly.

"Hello." A voice to her left caught her attention, and her eyes opened to find a woman looking at her.

"Hi." There was something vaguely familiar about the person, and she stood there trying to figure out why.

"You're Lucy, aren't you?"

She peered closer. The woman knew her, and she tried to grasp where she knew her from. "I am. I know you, don't I?"

The woman was probably in her early thirties. When she smiled there was a slight crookedness to it that made Lucy tilt her head, and there was a slightly accented tone to her speech.

"You probably don't remember me. I looked a little different fifteen years ago."

Fifteen years ago. She hadn't even been a physical therapist at the time. She'd been studying to be...

Recognition gripped her and tears sprang to Lucy's eyes. She grabbed the woman in a hug and held her tight. "Oh, my God! I've worried about you all these years."

The woman hugged her back. "I've wanted to thank you all these years. I felt like you were the only one who really heard me back then."

It was the Moebius patient who'd been struggling so much. Lucy let go of her. "I don't even know your name."

"It's Becky Collins." She smiled. "Well, it is now. It was Becky Moore back then. I'm married, with three little ones."

"I'm so happy for you. You got your surgery, obviously."

"I did. More than one of them. It was a fight every step of the way, but I just remember you gripping my hand and telling me not to give up no matter what happened. I didn't. And here I am."

Becky looked at her for a long moment. "I came because I saw your name on the list of the team and asked to come along, although I had to shift some of my patients around."

"You're a doctor." Lucy breathed the word, unable to believe this was happening.

"I'm actually a physical therapist."

A ball of emotion lodged in her throat and wouldn't let go. Hers was the empty seat on the podium.

Becky touched her hand. "I'm so glad to know you'll be helping more people like me. I've dedicated my life to doing the same."

How could Lucy tell her that she'd been toying with

dropping off the team? Her problems suddenly seemed so minor. Well, they weren't. But in the whole scope of things they were. MMH wasn't the only hospital that was building a program like this. There were other places out there doing this too. It was a growing field offering people a chance to be able to freely express their emotions through their facial muscles.

Like the ones she was currently suppressing? The ones that had her feeling she was slowly dying inside even as she kept on smiling on the outside. She didn't have to give up this dream. She just had to decide *where* she was going to do it.

"What's wrong?"

Becky was looking into her face, twin frown lines appearing.

God. It really was miraculous. She grabbed Becky's hand. "I know you have to go inside and be on the panel, but can I talk to you later?"

"You can talk to me right now. You took the time to listen to me when I needed it the most—the least I can do is listen to you."

So even though they were basically strangers, Lucy felt an affinity with Becky that had her spilling out everything that had happened over the last month, how she'd slowly fallen in love with the new department's team leader and that she was thinking of resigning from her position.

"Did you tell him how you feel?"

Lucy shook her head. "No. I just keep smiling and trying to suppress my emotions."

"Hmmm. Just because you're *able* to smile doesn't mean you should."

She blinked. "I'm sorry?"

"I was so happy to have muscles that obeyed my mental commands that I sometimes pasted a smile on my face just because I could. It became a problem. One my husband had to talk to me about. So now I'm more careful." Becky paused. "How is he going to know it's bothering you if your face doesn't match what's inside?"

"But I can't just tell him."

Her brows went up slightly. "Why not? If you're thinking of stepping down anyway, what do you have to lose?"

"Maybe everything."

Becky hugged her. "And maybe you have everything to gain. Maybe he's fooled by your smile and doesn't think you care about him."

Lucy swallowed. "But what if it doesn't matter to him either way?"

"If I were you, I would want to know."

"Should I draw two circles?" She tried to make light of her problems by referring to their meeting all those years ago.

Becky shook her head. "No. Because no matter what happens in the first circle, life is still worth living. I found that out. Thanks to you. Even if I hadn't had my surgeries."

"Thank you. Thank you so much."

She nodded. "Ready to go back inside?"

"I'm ready."

Sam sat in his chair, a pain in his head that just wouldn't quit. He'd come down those stairs and glanced across the audience and seen Lucy. That was when it hit him. The pain. The pain in his head. The pain in his gut. And the pain in his chest. It had nothing to do with being sick or anything else. He'd caught Lucy at a time when she hadn't been smiling or laughing or joking about something, and he realized how much he missed all of those things.

This week without seeing her had been a strange one. It was like the joy of living had been sucked right out of him. At first he'd thought it had been just coming off the adrenaline rush from getting this Q&A organized and off the ground. But then when he saw Lucy, he knew exactly what it was, and it floored him. He was in love with the woman.

God, he didn't want to be and knew he didn't deserve someone like her and couldn't ask her to take a chance on him, but it had hurt to look away. And then when he'd chanced to glance back there again, she'd been gone. And he wanted nothing more than to run out that door and find her. But of course he couldn't. And he shouldn't.

She was doing just fine without him—she'd made that very clear the last time they'd spoken. So he should just let things rest the way they were.

But how was he going to work with her?

He didn't know, and that was something he'd have to sort through later. There would be a time and place for all of that. But it wasn't now.

After an hour and a half, there were finally no more questions. Todd went up to the front and stood at the microphone. "Our guest panel has been kind enough to offer to stay afterward for a while and answer any questions you may not have wanted to ask in an open forum, but one member of the panel has asked to say something to all of you."

A woman came to the microphone and stood with Todd. She looked a little uncomfortable standing in front of everyone, but she smiled.

"My name is Becky, and I have Moebius syndrome."

Sam's gaze sharpened. She'd been on the panel and had answered questions just like the other members of the team, and he hadn't noticed anything specifically different about her.

She went on. "I can't tell you how important the facial-reanimation field is, but you all feel it, or you wouldn't be here. I have a special friend here who gave me hope at a time when I felt I had none. You'll never know how happy I am to see her on this team and to see her here today. I hope she'll never doubt her importance to this field, no matter where she may find herself. Thanks to all of you."

She then went back to her seat.

Sam's gaze jerked back to where Lucy was sitting and saw tears streaming down her face, and he knew in a moment who that woman was. But why had she said *no matter where she may find herself*? Was Lucy thinking of leaving MMH? Surely not.

Hell, he surely didn't want to be the reason for that—although she'd seemed fine when he'd talked to her, so he might have misconstrued the woman's words. But the thought of never seeing Lucy again? The pain in his midsection grew in intensity. He'd only felt relief after he and Priscilla broke up. And he hadn't missed her since being back in the States. But Lucy?

That was another story. He already missed her, even though they worked in the same building.

So what was he going to do about it? He wasn't sure, but he'd better figure it out pretty damned quick.

Lucy was gone. He'd finished saying farewell to the last of the visiting experts and had gone and personally had a word with Becky, thanking her for her words and for being willing to put herself out there for others who needed the same life-changing surgeries. She'd smiled. "I feel like I already know you. But thanks for your kind words."

With that she was gone. She felt like she already knew him?

Had she spoken with Lucy and been told that she was thinking of going somewhere else?

When he'd looked for her, the room was empty and she was nowhere to be seen. Sam glanced at his phone, and the screen was blank. No texts. So she hadn't tried to reach him. Maybe she was down in her department. If so, he needed to find her and tell her the truth. If she didn't feel the same and thought they couldn't work together, he would understand. But why should she be the one to leave a place she'd worked for her entire career? If anyone should go, it should be him.

And he was going to make that clear.

With that in mind he headed out the door and started in the direction of the elevator until something to his left caught his eye. He glanced over there and saw Lucy, standing there all by herself.

Okay, there she was. Let's see if he could do what he said he was going to do. He went over. "Can I talk to you for a few minutes?"

"Yes. I was just waiting for you, actually."

So she *was* leaving. She'd just stayed here tell him.

"Let's go to my office."

She shook her head. "I'd rather go to that quiet little waiting room just down the hall from there. There's rarely anyone there."

"Okay." That didn't bode well for whatever it was she wanted to say.

The conference room was housed on the same floor as the plastic-surgery wing, so they went just around the corner and found the area she was talking about.

She led the way and went to the far back corner and sat down. He joined her, careful not to touch her. His heart ached in a way he'd never known. But he had to do this now, or he'd always regret it.

"Are you thinking of leaving MMH?"

Lucy nodded, and none of her customary exuberance was on display at the moment. "I actually thought about stepping down from the team, but then I saw Becky in the hallway and she convinced me that I should rethink that. That if things couldn't work out here, and if I really cared about the facial-reanimation field, I should find another place where I can plug in. And I really do care."

"Why? Why do you want to leave?"

"Can't you guess?" She gazed into his eyes, and he saw nothing but Lucy. The Lucy he'd come to know.

"Is it because we slept together?"

"No. It's because of what I realized after it happened."

He took a deep breath. "And what was that?"

"That I'd fallen in love with you and that it was going

to be hell to work on a team where I saw you each and every day." Her eyes held steady.

"But down in your treatment room you seemed so happy and even said—"

"I was lying. And Becky helped me to see that when my facial expressions don't match what I'm feeling inside, it means I'm not being truthful to myself or to the person I'm addressing. I need to learn the importance of being authentic."

"Well, then I've been lying too. Only I just realized it during the Q&A."

"And what were you lying about?"

Now she was frowning. And it made him smile. "I kept telling myself that these feelings I had for you would go away even when deep down I knew they wouldn't. I love you. And when your friend Becky stood up and hinted that you might be leaving, my world might as well have imploded. I don't want you to leave, Lucy. I want you to stay. And work with me. And be beside me always. In good times and bad."

"But you said you didn't want to be with anyone."

"At that time, I didn't. Because of my upbringing. Because of Priscilla. Because of the lies I told myself all along the way. I didn't believe I could be fully engaged with anyone emotionally. But our night together…let's just say it made me rethink that. Not just physically. But yes, emotionally. I've never felt more in tune with another human being than I do when I'm with you. And it wasn't just that night. It was when I saw you with Devon. When we walked in the park and talked about things that were more than just superficial." He shrugged. "When I told you about my arrest. I love you. That's the only explanation. And if you can help me get past the times when I have problems being like you said…authentic, or at least hold me accountable, I'd like to try to make this work."

"Are you serious?"

He smiled. "About holding me accountable or trying to make this work? Because I'm very serious about both of those things."

"Then, yes, Sam, to both." She took his hand. "I sat in that conference room thinking I couldn't go through with being on the team, and then I saw Becky in the hallway. She convinced me to come talk to you and tell you the truth."

"She didn't tell me exactly that same thing, but she convinced me to do the same."

Lucy sighed. "She's a special lady."

"Yes, she is." Sam leaned down and kissed her on the mouth. "I love you, Luce."

"I love you too." She smiled. "*Dios*. It's good to smile and have it feel real."

"It's good to see you smile and know it's real." He stood and held out his hand. "Shall we?"

She took his hand and let him pull her out of the chair. Then with his arm around her waist, they walked out into the corridor. "What are people going to think if they see us like this?"

"Who cares? They can either be happy for us, or they can go to—"

She put her hand over his mouth to stop the word before it came out. "Let's just hope they're happy for us in the same way that I'm happy for us."

Sam dropped a kiss onto her head. "I am too."

A coy smile appeared on her face, and she glanced up at him. "So is that extra spot in front of your apartment only available on street-sweeper days?"

A laugh bubbled from his chest that felt good and healing and right. "It's available anytime you want it to be. And I'm hoping it's every single night."

"Oh, mister, you may regret saying that."

"Never. I'll never regret anything when it comes to you."

And they walked down the hallway smiling at anyone who happened to look their way, knowing they were heading into a future that would make a difference. Not just for them, but for lots of other people who would walk the halls of MMH in search of answers and hopefully find what they were looking for.

EPILOGUE

SAM AND LUCY stood at the front with only their closest friends and relatives gathered around them. Sam had not been interested in big festivities—he wanted this to be done like he'd lived most of his life: simply. The fact that Lucy had been the one to bring it up first had confirmed for the millionth time that he could do this emotional journey. He'd just needed the right partner by his side.

Surprisingly his parents had not argued for a huge elaborate wedding. Maybe they'd learned their lesson from what happened with Logan and Harper. But he had to say grandparenthood looked good on both of his parents. They doted on his brother's baby girl, and Lily, in turn, seemed to adore them.

His dad had softened in ways that were unimaginable. His and Sam's relationship would never be perfect—they wanted different things out of life—but for the most part they had come to an understanding. And Sam had told him he loved him and had meant it.

The officiant repeated words that Sam had heard so many times before at other people's weddings, but this time each syllable became an oath that he vowed to keep. He loved Lucy more today than he had eight months ago at their first meeting. And when they'd started the Pediatric Microsurgery and Facial-Reanimation Department, they never could have imagined how successful it would come to be. They'd already performed and done physical therapy on ten kids, all of them with hopeful outcomes.

But as successful as it was, he and Lucy had carved out a month of time away from the hospital to go to Paraguay and spend time learning about Lucy's heritage. And where she could curse in Spanish without heads turning in her direction.

She was beautiful. Both inside and out, and he was so, so lucky to be able to share this life with her.

Becky was standing beside her as her maid of honor, along with Lucy's sister, Bella. Lucy and Becky had reconnected in a way that went beyond friendship, and she'd become like family, along with her kids and husband. They visited whenever they could.

The month away would also give them time to start trying to have a family of their own away from the stressors of the hospital and craziness of life. They could lounge around and enjoy each other and revel in the chance they'd been given.

"Repeat after me." The man glanced at Sam and then back again when Sam couldn't stop the smile that spread across his face. He'd decided that he'd fallen in love long before he realized he was in love. It was the time Lucy had worn those parrot scrubs with its motto scrawled across them and he'd decided he needed to make that motto his own.

"Sorry," Sam said. "Inside joke."

When he glanced at Lucy, she was grinning too. He was probably lucky she hadn't stuck a puppet onto his hand and asked him to do his vows in animal voices.

But if she'd asked, he would have done it. Anything for this woman.

They each repeated what the minister recited, and Sam's eyes never left his bride's. When he finally told them they could kiss each other, he'd swung her up into his arms and kissed her in tiny little touches that he hoped paved the way for some longer and sexier kisses later. But first they had the reception to get to.

Like the ceremony, it would be held at the hospital in its little courtyard that had been reserved for just this moment.

He carried her past family and friends and finally set her down just outside of the small chapel. "I love you, Lucy Galeano-Grant."

"I love you too, Sam. And I can't wait to introduce you to…" She pulled a plastic strip from somewhere inside her wedding dress and held it up to him.

He glanced at it, baffled, before realizing what it was. "What? Already?"

"Yep. We can go on our honeymoon without worrying about at least one thing."

He put his hand on her belly and whispered, "Welcome to our family, little one. Get ready for a wild ride."

"Sam!"

"What?" He gave her a naughty grin. "I was talking about life, not…"

She laughed, and that sound carried with Sam as they went out into the courtyard…as they headed for the table with their wedding cake…and as they headed into their future together.

* * * * *

*If you missed the previous story in the
Sexy Surgeons in the City duet
then check out*
Manhattan Marriage Reunion
by JC Harroway

*And if you enjoyed this story
check out these other great reads
from Tina Beckett*

Las Vegas Night with Her Best Friend
Reunion with the ER Doctor
ER Doc's Miracle Triplets

All available now!

MILLS & BOON®

Coming next month

NURSE'S DUBAI TEMPTATION
Scarlet Wilson

Theo's presence in the room made her catch her breath. She tried not to notice how handsome he was, or the way her body reacted to the smell of his aftershave.

He looked up in surprise at Addy. 'What are you doing here?'

She raised her eyebrows. 'You mean you aren't part of the plot to destroy me?'

He sagged down into a seat with a look of bewilderment.

'I've not been here long enough to plot anything,' he said easily. 'And I'm not important enough, and I don't have enough hours in the day. But—' he took a breath and looked amused '—I might be up to plotting some kind of coup at a later date.'

She leaned forward. 'And why would that be?'

He sat back and folded his arms. 'Let's just say I'm watching and waiting. Biding my time.'

'Are you planning on becoming leader of the world?'

He shook his head and grinned at her. 'You forget I have a three-year-old. Leader of the world is tame. He'd expect me to be leader of the universe.'

Continue reading

NURSE'S DUBAI TEMPTATION
Scarlet Wilson

Available next month
millsandboon.co.uk

Copyright © 2025 Scarlet Wilson

COMING SOON!

We really hope you enjoyed reading this book.
If you're looking for more romance
be sure to head to the shops when
new books are available on

Thursday 24th April

To see which titles are coming soon, please visit
millsandboon.co.uk/nextmonth

MILLS & BOON

FOUR BRAND NEW BOOKS FROM
MILLS & BOON MODERN

The same great stories you love, a stylish new look!

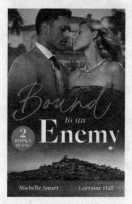

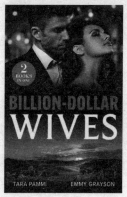

OUT NOW

Eight Modern stories published every month, find them all at:

millsandboon.co.uk

Afterglow Books is a trend-led, trope-filled list of books with diverse, authentic and relatable characters, a wide array of voices and representations, plus real world trials and tribulations. Featuring all the tropes you could possibly want (think small-town settings, fake relationships, grumpy vs sunshine, enemies to lovers) and all with a generous dose of spice in every story.

♪ @millsandboonuk
⊙ @millsandboonuk
afterglowbooks.co.uk

#AfterglowBooks

For all the latest book news, exclusive content and giveaways scan the QR code below to sign up to the Afterglow newsletter:

afterglow BOOKS

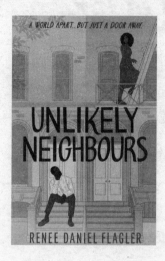

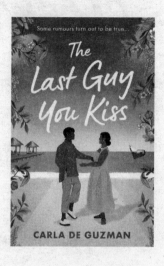

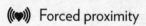 Forced proximity

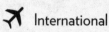 International

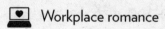 Workplace romance

 Slow burn

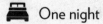 One night

 Spicy

OUT NOW

Two stories published every month. Discover more at:
Afterglowbooks.co.uk

LET'S TALK

Romance

For exclusive extracts, competitions and special offers, find us online:

f MillsandBoon

X @MillsandBoon

⊙ @MillsandBoonUK

♪ @MillsandBoonUK

Get in touch on 01413 063 232

For all the latest titles coming soon, visit
millsandboon.co.uk/nextmonth

OUT NOW!

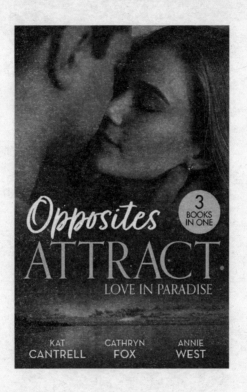

Opposites ATTRACT

LOVE IN PARADISE

3 BOOKS IN ONE

KAT CANTRELL   CATHRYN FOX   ANNIE WEST

Available at
millsandboon.co.uk

MILLS & BOON

OUT NOW!

Available at
millsandboon.co.uk

MILLS & BOON

OUT NOW!

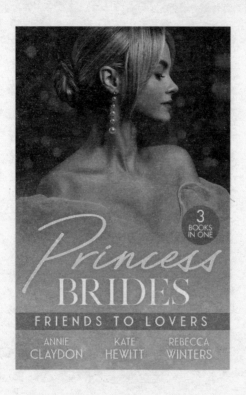

Available at
millsandboon.co.uk

MILLS & BOON

OUT NOW!

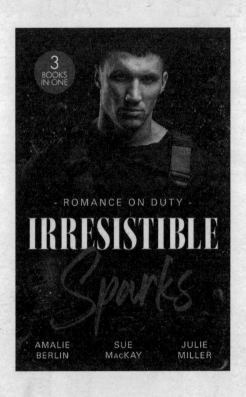

3 BOOKS IN ONE

- ROMANCE ON DUTY -

IRRESISTIBLE
Sparks

AMALIE
BERLIN

SUE
MacKAY

JULIE
MILLER

Available at
millsandboon.co.uk

MILLS & BOON

MILLS & BOON
A ROMANCE FOR EVERY READER

- **FREE** delivery direct to your door
- **EXCLUSIVE** offers every month
- **SAVE** up to 30% on pre-paid subscriptions

SUBSCRIBE AND SAVE

millsandboon.co.uk/Subscribe

MILLS & BOON

THE HEART OF ROMANCE

A ROMANCE FOR EVERY READER

MODERN
Prepare to be swept off your feet by sophisticated, sexy and seductive heroes, in some of the world's most glamourous and romantic locations, where power and passion collide.

HISTORICAL
Escape with historical heroes from time gone by. Whether your passion is for wicked Regency Rakes, muscled Vikings or rugged Highlanders, awaken the romance of the past.

MEDICAL
Set your pulse racing with dedicated, delectable doctors in the high-pressure world of medicine, where emotions run high and passion, comfort and love are the best medicine.

True Love
Celebrate true love with tender stories of heartfelt romance, from the rush of falling in love to the joy a new baby can bring, and a focus on the emotional heart of a relationship.

HEROES
The excitement of a gripping thriller, with intense romance at its heart. Resourceful, true-to-life women and strong, fearless men face danger and desire - a killer combination!

From showing up to glowing up, these characters are on the path to leading their best lives and finding romance along the way – with plenty of sizzling spice!

To see which titles are coming soon, please visit

millsandboon.co.uk/nextmonth